White Hot Holidays

An Ellora's Cave Romantica Publication

www.ellorascave.com

White Hot Holidays Volume 2

ISBN 1419956019

Cover art by Syneca

Electronic book Publication December 2005
Trade paperback Publication October 2006

Warning:

The following material contains graphic sexual content meant for mature readers. This story has been rated E–rotic by a minimum of three independent reviewers.

Ellora's Cave Publishing offers three levels of Romantica™ reading entertainment: S (S-ensuous), E (E-rotic), and X (X-treme).

S-*ensuous* love scenes are explicit and leave nothing to the imagination.

E-*rotic* love scenes are explicit, leave nothing to the imagination, and are high in volume per the overall word count. In addition, some E-rated titles might contain fantasy material that some readers find objectionable, such as bondage, submission, same sex encounters, forced seductions, and so forth. E-rated titles are the most graphic titles we carry; it is common, for instance, for an author to use words such as "fucking", "cock", "pussy", and such within their work of literature.

X-*treme* titles differ from E-rated titles only in plot premise and storyline execution. Unlike E-rated titles, stories designated with the letter X tend to contain controversial subject matter not for the faint of heart.

Contents

FULL MOON XMAS

Sherri L. King

Chapter One

Three days until Christmas

The snow was coming down heavier now, and it was all Terra Gillead could do to see the road ahead of her through the flurries. She tossed one long dark lock of hair back away from her face and focused on the road. Sleet, interspersed with the snow, made the steep, winding roadway even more treacherous than it normally was. The heater in her car wasn't working again, and her fingers were numb where they clenched the wheel at ten and two. She should have remembered her gloves.

The snow was blinding white, reflecting the brightness of her headlights straight back at her. The road felt squishy—slippery—beneath the steady rolling of her tires. It would only get worse as she made her way farther up the steep mountain slope. She decided it was best to speed up now before too much snow accumulated, making it even more difficult to navigate the road. She was only a few miles from her house—it shouldn't be too difficult a drive. Her foot eased down on the gas, just a little, and she began to make better time.

It was difficult to believe, but Christmas was already upon her. She had only just that day sent off the last of her packages. The trunk of her car was filled with goodies from her day of shopping—which had ended a lot later than she'd anticipated—with groceries for her Christmas feast, and a couple of presents for herself, from herself. Not to mention the Indian blankets she'd picked up from the post office—she'd ordered them over a month ago and they'd only just arrived yesterday. They were made of buffalo hair, tightly woven, warm and cushy as hell. She couldn't wait to put one on her bed.

The soothing sounds of Andean Nation filled her car, lulling her as the stretch of road lulled her into an almost hypnotic state. Not quite dreaming, but not quite awake, she sighed wearily and her breath misted in front of her face in the cold car, clouding the windshield with a hazy fog.

She didn't see him.

One minute she was driving steadily along, if a little fast given the treacherous weather, and the next, she was seeing the form of a man lying in the road in a heap. She swerved wildly to miss him and her car went into a terrifying spin. She screamed and tried to regain control of the car, to turn into the spin as she had been taught, but it was no use. She let the car have its way, praying that she didn't run over the man in the snow. After what seemed like an eternity, the car slid to a slow stop and she let out a sob, so relieved that she had made it through without a scratch.

"Oh my god, ohmygod, *ohmygod*," she said over and over like a mantra, hyperventilating. She rocked back and forth in her seat and fought against terrified tears. "I didn't just do that," she wailed. "Oh god." She unbuckled her seat belt and opened her car door all the while talking to herself in an effort to find some semblance of calm in the face of this emergency. She stumbled clumsily from the car. "Shit—what the hell is he doing in the road like that? Oh please let him be all right. Jesus, what was I thinking, driving that fast in this mess? I could have hit him. I'm an *idiot*! Please, *please* let him not be hurt." Her words streamed together into one long, rambling sentence and her voice shook as much as her frozen hands. In fact, her whole body was shaking uncontrollably.

Moving cautiously, she walked around the car and saw the man's limp form sprawled inelegantly on the ground, just as she'd first glimpsed him. He looked as if he'd been hit by a car, but any tire tracks must have long since been covered by the heavy snowfall. His shoes had been knocked from his feet—he was completely barefoot, without even the protection of socks—and for some reason this was the most horrific thing to her. She looked around, dazed, trying to see where his shoes might have landed.

The man groaned and rolled over. Terra screamed again, covering the sound at the last minute behind her hand to keep it silent so as not to scare the man any further than he already must have been. She gathered her failing courage and bent down to the man. She brushed his thick, long, golden brown hair away from his face and gasped softly.

He was beautiful. There was no other word to describe him. Oh, he wasn't beautiful in the traditional sense, not at all like the current metrosexual trend, instead he was all man, from the top of his head to the tips of his bare toes.

The man groaned again, jolting her out of her admiration of his body. "Sir," she started. "Can you hear me?"

He groaned again and the lids of his eyes trembled as if he were trying to open them, but couldn't quite accomplish the feat. Terra took the opportunity to look over him thoroughly—not as she had before, surprised by his beauty, but assessing to see how badly he was injured. She couldn't say for sure, but it looked as if the only external injury was a bloody gash in his head, right at his hairline.

"Wait here," she said, brushing his hair with her hand once more in an attempt to soothe both him and herself. She shrugged off her coat and draped it over him, tucking the edges in about him. "I'm going to go call for help," she said and rose hurriedly.

The man reached out and grabbed her ankle in an iron grip. His eyes opened and Terra found herself staring into the clearest, goldest eyes she'd ever seen. They fairly glowed.

"No doctor," he growled. His voice was deep and gritty with a hint of some exotic accent. "No help," he said.

"But you need medical attention right away," she insisted, trying and failing to free her ankle from his tight grip.

"No doctor, no hospital." He tightened his grip even harder. "*Promise.*"

"I promise," she lied, knowing instinctively that he wouldn't let her go until he heard the vow.

He let her go, releasing her so suddenly that she stumbled backward before catching herself. His strange eyes closed once more and his features smoothed, as if he slept, dreaming.

Terra slipped and slid her way back to the driver's side of her compact little car. She turned the caution lights on and rummaged through the glove box, finding and grabbing her rarely used cell phone, her fingers shaking so badly that she could barely dial the numbers. She listened for the dial tone…waiting…

Nothing happened.

She looked at the face of her phone and noted with dismay that it didn't have any juice. Swearing a blue streak, she smacked her phone against her thigh and checked once more with blind hope—no luck.

"Oh hell, what do I do now?" she asked herself, the sound of her voice startling in the stillness. She curled her fingers into the palms of her hands and breathed onto them in an attempt to regain some feeling.

It was too cold to leave him out here while she went for help. And besides, she couldn't just abandon him on the side of the road, no matter the weather. He was hurt, there was no way she would abandon him.

She walked away from the haven of her car and knelt down by him once more. Prodding his shoulder gently, she tried to rouse him enough to enlist his help.

"Sir, I've got to get you in my car. Can you help me do that?" she asked softly.

The man groaned and opened his eyes, but only barely. "No doctor," he said again.

Terra nodded. "No doctor," she said. "Even though I know I probably shouldn't move you, I've got to get you off the road and somewhere warm. Come on." She knew she was babbling, but she couldn't stop. Her lips were trembling from the cold—she could only imagine how cold the man was as he lay, barefoot, in the snow.

She slung his arm around her neck and pulled him up into a sitting position. "I need your help," she said, face close to his. She couldn't help but notice how delicious he smelled—like the forest on a rainy day.

"Come on," she said, hoisting him up with all the strength she had to spare. They made their way slowly to the car. Terra opened the back passenger door and eased him into the tight space. "Just lay there. We'll get you home and warm soon," she said, regaining her place behind the wheel.

"Shit, I hope this is the right thing to do," she murmured to herself as she started the car and began the ascent once more—slower this time in the heavy snow.

* * * * *

There would have been no way in hell she could've gotten him up the porch steps and into her living room, had he not helped. He was still woozy—she could tell that much easily enough by the way he swayed on his feet—but he was able to walk from the car to her couch with only a little support from her. However, as soon as he touched the couch, he collapsed onto it and promptly passed out.

Terra tried to turn on a lamp and realized with much dismay that the power was out. Damn. Terra knew she had to get a fire going in the woodstove before the cold settled into the house, and set about to do just that. As soon as she had the fire lit and burning, she gathered her many oil lamps and lit them, illuminating the living room with warm, soothing light. She made her way back to the couch, where the stranger lay so still that she worried for one terrifying second that he might be dead. When she saw his chest rise and fall she let out a whoosh of pent-up breath she hadn't even known she'd been holding.

She bent down next to him and brushed his hair back from his face to better see the gash in his forehead. It had already stopped bleeding. Terra wondered just how long he'd been lying out on that road in the freezing ice and snow. The road was a remote one, leading to only a few cabins along the side of the mountain. It was possible he'd been out there for hours. She hoped he didn't have any more serious injuries.

Terra would have to search him from head to foot, and hope.

His clothes were wet and clinging to his every contour. It took nearly all her strength to remove his black leather coat and tight, earth-brown T-shirt. Terra looked over the heavy muscles of his shoulders and chest, heart pounding despite her attempts to remain unmoved by the half-naked man on her couch. He looked all right. She breathed a sigh of relief.

Once she was sure he wasn't badly injured, her thoughts turned wholly carnal.

There was such strength in his body. He looked like a bodybuilder with all the tight, bulging muscles on his chest and arms. His skin was golden and smooth, not a blemish to mar its perfection. The wild, untamed scent of him was stronger now that he was half naked and she breathed the perfume deep into her lungs, savoring it like a fine wine.

She shook her head over her fanciful notions and tried to ignore her raging libido. It was impossible. She had to touch him. Hands shaking, she ran them over his massive pecs and down over his hard, washboard stomach. God! He was so smooth.

Now his jeans. They would be difficult to remove, but it must be done. She couldn't let him lie there in wet clothes and catch pneumonia on top of everything else. At least, that's what she told herself as her still-trembling hands moved to the button of his fly. She peeled the denim from him as she might have peeled the skin off a peach. And what she revealed stole all her wits.

God! He wasn't wearing any underwear!

She looked him over, at all the bare skin she'd revealed, and trembled. He was big all over. His cock, though flaccid amidst the bed of dark pubic hair, was very large. He was so thick and so long that he stole her breath away—and he hadn't even laid a hand on her. She shivered at that the very idea of him touching her. Sighing, she realized she could look at him for hours.

But she didn't have hours. She brought her mind back to the task at hand and searched him thoroughly, eyes missing not one inch of his form. She struggled to turn him over, to check his back. He had lived a hard life. It was apparent in the scars on his back and legs. But the scars were old and healed so she ignored them, though she felt some sorrow that he'd clearly suffered so.

The only other injury she found was a large, ugly bruise on his right leg, but otherwise he seemed totally unharmed. That didn't mean much, she knew. He could have sustained other injuries she couldn't see. But there was no getting back out in the storm tonight and her phones were all cordless—useless without power. She would have to keep close watch over him through the night and hope for the best.

Terra put her coat back on and ran out the front door to her car. She slipped and slid on the frozen ground, but somehow managed to maintain her balance. She gathered her purchases and took them inside, shaking the snow from her hair as she entered the house. She dropped her bags at the door and grabbed one of the buffalo-hair blankets. Approaching the man cautiously, Terra laid the blanket over his sleeping form and tucked the edges around his body, careful not to jostle him.

The gash on his head needed dressing, so she gathered what first-aid supplies she had on hand and knelt once more beside him. She gently dabbed the wound with peroxide and wiped the blood from his skin. Finding a large square of gauze, she used the last of her medical tape to affix it to the wound. It wasn't a professional job by any means, but Terra felt sure it would do for now.

Using the remaining buffalo-hair blanket and a pillow from her bed, Terra made a pallet on the floor by the woodstove and lay down upon it. She didn't want to leave his side again, so she reached under her sweater and slowly removed her bra. She would sleep in her clothes, but she would have this small comfort.

As she peeled the cotton of her bra away, it scraped over her nipples, and they grew instantly erect. A quick glance at him showed that he was still asleep. She breathed a sigh of relief and massaged her breasts to relieve the tight, desperate ache that reached from her chest straight to her womb.

She faced the man on her couch, eyes never leaving him, even as her lids began to grow heavy. Despite her best efforts, she was asleep within moments, the stress of the past few hours catching up to her all at once so that she was powerless to fight off her fatigue. Her last thoughts were about how incredible sexy the stranger was, how powerful and male, even while passed out. She wondered what he'd be like when he was awake and she trembled, drifting off into oblivion.

* * * * *

Two days until Christmas

Terra awoke with a start as her lights came on. Daylight was already growing outside and snowbirds were twittering outside the windows. Unbelievably, considering how uncomfortable her pallet had been, she had slept the whole night through without once waking.

She glanced at the couch and gasped as memories of the night before bombarded her. Letting out a sigh of relief to see that the man was still breathing, she approached him on quiet feet. First things first, she needed to check and see if he was still all right. She looked him over—determined not to lower the blanket to see his glorious nudity as she so longed to do. His hair had dried to soft, brown waves, interspersed with bright gold strands. But for the gauze on his head, there was no way to tell he'd been through so much in the past twenty-four hours. He was, simply put, lovely.

Curiosity got the better of her, despite her resolve. She shifted silently and lifted the blanket. Afraid that he might have suffered frostbite—something she hadn't thought to look for the night before—she examined him closely, growing breathless at the sight of his sleeping member. She checked his toes and legs, trying to ignore that most masculine part of him, and realized with a start that something was different.

His bruise was gone.

The big black and green bruise that had marred his right leg was no more.

Terra stared in fascination at the smooth, unblemished flesh of his leg. How had he healed so fast? She knew she hadn't imagined the injury—she'd seen it as plain as day. Yet it was gone. She couldn't believe it.

Curious now, she checked beneath the gauze on his head and almost cried out, putting her hands to her mouth to choke back the sound lest she wake her charge. The wound was now only a faint pink blemish on his skin. There was no angry, bleeding gash. Terra traced her fingers gently over it, feeling the newly formed skin, smooth as silk beneath her touch. It occurred to her just how strange the moment was. There was a naked man on her couch, and his delicious body had just performed a miracle of swift healing within a matter of hours.

She felt the hair on the back of her neck rise.

Struggling to hold back her swift, nearly panicked breaths, she looked away from the wound and let her eyes trip over his body, studying him closely. Then she closed her eyes tight, the image of his incredible body seared into her brain, before forcing herself to look at him again.

His eyes were open, waiting.

He breathed deep and Terra realized with a start that he was taking in her scent, capturing it in his lungs to savor.

Terra gasped and stumbled back, their gazes fused together.

His eyes glowed a warm golden honey, bright and clear. She'd never seen eyes like his in all her life. It would be easy for a girl to get lost in them. Heavy-lidded, almond-shaped orbs of such incredible color that she was swept down into their depths with but one glance. They were full of mysterious magic. In some elemental way she felt almost…hunted when he looked at her.

"A-are you all right?" she asked. "How are you feeling?"

He looked confused for a moment then his face settled into a stoic mask, as if he were hiding his confusion. "Water," he said, his voice as deep as a well.

Tripping to her feet she rushed into the kitchen and grabbed a glass, filling it with filtered water from the tap. She made her way back to him in record time and handed him the glass. He downed the entire thing with two gulps and handed the empty glass back to her with a satisfied sigh.

"How are you feeling?" she asked again.

"Fine." He sat up, taking in his surroundings. "Who are you?"

"Terra Gillead. What's your name?"

"Cassius del Morte," he said, and the name gave her shivers. He sat up and she stumbled backward to put more space between them. "Why am I here?"

"You were lying in the middle of the road. I almost hit you—hell, anyone could have come along and killed you. I took you home to get you out of the weather."

"I was walking home," he said blearily.

"Well, you're lucky to be alive," she told him. "Why didn't you want a doctor by the way? Or shouldn't I ask?"

He ignored her question, closing his eyes for long seconds. When his eyes opened they were hot and intense. He looked at her, making her feel like a deer caught in a hunter's headlights. She felt like prey to his predator. "I hunger," he said at last, eyes leaving her so that she could once more breathe easily.

"Oh, right." She laughed nervously. "I'll just go make us some breakfast." She rose, leaving him there, wondering if she was making a mistake turning her back on this stranger, and made her way once more to the kitchen.

Terra was facing the sink, opening a package of bacon, when great, strong arms came around her from behind. She stiffened and tried to pry the arms from around her. It was no use, he wouldn't budge. She whimpered, fear doubling. Cassius put his face in the curve of her neck and shoulder and breathed deeply. She shivered and tried to ignore the effect his nearness was having on her. "I hunger *for you*," he breathed softly into her ear, tightening his hold on her, lips tickling her flesh. The rough scrape of his shadow-beard branded her. She moaned and stopped struggling.

She grew immediately wet, knees weakening so that she leaned back against him for support. His hips cradled hers and there was no mistaking the fierceness of his arousal as it pressed hot and heavy and hard against the swell of her buttocks. He licked the side of her face and she gasped softly. The feel of his tongue was so hot against her skin that she felt scorched. He nuzzled her throat, heated lips wandering over her skin as if he were thinking about eating her, and she cried out in mounting desire.

There was no hesitancy about her need for him. It was like a runaway freight train, sweeping her along without mercy. Something about him resonated deep within her, his magnetism impossible for her to resist, and she was powerless in the face of her relentless desire.

His hands grasped her upper arms, fingers biting into her flesh, pulling her tighter to him. He bit her neck, shocking her into a gasp, and immediately laved the bruise with the tip of his tongue. Her nipples lengthened, growing impossibly hard, swelling against the brush of her soft knit sweater.

His breath moved the hair at the nape of her neck. Her clit swelled as if kissed and ached with an intensity that nearly had her weeping. His hands turned her to face him and he kissed her, stealing what little breath she had left.

The feel of his lips moving over hers was exquisite. His tongue probed at the seam of her lips and she opened her mouth wide to suckle it hungrily. He tasted like the outdoors, of fresh air and rain and earth. He smelled the same, swamping all of her senses until she was mindless to all but the feel and scent of him.

Emotion swelled in her breast, making her heart hurt. She had never felt the like. She hoped that it would last forever, kissing this stranger, touching him, feeling him—she never wanted harsh reality to intrude again. Terra tangled her hands in his hair, sighing into his mouth as she felt the cool, smooth, silken strands slide between her fingers.

He kissed her as if he would eat her from the mouth down. His tongue swept through her mouth, leaving behind no secrets for her to hide behind, filling her with the wild flavor of him. Her senses reeled—there was too much stimulus for her to cope with—and she grew dizzy, drunk on his kiss. He bit the tip of her chin, delicately scraping her skin, and she moaned, knees turning to butter.

One of his hands found her breast. He stroked it from base to tip through the thick material of her sweater, but it felt as if he were touching her bare skin. Her nipple grew tighter, harder and longer until it stabbed at the material, begging to be caressed. He found the hard nub and twisted it gently between his thumb and forefinger. Terra cried out and leaned further into him, raising her mouth to be kissed once more with such fierce intensity that it stole her breath completely away.

He lifted her suddenly, high up against him. She wrapped her legs around his waist and held on for dear life. The thick, hard demand of his cock pressed tight to her cunt, making her pussy weep, making it ache and pulse with want.

He growled into her mouth, a wild and untamed sound that vibrated through her mouth and straight to her heart, setting it aflutter. Something deep and unnamed within her flared to life at the animalistic sound, something elemental and raw. If she'd had any misgivings before about making out with a man she'd only known a handful of hours, they were cast aside. Instinct took over and she was lost.

She clutched his head, fingers tangled in his silky hair, and nuzzled his throat, kissing and suckling and nibbling until he was panting heavily in her ear. All of his naked skin was hot to the touch, electrifying, and she couldn't resist running her hungry hands all over his massive chest. Terra bit his shoulder and laved the hurt with her tongue and he nearly roared.

Lowering her to the ground, he put his hands on the collar of her sweater and ripped it clean in two. Her breasts were bared to his gaze and he ate her up with his eyes before he palmed both her breasts in his hands. With slow, erotic strokes he ran his thumbs over the protrusion of her nipples, making her cry out and clutch at him for balance as her knees gave out.

Every breath she drew was infused with his scent and she grew drunk on the masculine perfume of him. Arching into the touch of his hands as they kneaded her breasts, she gasped and shivered, cut adrift in a storm of desire. There was no part of her body that wasn't screaming for his possession, regardless that he was a stranger to her. It didn't matter. She wanted him. Bad.

His cock was thick—thicker than her wrist—and long. It bobbed up and down with his every movement, like a dowsing rod sensing water. It must have sensed that she was as wet as an ocean and was just as eager as he for the floodgates to open wide and accept him.

Oh god. He was going to stretch her wider than she'd ever been stretched before. She couldn't wait.

His hands found the waistband of her jeans and within seconds he had them pushed down around her ankles. He bent before her and hooked the edge of her thong panties with his teeth. He peeled them down roughly, demandingly, and let them fall at her feet along with all her other clothes.

With a gasp of mounting excitement, she watched as he buried his face in the vee of her thighs and sniffed deep of her scent. She cried out, a wild sound breaking over the noise of their panting breaths, and he speared her with his tongue.

His fingers spread her labia and his tongue—god, it was long!—unerringly found her clit. It flicked over the swollen nub, stroking and rubbing. He suckled it, like a nipple, and impaled her with one wide, strong thumb. It sank deep into her, its way eased by the plentiful moisture he had called forth from her pussy with his deep kiss. His tongue speared her again, impaling her alongside his thumb, tasting her deeply. She cried out again and sank, limp, against him.

Cassius held her up with his hands as if she weighed no more than a feather. He lifted one of her legs and hooked it over his shoulder, opening her wider for his mouth and fingers to explore. He licked her like he would an ice-cream cone, tasting her from anus to clit over and over until she was crying out uncontrollably with each pass of his tongue.

One of his fingers found the moue of her anus and traced little circles into the sensitive flesh. No one had ever touched her there before—she simply hadn't allowed it. But it felt so wicked and wonderful when Cassius did it that she had no will to object the bold caress. He entered her, one knuckle deep, and sucked violently on her clit.

His gaze bored into hers, his golden eyes glowing. The look he gave her was so hot, so wicked, that she felt her cunt pulse excitedly.

Terra would have collapsed completely had he not held her up. She wanted to fall to the floor and beg him to take her. She needn't have worried. Cassius promptly stood and turned her around. He bent her gently over the small breakfast table, so that her ass faced him. He came behind her, stroking his hands over the generous globes of her bottom as if in worship, and she trembled delicately.

The press of his cock was a shock, but not at all unwelcome. The wide, thick head penetrated her, stretching her. She cried out and wriggled to relieve some of the pressure, but his hands pressed into the small of her back, halting her struggles. He pressed inexorably deeper into her, stealing her breath, splitting her wide with his massive girth.

Short, high-pitched shrieks broke free of her lips as he drove himself slowly home. He filled her until she felt as if her body would tear right down the center. Pleasure and pain blended together so that she couldn't tell them apart. Cassius bent over her and sank his teeth into her shoulder and she did scream then, so loud it reverberated off the walls.

He held her still with his teeth as he began to move over her. His cock was so fat, so long, that it took several seconds to complete each thrust and withdrawal. Wet, sucking sounds accompanied his every movement, her body growing so wet that moisture slipped down the inside of her leg like teardrops. Her body literally wept with need for him, and she thrust her bottom at him in a demand for more.

He began to pound her, his balls slapping hard against her pussy. The table skidded across the floor and he followed it, pressing even deeper into the wet, clinging flesh of her cunt. Terra dug her nails into the wood, leaving faint scars behind, and pressed tighter back against him. He increased his pace and doubled his force so that she was sobbing, laid completely bare for his delectation.

His hands came around her and cupped the swinging orbs of her breasts, thumbs and forefingers pinching her long, hard nipples. Terra ran her hand over her pussy, finding her clit, and began to rub demanding circles into the tender flesh.

"Oh god, I'm going to come, Cassius," she cried out, shuddering.

Cassius growled and pounded harder into her.

Her climax was swift and debilitating. Her whole body seemed to shut down, only to focus with searing intensity on the milking pulses of her cunt. The walls of her channel trembled and squeezed his cock, making her see stars as he struck her womb over and over again. She cried out uncontrollably, knees giving out completely so that he had to hold her up over the table. He thrust into her over and over until, with a mighty grunt, he spilled his hot, thick, silky come deep inside her.

He lowered her gently to the floor, his carefulness in sharp contrast to the violent storm of passion they had just shared. Light pulsations still rippled through her pussy, caressing them both. Her body milked him of every last drop of his desire and they lay there, together, her trembling body beneath his, both panting uncontrollably.

"Holy shit, that was amazing," she said, dazed, voice shaking.

Cassius took a deep breath. "You smell of me," he said, voice satisfied and possessive. He rolled them, so that she sat on top of him. He lifted her and twisted her around, moving her on his thick stalk, his way eased by their combined fluids. His finger found her clit and began to stroke it.

"Come for me again," he said, guiding her to ride him.

His words were like magic. She increased her pace, breasts bobbing with her every movement. Panting, she braced herself with her hands on his large, smooth pecs and rotated her hips on him. They both gasped. He filled her so tightly, so deeply, that each movement brought her closer and closer to the edge.

Her body clenched on his. They both cried out. Cassius howled like a wild wolf and he pounded up into her. Terra clenched at him, digging her nails into his flesh. She came, eyes blinded, hard and absolute.

Orgasm after orgasm tore through her. Cassius roared beneath her and surged upward, finding his release yet again. Terra was so wet with his cum that their bodies slid easily against each other. She screamed as yet another—and still another—release consumed her and she arched back over him so that her long dark hair tickled her ass and his legs.

Terra collapsed against him and fought for breath that didn't smell of their sex. It was impossible. The perfume of their naked, sweating bodies filled the room, drugging her. She buried her face in his neck and lay there until her shuddering stopped and she found reason once more.

"How did you do that?" she asked. She'd never had multiple orgasms before—didn't even know it was truly possible. That she had done so with him was somehow so special that it brought tears to her eyes.

"I don't know," he said. "It was my first time."

Chapter Two

"What are you talking about?" she exclaimed.

"I was a virgin," he said, eyes glowing.

Terra scrambled up off him, gasping as his cock left her body. She stumbled and only just managed to sit in a chair by the table. "That's not true," she insisted.

"I wouldn't lie to you," he said softly, a growl underlying his words.

Terra frowned furiously. "How is that possible in this day and age? What are you, like thirty years old?" she asked.

He smiled, revealing a row of very large, very white teeth. "Actually I'm fifty-seven, but who's counting?"

She burst out laughing. "You're teasing me."

Cassius shook his head. "No I'm not. I'm very serious, I can assure you."

Terra sobered and eyed him. "You're not fifty-seven. You can't be."

He nodded. "My family is known for its longevity. We age well."

"No shit," she said flippantly. "Can I see your driver's license?" she asked.

He looked around. "Where are my pants?"

"Hanging on the back of the recliner in the living room."

Cassius rose, uncaring of his nudity, though Terra fairly drooled over him, eyes wide to drink in the sight of him. His butt was perfect, round and taut and toned. God but he was magnificent! He disappeared into the living room and came back almost immediately. He handed her his license and she reeled to see that he was telling the truth. Wow. He really did age well.

"I'm told my grandmother lived until she was one hundred thirty years old. My grandfather made it to one hundred ten. No doubt I shall live as long if I am lucky."

Terra frowned. "What about your parents?"

His face darkened, his eyes dimming somewhat. "They were both killed when I was nine."

"Oh," she said, sadness welling within her at the pain she heard evidenced in his voice. "I'm so sorry, Cassius."

"Such is the way of the world," he said with a shrug. His hair, shaggy and disheveled after their storm of lovemaking, fell over his face, shielding his expression from her.

"Well," she said, dropping the subject. "I don't know about you, but I am famished." She rose and went back to the sink, preparing to make bacon, eggs and toast. It was strange, but she felt very aware that she had turned her back to him. He wasn't a threat to her, she knew it instinctively, but he still seemed the sort of man one shouldn't turn a blind eye to all the same.

"How do you like your eggs?" she asked.

"Over easy," he replied, coming up behind her and running a fingertip down the crease of her back, reminding her that they were both still nude. Somehow, though, it just felt right to be naked with him.

"How about your bacon?" she asked breathlessly. "Crispy or tender?"

"Raw," he said.

Terra laughed. "No, really."

"I like all my meat raw."

She met his gaze. His eyes were glowing again. "You can get sick from that, you know, especially with pork," she laughed.

"No. I won't," Cassius said softly, his breath tickling her ear.

Terra laughed nervously. There was just something so strange about him. She couldn't put her finger on it, but it was there all the same, tickling at her mind. She didn't feel threatened, not really, but something about him gave her pause. He was just so strange.

"Now tell me the truth," she started, laying out raw bacon on a plate for him. "Were you really a virgin?"

"Yes. My kind chooses one mate and one mate only."

"Your kind?" she asked. "I don't understand."

"Yes," Cassius answered evasively.

"What, are you, like, a foreigner?"

"I am from here in Washington. From the woods."

"You live in the woods?" she asked.

"Yes. Well, I have a house in Seattle, but I rarely go there. I prefer the forest over the city any day."

She sat a plate with steaming eggs, toast and raw bacon on the table for him. Cassius immediately took a seat and tore into the meat, wolfing down strip after strip with large, single bites. She took a seat opposite him and ate her toast, watching him eat the food with a ravenous appetite that warmed her heart.

"What do you mean, exactly, when you say you only mate once?"

"I mean exactly that," he said, sopping up some runny yolk with his toast. "You are my mate. I know that now. My one and only."

Terra laughed uncomfortably and played with one long dark lock of her hair. "You don't mean that," she said. "You don't have to woo me with lies, if that's what you're doing. I don't want a commitment from you. I barely know you."

Cassius swallowed the last of his food and met her gaze with his. "I wouldn't lie to you," he said once more. "Do you know, you have the most beautiful brown eyes I've ever seen?"

Terra blushed. "Quit sweet-talking me or I'll jump your bones again."

His gaze turned positively wicked. "How about I jump on yours?" he said and pounced across the table, taking her to the floor with a jarring impact.

Cassius spread her legs and bent his head between her thighs, pressing a hot kiss to the crown of her sex. Terra cried out, surprised, but quickly recovered. She pulled him up over her and reached down to take his thick stalk in her hand, pumping him over and over until he was hard as marble. It thrilled her heart to hear him cry out his response to her caress. A droplet of pre-cum seeped from his opening and she brought the drop to her lips to taste. He was so sweet, so decadent. She'd never tasted a man with such a wild, delicious flavor.

His mouth found hers and he plundered it, plunging his tongue deep. Terra sucked on his tongue, relishing his flavor. His hair was a curtain about their heads, smelling so thickly of spicy woods that she reeled dizzily. His fingers found her nipples, long and thick and hard, and squeezed them gently until she was gasping for breath like a fish out of water. All the while he kissed her, until she was mindless to all but him. His touch. His scent. His flavor. It was all too intoxicating.

The rough tips of his fingers spread her pussy lips, and she helped to guide him into her opening. Her fingers, unable to reach completely around the base of his cock, guided him until he was home, sliding so deep into her that he stole her very breath away.

This time he was gentler with her, rocking on top of her, thrusting his cock in and out of her pussy with such tender care that it brought tears to her eyes. He popped a nipple into his mouth and suckled it, rooting like a babe. Terra found a heretofore undiscovered connection between her breast and her loins. With each draw of his lips, her pussy gushed with liquid warmth, milking him and sending her reeling. Heat pooled low and deep in her belly, and each time he moved inside her, that heat intensified.

He lifted her legs and she wrapped them around him, hooking her ankles at the small of his back. This allowed him to penetrate her even deeper, if that was even possible, wringing forth cries from her mouth that sounded like a stranger's voice and not her own.

The sharp bite of his teeth bruised her nipple, but Terra welcomed the pain as it melted into pleasure. He would leave a mark behind, as he had left other marks with the burn of his shadowy beard.

For some strange, alien reason, it felt to Terra that they were doing more than just fucking. They were even doing more than simply making love. It felt as if something deep inside her was giving itself over to him, and that something in him was being gifted to her. She'd never felt such things. It was as if they were one being, one mind, one heart. This type of communion had never been part of her lovemaking before. It was unbelievably wonderful and welcome. Terra felt as if they belonged together.

She shook her head violently to clear it of such fanciful thoughts.

"What's wrong?" Cassius asked, mouth at her ear.

"Nothing," she said, gathering him closer. "Nothing at all," she sighed happily.

Cassius growled, the sound echoing through the house, so deep and so loud that it vibrated through her bones. It was a sound of total satisfaction. His fingers found her clit just as he exploded inside her. She felt the hot, creamy scald of him deep within and then she, too, was flying through ecstasy.

"Terra, Terra," he cried out, shuddering in her arms. "Take all of me."

Her orgasm brought tears to her eyes, and her body milked his until they were both mindless. He thrust into her again, over and over, until finally collapsing, sweating and breathless, on top of her.

It took some time before Terra could think clearly again. She felt Cassius withdraw from her body and moaned when he left her. He wasn't gone long. He came back with a wet paper towel and spread her legs once more. He cleaned her with soft, gentle strokes, soothing her raw flesh. But with every brush of the cool cloth over her clit, she bucked her hips and gasped.

"You're mine, you know," he said softly, glowing eyes meeting hers.

Terra laughed. "You don't even know me," she said awkwardly.

"We have our whole lifetime to get to know one another. I, for one, am looking forward to it."

She shook her head and reached up to tuck one golden brown strand of hair behind his ear. "You're so weird," she said. "I don't understand you."

"I have been a lone wolf my whole life, looking for somewhere I could belong. I belong with you, Terra. Forever and always. I know it in my soul," he said passionately, holding her palm over the beating of his heart.

Terra pushed him back and got to her feet. He knelt there, looking up at her with his strange, golden eyes. "Stop saying such things," she told him breathlessly.

"I am only telling you the truth," he said.

Terra shook her head and squeezed her eyes shut. He was so beautiful, looking up at her with such longing, such desire, that she couldn't bear to see him just then. "I think I need to get dressed," she said and left him there, going to her bedroom in the back of the house.

When she came back, Cassius had donned his jeans and was sitting at the kitchen table once more, muscular chest still bare. His skin was golden-hued and smooth as marble. His hair, reflecting the light from the windows, looked more blond than brown today. His eyes were still aglow, and when they met hers they sizzled. He looked utterly delicious.

"Please, sit. I must talk with you," he said, motioning to the other chair. He had grabbed a pop from the fridge and sat it in front of her, bidding her to take a drink.

"What do you want to talk about?" she asked suspiciously.

"I have been alone since my parents were killed," he started. Terra gasped, surprised at what he was saying, considering that his parents were killed when he was nine. Who had raised him?

"When my parents were gunned down by poachers, I retreated into the deep woods and lived there until my twentieth year. I built a cabin there and kept the city house my family had lived in with the help of a trust fund my parents had set up for me. I seldom go to Seattle anymore—I make my living going from one job to the next, always moving—but the city house is there whenever I need it."

"Is your cabin far from here?"

"Not far," he said. "Just a couple of miles east of here. I was returning last night from a short stay in Seattle. A car struck me as I was trying to get home."

"Barefoot?" She chuckled. "It's a miracle you aren't dead," she told him.

His eyes met hers, gaze deep and hot and passionate. "I'd like to take you to see my cabin," he said.

Terra chuckled. "What, you mean now?"

"Yes."

She shook her head disbelievingly. "I don't even know you. You could be a murderer for all I know." She didn't believe that lie for even a second.

He smiled softly. "You know I would never hurt you," he said.

"No, I don't," she insisted stubbornly.

"Search your feelings. You know me in your heart. In your soul. You *know* me."

He was right. For whatever reason she couldn't explain, she did trust him not to hurt her. She trusted him to the ends of the Earth and beyond. "Okay. Let me just get my coat and boots on. Oh. You're barefoot. We'll need to drive."

"My feet will be fine for our walk. I was walking barefooted last night through the storm. The cold won't bother me, I promise you." He donned his T-shirt and jacket, zipping it as he spoke. "Nor will it bother you. I won't let it." He smiled at her.

Terra shook her head again. "You are *so weird,*" she told him once more. "Here you tell me you're almost sixty, you've lived alone since you were nine, you survived being hit by a car and you walk barefoot in the snow. What sort of superhuman are you supposed to be?"

"I'm not a human at all," he said simply. "I'm a werewolf."

* * * * *

Terra was speechless. She eyed him from head to toe, noting everything about him. He was gorgeous as ever, rough and tumbled-looking, but well and fit all the same. It was too bad he was completely crazy.

"A werewolf," she stated dubiously.

"Yes," Cassius returned, his gaze never leaving hers.

Terra took deep, calming breaths, but each was heavy with the scent of their bodies combined. It made her head spin even more than it already was. "I don't believe you." She managed to force the words out.

"I know," he replied. "But the full moon is Christmas Eve. You'll know then that what I say is the truth."

"Who says I'm going to let you hang around until then?" she asked angrily.

He looked hurt, mortally so, for all of a second, then a mask fell over his face, hiding his emotions from her. It made her feel bereft, this mask, but there was nothing she could do about it. Or so she told herself.

"You cannot deny me."

Terra growled, the sound startling her. "I can do whatever I want," she said angrily. "Now get out of my house."

"I'm not leaving you like this," he said.

"Get out of my house, Cassius. Now," she shouted, pointing toward the door.

He rose from his seat and came to stand before her. "Can you look me in the eye and tell me to go?" he asked.

She met his gaze.

And something faltered in her. Her anger dissipating as if it had never been.

She licked her lips. "I can't," she admitted. "But what else am I expected to do? Just wait around until you turn furry—or not, as the case may be?"

"Yes," he said insistently.

"Cassius, you are by far the strangest man I have ever met."

He smiled and tucked a strand of hair behind her ear. "Come on. Let's go to my house. I want you to see where I live."

"No," she protested. "You go home and call me later, okay? The power's back on, so my phone will actually work. I'll be here waiting patiently."

"I'm not letting you out of my sight," he growled and the sound made the hackles on the back of her neck stand at attention.

Terra sighed, admitting defeat, and went to get her coat and shoes. Though she didn't want to admit it, even to herself, she didn't want him out of her sight either. With one last look around, she grabbed one of the buffalo-hair blankets and left the house.

They stepped out into the cold day. The snow from the night before had accumulated on the ground so that several inches of it covered the tips of her boots. True to his word, Cassius walked barefoot without a qualm.

"This is insane," she said, boots crunching the snow underfoot.

"I can regulate my body temperature as climate demands," he said, taking her hand in his. "I have no fear of hot or cold."

"Well, neither do I, but you don't see me walking around barefoot in this mess."

Cassius laughed and the sound washed over her like honey-drenched silk. It was the first time she'd actually heard him laugh, and the sound of it made her heart race. She vowed then and there to make him laugh more often.

"Here," she said, offering the blanket to him. "I thought you might like to keep this," she grinned. "As a keepsake."

He took it, returning her smile, and tucked it under one massive arm.

They made it to the tree line and crossed over into the woods. Terra's cabin sat atop a hilly clearing, but was surrounded on nearly all sides by thick forest. They headed east, just as he had said, and the sight of her home faded in the distance behind them.

Cassius took her hand more tightly in his and directed her to stand still before him. "I have to have you again," he said, voice rough and gritty.

Terra laughed. "What? Here? We've only just made it into the trees."

"No one will see if that's what's bothering you. There isn't a soul about for miles," he said.

"Oh god," she laughed, and hurriedly began to unfasten her clothes. Cassius gave a feral grin and freed his cock from its confines, undoing the fastening of his jeans so that it bobbed free and bounced in the chilly air.

God he was huge, even in the cold!

Terra tore off her shirt and her bra with swift, eager motions as Cassius laid the blanket out on the bed of snow. Her hands went to the fastening of her jeans, and she kicked her boots off. When they were both nude—Terra shivering in the brisk cold—she sank to her knees on the blanket and sucked his cock into the back of her throat.

He tasted wild and untamed, like the forest surrounding them. She palmed his sac in her hand and squeezed it gently, rolling his testicles expertly. Cassius threw back his head and howled, his voice echoing back from the trees. She opened her mouth wide over him, using her tongue to tease him deeper past her lips. She made wet, sucking sounds over his sensitive flesh, using her spit to moisten his velveteen skin so that it could slide deeper inside.

He pulsed in her mouth. He was so hot that he nearly singed her lips. He smelled of earth and green, growing things, the luscious scent driving her wild. Her body shook with the force of its need, her nipples hard and long and tight, her pussy wet and aching for him.

"Fuck me," she murmured against his flesh, licking him from base to tip. "Fuck me like a wild wolf would fuck its mate," she said.

Her words inflamed him. He growled low and pushed her back onto the blanket. He kissed her hard and swiftly turned them so that she sat atop him. The cold was forgotten as he raised her blood temperature by popping one of her nipples deep into his mouth.

Cassius thrust into her with one fierce thrust. Terra screamed as he slid home and wriggled over him. He filled her so deep and so tight that she could hardly breathe. He bounced her up and down with his hips, grasping hers tight in his hands to help steady her.

His fingers found her nipples and twisted them delicately. Terra arched into his touch, her head falling back so that her hair tickled over their heated skin. His hands roved over her body, down over her stomach and straight to her clit. He rubbed her most sensitive flesh and thrust deeper, harder into her.

"Do you like it when I fuck your tight, wet hole?" he asked, his voice a gasp.

"Oh god, yes," she answered. "Yes, yes, *yes*!"

"You're so fucking hot. So fucking tight. It feels like a fist is wrapped around me," he said. "And your tits! Shit, your tits are the most beautiful in all the world."

"How would you know?" she teased.

"Oh trust me, I know it for certain." He grinned cheekily up at her and thrust home particularly hard. "You're so wet. So silky. You make me want to fuck all day."

"So do it. If you're man enough," she goaded.

"Don't ask for something you can't handle. I would never hurt you."

"It won't hurt me to get banged all day," she laughed. "Come on. Give me all you've got."

He roared and thrust into her, jarring her from head to toe. He pounded so hard into her that she saw stars. Pleasure and pain blended into bliss, and every breath she took was just enough for her to moan, or shout, or scream.

"Milk me, Terra. Come for me."

Terra cried out and rode him harder. Her clit ground down on him and she screamed, a harsh, rough sound that echoed off the trees. Her body clamped down hard on him, locking them both together, and they found release in the same heartbeat, the same breath.

His cum jettisoned into her body, burning her, bringing her. She felt her pussy clench over and over, the pulsations in rhythm with her erratic pulse. "Oh god, *Cassiusssss*," she cried out.

He held her to him and let her come, filling her at the same time with his scalding cream. When they were spent, she collapsed down upon him, breath bellowing out like a freight train. She rubbed her face in his neck and kissed his mouth, licking his lips delicately.

"That was awesome," she said.

Cassius laughed.

Chapter Three

Christmas Eve

Once they made it to his cabin the day before, they made love all day, with hardly a word spoken between them.

It felt so right to be in his arms.

They made love into the night and on until the morning. They showered together, each pleasuring the other with eager mouths. She tasted his come, and he tasted hers in turn. Then they soaped each other's bodies and fucked right there in the shower.

He fucked her in the ass with his finger and she rode his cock until they were both raw. Then she took him in her mouth and made him come again. The delicious flavor of him filled her senses, drugging her, and she swallowed every last drop he had to give, reveling in the thick, creamy texture.

They stopped only to eat and speak a few words to each other then the evening was upon them.

"Will you watch me as I change?" he asked, pinching her nipples over and over with his fingers.

Terra licked his lips and spread herself for his pleasure. He buried his face in her pussy and licked her from anus to clit, breathing deeply of her scent in that most secret place. He inserted three fingers into her fuck hole and thrust them in and out, over and over, until she was panting for breath.

"I suppose so," she said. She hadn't really given his claims of being a werewolf much thought since they'd made it to his small, cozy cabin deep within the woods yesterday.

Had it only been yesterday? To Terra it felt like a lifetime. She could no longer imagine how she'd lived without Cassius at her side.

"Will you be scared?" he asked, gently inserting his thumb into her anus.

"Probably," she gasped, stretching wide to receive him as he guided his dick into her body.

"Don't be," he said. "I would never hurt you." He began a slow, rhythmic thrusting into her body. Over and over again, stretching her until she was so full of him she could hardly breathe. He rocked her, hips slamming home, holding her head still for his thrilling kiss.

He took her nipple into his mouth and suckled it, wet sounds filling the quiet around them. His finger found her clit and rubbed little circles into it. Her body tightened around his, and she arched up beneath his caress.

She came with a wild cry that he returned. He slammed into her and filled her with his essence until her body overflowed with him and wet the mattress beneath her. They came back to Earth shuddering and breathless.

The dark gathered outside and Cassius stood. "Come. The time draws near," he said, reaching for her hand.

The moon was full, just as he had said it would be, casting its silvery glow over the white land, turning it to sparkles. Cassius left the porch and stood beneath it, motioning for her to follow.

"Isn't the moon beautiful?" he asked, the word "moon" long and drawn out like a small howl.

"It is," she said and rubbed her arms with her hands nervously.

"Don't be afraid," he said and his eyes were a warm, brilliant gold. "I'll come back in a few hours after I've hunted," he said.

He looked back at the moon and something miraculous happened.

Terra hadn't believed him to be a werewolf for a second. But now she was forced to acknowledge the reality. Cassius' form blurred and a brilliant golden glow suffused his form. A long, lone howl sounded out over the night, stirring the stillness. The glow dimmed, but only just, and in Cassius' place there stood a dark brown wolf.

"Holy. Shit," she said, backing away.

The wolf came to her and sniffed at her hand. She jerked it back, shrieking. The wolf, eyes glowing gold, licked her knee and she nearly lost it.

"I don't believe it," she said.

The wolf huffed its breath as if it was scoffing at her words. It turned and fled into the forest.

"Oh my god, he *is* a werewolf," she said as she watched him retreat. "What am I going to tell my mother?" She laughed hysterically and walked backward into the house.

She thought about locking the door, but knew it was Cassius' house and she couldn't bar him from his home. Besides, she was getting over her upset. Slowly but surely.

Terra returned to Cassius' bed and lay down upon it. The smell of him was thick here, comforting her, arousing her. She buried her head in his pillow and breathed deep. With a growl she flung the pillow across the room.

She got up and made her way into the kitchen. She grabbed a bottle of whiskey from Cassius' fridge and went to bed with it, determined to drown out her current confusion with the confusion of drink. Eventually she fell asleep, the bottle falling empty to the floor…

When she awoke a few hours later it was to find the furry form of Cassius lying in the bed with her. The wolf turned its head and looked at her with human eyes and she was lost. "Oh Cassius," she said, rubbing her hand over the soft, silken muzzle of the beast. "I love you."

The wolf seemed to smile and licked her cheek. The effects of the drink still heady in her system, Terra smiled…and promptly passed back out.

Epilogue

Terra and Cassius returned to her home to gather her things, so that she could start moving into his cabin. They held hands as they walked and made love twice along the way. Terra had never been so happy.

When they stepped onto her porch and Terra reached for the lock, she noticed a small rectangle of paper wedged in the doorjamb.

"What's this?" She frowned, freeing the paper.

Cassius reached over her and took the card.

World of the Living Forest
Adrian Darkwood

The words were in bold type on the front. Cassius turned the card over and read the elegant, masculine scrawl on the back.

Been looking for you. Will come back at a better time.

P.S. Congratulations on finding your mate.

"Do you know this person?" she asked curiously.

He smiled up at her. "He knows you're my mate, whoever he is."

"Did it say when he'd come back?"

"No. But I doubt he'd have any trouble finding us if we didn't wait here."

Terra laughed. "Let him find you. It seems like he knows what you are. Maybe this Living Forest thing can help you find more beings like yourself."

"I'm happier with it just being you and me," Cassius said with a grin and a quick kiss to her cheek. "Come on, let's get your things. I'm eager to get you home so we can try out the warm spring on my property."

Terra laughed and rushed to gather her belongings.

She couldn't wait for the trip back home.

Also by Sherri L. King

Bachelorette
Beyond Illusion
Ellora's Cavemen: Tales From the Temple III (*anthology)*
Fetish
Horde Wars: Ravenous
Horde Wars: Wanton Fire
Horde Wars: Razor's Edge
Horde Wars: Lord of the Deep
Manaconda *(anthology)*
Midnight Desires (*anthology)*
Moon Lust
Moon Lust: Bitten
Moon Lust: Feral Heat
Moon Lust: Mating Season
Rayven's Awakening
Sanctuary
Sin and Salvation
Sterling Files 1: Steele
Sterling Files 2: Vicious
Sterling Files 3: Fyre
The Jewel

About the Author

ജ

Sherri L. King lives in the American Deep South with her husband, artist and illustrator Darrell King. Critically acclaimed author of *The Horde Wars* and *Moon Lust* series, her primary interests lie in the world of action packed paranormals, though she's been known to dabble in several other genres as time permits.

Sherri welcomes comments from readers. You can find her website and email address on her author bio page at www.ellorascave.com.

CHRISTMAS TO REMEMBER

Annie Windsor

ꙮ

Dedication

ꭓ

To Dot the Ever-Wicked, at http://www.devilishdots.com.
Thanks for the toy info!

Chapter One

"You're fired."

Megan Caulfield didn't think she heard the man right. She shifted in the conference room chair and stared at the skinny little pencil pusher in the black suit, the one who had just spoken the two words sure to ruin her life.

Dwayne Grenchler, the new CEO of Sweet Dreams Cosmetics, sat across the huge oak table with his fingers spread across a file in front of him. Damn, but he looked pleased with himself. The weasel-bastard actually *smiled* at her.

In a window overlooking Central Park, snow started to fall. A dull ringing plagued Meg's ears. Stark white walls and hunter green carpet squeezed in on her. The room suddenly felt so small she didn't think she could breathe. Her hands clenched into fists in her lap. "I'm the best chemist you have. I created the entire Dreamwalker perfume line." Then, as if it made any difference, "It's a week before Christmas—and I promised the Children's Fund half of my December check. How can you fire me a week before Christmas?"

"Holidays are just another number on the calendar." Grenchler's condescending smile never faded. "If you had your head in Sweet Dreams instead of kiddie charities, you'd understand that. And you should read your memos. I terminated the Sweet Dreams dollar-for-dollar contribution to that free-ride waste of time the first day I was here. "

Meg's insides curdled. She bit her lip to keep from screaming at Grenchler, or slapping him, or worse—crying. The Children's Fund depended on Sweet Dreams! Without employee contributions and the corporation's matching funds, the big Christmas Eve shopping spree would have to be cancelled.

Hundreds of children would wake to a cold Christmas morning with no presents, no food—nothing.

She wouldn't cry, damn it. Not yet. What a bastard!

Grenchler gestured to the other man in the room, the one standing near the door. "Personnel's here to go over termination papers, a generic reference and insurance continuation issues."

Meg couldn't even look at Nick Myra's achingly handsome face. She wanted his muscled arms around her. She wanted to wrap her fingers in his thick black hair and hear him tell her to wake up, that Grenchler and his "company slim-downs" were just bad dreams. But she was getting fired. That fantasy would never come true, would it? She'd leave the company, and she and Nick would never see each other again—and she had been so sure the man was an inch from asking her out, despite company rules about fraternization with fellow employees.

She would have said yes, too.

Normally, Meg was all about rules. Her roommate Nancy even called her "tightly wrapped." Nick Myra could tear through the most well taped package, though. Of that, she had no doubt.

At last, she managed to raise her chin enough to see Nick. He stood with his head down and his arms folded, as quiet and unreadable as ever.

Grenchler tapped the file on the table. "While you two talk, I'll have someone pack your desk and locker, and Security will walk you out." He stood to leave.

"My desk—my locker?" Meg got to her feet almost as fast as Grenchler did. "Security? You've got to be kidding. I've worked here for ten years! You think I'd cheat my own company?"

"My company, Ms. Caulfield." Grenchler's weasel-bastard smile turned smug. "I expect you out before lunch."

He started for the door.

Heat flared across Meg's cheeks. She hurried to follow him. "You've only been at Sweet Dreams for four days. You don't know me. You don't know what I can do!"

Grenchler paused at the end of the table. His eyes swept over Meg, head to toe and back again. "Unlike the previous CEO of Sweet Dreams, I pay attention to numbers, not…other assets."

From the corner of her eye, Meg saw Nick's head snap upward. His arms dropped to his sides and his fists clenched.

Grenchler's high-pitched chuckle stabbed through Meg's ears and lodged in her brain. Before she could stop herself, she clenched her own fists and raised them. "Other assets? What the hell does *that* mean?"

Chapter Two

Nick moved before Grenchler even opened his mouth.

By the time the CEO started to shout for Security, Nick had stepped in front of Meg and blocked Grenchler's view of her. Nick had never been one to use his powerful build to intimidate, but in this case, looming over the sniveling worm had the desired effect. Grenchler snapped his mouth shut and backed toward the door.

"I'll take care of Ms. Caulfield," Nick offered with as much professional courtesy as he could muster, but he let his tone communicate his true feelings. *One more word and I'll give you a bird's eye view of Central Park.*

Grenchler nodded. His lips smacked as he swallowed repeatedly. "Well, then," he managed between conspicuous gulps. "See that you do. I'll have her things taken to the front desk."

From behind Nick, Meg said a few harsh words under her breath.

Grenchler whirled and stalked out of the conference room. The door slammed behind him.

Nick turned back to Meg, half expecting her to attack him next. If she wanted to, he'd let her. He'd do anything to soften this blow.

Instead, she just stood there with her arms wrapped around herself, looking so fragile he wanted to hold her. Her rich brown eyes misted and her mouth trembled.

Nick couldn't stand it. How could any woman be so perfect and not know it? She hid herself behind thick sweaters and an even thicker silence, lost herself in her work, but Nick sensed the fire in her heart. She was locked inside herself, and he wanted to set her free. He wanted to claim her. What wasn't to adore? Brilliant thinker, chestnut hair pulled back so tightly her eyes slanted, that lush, curved figure like a Rossetti painting come to life—and those eyes. Those unbelievable eyes.

If she started to cry, Nick thought his heart would tear in half.

Before he could stop himself, he strode forward and put his hands on her shoulders. She didn't resist as he pulled her close, even leaned into him and rested her face on his chest. The soft press of her body against his, and her whisper-soft scent of warm vanilla captured his senses completely. He thought about icebergs and the north wind and his ugly aunt Gertrude—anything to make his cock behave. Everything about Meg Caulfield threatened Nick's self-control, but he couldn't take advantage of her now, not when she'd been wounded by that prick Grenchler.

I tried to give him a chance, spirit of the season and all. But he'll get his, very, very soon.

"I'm sorry," Nick murmured, resisting the urge to press his face into Meg's hair, tug it loose, and stroke the soft waves as they cascaded down her back. "I had no idea until he ordered me to bring your file up here. I would have warned you."

Meg sighed as she pulled back. Tears glistened on her cheeks. "Thanks. But the Children's Fund. Grenchler's a monster to strand all those kids."

"I know." Nick wanted run his lips across her cheeks and brush away her tears. He wanted to tell her not to worry, that he'd make everything okay, but how could she believe that? She didn't know him, except for the six months they'd worked at Sweet Dreams. She didn't know who he was, or anything about his unusual family and friends.

Damn it, he should have asked Meg out after the takeover meeting last week. He'd thought she might be ready, maybe even willing to consider some alone time with him—but again, she'd been vulnerable. Afraid about her future.

Meg reached up and touched his cheek. "Let's go over my benefits and get this over with. I think I need some alone time."

God, he wanted to kiss her.

But how?

When?

This woman deserved perfection. He had to show her how he felt at just the right time, just the right place, in just the right way. Maybe then she'd trust him enough to relax, to turn loose, let down her hair—in every way—and let go all that trapped passion he sensed in her fascinating depths. And maybe she'd believe him when it came time to tell her the truth about a few little secrets, like why he'd left home and come to New York in the first place.

Yes. Maybe he could salvage some good from Grenchler's debacle.

I have to do it right. I have to win this woman's heart. After all, she took mine the day I met her.

* * * * *

Meg hadn't been gone thirty seconds when Nick pulled out the special red phone he kept in the hidden pocket of his suit jacket.

He didn't have to dial. The phone activated when he flipped the lid, and responded to the read of his thumbprint by dialing the only number it could.

His cousin answered on the first ring.

"Yo, Nick!" Chris shouted over the din of hard rock Christmas carols and raucous laughter. "It's been a while. You have enough of New York yet? You're missing the parties. Come home!"

Nick cleared his throat and got ready for the teasing. "I need your help."

A distinctly female voice giggled nearby, and Chris turned loose with a drunken belch before yelling, "What?"

Nick ground his teeth and tried again, this time shouting into the phone. "If you want me to come home, I need your help!"

The music turned off in a split second. Nick heard Chris excusing his guests, and when his cousin came back on the line, he actually seemed sober.

"I'm here, buddy. Nick? You still there? You sounded way serious."

"Dead serious." Nick let out a breath of relief. For the first time since Grenchler buzzed him that morning, his muscles relaxed.

"Let's get to it then. What can I do you for?"

Nick explained in as much detail as he thought Chris could remember, then said, "Now I've got another call to make. Oh, wait. I almost forgot. Dwayne Grenchler." Nick gave the CEO's birth date and address to his cousin. "That asshole goes on the naughty list. Way up toward the top."

When Chris laughed, Nick could feel the arctic chill through the phone. "Done, Cousin. And I hope I see you soon."

Chapter Three

Meg walked home through Central Park with her head down, carrying two bags of office supplies. Staplers, paper clips, notepads full of organic, animal-friendly formulas she'd never get to test, and way too many pens and pencils. After ten years, her career boiled down to sticky notes and highlighters. Oh, and an insurance continuation letter, and her last paycheck—a third of what she needed to make her bills, forget about her charity contributions. This would be a Christmas to remember.

Not.

No Nick. I also have a complete absence of Nick.

Meg sighed at the memory of being in his arms for those few wonderful minutes. Snow dampened her hair and kissed her face in all the places she wanted to feel Nick's warm lips.

I didn't even get his phone number. I could have said something, for God's sake.

Tightly wrapped. Yep. Nancy had a point. Her bags got heavier and heavier, but she made herself slog past Lennon's memorial at Strawberry Fields, and onward, toward the apartment she shared with her best friend on the Upper East Side.

An apartment she suddenly couldn't afford.

"I need a job," she muttered to a passing cart and horse.

The driver didn't look up. Inside the carriage, a couple snuggled underneath a Christmas-red blanket. They were laughing and kissing.

Meg wanted to sob.

What am I going to do?

* * * * *

"Sell sex toys, of course!" Nancy shifted her ample bosom in her bustier, and straightened the lace on her French maid costume. "You'll make a fortune—and best of all, you'll have me for a boss. *Decadence* is so ready to grow. I told you last month I can't keep up anymore. I need you."

Meg sat in their apartment rocking chair and felt her face turn red. She gaped at "sassy maid" Nancy, who looked remarkably like an erotic version of a children's doll she dared not mention, lest Nancy shove a vibrator up her nose. Blonde and way past built, Nancy had heard that particular comparison one too many times in her life.

"You're delusional, Nance. I can't sell sex toys. I can't even *say* 'sex toys' without turning red as a candy cane stripe."

"Get over it." Nancy grabbed Meg's arm, pulled her out of the rocker, and hauled her toward the table where Nancy had spread out her—er—wares. "Besides, tell me one other job—well, *legal* job—you could get, Ms. Chemist, that would cut you a big fat check tomorrow night."

Meg's face grew hotter as she did her best to ignore the display of eggs, bullets, pocket rockets, dildos, dongs, vibrators, gels, creams, beads, clamps and clips. Especially that thick, motorized monster dick that looked so real. The one with scary-looking coils and controls that rivaled some of her lab equipment. That vibrator made her squirm just thinking about it. "I can't let you give me money."

"Give, hell. You'll work your cute little buns off for every dime." Nancy lovingly ran her fingers across her impressive array of toys. "I double-scheduled myself by accident, and I was going to have to cancel one of the toy parties. Now, I'll do Duke's, and you take the one at Spirits of the Season."

"Spirits of the Season? That bar with the stage and the dancers—and the waitresses who wear their boobs pushed up to their nose?" Meg stared at the monster dick even though she didn't want to. "Nancy, those girls look like they stepped out of a chorus line. They won't buy sex toys from someone like me."

Nancy laughed. "S-O-S girls know how to heat it up, and you don't have anything to worry about. The toys sell themselves." She picked up the motorized monster Meg couldn't quit looking at, the thick one with all the ridges, and she turned on the controls. The vibrator hummed…and its coils started to pump. Hard. Up and down. Up and down.

Meg stared at the thrusting wonder and licked her lips.

Nancy's grin turned positively wicked. "See what I mean? This one's called The Satisfier. Wouldn't you pay money to find out why?"

* * * * *

A little over twenty-four hours later, Meg found herself walking down East Sixty-Fifth wearing a full-length leather coat, a lace body stocking with bow patterns all over it and spike-heeled ankle boots, wondering what in the name of all sinners and saints she was doing.

If the wind caught her coattails, she'd probably get arrested for indecent exposure. Never mind if she dropped the display case she was carrying. And damn, was it ever cold outside! Fresh snow crunched beneath her three-inch spikes, and every now and then, a breeze made it under her coat to tickle her nearly bare ass. The few times the chill slipped between her legs, she thought she'd scream—or moan. She couldn't decide.

And she couldn't be doing this.

Not her. Not Meg Caulfield, chemist and avowed champion of the tightly wrapped. She sure as hell couldn't believe how her body responded to the forbidden feel of that body stocking. It held her full figure as tight as any lover, rubbing, stroking and teasing every inch of her skin until her eyes wanted to cross. She couldn't keep getting wet, or her clit would freeze.

"Think about the Children's Fund," she mumbled to herself as she made it another block. No *way* was she calling a taxi dressed like this. She'd probably end up on some cable exposé like *Chemists Gone Wild*.

"Think about the kids. Just get through tonight, and you can make your Fund contribution plus a little more since that bastard Grenchler cut them off. You can survive until next month. Find another job. Put on clothes. Return to sanity."

The wind gave her ass another tweak, along with her stone-hard nipples. "Whatever you do, don't think about Nick."

She didn't need to trash her makeup by crying, and she sure didn't need to get any more aroused before she had to take off the leather coat and see if she remembered anything about Nancy's crash course in pleasure aids and sensual adult toys.

By the time she reached the wreath-covered door of Spirits of the Season, she was shaking not just from the cold, but from absolute terror.

A sign hung in the window, noting that the bar was closed for a private party.

Right.

Meg knew she *was* the party.

She was a chemist. She made environmentally friendly perfume, for the love of God.

How could she be a party?

Trying to breathe, she put her hand on the door handle, but couldn't make herself turn the knob. She'd been to Spirits once before for a bachelorette party, and it definitely wasn't her kind of place. Loud, rowdy, lots of sloshing beer, hot wings and peanuts—nope. Not her scene.

But, like Nancy mentioned at least ten times before sunrise, the waitresses got paid well, tips flowed like all that alcohol and they had plenty of money to spend.

Think about the kids. Think about the kids. You've got to do this.

Meg opened the door.

The entry was dark, and no one manned the podium to collect cover charges and check IDs. Soft strains of Christmas music wafted through a small crack in the heavy oak doors leading into the bar. Before Meg could open them, a little redhead in an elf suit came rushing out to greet her. If not for the skimpy costume—lots of velvet and lace, boobs shoved up to the nose—Meg would have taken the woman for much younger. A child, even.

"You're here!" The woman-elf sounded excited. Her eyes moved from Meg's face to the heavy case she carried. "Go right in and set up on the stage. I'll just lock up behind you, so you're not interrupted."

"Thanks," Meg managed. She wanted to scream instead. She wanted to run. But she opened those oak doors, marched into the bar—and stopped, stunned.

Spirits of the Season had been completely remodeled. Gone were the rough wood tables and board floors, and the stench of aged beer and filth. The walls had been painted a soothing, clean cream. Fine prints and oils hung at tasteful intervals. Fires burned in two fireplaces, one on the left and one on the right, and large, comfortable-looking pillows had been casually tossed on the carpeted floor in front of them.

Wow. Those fireplaces were real. Genuine firelight danced against polished, carved mantels, and the air smelled faintly of cedar.

A handful of tables covered with starched white cloths took up the center of the floor. Each one held a candle nestled in a rosemary or holly topiary trimmed like tiny Christmas trees. Red and white poinsettias filled the rest of the room, along with sprigs of evergreen laced with splashes of clear lights.

Meg felt herself relaxing into the beautiful scene until she looked at the stage.

The stage where she was supposed to set up her sex toy display.

Yep. This is a Christmas to remember, all right. I rank it right up there with starting my period and getting my first yeast infection.

A single long table waited for her, this one also covered with a crisp white cloth, and trimmed with several small wreaths. Meg glanced around, but she didn't see any waitresses. They must be changing into more comfortable clothes. At least she hoped they were. She didn't think she could talk about vibrators to a bunch of fashion models dressed in elf costumes.

You're doing this for charity. Get a move on, Caulfield.

Refusing to make herself any more nervous, Meg strode up to the stage, unfastened her case, and unloaded her displays onto the long table. Gels, creams, clamps, clips and beads along the top, like Nancy told her. Eggs, bullets and pocket rockets on the right. Dildos and dongs on the left, and scattered between them all, various sizes of the bow lace body stocking she was wearing for demonstration. Dead center she set up the vibrators, making sure to give The Satisfier a place of honor, right in the middle.

Now for the harder display.

Her.

In the body stocking.

Meg squeezed her eyes shut, but tried to remember what Nancy had said. *It's just you and the girls, honey. Everybody likes to look sexy. Show 'em how to do it!*

Heart hammering, Meg slipped off her leather coat, folded it and bent to slide it under the table, incredibly aware of the sheer fabric covering her ass and pussy.

A strangled cough made her stand up straight.

Oh, God.

That cough hadn't sounded feminine at all.

Were there male waiters at Spirits?

Meg wanted to snatch back her coat, but she'd have to bend over again to get it. She'd kill Nancy. She'd kill her dead and fling her body off the Empire State Building. Damn! How could she turn around?

What if Spirits was a gentleman's club now and she found herself facing a room full of hunks in tuxedos?

Shit.

Why did that make her wet?

Her face felt so hot she wondered if flames from the fireplaces had jumped across the room to burn her.

I want to die.

She didn't die, though.

She turned around.

Nick Myra stood, arms folded, in front of the tables and topiaries, looking like a Greek god in a silk tuxedo. His night-black hair glistened in the firelight, and his dark eyes studied her with an intensity that threatened to melt her to nothing but tallow.

"Merry Christmas, Meg," he said in a deep, husky voice. His gaze traveled from her face to her lace-clad nipples, and lower, to the barely covered dark patch of hair between her legs. "Damn, woman. Happy New Year, too."

Chapter Four

Nick fought an impulse to storm the stage, kiss Meg until she begged him for more, and take her right there on the table, in the middle of all the plastic dicks and dongs. His hard cock throbbed. His breath hitched and caught, and his mouth watered at the thought of tasting her full, parted lips.

Her tightly bound chestnut hair shimmered in the candlelight and flickers of fire, and her gorgeous brown eyes had gone wide with shock. The pattern on that beyond sexy body stocking covered the tips of her nipples, but mouthwatering wine-red circles peeked through the sheer fabric. Her curves would tempt a monk to debauchery. Made for squeezing. Made for a man's hands to stroke and coax—and between her legs, the dark shadow of curls barely contained by the stocking's netting and bows…

"You aren't a waitress," she whispered, sweetly confused, and he fell in love with her all over again.

Keep it together. Do this right.

"I can be a waiter." He cleared his throat to control the raw rasp of desire. "I can be a barkeep or a cabbie or street vendor if you like, or a personnel director who worked with you and watched you and admired you. A man who wanted you but never found the right moment to ask if you wanted him, too."

Meg's eyes got impossibly wider.

He wanted to kiss her in the worst way, brand her lips with his, demand her passion with his tongue and fingers and cock until she moaned and opened wide for him, only him, always him. But he had to be careful. He had to be sure. If she had doubts, if she didn't return his feelings, it would hurt like hell, but he wouldn't press his advantage with any woman.

When she said nothing, he took a slow breath. "I rented the restaurant. The waitresses moved their *Decadence* party to another day—but your payment's taken care of no matter what." He gestured toward the bar's entrance. "It's on the podium by the door, twice your fee, plus a separate donation to the Children's Fund to cover the Sweet Dreams shortfall."

Meg still didn't speak. She just gazed at him with those bright, beautiful eyes.

Nick's cock ached so badly he wanted to groan. Instead, he made himself try again. "You don't have to stay, Meg. No tricks, no traps, no questions asked and you get paid anyway. I'll call you a cab or drive you myself if you want to go home."

She blinked. Her mouth opened and closed. Opened again. When she answered, her silky whisper seemed to wrap around his cock and give it a slow, deep squeeze. "I don't want to go home."

For a moment, Nick couldn't speak at all. He felt like someone had him by the balls and heart at the same time.

"You rented the restaurant," she said slowly.

He had to work to get his voice to cooperate. "It belongs to my cousin. He owes me a few favors."

"How did you know I'd be here?"

"I broke a rule," he admitted. "I used the number in your file and talked to your roommate before you ever got home."

"And how did you get Nancy to agree to all this?"

Nick shrugged. "I'm persuasive. And I promised her a great Christmas gift."

"Bet you did." Meg shook her head, still looking amazed. "What do you want from me, Nick Myra?"

His throat went dry, but he told her the truth. "Everything."

Her whole body turned an appealing shade of pink under her body stocking, but she didn't ask to go home.

"For starters," he said, "let your hair down. I want to see you like I've dreamed so many nights."

Meg's lips parted again. The surprised expression on her face shifted to doubt, but she raised her hands and tugged at her thick bun. He couldn't help staring at the way her heavy breasts thrust forward, at the hint of nipple teasing him behind the body stocking's lacy black bows.

Her hair tumbled free down her shoulders, chestnut waves rich and lustrous, every bit as luxurious and enticing as he'd imagined. God. What would the rest of her be like?

"Beautiful," he murmured, and she rewarded him with a shy smile.

Could his cock get any harder?

Nick gestured to the table behind her. "What did you bring to show me, Meg? I'd like my demonstration."

Her cheeks turned redder than holly berries. "Nick. I—I can't. I—ooooh." She fanned herself with one graceful hand, stirring wisps of hair around her flushed cheeks.

He grinned at her and wondered if his erection would rip through his pants. "You're standing on a stage, honey. Don't disappoint your audience."

Meg's eyes drifted from his face to his chest, to the unmistakable bulge of his silk-restrained cock. She gave him another smile, this one decidedly less shy. When she met his gaze again, he could have sworn he saw a wicked little spark in those warm, inviting depths.

His cock gave up throbbing and started to burn.

When she picked up a tweezer nipple chain with red flowers and little silver bells, he almost came.

"Well, sir. As you know, foreplay is essential in a satisfying sexual relationship." Meg's voice trembled as she gave the sales pitch, but the spark in her eyes grew brighter. She stroked the top of one breast with the chain, letting the bells dangle against her bow-hidden nipple. "Here we have a seasonal treat guaranteed to leave your woman moaning more." Up and down went the bells. They tinkled each time they bounced across the swelling center of that bow. "With this sliding ring, you can take her from tweak to pinch in the blink of an eye. These clamps are durable, easy to manage and sure to stay on even under the most passionate assault."

I'm going to die, Nick thought as everything inside him caught on fire. *I asked for this, and I'm going to die.*

Picking up speed, Meg turned back to her display table. The next thing she selected was a tube of crimson lotion. "This is Liquid Fire, our top-of-the-line warming lotion." She opened it, squeezed a little of the fluid into her palm, then began rubbing it in her cleavage.

Nick couldn't stifle his groan.

He'd known she had this streak, that she could turn wild and hot with just the right nudge, but *damn*.

Meg let her hands slip beneath the body stocking to the full swells of her breast, where she stroked and massaged, and added, "It comes in several flavors, like apple, cherry, strawberry and chocolate—but I prefer cinnamon. A little more spice, don't you think?"

He couldn't have answered if she paid him.

Back to the table she went, and this time, she turned around with the biggest vibrator he had ever seen. Just the sight of her standing there with that plastic dick between her damp, lace-clad breasts almost finished him.

"Our most popular vibrator. The Satisfier." Meg's hot brown eyes bored into his as she ran her fingers up and down its length, hesitating on the head. "Thick and pleasing. Just what a woman wants." She lowered her head and slid the tip into her mouth, pulled it back out, and smiled. "And best of all, realistic action."

She turned the damned thing on and it started to pump.

Nick stared, transfixed, as she caressed the thrusting dick with her tongue, then lowered the vibrator and ran it across the tips of her breasts.

Lower. To her belly.

Lower again. To the dark curls between her legs.

The vibrator hummed and slammed against her pussy, and she moaned.

That was it. All he could take. His self-restraint shattered.

One minute, Nick was lounging by the tables and topiaries, and the next he was on that stage, standing right in front of her.

Meg switched off the vibrator and dropped it on the table behind her without looking. The mischievous glint in her eyes blazed into serious fire.

Nick grabbed her by the waist and pulled her to him so fast and hard that he lifted her off the stage. She melded against him, wrapped her arms around his neck and held on tight as he kissed her fiercely, blindly, feeding his desperate desire into each questing thrust of his tongue.

Her feather-soft lips parted as he slid his hands down and cupped her ass, squeezed the firm, warm flesh again and again. Meg tasted like mint and heat and everything female. She smelled like vanilla and cinnamon and he wanted to eat her whole like a Christmas treat.

Tongue to tongue, chest to chest, he kissed her and she moaned into his mouth. He felt the push of her breasts through his silk shirt, and he wanted the clothes gone. He wanted her naked, too. He wanted to feel every inch of her with no netting, no bows, no barriers at all.

Her body stocking shifted under his palms as he stroked her ass and let her slide toward the stage until her feet once more found purchase.

When he finally released her lips, she pulled his head down, down, back toward her mouth, and whispered, "Don't stop. I want you. I want you hard and deep. Now. *Please.*"

She didn't have to ask him again.

Chapter Five

Meg's thoughts spun out of control.

When she'd seen Nick standing in front of the stage, she'd almost fainted. When he asked about the toy display, she'd wanted to crawl under the table and hide. Then she'd seen the scorching flash of desire in his eyes, heard it in his voice and saw it in that incredible erection.

As for their first kiss—mother of God.

Fire flowed underneath her skin, blazing hotter everywhere his strong, sensual hands gripped her. She couldn't believe herself, how she'd teased him, and now, how she was begging him to fuck her.

But sweet heaven, if he didn't do it soon, there'd be nothing left but a puddle of Meg on the Spirits stage.

Nick's dark eyes drove into her.

Like black jasper, polished to a perfect shine.

She ran her palms against his rough cheeks, and he captured her mouth again with a deep, rumbling growl she felt from her tongue to her curling toes. His scent of cedar smoke and some bewitching spice made her dizzy, and his firm, demanding lips made her wet and wetter still. He tasted faintly of expensive wine. Every inch of the man had to be made out of steel, especially his cock, hard and hot against her belly.

She slid her hand down as their tongues danced and tangled, and she brushed her fingers across the heat of his silk-covered erection. He groaned and bit her lip just hard enough to make her gasp.

"You're killing me," he murmured. "You've been killing me since you walked in here." Then his mouth moved across her cheek, down the line of her jaw, to her neck. When he bit the sweet spot just below her ear, her nipples hardened into throbbing nubs. Hot juices trickled down her legs, drenching the body stocking.

He nipped her again and Meg shuddered from the exquisite sensation. She clenched her fingers on his cock. She wanted him inside her. She wanted that sensual biting on her shoulders, her belly, her nipples, her clit.

"Please," she heard herself moaning. "Please, please..."

He swept her into his arms so easily she might have been weightless. His lips claimed hers again as he carried her, muscles rippling through his tuxedo against her barely covered skin. She slid her hands into his hair and tugged at the thick, silky strands.

Kissing her, caressing her even as he held her, Nick carried her down the stage steps and over to one of the fireplaces. Once more, he set her on her feet, this time amidst a bunch of red and green pillows, and pulled back to look at her.

"You're an incredible woman, Meg." The low purr of his voice made her shiver with anticipation. He stroked her hair, then brought his hand to her face and traced her jaw with his knuckles. Bolts of pleasure fired down her neck, across her nipples and straight to her throbbing clit. "A genius at what you do, generous and unbelievably attractive. I wanted to touch you the first day I saw you."

"Handsome," she said over the pound of her heart. "Graceful and mysterious. Where do you come from, Nick Myra?"

His smile made her melt every time she saw it. "North. From the cold and snow."

"I love snow." She kicked off her cumbersome heels. The carpet felt cushioned and soft under her toes as she stretched up to kiss him, as she savored the strong feel of his mouth and that distant hint of fine wine. When she pushed at Nick's jacket, he released her mouth long enough to shrug out of the coat and send his tie with it to the floor.

Meg made short work of his buttons, and she was gratified to touch bare, muscled chest as she pushed his shirt open. Toned. Cut. Pure male, like the cedar and spice she smelled each time he kissed her. He let her take his shirt off, let her squeeze and sample his rock-solid biceps, the tight cords of his shoulders, and lower, to the rippling perfection of his pecs.

With another rush of that mischief that seized her on the stage, Meg ran her nails across both of his nipples. He answered with a rumble of surprise and pleasure, and another bone-melting kiss. Before he could let her go, Meg had his silk trousers undone. Feeling fire in her cheeks at her own boldness, she ran her hands down his abs and kept going to the pulsing iron of his cock.

He pulled back and sucked in his breath as she captured it with both hands, marveling at the girth, thrilled by the dimensions, dying to sample it every way she could imagine.

Talk about The Satisfier…

"Be careful, honey." He pinned her with his polished jasper eyes as he gently squeezed her ass. "I can't take much. You've got me too damned excited."

Meg freed his splendid erection from his pants but kept it tight in her hands as she gazed into his eyes. She wasn't sure she had ever wanted any man this much in her life. She'd had a handful of boyfriends, even a few serious relationships—but nothing this exciting. Not even close. Nick made her feel scandalous and daring and oh-so desirable. And that made her bolder.

Still holding his cock and staring into his fathomless eyes, Meg sank slowly to her knees. Her body stocking pulled and stretched, scrubbing her nipples and clit with each movement. Her breasts shifted, and she knew they were close to bursting out of the lace holding them in place.

Nick watched her with frank lust, and when she gave his erection a teasing squeeze, she saw him grind his teeth. Eager to sample him, Meg flicked her tongue against the swollen head, tasting a bead of salty pre-cum as he clenched his fists in her hair.

What power I have. A smile tugged at her lips. *I think I like being naughty.*

While he watched her, she guided his cock to her lips and sucked him deep into her mouth.

"Meg. God." His grip on her hair tightened.

She sucked him again, this time harder, deeper, feeling her cheeks expand and her throat spread to accommodate his impressive length. He tasted so good, so earthy and male, and the soft skin rippled as she moved her tongue against it.

Nick never closed his eyes. He watched her intently, moving his hips, sliding his cock in and out of her mouth.

He wants to see this, she thought with a major thrill. *He doesn't want to close his eyes because I'm his fantasy.*

Meg hummed her pleasure against his hard, throbbing flesh, and he groaned. She wanted to give him more, and more still. Using her fingers and lips and tongue, she worked his cock up and down, up and down until he groaned again and pumped with more force.

Yes. Yes. Yes. Like that. Let go. Let me have all of you.

Her breasts lurched in her body stocking. The lacy bows rubbed her straining nipples. Her pussy was so wet she could smell her own arousal, and still he watched her, watched her as he fucked her mouth harder, pulling her hair now, guiding her head.

"Meg," he said, hoarse with need. "Meg. I'm going to come. Meg!"

She loved hearing him say her name, loved being his fantasy. She sucked Nick and sucked him and cupped the swollen sac behind his cock, massaging his balls until he exploded in her mouth with a low roar.

Hot, salty fluid blasted down her throat, and she drank it, feeling naughtier than ever.

Meg didn't want to stop. She wanted to suck Nick's cock until he got hard again, until she made his knees weak.

Nick pulled away just enough to slide his cock out of her mouth, then carefully lifted her to her feet. Her breasts finally spilled over the top of her body stocking, and his gaze fixed first on her swollen, aching nipples, then back on her eyes.

"Now it's my turn, honey," he said in such a dangerous, hungry voice that it was *her* knees that went weak instead.

Chapter Six

Nick stepped out of his pants and allowed himself a few seconds to drink in the sight before him.

Meg.

Beautiful Meg, bow-patterned stocking low around her shoulders, face flushed, eyes eager, mouth wet and her lips swollen from sucking his cock until he had one hell of an orgasm. Her lavish hair lay across her bared breasts. He brushed aside a curvy wave of chestnut, then rubbed one taut nipple with his thumb.

She gasped.

Her whole body rippled with pleasure, and Nick knew he should tease her at least as long as she teased him—but his cock had other ideas. He was already getting hard again, and he knew he couldn't wait long to be inside her.

"What do you want?" he asked as he slid the body stocking down and off her arms. When she didn't answer, he pinched her nipple gently. She moaned and arched toward him, offerin herself to his hands, his mouth.

He wasn't a man to turn away such splendid gifts.

"Tell me what you want, Meg." He pinched both nipp this time, hard, and held on as she trembled and let out a ragg breath. "Let me hear your sexy voice."

"I want your mouth," she managed as he tightened hold. Her eyelids grew heavy, and her brown eyes misted desire.

"Where?" he demanded. Damn, she was splendid. "Sa

Meg's cheeks flushed. Still shy, but wanting to be wild. "Suck my nipples, Nick. Please. I want to feel you sucking my nipples."

He couldn't help a growl as he cupped one breast, leaned down, and took the pebbled tip in his mouth. It tasted like cinnamon, sweet and warm as he teased the rough point with his tongue.

Meg moaned and gripped the sides of his head. "Yes. God, yes!"

Nick sucked the tender flesh between his teeth, biting softly, reveling in her throaty cries. When he bit down harder, she yanked his hair. At the same time she pushed her breast against his mouth asking for more.

He'd give her whatever she wanted, and then some.

Squeezing and sucking, he moved from breast to breast until she pulled his hair so hard his eyes watered.

"Please," she whispered.

Each time she said the word, his cock got harder.

"Please—what?" He stood and kissed her, tilting her head back with the force of his embrace.

It felt so right to hold her close to him, to stroke the satin skin of her bare back. He surrendered her lips long enough to push the body stocking down over her shapely hips. "What should I suck next? Tell me. Your neck?" He nipped the soft flesh under her ear. "Your lip?" He kissed her again and nibbled her bottom lip.

Each time he spoke, each time his lips touched her, she trembled. He felt her muscles tense with excitement, smiled at the gooseflesh breaking out across her shoulders.

The body stocking dropped lower. To her knees. To her ankles. Meg stepped out of it, naked, flushed, her nipples damp and swollen from his tender sucking. Nick could still taste the cinnamon on his tongue.

His.

She was his.

He wasn't letting her go, now or ever.

He kissed her again, squeezing her bare ass, rubbing her breasts against his chest. Then he picked her up, knelt and stretched her out on the soft carpet in front of the fire. Her hair spread across the red and green pillows like a Christmas angel come down to grant his every wish. He sat back, studying every aspect, from her brown eyes to the curve of her belly, to the damp hair and swollen folds of her pussy, ready and waiting for him.

His. Definitely his.

"You're the most amazing woman I've ever known, Meg."

She reached out and trailed her nails down his chest. "They don't have women up north in the cold and snow?"

Nick laughed. "Yes, but they're— Let's just say I'm a little too tall for them."

She looked confused, but she didn't ask any more questions because he stretched himself out on top of her and kissed all her questions away. All her answers, too, except for one. The one he wanted to hear.

"Where do you want my mouth, Meg?" He slid his hand into the wet heat between her legs, making her moan and writhe. She tried to talk, but he stole her words by sliding one finger into her pussy, slowly, slowly, in and out, then up to swirl around her clit. When she raised her hips to meet him, he stopped, and she smacked his arm.

"Tease," she gasped.

He ran his tongue across her lips. "So wet for me. I want to make you wetter. I want to make you scream. Tell me what you want, Meg, or I'll tease you all night."

She moaned as he cupped her pussy, and she arched her hips again. "Nick. Now *you're* killing *me*."

"I like to see you blush. I like to hear your voice, asking me to give you pleasure. Letting me know you're mine. Say it, Meg. What do you want?"

She did blush, and she sighed, and she moved against his merciless hand.

"Lick my pussy," she whispered, and blushed harder. "Make me come, Nick. Please. Please!"

Chapter Seven

Nick's smile made Meg's blood boil with need.

This wasn't a dream. This was really happening.

She was here with Nick, naked in his arms, feeling the press of his renewed erection against her thigh as he moved on top of her and slid down, down between her legs.

Meg's body throbbed and burned for release. Hard to breathe, hard to think, hard to speak. And she knew she had to be red everywhere, admitting what she wanted, begging for it, using forbidden words for his ears only.

Moisture coated every inch of her lower lips and curls. God, she was losing her mind, or at least she thought she was until he buried his face in her pussy and ran his tongue from channel to tip and back again. Over and over he drank her in, pausing to taste her clit. Little licks, small nibbles, like he was enjoying a gourmet meal.

Rushing toward the edge, Meg raised her hips and pressed her sex into his face. He slid his hands under her ass and pulled her closer. His lips fastened on her clit and he sucked, and she really did lose her mind.

"Oh, damn. Oh, yes. There. Please. There!" Her fingers found his hair and she tugged him closer still. "Don't stop. Please don't stop."

White-hot rivers of ecstasy spread through her hips, up her belly, to her chest and down through her arms. Her nipples jutted higher, and her breasts seemed to swell, too, heavy with want.

Nick stopped sucking, but only long enough to murmur, "Beautiful. So beautiful, and you taste so good."

The he took her clit in his mouth again and she bucked from the force of the bliss. Meg felt like Nick's tongue was everywhere, flicking that sensitive spot, then lower, delving into her clenching channel, then higher, sliding along her inner lips in a maddening pattern designed to claim her sanity. He bit those lips softly, sucking and tasting, then turned them loose and raised his head.

"Pinch your nipples," he said in a forceful rumble that would have made her do anything, anything. Her hands flew up to her breasts, and she took her own nipples between her thumbs and forefingers and pinched.

The sharp sensation shot straight to her clit as Nick groaned his approval and fixed his mouth back on the swollen, pulsing button once again. As he did, he thrust two fingers deep in her channel.

Meg rose up again to look at him, to watch what he was doing to her. He was her fantasy, too. Damn, yes. And so much better than she'd let herself imagine.

The pressure on her nipples, the image of Nick between her legs, licking her pussy, sucking her clit, and the feel of his fingers inside her sent her straight over the edge.

Meg's orgasm hit her so hard her head slammed back against the red and green pillows. A wave of molten heat traveled every inch of her skin. She heard the force of her moan, felt her channel clench tight around his pumping fingers.

Nick's tongue darted and touched, pressed and tapped as he drew out the waves of pleasure until she thought she'd melt into nothing, just fade into that soft carpet and never get up again.

He eased up, then pushed himself over her and settled his chest against hers, arms to either side of her head. When he kissed her, she tasted herself on his mouth and started blushing all over again. She had never done that before. New risks. New naughty excitement.

This man had her so bewitched he could have collected her soul in a jar and she might not have noticed.

"Incredible," he murmured against her ear, sending a new round of chills all over her. "I could touch you forever, Meg Caulfield."

"I'd let you," she whispered back, and kissed him, losing herself in his cedar-spice scent, in the smell of her pleasure on his face and lips.

"But you know the rules, honey." His cock pressed between her thighs, sliding along the length of her pussy, nudging at her wet, ready channel. "Tell me what you want. Let me hear you say it."

Meg gazed into his polished jasper eyes, knowing her cheeks had started to flame, but not even caring. She wanted this. She wanted him now, right now, and she'd say whatever it took to get that thick, hot cock deep inside her pussy.

"I want your cock inside me. I want you deep. I want you hard. Fuck me, Nick. Fuck me now. Please!"

His ravenous grin made her insides turn to mush. She loved how her words excited him, loved how he wanted her so completely, so absolutely.

Nick eased back down between her legs and sat back on his knees. In quick, deft movements, he grabbed his silk pants and removed a condom from the pocket. Never taking his eyes off of hers, he tore it open and slipped it on, sheathing himself while she watched and waited and wanted.

Oh, how she *ever* wanted.

He finished and shifted her on the pillows, pulled her closer and slowly, with deep, sensual caresses, lifted her legs up on his shoulders.

"Keep your eyes open," he said in his hypnotic bass. "Let me see inside you while I fuck you."

His fantasy.

My fantasy.

Meg's heart pounded so loudly she knew he'd hear it as he rocked her back on the pillows and spread her legs.

"Yes," she whispered. "Fuck me."

And oh, God, he did.

Nick's muscles flexed as he drove his cock inside her, all the way inside her, filling her up, stretching her pussy so wide she ached from the joy, that she cried out from the absolute possession.

He stayed still a moment, holding her legs tight against him, gazing at her like she was the only woman on the Earth, and all he would ever want.

Then he moved his hips with a slow, heart-claiming rhythm. Meg watched the point where they joined, watched his iron-hard cock move in and out, in and out, slick and shining with her ample juices.

"So deep." She touched his hands on her legs. "So good!"

Fire danced in his eyes as he plumbed her channel deeper still, pulling her against him with each slow, sensual plunge.

Meg's coherent thoughts gave way to sensations. She saw the fascinating dark of his eyes, the way his lips pulled back in an untamed smile. She felt his grip on her legs, the strength in his arms as he held her there, fucking her, fucking her so deep she rocked with each thrust.

Faster now. In and out. In and out. Her back scrubbed against the soft carpet while the pillows held her head and Nick had complete control of the rest of her.

She was at his mercy.

And she loved it. Loved every second of it.

His balls slapped against her ass as he pumped deeper, faster, spreading her wider each time. Her channel walls clenched and unclenched, and Meg moaned again and again. She couldn't stop. She didn't want to stop. She wanted his cock inside her forever, thrusting, thrusting, making her pussy his from the inside out. It was his. *She* was his.

The hot musk of sex filled the air, mixing with a touch of cedar smoke and evergreen and fire itself.

"Harder," she begged, and he obliged. Rhythmic thrusts became insistent pounding, pushing her, stretching her, filling her up and up until she thought she would burst.

"Wait," he ordered as he slammed his cock into her pussy again, and again, and again. "Just another second. Just another minute."

Meg dug her nails into his arms and scratched, drawing a hiss of mixed pain and pleasure.

She couldn't hold off. She couldn't!

But the spark in his eyes made her want to. The way he looked at her with so much passion and affection made her determined—and somehow, she did hold back.

She bit her lip. She held her breath. And the heat built and built. Sweat broke across every inch of her. Her muscles gathered into tight, ready knots. Her belly clenched with her pussy, grabbing his cock, holding on as he drove in and out of her channel until the wet slap of flesh on flesh was all she could hear, mixed with the thunder of her own heartbeat.

"Now, Meg," Nick shouted. "Come now!"

Meg turned loose her breath in one big rush, screaming as her body exploded.

Her teeth slammed together as liquid fire tore through each muscle, burning her so, so sweetly, forcing her up and up and up until she thought she might fly forever.

Her pussy spasmed over and over, clamping tighter on Nick's cock as he roared with his own orgasm. He kept thrusting, slower, slower, sending aftershock after aftershock streaming through her spent body.

Nick fucked her slow and easy, bringing them both down until Meg could breathe again—but only in short, forced gulps.

She had never felt anything like that in her life.

Merry Christmas to me…

At last, he slid out of her, rolled over and cradled her against him in front of the soothing, beautiful fire.

Meg didn't want the magic to end. She didn't want to fall asleep, but she had nothing left inside her. Not even the energy to hold up her drooping eyelids.

"Go ahead, honey," Nick whispered. He kissed the top of her head. "I promise I'm not going anywhere."

Chapter Eight

Nick held Meg long after she fell asleep, listening to her breathe. It was the sweetest sound he had ever heard, except for her moans and screams of pleasure.

When he finally dozed, he dreamed of making love to her, and when they both woke a few hours later, he pulled her into his lap and slid his cock inside her sweet, hot pussy again.

She rode him as he rocked his hips, sensual lips parted, eyes fixed on his, nipples rubbing against his chest. He pressed his hands against her back and felt the silk of her hair tickle his fingers. Perfect. Perfect for him. Meg Caulfield was everything Nick had ever wanted.

This time, she came with her lips against his, gasping, moaning, bucking against his cock until he spilled so hard into his condom he was scared it would break from the load.

Afterwards, he held her against him, and she seemed content to stay right there, keeping him tight inside her warm channel.

"What time is it?" she finally asked after kissing his neck.

"A little after midnight, I think."

"When do we have to leave Spirits?"

"Never." He nipped at her shoulder until she shivered.

Meg gave his hair a tug. "Be serious, Nick."

"I'm always serious. Ask my cousin Chris—no, wait. Ask my cousin Noel. They'll both tell you." He moved his thighs against her ass. A few more times, and he'd probably get hard again. "I have a lot more cousins, and they all have similar opinions. Especially Klaas and Juleman. They—"

"Nick..."

He sighed. "Okay, okay. How about I have one of my el—er—employees pick up the checks and take them to the Children's Fund before Christmas Eve, and you stay here with me?"

"Very funny. I know your employees." Meg bit his earlobe, but she still didn't move. "Why don't you go with me to take the money?"

At that, Nick shifted from nerves more than desire. Being in a room full of little kids might be a bad idea, especially this close to Christmas Eve. As much as he didn't want to, Nick gently lifted Meg off his cock and laid her back on the pillows, then got up and quickly got rid of his condom.

When he came back, he kissed her nose as he laid back down beside her. "I'll drive, but you have to go in. It's your good heart that made me realize how important the Fund was—and what harm Sweet Dreams did by backing out."

Meg stretched next him like a cat about to start purring. "We've got a lot of cleaning up to do around here. All those toys—"

"Nah." He kissed her chin this time, then her neck. "I'm buying the toys, so we can just stash the loot in one of my bags."

"What do you plan to do with a table full of sex toys, Nick Myra?"

"Use them." He slid down and took one of her nipples in his mouth, and sucked once, twice, then let it go. "One a night, for the next year. I want to see how the clamps look on your nipples…your clit…oh, and how each one of those dildos and vibrators looks inside you, in your mouth…you get the picture."

He sucked her other nipple, and this time he didn't let go until she moaned and wriggled underneath him.

"Like I said when I got here, Merry Christmas, honey." He bit her lip next. "And happy New Year, too."

* * * * *

Late the next afternoon, snow fell heavier on New York, and the city turned into a beautiful white vision—everywhere but the roads, of course, which backed up to a near stop. Nick's driver had to take them around the block to make a better approach to the Children's Fund office.

Meg hadn't said much when Nick loaded her sex toys into a green velvet bag and handed them to the driver to put in the trunk, and she hadn't argued when the driver held out a package holding the svelte red dress, silky hose and red pumps Nick had special-ordered from his cousin Noel, the fashion freak.

Now, looking at her in the back of the limo all decked out in racy colors with her hair loose, her face flushed and her eyes wide with joy as she looked out at the snow, Nick wished he'd kept the sex toys with them. He could have had a little fun with that Satisfier vibrator right about now. But that would probably lead to a pumping action of his own, and they were getting pretty short on time.

Nick ran his hand along Meg's silk-covered thigh, gratified at her sigh of enjoyment. "Have you given any thought to what you want to do next? For a job, I mean."

She gave him a wry smile. "Sell toys for a while until I get my résumé together and start interviews. Nancy does well with *Decadence.* Maybe if I work with her, I'll keep loosening up."

An image of Meg demonstrating The Satisfier to a room full of eager men seized Nick, and for a few seconds, he saw way more red than Meg's dress. "Yeah." He coughed. "I think I like your current level of looseness. Probably loose enough. Definitely loose enough."

Meg let her hand slip across his trousers and settle on his cock. "I don't know. I think I could use some practice."

She squeezed.

He groaned and had to force himself to pull her questing fingers away. "I have another idea. Why don't you consider working for my family business?"

She got her fingers loose and went for his cock again. "You have a family business?"

"Sure. But it's up north, like I said." He caught her hand again. "Honey, if you don't stop that, I'll fuck you here and now. In the car. On top of the car."

"Mmm-hmmm." Her smile made his erection worse. "If you have a family business, what are you doing in New York working for Sweet Dreams?"

Here comes trouble… "I was hunting for a chemist. My Aunt Jessie wants to scale back, but we've had a hard time finding the right woman to replace her. I spent a year each at three other companies before I tried Sweet Dreams." Nick kissed Meg's hand, hoping she wasn't about to start looking at him like he had a few berries off his mistletoe. "I think you'd like Aunt Jessie. You'd definitely like her job."

She looked at him like he had few berries off his mistletoe.

He sighed.

She kept staring. "How far north are we talking about?"

"Um, pretty far." He let go of her hand. "Like all the way north. A place most people call the North Pole. It stays snowy all the time."

"North Pole," she said slowly, suspiciously. "I do love snow, but—well, what would I be doing?"

"Coming up with new formulas, just like at Sweet Dreams—only a lot more. Perfume, soap, bath oil, cosmetics, candy—pretty much everything. Anything you wanted to try."

Meg's brown eyes grew sharp and serious. "And the salary?"

"The salary's not what you're used to," Nick hedged, "But you can't beat the benefits and the job security."

Silence filled the limo.

Nick clenched his jaw, took a breath, relaxed. "I'd be going north with you—going home. My cousin Chris would probably give you a great big bonus to say thank you. He's tired of handling our holiday crunch without me."

The limo pulled up in front of the Children's Fund office, and Meg gave Nick another appraising once-over. "Anything else I should know about this job?"

"You'll have fun every day." He tried to smile. This wasn't going well. "You'll laugh all the time, and never ever grow old. Oh, and I'll be right there to help you try out all those *Decadence* toys."

This, at least, made her beautiful eyes spark. She rested her hand on his. "One at a time. Every night for a year. Is that a promise?"

"Solemn promise," he murmured, feeling it in the depths of his heart.

On cue, sparkly white snow flittered inside the limo, coating Meg's hair and shoulders.

Damn. I forgot how strong the magic gets close to Christmas Eve.

Meg stared at him and jerked her hand away. "What's going on, Nick? The North Pole. Snow in the limo. Are you trying to convince me you're—what? Some sort of Santa Claus?"

"Here we are at the Children's Fund office," he said in a hurry. "Go take care of the checks. We'll talk when you get back."

"Yeah." She kept staring for a moment. Then she got out and rushed inside the charity without looking back.

Nick groaned and banged his head on the limo door. Great. Just great. Blowing it didn't quite describe the current disaster.

The little green-coated driver got out at the sound of Nick's thumping head, and quietly opened the door. "Problem, sir?"

"You could say that." He got out and gazed at the now closed door of the Children's Fund. "The lady thinks I'm crazy."

"Well, then, sir, perhaps you should prove your insanity."

Nick regarded the old elf with affection—mixed with a desire to choke him for being so wise. "You're probably right."

"I'm always right, sir."

Without gratifying the elf with a direct response, Nick pulled out the red phone and pressed his thumb against the sensor. One ring. An immediate answer.

Thank God.

"Yeah, Chris?" Nick rubbed his free hand through his hair. "Help me out again, buddy. Here's what I need."

Chapter Nine

Meg stood at the desk of the Children's Fund director and picked at her fingernail. *I slept with a crazy man who thinks he lives at the North Pole. I wantonly* fucked *a crazy man. Several times!* She looked down at her red dress, at the silky hose and sexy pumps and wanted to cry. *I finally find the perfect man, but…*

"Hello, dear!" The director, a kindly looking woman with long white hair bustled into the room and took Meg's hand.

"He thinks he's St. Nick," Meg said miserably.

"Excuse me?" The director gave her a confused smile.

"Nothing, sorry." Meg took her hand back and gestured to the checks. "Here's my contribution, and a donation to make up for the Sweet Dreams shortfall, just like I promised when I called."

"Thank you so much! Now come with me. We have a little surprise for *you*."

Before Meg could object, the director pulled her toward the office door. Out of the office they went, and down a hall, while the director chattered about generosity and rewards. The next thing she knew, she was dragged into a cafeteria packed with children and lots of red and green streamers.

"Here she is!" the director shouted. "This is Meg, children!"

"Merry Christmas!" shouted dozens of little voices.

Little eyes. Little smiles. Little waving hands.

Meg wanted to cry worse than ever.

For the next fifteen minutes, she was besieged by kisses and thank-you cards…then weird things started to happen.

One little girl with red curls stuffed a list in her hand and whispered, "I know you'll give this to him."

A boy with a blond crew cut slipped her a bag of rock-hard chocolate chip cookies sealed lovingly into a smudged and torn plastic bag. "These are for him," the boy told her with a stoic nod.

And so it went.

By the time Meg extracted herself and fled toward the front door of the Children's Fund office, she was carrying the note, the bag of cookies, a carton of milk, one doll, two candy bars, and three carrot sticks. And to make matters worse, she almost ran straight over Nick Myra's driver, who was standing in the lobby.

Odd.

She didn't realize the guy was so short when he picked them up.

I was distracted from fucking the crazy man. Must have melted my brains.

"Here, Miss Caulfield. Let me take those." From somewhere, the little man produced a small red sack, and relieved her of her gifts. "Mr. Myra wants to show you the family business. For that, we need to go to the roof."

"Oh, right. A helicopter? Because this building's too small to land a jet—and rich doesn't make up for nuts, just so you know." She folded her arms and waited for the driver to defend Nick.

"Yes, ma'am," was all he said.

Meg sighed. She could always make a break for it and run screaming down Broadway.

But she didn't. She followed the driver into the elevator.

Less than two minutes later, Meg Caulfield's world changed forever.

* * * * *

"Nick." She had him by the arm, almost too shocked to notice the bulge of his biceps. The driver had already beaten a quick retreat, saying something about finding his own way home. "Nick, those are real reindeer. And that's a real sleigh. Purple, with racing stripes and neon running lights."

"It's not mine." Nick sounded miserable, though he looked like a splendid god in the golden-streaked sunset. "It's Chris'. He *wrecked* mine."

Meg wondered if she had slipped on her way out of the cafeteria, fallen, and knocked herself silly. Tomorrow, she'd probably come-to in a hospital with a serious headache—and Nancy showing the staff how to wear Naughty Nurse costumes and use The Satisfier.

God, she hoped she hadn't hallucinated that whole night and day at Spirits of the Season.

Deep breath.

Deep breath.

Better enjoy this while I can. It's gonna be hell when I wake up. "Okay. So…what happens if I get in the sleigh?"

Nick gave the tricked-out sleigh a last rueful glance before he turned his full attention to her. Immediately, the lines of his face softened and his sexy black jasper eyes studied every curve she had. When he spoke, his voice had that telltale rasp, and she knew he wanted to kiss her.

"If you get in the sleigh, we become invisible to New York—to everyone—until we get to my place. If you get in the sleigh, we go visit my family and you can try out that job we talked about." He pulled her close to him and brushed his lips against hers, creating a wave of delicious shivers up and down her body. "If you get in the sleigh, you can try *me* out as many times as you like."

Okay, so, Nick might be crazy.

And Meg knew she really might be unconscious in some hospital while Nancy showed off her sex toys to the nurses.

But damn, could the man ever make her wet in a hurry.

Meg kissed him slow and deep, pressing herself against the hard, carved iron of his chest—and his swelling, tempting cock.

I'm his fantasy…

He's mine…

When they at last pulled back for a breath, she managed to ask, "And if I don't like your home? The job?"

"I'll bring you home with a few memory modifications, but I have to tell you now, you won't be forgetting me—and I won't be giving you up."

He kissed her again, and a third time. Meg knew the cold should be bothering her, but she didn't feel anything past that liquid fire igniting under her skin.

As his hands roved up and down her soft, formfitting dress, she murmured her next question against his mouth. "What if I like it all?"

His deep, rumbling chuckle made her nipples hard. "Then it's all yours. Forever."

"Are you Santa Claus, Nick Myra?"

Another clit-tickling chuckle. "No. That would be my uncle. But we help out—me, and all of my cousins. I have way too many cousins, Meg."

"Are they all as handsome as you?"

He pinched her ass until she squealed. "Absolutely not. Get in the sleigh."

*****

Flying.

Truly flying.

No wind, completely safe, but flying!

Nick took the sleigh for a wild, long spin around New York City. Meg gazed down at the crystalline tableau and almost couldn't breathe. Nick explained that she couldn't fall out of the sleigh, but she couldn't quite believe that. She sat in his lap and hugged him tight, and now and again rubbed her hip against his erection just to hear him groan.

"This is real," she said over and over again.

Each time, he kissed her.

Each time, she fell in love with him a little more.

A little while later, as he got ready to take the sleigh north, she snuggled her head under his chin and closed her eyes to remember her last long look at the city she had called home for most of her life.

"What about Nancy, Nick?" She ran her fingers along the strong line of his jaw. "Does she know? Will I be able to talk to her?"

"She knows." He captured her fingers and kissed them. "You can call her and see her any time you want, but she'll keep her mouth shut."

"How do you know that?"

He nibbled at her wrist. "She signed a contract. I gave *Decadence* an exclusive with the elves—and will they ever keep her busy."

Meg let herself get lost in the feel of Nick tasting her thumb. Her nipples got hard as she thought about his teeth, his tongue, the wet heat of his mouth on her breasts, between her legs…

Something niggled at the back of her brain, then exploded to the front of her thoughts. She pulled her hand away and scooted out of Nick's lap. On the big, wide seat of the purple sleigh, she turned to face him. "Wait. Stop. We can't leave yet."

He tugged at the reins and slowed the reindeer, his face tense with concern. "What is it, Meg?"

"Grenchler. He can't stay at Sweet Dreams! What about all the people we used to work with?"

"Oh, him." Nick laughed. "Don't worry about Grenchler, honey. I've got these three cousins—Dorian, Bacchus and Furio—they like to dress up like ghosts and scare scrooges into next week. Leave it to the terrible triplets. By morning, that bastard will be running through the streets of New York buying Christmas turkeys and presents for every kid he sees. "

Meg shook her head, amazed. "You really do have a lot of cousins."

"Way too many. Don't say I didn't warn you." He winked, and Meg's pussy flooded.

How would she ever get enough of this man?

"Pinch me." She sighed. "I know I must be dreaming."

Quicker than the reindeer could speed up again, Nick slipped his hand into the neck of her dress, found her taut nipple, and gave it a good pinch.

Meg cried out and slapped his fingers, but he only pinched her nipple again and grinned.

"What?" His smile was devastating as the pinches turned to caresses she felt everywhere at the same time—especially her clit. "You told me to!"

She got his hand loose and sank to her knees beside him in the sleigh, nipples aching, pussy throbbing and ready for a good, hard pounding. "I hope this thing has an autopilot."

"Why?" he asked, sounding a little nervous as she plunged her hands into his pants. "Meg—oh, God. Honey. What are you doing?"

She freed his thick, delicious cock and brought it toward her mouth, making sure to stroke him slowly, slowly, oh-so slowly, so he was too busy groaning to put up much resistance.

"Hold on, St. Nick. I'm about to give *you* a Christmas to remember."

Also by Annie Windsor

Arda: The Captain's Fancy
Arda: The Sailkeeper's Bride
Arda: The Sailmaster's Woman
Dungeon Heat: Hot Lessons
Dungeon Heat: Throwback
Cajun Nights *(anthology)*
Ellora's Cavemen: Tales From the Temple IV *(anthology)*
Equinox *(anthology)*
Legacy of Prator: Avalon's Price
Legacy of Prator: Cursed
Legacy of Prator: Redemption
Redevence: The Edge
Vampire Dreams – with Cheyenne McCray

About the Author

Annie Windsor lives in Tennessee with her two children and nine pets (as of today's count). Annie's a southern girl, though like most magnolias, she has steel around that soft heart. Does she have a drawl? Of course, though she'll deny it, y'all. She dreams of being a full-time writer, and looks forward to the day she can spend more time on her mountain farm. She loves animals, sunshine, and good fantasy novels. On a perfect day, she writes, reads, spends time with her family, chats with friends, and discovers nothing torn, eaten, or trampled by her beloved puppies or crafty kitties.

Annie welcomes comments from readers. You can find her website and email address on her author bio page at www.ellorascave.com.

LONG HARD WINTER

Rachel Carrington

Chapter One

The naked woman stunned him.

With hair the color of hewn wheat and long golden limbs kissed by the sun's rays, she lay atop the boulder like an offering to the gods.

At first glance, his cock reminded him he was alive and it grew harder with each move the angel made, throbbing and straining against the thickness of his jeans. He dropped his backpack and allowed his eyes to follow the smooth curves of her full breasts before traveling lower to the concave stomach and then to the light blonde hair covering the mound of her pussy.

Keane swallowed hard, but didn't attempt to try his voice. Words failed him. Did the woman even sense his presence or was she so enthralled with her enjoyment of the crisp afternoon that her very thoughts hid him?

She leaned back against the rock and spread her arms wide, giving him full access to the taut nipples and sleek limbs. Blood spiraled downward and Keane winced. His erection had become painful.

He'd never been enraptured in such a way, but the sunbathing goddess mesmerized him. The sun began to sink lower, and like a bullet discharged from a gun, the beauty leaped to her feet, cursing below her breath. She lifted her head and her gaze shot toward him.

Keane took a step back, but he'd already fallen into her line of vision.

She clamped her hands on her hips, unmindful of her nudity. "Who are you?"

His eyes slid up and down her exposed body, lingering on her nipples long enough to be indecent. When he didn't immediately respond to her question, the beauty snapped her fingers in front of his face.

"Do you not have a voice then?"

He liked hers. The rich, cultural sound of London.

"It's impolite to stare," she reprimanded, casually lifting a blouse of white silk from the ground next to the boulder. "Have you never seen a naked woman?"

Keane's lips curled into a smile. "Not one who didn't seem to mind being caught naked."

She tossed him a saucy look over her shoulder. "I have nothing to be ashamed of. Do I?"

He liked her confidence…and her body, especially her body. His smile widened. "Absolutely not, but it is the middle of winter." His eyes rested on her ass as she turned her back to him, stooping to pick up a pair of jeans he hadn't even noticed.

Draping the denim over one arm, she winked at him over her shoulder. "I'm glad you appreciated the view."

"How could I not?" Even now, his cock throbbed.

Tossing the jeans onto the boulder, she slid her arms into the blouse. The material drifted toward her thighs but didn't fully cover the thatch of curls between them. Sweet Jesus. He was going to explode just from watching her.

The woman then turned her attention to her jeans, stepping into them with the grace of a gazelle. Keane noticed she hadn't bothered with the silky thong dangling from her right wrist, and his mouth went dry.

"Aren't you cold?" The words came out on a croak.

The smile she gave him was devastating. "I like the brisk air."

"Who are you?" he demanded. He had to know more about her, needed to know. No woman had captivated him with just one look at her body. But this one had and with the lyrical tone of her voice, she entranced him.

She waggled her finger and Keane caught the hint of mischief in the depths of her ocean eyes. "I asked you first."

He folded his arms over his chest. "Keane Brady." It took every effort to get the words out.

The goddess took her time sweeping her eyes from the top of his head to his booted feet. By the time she completed her journey, his body hummed. "Well, Keane Brady, I'm Allyn Reynolds and I daresay I'm lost."

Keane's lips twitched. "Lost? Do you always take time to sunbathe when you're lost?"

"Clears my head. I used to have a good sense of direction, but—" she lifted her shoulders in the barest of shrugs, "all good things must come to an end, I suppose."

Keane rubbed his finger under his nose, trying to regain his composure. "So what made you lose your sense of direction?" He stooped down to rescue a thin swatch of lace, allowing it to dangle from one finger. "I presume this is yours?" Resisting the urge to curl it into the palm of his hand, he extended it toward her.

Allyn took the flimsy white bra from him and rolled it into a ball. "Damnable things. Never have cared for them."

His gaze dropped to her breasts. He could see the pert nipples and the darkness of her areolas outlined beneath the silk. No doubt about it, he definitely liked her better without it. "So where are you headed?" And why are you here? He kept that question to himself. Could the Fates have actually been kind enough to drop this woman at his feet?

She squinted her eyes and tipped her face back to the waning sun. "Newgrange."

"On foot?" Though he continued the conversation with her, his mind was elsewhere, like on the way the denim hugged her hips. And the knowledge that bare pussy was just behind that zipper made his knees wobble.

The perky blonde grabbed her thick wealth of hair and deftly twisted it into a misshapen bun before securing it with a stick she'd picked up from the ground. "I don't own a car." Her eyes lit up. "Do you?"

Keane couldn't tell her he had no use for a vehicle when he had other means of travel. Instead, he shook his head slowly and reached for his backpack. "I like to walk." As if he could now.

"Bugger," she muttered before slapping her hands against her thighs. "Well, then I guess I must be off once more." She came forward and stuck out her hand. "It was a pleasure meeting you, Keane Brady. You're more than easy on the eyes." Giving him a wink, she crammed her lingerie into the pockets of her jeans and started walking.

He watched her walk for a few seconds, enjoying the sway of her hips. As she continued her stroll in the wrong direction, Keane realized he didn't want her to go…at least not without him. At the very least, he could steer her east.

"Miss Reynolds," he called, jogging to catch up with her.

She stopped and fixed him with a smile which could stop traffic in the city. "Yes, Mr. Brady?"

"You do realize that Newgrange is about one hundred sixty kilometers." He took her arm and gently turned her around. "And it's east not west."

Blue eyes met his for a long moment before her lips pursed. "My bloody sense of direction is completely gone, I tell you. Now, which way is west again?"

Keane caught the scent of English roses in her hair and for a moment, lost his train of thought.

"Mr. Brady?"

"Oh." He cleared his throat and pointed straight ahead. "This way." Allyn squinted again and Keane leaned closer to her face. She was even more beautiful up close. "Is there something wrong with your eyes?"

She burst out laughing. "Oh, well, I guess that much is obvious, is it not? Had a run-in with a bad-tempered witch. I know it probably doesn't seem like it but I can be a bit of a smartass. Anyway, the witch didn't like my 'attitude' is what she called it and here I am."

"So you pissed this witch off and her only retaliation was to drop you off in the center of Ireland without a road map?" Keane figured the blonde had gotten off easily.

"Well that and the loss of my eyesight."

Keane's mouth dropped open. "You're blind?" He waved a hand in front of her eyes to check for himself as suspicion crept up the back of his neck. Okay, so maybe she wasn't an offering as much as a test.

She swatted his hand away. "Not yet but I will be unless I make it to Newgrange before Winter Solstice."

"Ah," Keane murmured as realization arrived. "The sun streaming down through the chambers. That's supposed to restore your vision?"

Allyn squared her shoulders and nodded briskly. "Of course it will."

"That's a myth, you know." But something told him she believed it anyway and if he hung around her for a little while longer, no doubt, he'd start to believe it himself.

She tipped her head to one side and glowered at him. "And I suppose you think Winter Solstice is a myth, too?" Her hands fisted on her hips. "Why don't you tell the Mesopotamians that their festival of renewal is useless, too?"

"I would if they were alive, but I never actually said I don't believe in Winter Solstice. It's fine for those who want to celebrate it."

"Has anyone ever told you that you have a very pessimistic attitude?"

He took hold of her arm and chastised himself at noticing the softness of her skin. A relationship wasn't what he was looking for. "It doesn't look like we're going to get much walking done this evening. Sun's already setting and the last thing I want to do is have to lead you around in the dark."

Tugging her arm free, Allyn took a step away from him. "You don't have to make me sound like a burden. I'm perfectly capable of taking care of myself and I don't recall asking you to lead me anywhere."

The snap of the words brought another smile to Keane's face and he realized he'd smiled more in the past twenty minutes than he had in the last three years. The knowledge sobered him. "I'm certainly not going to let you wander off by yourself now that I know you're losing your eyesight." Besides, he wasn't ready to let her go.

With a toss of her head, she brushed past him. "Fine. But don't expect me to follow your commands like a docile woman. I've never been one to obey very well."

That he could believe. The wiggle of her hips made Keane's gaze drop to the pockets of her jeans where the tight denim covered her firm ass.

"Are you staring at my bum? That's not polite, you know."

He doubted she'd be so smart if she knew he could singe that lush ass with just a flame from his fingertip. "You're going to talk yourself out of an escort," he warned. Not likely. The woman had entranced him and he could do no more than to follow her scent.

Allyn laughed aloud and the musical sound drifted across the hills. "So what are you doing out here all by yourself, Mr. Brady?"

She said his name like a caress and it skated over her skin in the same manner. He picked up the pace toward the mountains. "I like being by myself."

"Well, then, I guess I can shelve my charms for the evening."

Keane stopped walking. He mentally counted to ten, but then the vixen laughed and the sound sent a spark straight to his heart. "Who are you?" he demanded. He swore if the Fates sent her here to further aggravate him, he'd—

"I've already told you who I am and even why I'm here, but you have not shared the same information with me."

"I'm not the one who's lost." He managed to make up the distance between them and fell into step beside her.

Allyn nodded her head and the last rays of the sun glinted off the gold in her hair. "True, but from where I stand, you might just need me as much as I need you. Though I don't know you very well, I know you have some issues, Mr. Brady."

"Don't we all?"

"That we do but yours are…well…visible."

He glanced at her and saw her delightful smile. For someone who was losing her sight, she was in a damned cheerful mood.

"Since we're going to be traveling companions, perhaps you'd like to tell me a bit about yourself then."

Keane stiffened, suspicion taking the forefront again. "Did the Fates send you here?"

"Why would you ask me that?"

"Because only they would send such a beauty to pry information out of me."

"My, but you have a vivid imagination."

Her words did little to assuage the uneasiness settling in the pit of his stomach.

Chapter Two

As Keane walked on ahead, Allyn couldn't resist admiring the tight ass which led down to muscular thighs. She imagined he'd be a rousing ride between the sheets. "Thank you," she whispered not certain whether or not the Fates would be pleased with her gratitude.

"What are you thanking me for?" Keane queried, coming to a standstill.

Realizing her faux pas, Allyn hurried to his side. "Nothing. Just talking to myself. Don't you ever do that?" Unable to resist his magnetism, she touched his shoulder and he jerked.

"What are you doing"

"Touching you."

She heard a sound, almost like a growl and dropped her hand. "Do you like being out here alone then?" When he didn't respond, she tried again. "Don't you have a family who is worried about you?"

Keane resumed walking at a much quicker pace. "We'll make camp straight ahead and at daybreak, I'll point you in the right direction."

Allyn felt the lash of his anger even though he changed the subject. "You don't like to talk about your family."

"Not with strangers," he bit out.

"I see." She stuffed her hands into the pockets of her jeans and trudged alongside him. "What do you do in the evenings then?"

Keane let out an explosive breath. "Do you ever stop talking?"

Allyn stopped walking. "Occasionally."

"When?" he called over his shoulder.

"When I don't mind the silence." She lifted her shoulders in a halfhearted shrug. Keane dragged his hands through his hair and by the light of the new moon beginning to climb in the sky, Allyn read the agitation on his face. "Allyn, look, I don't mean to snap but..." he broke off and cursed. "I'm just not good with words."

Her eyebrow arched. "Then what are you good with?"

The breath exploded from his body. "Could we just keep walking?"

Allyn assessed his sincerity for a brief moment before nodding slightly. "All right, but I'm warning you, I don't know how much more of your foul mood I can contend with." She marched past him, head held high.

And she swore she heard him call her an unpleasant name. But that was okay for now. She'd change his attitude. It was all a matter of time and she intended to enjoy every minute of it.

* * * * *

Allyn poked at the blazing fire with a stick, her brow furrowed. She felt the need to broach the subject of Keane's family again but she preferred not to have to drag it out of him. Men were such irritating creatures at times.

Keane hunkered down across from the fire and the glow cast his features in full light. She drew her eyes over the sculpted lines of his face, the full lips any woman would envy and thick, curling eyelashes. His eyes, a blend of green and gold catastrophic for a woman's peace of mind, remained lowered.

"What are you thinking?" she whispered, seizing the opportunity to open up the lines of communication.

Keane scratched the back of his neck and adjusted a piece of wood on the fire. "Nothing much."

The flames licked at the wood, spitting and hissing and Allyn couldn't take her eyes off the hardened planes of Keane's face. She'd never seen a man who could only be described as beautiful at least not before now. Everything feminine within her wanted him. The thought shocked her as much as it subdued her. She wasn't supposed to want him. Was she?

The silence thickened until Keane chuckled. She looked up. "What are you laughing about?"

"You must not mind the silence now."

She smiled in return. "It's very peaceful out here. I'm not used to it."

He sat down on the ground and rested his back against a downed tree. "You live in a city?"

She drew her legs up to her chest. "Always have. My family lives in London and I just recently left for Ireland." Well, it wasn't totally a lie. "I miss them."

Keane dusted off the toe of his boot. "Then why don't you go back?"

"Because that's not where I'm supposed to be."

His face shuttered and Allyn knew the moment for further conversation was passing rapidly. She quickly changed tactics. "Do you spend a lot of time with your family?"

He shifted and shot her a glare across the flames. "That's the second time you've asked about my family."

"I know. I'm curious. You seem...well...I don't know a better way to describe it other than sad."

"I'm not sad."

"Then what is it?"

"It's none of your business," he retorted.

Allyn sighed and rested her chin on her knees. "I suppose not but I'm more than willing to tell you about mine." She liked the way his eyes crinkled when he smiled.

He got to his feet. "I don't imagine there are too many things you won't talk about."

She stood as well. "I disagree. I won't talk about my weight, my age or my first haircut." She lifted a finger in an admonishing waggle. "But talking about my family is no secret. Neither should yours be."

Keane stared at her across the distance, a tiny frown marring the perfection of his face. "Who are you really?" The words came out on a croak.

Allyn's heart began to hammer within her chest. "I'm just a woman with an insatiable curiosity and an affinity for handsome, distressed men." Oh, it was much more than affinity now. It was a deep hunger to know more about this man with a wealth of sadness in his eyes. Now, he was her mission.

He began to walk toward her. "Is that what you think I am? Distressed?"

She held her breath as he closed the space separating them. "You forgot handsome."

"No, I didn't." He lifted a strand of her hair. "Why is it that I feel like I know you?"

Her breath snagged in her windpipe. "I wouldn't know. We've never met before."

She swallowed when his fingers slid down her neck. She should stop this now. This shouldn't be happening but the Fates had to know how much she wanted it. "You know, we should…" she broke off and licked her dry lips. Then felt his eyes on her lips. He moved in closer and…she pressed her hand against his chest.

"You can't kiss me" Even she realized how inane the words sounded.

He raised one eyebrow. "Why not?"

A reason? He wanted a reason? She didn't have a bloody reason. "Because I don't kiss strangers." She effectively used his reasoning against him.

Keane's lips inched even closer to hers. "Are we really strangers?"

Her heart skipped a beat. "You say we are." *But please change your mind.* She desperately craved the feel of his lips against hers.

"I think you're much more than a stranger and while I'm not sure who you really are, I will find out." He twisted a strand of hair around his finger. "So if you have anything to tell me, you should probably confess right now."

The panic intensified and Allyn knew only one way to change the subject. She wrapped her arms around his neck and dragged him closer for that kiss he wanted.

She sank against him until her breasts melted against his chest. She couldn't think of one good reason why they shouldn't kiss. Her murmur of approval provided all the impetus Keane needed for him to deepen the kiss. And Allyn felt the ground tilt beneath her feet.

Chapter Three

Passions collided and a savage intensity overtook them. Holding her, Keane backed her against a tree and with a savage growl, he allowed primitive instincts to take over.

He curled his hand around the back of her neck and sought the sweet taste of her mouth. Need soared within him, struggling for freedom. Heat enveloped him as desire pummeled him from head to toe. His self-control completely depleted, he was helpless to fight the emotions battering him.

Sweeping one hand under her thin blouse, he encountered the sweet softness of her skin, the fullness of her breasts, the nipples which pouted with invitation. The longing to touch her was so powerful it nearly made his knees buckle. Though a wizard, he knew then the urges swelling within him were altogether human.

He could take her here. Now. Instincts urged him to, that primitive male animal writhing within him ordered him to claim her body as his own.

Allyn stopped kissing him to stand on tiptoe to nibble his neck, then his earlobe, destroying his ability to listen to any reason his conscience might offer. His kisses deepened and the nature of the beast took over.

He touched her everywhere, his hands learning each and every curve, tweaking her nipples, gliding his fingers over her spine. And when her hands began to tentatively explore his skin, he fell helpless beneath her touch.

His breathing ragged, he lifted his head to stare into liquid pools of blue. "What are you trying to do to me, Allyn?"

She licked her lips and Keane figured it was more to tantalize him than any need for moisture. Fascinated, he stared as her lips began to glisten. The breath whooshed out of his lungs and hunger clawed at his insides, a living, breathing enemy.

Without further thought, he unbuttoned her jeans, yanked the zipper low and shoved the thick denim over her hips. One hand sought her pussy's heat and encountered slick flesh, already wet.

Her labia was swollen, pumping with blood, her clit engorged. With just the barest flick of his finger, he made her jerk. Her fingers dug deep into his shoulders, nails scoring his skin. She could be the enemy as far as he knew but for now, she was his feast.

* * * * *

Allyn pushed against his hand, inviting his touch, his exploration. She burned for him. Fuck the Fates. Right now, she hoped they weren't looking.

Her skin craved each sweep of Keane's tongue, each stroke of his hand. And she'd damn any repercussions to keep feeling the sensations writhing inside of her. And when his fingers dipped into the creamy moisture bathing her clit, she ignited.

She couldn't think, couldn't breathe and as he stroked her, she felt herself coming alive for the first time in years. Sexually vibrant and aware, she yielded to his every command, arching at his beck and call.

Making animalistic noises, Keane pushed her harder against the tree, grinding his index finger against her clit while the fingers of his other hand sank deep into her wet cunt. He pressed his lips to her ear, nibbling lightly at the tender lobe. "Give yourself to me."

Allyn had no choice. Her body reacted as much to his words as his touch and the orgasm wrapped her in its magical spell. She cried his name and grasped his wrist, not yet willing to release the promise of his fingers.

With his free hand, Keane turned her face to his and found her lips again. He kissed her until the spasms subsided and with one final sweep of his tongue, he withdrew.

He pressed his forehead to hers. "Very nice diversionary tactic."

*****

Allyn was too satiated to take offense. Her body hummed with pleasure. "Are you always so suspicious?" She eyed the thick bulge at the apex of his jeans while stepping completely out of her jeans.

"Only of perky blondes who seem to have an inordinate amount of interest in my family." His strangled voice couldn't be her imagination. That erection had to hurt like hell.

Though the Fates might frown on her methods, she had at least stalled for some time. And had a helluva good time doing it.

Allyn wrinkled her nose and fluffed her hair with her fingers, moving out of his reach. "I wouldn't necessarily call it inordinate."

Keane watched her stretch her arms over her head and twist from side to side while her hips swayed in time with the movement. "Of course you wouldn't. You're the one being nosy." His eyes followed her body, presenting her shapely ass up for full view like an offering from the gods. "What are you doing?" His hands clenched into fists and sweat broke out on his forehead. God, every move the woman made sent a rush of blood straight to his cock.

Allyn splayed her legs and peered at him upside down, her long, blonde hair swinging forward to touch the ground. "Stretching exercises. I do them every evening."

Keane closed his eyes and drew in a deep breath of the fresh air. "Without your clothes?"

"I still have my blouse on, but does it matter? Besides, it is less restrictive to sleep this way. You should try it."

God help him. "You should get some sleep. I'll wake you at dawn." If his cock got any harder, it would burst right through his jeans.

"No need," she replied happily. "I'm always up before the sun. I love to watch it rise high in the sky while the city is just coming awake."

A muscle clenched in Keane's jaw. He didn't doubt she was a nocturnal person, too. The night air peaked her nipples and his eyes feasted on the stiff nubs through her blouse. It was going to be a long night. "You might want to," he jerked his head toward her breasts.

Allyn lowered her eyes briefly before lifting her head with an impish grin. "Feeling uncomfortable?"

"Feeling dangerous," he replied in a tight voice, hoping she'd take the hint. The next time he kissed her, he wouldn't stop.

"Have you ever been seduced, Mr. Brady?"

The words slammed into him and Keane fisted his hands at his sides. "I don't know what kind of game you're playing, but you should think before you speak. I'm only a man."

Her lifted eyebrow gave him cause for more suspicion. "Are you?" She rolled the hem of her blouse up to allow Keane a peek of her flat stomach. A sparkle captured his gaze and held it. A diamond. She had a bloody diamond in her navel.

"Put your shirt back down." After having felt the wetness of her pussy, there was only so much more he could take. His control was slipping.

She strolled toward him, lifting her thick mass of hair off the nape of her neck. Her blouse dropped back into place, but Keane breathed only marginally easier. The light in her eyes told him Allyn wasn't quite finished with him. "For some reason, I'm feeling extremely hot. How is that possible when the air is so nippy?"

His eyes narrowed. He knew the game the vixen was playing. What was worse, he doubted he could hold out much longer with her so close to him. "Look, Allyn, you should be satisfied. You've already gotten what you wanted from me."

She smoothed her palm over the wide expanse of his chest. "Not everything. I like to touch you."

Blood spiraled downward and made his cock throb painfully. He snatched hold of her wrist and forced her hand away. "You need to stop."

She blinked up at him, an innocent look on her face. "Why?"

"Because I don't want to take further advantage of you." Since when had he become such a martyr? A woman stood before him, offering herself like a virginal sacrifice and he questioned her motives? Would those motives matter in the morning?

"Can you really take advantage of someone who's offering herself?"

"And why exactly would you be offering yourself to me? You barely know me and I certainly don't know you."

Allyn brushed up closer to him and the scent of her hair, a mixture of sunshine and roses, tickled his nostrils. "Well, if you'd prefer to talk..."

He yanked her back to see her face. "Is this how you amuse yourself? Do you find it funny to torture a man with your sexy body?" His hands snagged in her hair. "Are you trying to test the limits of my patience?"

Allyn stared at him, her eyes blazing. He saw no fear in the icy depths and for a brief moment, he recognized the flicker of challenge.

"Does everything I do make you suspicious, Keane?" Her whisper warmed his skin while her hand caressed his thigh, causing him to catch his breath.

Throat tight, he couldn't speak while her fingers danced along denim. His eyelids drifted low and Allyn took another step closer to him. Her nipples pressed against his cotton shirt and his body reacted painfully.

He wanted her, but that seemed too mild a word to describe the craving clenching his muscles. The warmth of her skin was so close and with just the slightest movement, he could feel her. Satiny soft and perfect.

Allyn, you don't know what you're doing," he warned, his voice coming out on a guttural groan.

She nibbled gently at his collarbone. "Don't I?"

"I'm not an ordinary man."

She pressed her palm against the throbbing bulge between his legs. "You feel like a man to me."

His vision grayed. "Are you trying to drive me insane?"

"No, just over the edge."

His head snapped up and he caught her face between his palms. "Why? Tell me why, dammit?"

Allyn hooked one leg around his and brought her mound in direct contact with his hard thigh. She rubbed against him like a satisfied feline. "Did you not feel the instant attraction when we met, Keane, or was it my imagination that you were staring at me while I bathed in the sun?"

He ground his molars. "I cannot take you," he muttered.

A tiny frown marred the perfection of her face. "It doesn't feel as though you would have a problem in that area." Purring, she slid down his body, taking her sweet time in the exploration of the hardness of his thighs, the stiffness between his thighs. "In fact, I think you could handle it quite nicely."

Closing his eyes, he silently pleaded with her to stop but he couldn't say anything aloud. He needed this. The orgasm would engulf him and for a brief moment, take away the guilt clawing at his soul. But it wouldn't solve anything.

He released her instantly and pushed back. "You don't know what I am, Allyn."

She flung her hair over her shoulders and Keane couldn't mistake the blatant challenge in her eyes this time. "So tell me what you are then."

He thrashed his fingers through his hair. "I cannot."

"You can and you will."

He eyed her warily. "Or you'll do what?"

"I won't stop until you snap."

Realization dawned and Keane turned away from her. "You know, don't you?"

"I do." Approaching him so she could stand in front of him, she placed on finger against his lips. "But it doesn't matter right at this moment. What matters right now is that I want to taste you."

Sweet Jesus. "Allyn, you don't know—"

"Shhh." And as she began to drop to her knees once more, Keane bit his lower lip to keep from groaning aloud. Her fingernails crawled over his thighs before gliding upward to release the catch on his jeans. Inch by agonizing inch, she undressed him, freeing his cock from the pressure of the denim.

The sounds of approval she made only made him harder. She cupped his scrotum and the breath left his lungs on a rush of air. Applying light pressure, she massaged his sac while her cheek brushed the length of his cock.

Muttering imprecations, Keane couldn't take it anymore. He snatched a handful of her hair. "Suck, dammit!"

She licked instead and he nearly jumped out of his skin. "Not yet." The whisper nearly unraveled him.

Those same wicked fingertips tiptoed beneath his balls and tickled the sensitive area.

"Jesus," he cried, his hips surging forward.

Her lips replaced her fingers and Keane's ass clenched. She suckled his balls into the moist cavern of her mouth and his cock began to twitch.

"I don't know how much more of this I can take, Allyn."

Allyn stroked her way up his cock with her wet, clever tongue, making appreciative noises which drove him wild. Finding all of his erogenous zones, she tortured him, stroking

"Yes," she breathed, pushing up against his finger. "Push your fingers into me." The command surprised him, but her forwardness only made him harder.

He shoved three fingers deep into her pussy and her muscles clenched, convulsing around the digits. His lungs filled with oxygen as his imagination took flight. That same tight hold would be around his cock in seconds and he would burst.

Allyn began to wiggle, her breaths coming in staccato pants. "Now, fuck me." Her ass bumped back and forth against the oak.

Keane withdrew his fingers and positioned his cock at her opening. He stood there for several seconds, bracing himself for the ultimate impact of sinking into her tightness. And with that brief pause came the sudden realization this time was different. This woman was different.

And this wouldn't be just a fuck.

Without giving himself time to consider the consequences further, Keane flexed his hips and pushed his cock into her. Instantly, her muscles gripped him and stars exploded behind his eyes. Vibrant colors, bright lights and rippling waves of electrical sparks all combined together to nearly blind him.

Could such perfection exist in a woman? He didn't need to ask the question. As the walls of her pussy closed around his cock like a silky hand, he knew he'd found his own Utopia.

Allyn moaned and wrapped her legs around his hips as he pushed and thrust, harder and harder until sweat beaded on his forehead.

Her palms slapped the tree behind her and excited noises escaped her throat. Fingers digging into the underside of her thighs, Keane rammed into her one last time. Then her muscles began to spasm, the orgasm tearing through her, almost pushing her upright.

And the clenching and sweet heat of her cunt pushed him over the edge. His second orgasm of the night ripped a series of growls from his throat, wringing him completely dry until he collapsed against her.

Allyn began to stroke his hair. "It's nice to see you do keep your promises."

Laughter made his chest rumble. "Vixen." For some reason, this felt…right. It was the only word he could think of.

Her hands fisted in his hair, dragging his head upward so she could see his eyes. "You haven't seen nothing yet."

Slowly, he lowered her to the ground. "That…shouldn't have happened."

"Please don't tell me you're about to apologize. That would be a definite ding to my ego."

Keane tugged his jeans up and fastened them before dropping down to the ground. His hands fisted in his hair. "I'm serious. This shouldn't have happened. I let down my guard."

She sat down beside him. "And that's a bad thing?" When he didn't respond, she continued. "Why do you consider it such a curse to be a wizard?"

Keane looked away from her. He couldn't handle the softness in her eyes or the gentle touch of her hand on his leg. He tried to move away from her, but she followed, sliding along the ground until her thigh bumped his once more. "Allyn, please."

"Keane, look at me," she demanded in a stronger voice than he'd heard before.

His head lifted. "You wouldn't understand."

"That you carry a burden? Do we not all carry our own?"

He slid his hand along her neck and heard the swift intake of her breath. "Why were you so willing to give yourself to me just then?"

"I sense the pain within you. It needs to be released. You've kept emotions bottled up inside you for too long."

"And that's enough to make you fuck someone?"

Allyn didn't flinch at his words. Instead, she sat very still, remaining stoically quiet until Keane's hand fell away and his shoulders hunched.

"I'm sorry. I should not have said that."

"If it is what you believe, you have every right to say it."

He huffed out a breath. "I don't believe it. I've just never had a woman throw herself at me like that."

Allyn snorted in a most unladylike fashion. "Now that is difficult to believe." She grinned at him. "But since we're talking revelations, why don't you tell me why you try to hide what you are?"

Keane shifted on the ground until he turned his body away from her. "That's a topic I do not discuss."

She rubbed his back. "Oh, come now. You need to talk about it."

"Are you sure you're not a psychiatrist? Because if you are, I'm not paying you for this analysis."

She sighed and climbed to her feet. "Fine. Have it your way, but I'm telling you that these types of wounds never heal themselves."

"How do you know what type of wound it is?"

She looked over her shoulder and the sadness in her eyes impaled him. "Sleep well." As she started to walk away, Keane realized, he didn't want her to leave. He didn't know what it was about the petite beauty which magnetized him or perhaps he did, but he wasn't in the mood for his own analysis.

"Allyn?"

Her footsteps silenced. "Yes?"

"It was my family."

She turned to face him. "What about your family?"

Keane didn't want to say any more, but the words spilled out of him, forced from the depths of his soul. "They're dead because of me."

Chapter Four

Allyn closed her eyes for a moment, accepting the full brunt of his words and the pain wrapping them. Then, she moved forward and sat back down beside him. "Tell me," she encouraged.

He cursed below his breath. "I don't want to talk about it. And could you please put some clothes back on?"

Ignoring the anger in his tone, Allyn followed his command, standing to snatch her jeans and tug them over her hips. "There. Happy now?"

"Nowhere near it."

Her heart ached for him as she returned to the subject he didn't want to discuss. "You've told me the hardest part."

He fixed her with a harsh look. "No. Knowing I'm the reason for their death…that's the hardest part, Allyn."

She didn't touch him though she wanted to. She wanted to take him into her arms and comfort him, but she couldn't. He needed to exorcise the demons within his soul. She could only prompt him to open the wound.

"You didn't kill them."

"How do you know that?" he almost shouted. "Do you claim to know me so well that you know whether or not I could be monster enough to eliminate my family?"

A vein bulged in his temple and Allyn clenched her hands at her sides to keep from touching him. "I know what I've seen so far."

"And that makes you an expert."

The bitterness didn't dissuade her from her task. "I believe I'm an expert at reading people. I see what you might not want me to see."

He held his hands up in the air. "Oh, really? Then tell me what you see, Dr. Reynolds. Read me." He whipped his blistering gaze to her face. "I dare you."

Allyn nodded once. "Fine. If that's how you want it. I see a man, also a wizard, who's struggling to deny what he is."

Keane gave a short, humorless bark of laughter. "I can't deny what I am, Allyn. The Fates continually remind me by throwing obstacles in my path to tempt me to use my magic."

Allyn considered his words with a knitted brow. "You mean, you don't use your magic?"

The vein in his temple grew larger, if possible. "No."

She scooted the toe of her shoe across the grass at her feet. "Forgive me for pointing this out, but isn't that denying what you are?"

"No. It's choosing a different path."

This time, Allyn laughed. "You can't choose to be a mortal, Keane. I mean, look at you." She took hold of his hand and turned it over in hers. "Everything about you screams magic. You are one of the most powerful beings in the universe and you want to hide what you are because of something you had no control over."

He jerked his hand free. "How do you know I had no control over it?"

"I'm assuming," she hedged.

His eyes glittered. "Bullshit."

She scooted away from him as his anger blazed. "What?"

"You heard me," he replied in a stone-cold voice. "You know more about me than you're willing to admit and the question I have for you is how." She tried to stand, but Keane snatched her arm and secured her in place. "You're not going anywhere until I have some answers."

Allyn began to peel his fingers away one by one. "Let go of me."

"I'll let go when you tell me how you know about me, about my life and the death of my family."

She muttered under her breath and her shoulders sagged. Tears clogged the back of her throat and not just because she'd failed, but because she really wanted to help Keane. Now, she'd no doubt he'd send her on her merry way with some bitter words for the Fates.

"Allyn, I'm waiting."

She gave him a long, studious look. "And I'm thinking." Her gaze dropped to his fingers still encircling her flesh. "Do you mind? I think better when my arm isn't being held in a vise."

"You have to think about telling the truth?"

She let out a woeful sigh. "All right, fine, but don't blame me when you don't like what I have to say." She scooted her rump around so that her body faced his fully. "The Fates sent me."

Keane threw her arm away and surged to his feet with a string of words she didn't understand.

Allyn hurriedly climbed to her feet, but she didn't walk toward him. She didn't really know what to do next. "Keane, listen to me. They're worried about you."

He held up one hand. "Just stop. I don't want to hear anything you have to say. It's all been a lie from the moment I saw you sunbathing. You set a trap for me and it worked. I don't know what kind of promotions the Fates give, but you're definitely in line for one."

"No, I'm not."

"You did what you were sent to do."

She clamped her hands on her hips. "No, I didn't."

"Oh, really? Weren't you sent to remind me that I'm still alive, that I can't deny what I am and all that other nonsense you were spouting a few moments ago? Isn't that why we just fucked…so you could remind me that I was still a part of life?"

She'd never really had much of a temper, but since meeting Keane, she'd started to develop one. "First, it wasn't nonsense, and second, no, I was sent here to help you."

He whirled around and Allyn saw flames lighting his irises. "Help me? I'm a wizard, for God's sake. Do you really think you could help me?" He jerked his hand toward the ground and sparks shot from his fingertips, singeing the ground inches away from her feet. "I know what I am. I know what I'm capable of doing. Make no mistake about it, Allyn. I could never deny the magic within me. I'm a wizard. I will be a wizard until I cease to exist, should that day ever come, but neither you," he pointed a finger toward the center of her chest "nor those useless entities who call themselves the Fates can stop me from living my life the way I want to live it."

He started to walk across the grass, leaving Allyn standing next to the fire. She wanted to call out to him, to convince him she could help, but no words would come. Even from this distance, she felt his fury and knew he needed time to calm down, to regain control. She could give him that.

She dropped her head and let out a long sigh. Then her world went black. Panic crowded her lungs, making breathing difficult. The night wrapped its thick, dark arms around her and she let out an inarticulate cry.

Sinking to her knees, she searched for some sense of stability. Her palms encountered damp grass and as she continued to feel her way across the landscape, the heat from the fire scorched her face.

"What the hell!" Keane exclaimed and suddenly, Allyn felt strong arms circling her waist, lifting her to her feet. "What are you doing?" He shook her as if to snap her back to her senses.

"I…I can't." She drew in a deep gulp of air. Her lungs ached and tears trailed down her cheeks.

"You can't what?"

Allyn heard the tension in his voice, but she couldn't reassure him as she'd been sent to do. Her own fears now strangled her. "My…I…can't…see."

* * * * *

Keane watched Allyn sleeping after he'd finally managed to soothe her fears. He turned his hands over in the light of the fire, inspecting his palms. He'd sworn never to use his magic again but what if he were to use it for good? Would the Fates then think they'd won?

Allyn placed all of her hopes on arriving at Newgrange in time for Winter Solstice, believing the Fates would be kind enough to restore her sight. Perhaps they would since she worked for them. Keane didn't believe in leaving anything to the Fates. He could heal Allyn now. Then he wouldn't feel so guilty about leaving her.

She rolled over onto her side, making a soft, almost purring, noise. With her face relaxed and her blonde hair flowing around her shoulders, she looked like the angel she was, the angel he didn't want her to be.

He knelt down beside her and stroked her face. Her beauty made him catch his breath. Her skin felt like fragile crystal, smooth and delicate. Her full lips parted slightly and Keane's body reacted instantaneously, his mind conjuring the image of those slick, wet lips wrapped around his cock.

Had the Fates sent her here to torture him as well? Had he not endured enough with the loss of his parents and brother? He sifted his fingers through her hair and Allyn turned toward him, seeking out the warmth of his body. The night grew cooler and the shifting winds caused her nipples to peak again.

Keane slipped down to lie beside her, draping his arm over her narrow waist. She moved closer, her cheek pressing against the beat of his heart. One hand pressed against his stomach, just above the waistband of his jeans.

Her soft body captivated him and for the first time in a very long time, Keane didn't think about the past. He didn't relive the night he discovered the annihilation of his family and he pushed the guilt to the back of his mind. At least for now.

Allyn hooked one leg atop his and her heat scorched through denim. Keane's body began to ache. When had he last wanted a woman as much as he wanted this one? If the Fates had sent her to torture him, they'd chosen their tool well.

He slipped one hand down and cupped her firm ass. She moaned. He began to massage her through the fabric of her jeans. She let out a breathy sigh.

Keane gave up all pretenses and rolled her to her back. Though she stirred slightly, she didn't open her eyes and he wondered if fear made her keep them closed. Either way, she would encounter darkness. He wondered if she would hate the Fates now.

He inched her blouse up past her navel and stared at the diamond. With each of her breaths, the gem winked at him. He released the catch on her jeans.

"Keane?" her voice, raspy with sleep, made him pause.

"I'm here," he responded. Could she hear the longing in his voice?

"What are you doing?" The inane question brought a smile to his lips.

He lowered the zipper and slipped his palm across the top of her mound. "What does it feel like I'm doing?"

She bit her lower lip. "I can't see you." Panic edged her voice.

Keane quickly soothed her. "You don't need to see me. Use your other senses. Tell me what you feel." He inched her jeans down over her thighs and inhaled the scent of her womanly heat.

"Heat," she said instantly.

"Good." He parted the slick folds of her body and gently brushed his middle finger over the tiny nub of flesh. "Talk to me, Allyn. What do you hear?"

She sucked in a sharp breath. "The wind. My own breaths."

Keane moved his finger with more force and Allyn jerked beneath him. "And what about smell? Can you smell your pussy?" He lowered his head and brushed her lips with his.

She squirmed and Keane's lips traveled to her neck, her clavicle before he used his teeth to lift her blouse up toward her neck, exposing her bare breasts. His mouth caught one engorged nipple and feasted on its satiny smoothness while his fingers worked in and out of her sheath.

Allyn began to pant heavily. She raised her legs and spread her thighs, offering herself completely.

"What do you want?" he whispered against her skin.

She caught his head in her hands. "I want to see you."

He slipped out of her grip and licked his way down to her bikini line. "You will, baby. You will, but first, I want you to feel." He crawled down her body and for a few seconds, allowed her to lie there, exposed, trembling and anticipating. He tiptoed his fingers up the inside of one thigh and Allyn sucked in a sharp breath.

"Tell me what you want now, Allyn."

"I want to feel your tongue against me."

He licked the smooth skin close to her knee. "Here?"

"No." She sounded almost frantic.

Keane drew a circle around her navel. "Is that better?"

Her hands scrambled to find his shoulders. "Lower."

He moved to the top of her cunt and hovered. "How low?" he teased.

"Dammit, Keane," Allyn muttered as her breath exploded from her body. "Taste me. I want to feel your tongue inside me."

"Your wish is my command." He grasped the backs of her thighs and sank into her heated pussy. His tongue circled her clit, drawing out the sensations. Allyn whispered his name and lifted her hips to push herself closer to his mouth and tantalizing tongue.

He drew the nub into his mouth and suckled it tenderly while she bucked beneath him, digging her heels into the grass. Keane grazed the slick walls of her labia with the rough pad of his tongue before diving into her opening. He stabbed her with intimate flicks and Allyn's body began to rock.

He took his time, savoring every inch of her spicy sweetness before returning to her swollen clit. He cupped her ass and exhaled loud and long, raising his head a fraction of an inch. "Let me hear you come, Allyn. I want to hear you scream." His tongue captured her again, flicking and tormenting until Allyn had no choice but to do as he commanded.

His name pierced the darkness and perspiration drizzled down between her breasts as she came hard and fast. Her muscles clenching, she fisted her hands in his hair.

"That's it, baby," he encouraged. He moved back up her body, his cock throbbing for release. "Allyn?" he looked into her sightless eyes, surprised when she smiled.

Her hands reached for his zipper. "You don't think you're going to get to stop now, do you?"

Chapter Five

Allyn's heart pounded and the blood poured through her veins sluggishly. Satisfied and replete, she moved her hand languidly over the bulge covered by the silky boxer shorts Keane wore. She hadn't heard him remove his jeans but she'd heard every sound, the rasp of denim sliding down thickly muscled legs.

She even heard the sigh leave his throat and wished she could see his face. She massaged the thickness of his flesh and Keane groaned. She leaned forward and slid her lips across the corded muscles bulging in his neck. Fumbling for a second with the buttons on his shirt, she didn't ask for help. This was something she needed to do on her own.

She ran one hand inside the opening she created and crisp hair tickled her palms. She played with the nipples while Keane's breathing intensified. Dropping her free hand to his cock, she tested its length again, so thick and hard. She cupped the head and drew circles over the tip. Keane squirmed and made noises in the back of his throat.

Allyn smiled. She might not be able to see, but instincts guided her flawlessly. She hooked her hands in the waistband of his shorts and tugged them down over his hips. Allowing the cool air to bathe his skin for a second before she lowered her head, she sought his rigid cock.

Her lips brushed his engorged flesh and Keane snapped out her name. She stuck out her tongue and tasted him inquisitively. He lifted his hips, seeking the wetness of her mouth. She licked the tip, the saltiness bathing her tongue, before her lips created a suction cup around the top. With one hand at the base of his cock, she lightly scratched the skin close to his balls.

Keane writhed on the ground and she heard her name again, this time, more of a plea. She drew herself up over him and took the full width in her mouth. Keane's hands snagged hold of her hair while she suckled him. His hips pumped lightly.

"I'm..." Keane didn't get any more words out before a loud, disjointed cry spilled from his lips.

Allyn swallowed his juices and drew back slowly, licking her way to the top of his cock. The muscles in Keane's stomach quivered and she felt his hands holding her arms.

"Don't go anywhere," he instructed.

"I thought you weren't going to use your magic," she reminded with a hitch in her voice. Keane's hand climbed up her thigh and now his fingers stretched her sheath.

He chuckled low in his throat and rose up over her. "This isn't magic, baby. It's just the way with wizards."

Allyn released a heartfelt sigh. "Oh, thank God." She opened her thighs and felt his cock bump her leg. She shivered with anticipation. The smooth tip brushed her wet pussy and she whispered, "Yes."

Keane removed his fingers and guided his thickness toward her center.

Her opening stretched to accommodate the size of his cock and Allyn lifted her legs to press them against his ass. She wanted all of him, filling her, taking her.

When the base of his cock touched her dampness, Allyn demanded, "Fuck me. Fuck me now."

His fingers bit into her waist as he began to drive into her. The sensations cascaded over her and Allyn knew at that moment, she would give up her sight forever if she could keep what she had at that moment.

Relentlessly, he pumped into her, the harsh sounds he made adding to the frantic mating.

Allyn begged and pleaded, not even aware of what she said. His cock brushed her most sensitive area and she came up off the ground, her nails digging into his arms. "Oh my God," she screamed, the spasms ratcheting through her. The orgasm wrung her muscles and left her weak and exhausted.

Keane slowed the thrusts and came on a long, low moan before he collapsed on to top of her.

"Now, I'm scared," she murmured in his ear.

She felt his weight leave her body as Keane rose up on his elbows. "Scared? Why?"

She reached up and managed to connect her palm to his cheek in a soft caress. "How am I ever supposed to top this?"

Keane relaxed against her again. "Maybe you're not."

Allyn didn't respond, but inwardly, she knew he spoke the truth.

"Are you okay?"

She smiled slightly. "Why do you ask?"

"Because you're frowning." He touched a finger to the crease in her brow.

Allyn chuckled. "I didn't even realize it. Trust me. Nothing's wrong and I'm more than okay."

Keane took hold of her hand and brought it to his lips. Her palm tingled. "You're so beautiful."

She closed her eyes. "We should get some sleep. We have a lot of ground to cover and a short amount of time to do it in."

"We'll make it," he assured her.

"So you're not still angry with me?"

"I don't know that I was every really angry with you. The Fates are a different story."

"But if they hadn't sent me, we wouldn't be here now."

"Good point." Keane adjusted his body and pressed her head to his shoulder. A long moment passed before he asked, "Allyn, are you so sure you'll get your sight back once we reach Newgrange?"

"Of course." Even she heard the doubt in her voice.

"The Fates could have stopped the witch from doing this, you know."

Her fingers splayed across his chest. "Could we just not talk about this now?" Anxiety was a tight ball in the pit of her stomach.

"Okay." He kissed the top of her head. "Sleep now. I'll wake you at first light."

* * * * *

Keane wanted to stay close to her. The night only served to increase his feelings and now, as they walked together across the vivid green grasses and the wind blew their hair, he felt . . . content. He couldn't remember the last time the word applied to his life.

Allyn walked so close to him that her shoulder bumped against his from time to time. He didn't mind. He liked the trust she placed in him. When she seemed unsure of the path ahead, she reached for his arm and occasionally, she took hold of his hand just to touch him.

Keane began thinking about things he shouldn't be thinking. He studied their joined hands for a moment before finally breaking the silence. "Do you work for the Fates?"

"Not really. I guess they just chose me for this mission. Don't ask me why."

"I know why."

She wrinkled her nose. "You're thinking with your dick."

"Touché," Keane responded with laughter. "So tell me more about you."

Allyn's eyes took on a faraway look. "My family is a wild, rambunctious lot. We fight a lot, laugh even more, and we love one another ferociously." She drew her hand out of his. "I miss them all terribly."

"You don't get to see them often?"

She shook her head slowly. "Usually around Winter Solstice. We decorate an evergreen tree and hang holly. Mum always makes sure we have enough to hang at every window and we always fight over who gets to hang it over the front door. My brother, Samuel, is the tallest now, so usually, he wins. Then, we burn a Yule log on the third day of the Solstice. And the food," she pressed a hand to her stomach to emphasize her point. "It's almost shameful the amount of food that's prepared." She stopped talking for a long second and then picked up with, "We sing ancient songs each night and we always light the candles in the windows. It's a beautiful time."

Before Keane could change the subject, Allyn plunged on ahead. "So what do you and your family do for Solstice?"

"What makes you think we celebrate it?"

Her nose wrinkled. "I've never met anyone who doesn't. It's one of the biggest traditions for my family."

"In that case, why aren't you with them this year?" Keane suspected he already knew her answer.

Allyn kept her eyes straight ahead. "Because the Fates wanted me here."

"Do you always do everything they tell you to do?" The words came out harsher than Keane intended but he didn't apologize.

"I don't know. They've never asked me before. I knew it must be a special mission. Of course, my run-in with the witch wasn't really part of the deal. And speaking of that, we should get a move on. I don't want to miss that stream of sunlight."

He snatched hold of her shoulders and held tight. "We have plenty of time. You know I can get us there before the first day of Winter Solstice."

He saw the challenge on her face before she spoke. "How? By using your magic? I was under the impression you were too busy feeling sorry for yourself to do that."

Keane released her at once. "I don't feel sorry for myself, Allyn. It goes beyond that."

"Oh yes, the guilt." Her fingers sifted through her hair. "I bet you'll be glad that in a couple of days, you'll be free of me then so your wallowing can continue."

"You'll leave without completing your mission?"

Allyn nibbled the fingernail on her index finger. "I hadn't thought of it that way."

"You said you were sent here to help me."

"Yes, to help you, but you have to want to be helped."

Her words struck him and though he didn't want to admit she had a point, he relented a little. "Maybe."

"Do you want to be helped, Keane?"

"I've been okay on my own, Allyn."

"But do you still want to stay on your own?"

Before the previous night, he would have said yes, but now, with Allyn walking so close to him and smelling the sweetness of her skin, he had to be honest. "Not particularly."

She smiled. "At least we're making progress."

"So why don't we talk more about you?"

"Nice evasive tactic."

Keane chuckled. "I have skills."

Her eyebrows rose. "I've seen those already."

Keane laughed outright. Then sobered instantly. "I should have been with my family the day they were killed."

Allyn reached for him and he allowed her to take his hand. She didn't say anything and Keane knew she was keeping silent hoping he would continue his revelations.

"My family was killed because I was too interested in becoming a better wizard."

Chapter Six

Keane told the story in an emotionless voice, but Allyn quickly deciphered the pain behind the words. He spoke dispassionately of his father's decision to send Keane to school on the other side of the city where they lived. Obediently, Keane went and soon, he began spending more and more of his time away from home and even when graduation came and went, Keane decided to remain with his friends, learning more, expanding his skills and growing as a wizard.

He stopped talking to draw in a deep breath and though Allyn held tightly to his hand, she offered no other comfort.

"I couldn't believe I learned so much. I went home a couple of times and my family was so proud of me." His breath rattled out of his chest. "At least they were…until the weekend I came home too late."

Allyn squeezed his fingers.

"I'd always believed wizards were indestructible. We could sense when danger was approaching and deal with it accordingly, but there was one enemy not even we could see."

When Keane fell silent, Allyn prompted him. "Who was it, Keane?"

He turned to face her and the agony dripped from his voice. "My best friend. We grew up together, learned our magic together only his father didn't want him to learn more. Justin saw his magic pale in comparison to mine and like an egotistical idiot, I had to show him my new tricks each time I returned home. Soon, Justin began searching for other ways to improve his skills."

Allyn felt the guilt weighing each word. "He turned to the black arts."

"And he took to them well." She heard the shift in his voice and knew he'd moved away from her, not physically, but mentally, emotionally. "So well that he destroyed my entire family before they even knew what had hit them. I got home in time to see him standing over my mother's body and when he raised his head to look at me, all I saw were his eyes, two empty pools of hatred. I didn't understand it. I still don't." He ended the sentence on a note of defeat.

"What happened to Justin?"

Keane slipped his hand out of hers and Allyn heard the rasp of his palms against denim. "He escaped before I could recover quickly enough to attack him. I don't know that I could have destroyed him then anyway."

"Did you look for him?"

He gave a bitter laugh. "No. I didn't. I was too scared to."

Allyn frowned. Keane didn't seem like the type to be frightened by a rogue wizard. "Why? Wasn't your magic just as strong?"

His shoulder bumped hers once before he moved ahead of her. "It was stronger."

"Then why didn't you go after him? I don't understand."

"I knew if I sought revenge, I would kill Justin and that would make me no better than he is. Instead, I decided to give up what had created Justin in the first place… my magic."

Allyn followed the sound of his voice and caught up with him to snag hold of his shirtsleeve. "Let me get this straight. You stopped using your magic because you blamed yourself not only for the death of your family but also for Justin's ways. Did I sum it up correctly?"

His muscles bunched close to her curled fingers. "If I were you, I'd choose my next words very carefully."

His anger didn't scare her. Allyn released him and folded her arms over her chest. "Careful? Oh, I think you've cornered the market on careful. In fact, you're too busy being careful not to use your magic that you don't see you've allowed Justin to win. You think you honor your family's memory by adhering to his belief that using your magic somehow makes you the bad guy. Instead, what you've done is to create a person who doesn't really exist." She moved toward him and before he could back away from her, she captured his face in her hands. "Do you really want Justin to spend the rest of his life believing he's gotten away with this? Do you even know how many others he's killed now?"

He tried to shake free of her, but Allyn held fast. "His crimes are not my responsibility."

"So you'd rather be a martyr than to deliver justice?"

"I'm not a judge, Allyn. I'm only a man."

"You're a wizard!" she shouted her frustration.

He finally managed to extricate himself from her hands and he moved beyond her reach, so far that she wondered if he intended to leave her. "I didn't ask you to understand, but at least now you know why I've chosen the life I now lead."

"How long has it been?"

"Since what?"

"Since your parents died," she replied in an irritated voice. She wanted to shake him and hopefully, restore some of his common sense.

"Three years," Keane responded icily.

"So you haven't used your magic in three years?"

He didn't immediately respond.

"Ah. So you have."

"Once or twice."

"When?" She pushed him, sensing he'd left part of the story untold.

"I'm through discussing this."

Allyn stomped forward. "If you think you're getting off that easily, you're sadly mistaken. I want the rest of the story."

"This isn't about you, Allyn. So stay out of it."

"Isn't about me? The Fates sent me here because you're wallowing and for some reason, they believe I should be the one to save you."

"I don't need fucking saving!"

Allyn inhaled his distinctive scent and imagined his green-gold eyes narrowed in anger. She wanted to thrust her hands deep into the silk of his hair and drag his mouth down to hers. She wanted to kiss away the hurt, the sorrow, the anger. Instead, she dropped her head.

"You know, this is supposed to be the time of the year when the monsters of chaos are tamed for another year. If you believed in that, perhaps you'd find that forgiveness you've been seeking all of these years." She touched his arm. "You have to forgive yourself, Keane, and no matter how you used your magic in the past, you can use it for good now."

Keane's dragged his hands through his hair. "I don't want to talk about this anymore, Allyn. You should go on to Newgrange by yourself. I'm done." He began walking away again and Allyn stood in the middle of the grasses, allowing him to leave. She couldn't force him to stay and the Fates certainly couldn't say she didn't put forth a good effort.

* * * * *

Keane heard her footsteps receding and knew she'd taken him at his word. He didn't want his moral compass to get in the way of his anger. He didn't want to go back and take Allyn to Newgrange. For all he knew, her lack of eyesight could be just another one of the Fates' tricks.

He plunked down on the grass and pushed his head into his hands. He wished Allyn had stayed away. He didn't want to think about yesterday, today or even tomorrow. And he certainly didn't want to remember the past. The agony brutalized him. He didn't need the memories to batter him. The images remained clearly in his brain, stamped on his mind like a movie reel with no pause button. His mother's unlined face and gentle voice. His father's roaring laughter and his brother's eagerness. Keane missed it all.

He even missed the fights he'd had with his brother on a daily basis, his mother's exasperation at their antics and his father's lectures about being a man, the responsibility of a wizard and the need for control. He stared down at the grasses below his feet. And the longer he looked the more he realized it didn't hurt as much. Had that anything to do with Allyn or had he simply grown accustomed to the grief?

Maybe it was the time of the year playing with his emotions, but he could even think back to the last time he'd used his magic and it didn't hurt so much, either.

The monument he'd erected for his parents had been his last act, the last thing he could do for them before he walked away from all that he'd known. They would never see it but perhaps they would know he wanted to remember them.

As if he could forget and now Allyn had brought all of those feelings back to the forefront, forcing him to deal with the bitterness, anger and pain. He should hate her for that but something deep inside him wouldn't allow that.

As the shell around his heart began to crack, he heard a thump behind him followed by a soft curse. He jumped to his feet and spun around in time to see Allyn struggling to her feet, her rump swaying in the air. In seconds, he made it to her side, catching hold of her elbow to lift her up.

"Let go of me," she instructed him in a haughty tone of voice. "I can make it on my own."

"Oh, you can, can you? Then I suppose you meant to trip over—" he broke off and looked down at the ground. "Exactly what was it that you tripped over anyway?"

Allyn snatched her arm free and brought it to her side. "Never mind. I'm going to Newgrange."

There's no need to go."

"Really?" She pointed to her eyes. "You might have forgotten about these, but I haven't."

"I didn't forget." With a sigh of resignation, Keane waved a hand in front of her face.

* * * * *

Vivid blues and greens swirled in front of her eyes and Allyn swayed on her feet, clutching Keane's forearms tightly. "I can see! You did it! You used your magic."

"And now your mission is complete." He took a step away from her. "You can be on your way."

Allyn blinked at him. "Not on your life."

"What? You did your job, Allyn. You can go home now."

Her teeth nibbled her lower lip. "But I don't want to go."

"The Fates will want you to go."

"They asked me to come here, Keane. They didn't make me."

"Another lie?"

"Just a little fib. They told me about you." One hand lifted to caress his cheek. "And when I saw the pain you were in, I had to come." She grinned. "No pun intended."

"And you left you family to help someone you didn't know?"

"In the spirit of the season, yes. Oh, and because I thought you were hot."

Keane reached for her, pulling her into his arms. "You take my breath away," he admitted, lowering her gently to the ground. The fresh smell of rose petals wafted up to greet them and Allyn smiled.

"Nice touch, wizard."

His hand slid across the flat planes of her stomach. "No. This is a nice touch." With one thought, he unclothed them.

How could this woman have penetrated the deep layers surrounding his heart? He couldn't have allowed it. He didn't remember allowing it, but as he rose up over her, his cock straining to push into her glimmering pussy, he gave himself permission to believe that he could forgive himself. He had to if he wanted to make room for Allyn in his life.

He took possession of her body with slow, even strokes. She curled herself around him, her warmth beckoning him to press against her until they became one in every aspect.

"I don't want you to make love to me, Keane." Allyn's words startled him out of the hazy reverie.

He brushed her hair away from her face and went completely still. "What? What's wrong?"

She gave him an impish smile. "I want you to fuck me just like you have before. We'll have plenty of time to make love after today."

Every ounce of blood rushed from his head and pooled between his legs, lending strength to his cock. He plunged into her again and Allyn cried out, unintelligible words urging him to take her.

Keane forgot about the past. He forgot everything save for the feel of Allyn's tight sheath milking his cock and her small heels digging into his ass. He drove into her over and over until she began whimpering his name and then he slowed the thrusts, titillating her with each rub of his thick cock against the walls of her pussy. He pushed her to the edge and then refused to let her tumble over.

Allyn's nails scored his shoulders and she braced her feet against the damp grass to push her hips upward. "Keane," she whispered.

He touched his lips to her neck and licked the salty taste of her perspiration. "Tell me what you want."

"I've already told you," she returned, moving her nails down his back.

He pressed his palms against the ground and looked down into her flushed face. The sunlight washed over the perfection, highlighting her moist lips and glittering eyes. He dipped his head and kissed her gently. "I want to watch you come." The second he said the words, he saw her lips curve into a smile.

She brought one hand to his cheek. "Is that all?" She shifted beneath him. "I think I can handle that request."

He came to his knees and grabbed hold of her hips, his eyes never leaving her face. She clenched the muscles inside her and Keane's breath exploded from his lungs. "Don't do that," he emphasized each word.

Allyn's smile broadened and she wrapped her legs around his hips. "You don't like it?"

He began to move again. "Oh, I like it all right, but this isn't about what I like."

Her hands slid restlessly over his chest. "Yes, it is." She reached down between their bodies and lightly caressed his balls with her fingertips. He jumped and cursed and throwing away good intentions, he pounded into her, his muscles straining with each pump of his hips.

Allyn drew his head down close and pressed her lips against his ear. "I'm close," she whispered.

The orgasm ripped through him and he closed his eyes as the sensations gripped him. He groaned and dropped his forehead to hers. For a brief moment, he couldn't breathe. Then Allyn moved beneath him and he rolled to one side. She didn't allow him to go far.

"Thank you." His words reached her through the haze of serenity and Keane brushed his lips over the top of her hair.

"You're thanking me?" She chuckled. "For what?"

"For saving me."

"Deep down inside of you, you've always been good, Keane. One bad decision doesn't make you an evil person nor does your inability to save your parents make you weak." She thumped her palms against his chest. "You don't allow yourself to feel the human emotions which are a part of you."

He raised one eyebrow. "So is that what I'm feeling now? Human emotions?"

"Let's hope so."

"Stay with me. And before you say no, listen to me. I know I need to go home. I have to make peace with the past but—"

Her finger touched his lips. "You want me to go with you to your home. Why?"

"Because now that I've found you, I'm not letting you out of my sight." Jumping to his feet, he grasped her around the waist, holding her tightly against him. "But first, we'd better put some clothes on." He nibbled at her ear before releasing her.

In seconds, he'd caught her back up in his arms, and Allyn laughed as Keane's hand slipped down over her nose, his splayed fingers giving her a peek of the landscape ahead. "Where are you taking me?" she asked as the world whipped by in a blur of blues and greens.

"You'll find out soon enough."

"I was actually hoping to see Newgrange one more time before Winter Solstice ended."

"Oh, you'll do more than see it, my sweet." Keane put his lips against her ear. "Look behind you." He slowed their pace as the circular structure came into view.

Allyn squirmed out of his arms. "Newgrange." She ran forward and pressed her palm against the stones.

His arms circled her from behind. "Let's go inside."

She hesitated. "Keane, don't you think this is all too sudden?"

He stopped moving. "You tell me. You're the one who came to me."

She bit her lower lip. "You know why I came."

"But why have you stayed? Once I used my magic, your mission was complete."

She gave him an impish grin. "Because I've never had such amazing sex before."

He laughed out loud. "Now that's honesty I can deal with." He tugged her closer to the entrance. Then bracing his arm overhead, he looked down into Allyn's upturned face. "So I guess this means you're staying."

Allyn gave him a pensive look. "It's something I'll have to think about."

"Well, while you're thinking, think about this," he whispered a naughty thought in her ear and Allyn swatted at him.

"All right. I'll consider it, but just this once." She waggled a finger in mock admonition. "I would want you to get spoiled or anything."

Rock hard, he took her hand and brought her index finger to his lips. Suckling gently, he watched her face change, becoming softer as she surrendered. "Let me feel you again, Allyn. I can't get enough of you."

She rocked forward, her breasts bumping against his chest. A low, husky moan spilled from her lips and she locked her arms behind his head, dragging him down for a kiss. Keane went willingly, sinking into the warmth of her lips caressing his.

He couldn't understand the maelstrom of emotions storming his soul or why this woman created them. Soft and pliant in his arms, she shattered his defenses, crumbled his walls. After just one day. He could only imagine what spending the rest of his life with her was going to do to him.

Allyn snatched his hand and brought it lower, settling it between her firm thighs. His palm pressed against her heat and his eyes glazed. Her dampness bathed his fingers and the feeling was as powerful as an aphrodisiac.

Tangling his hand in her hair, he dipped his head to feast on her golden skin, his tongue swirling and tantalizing until he felt the torture as much as she did. "God, Allyn," he whispered against her pulse point. Sinking his fingers deep into her cunt, he felt her arch against him. She pushed into his hand, wanting the release as much as he needed to give it to her.

Wild, wanton and without reason, they tore at each other's clothes, needing the feel of flesh on flesh. Keane felt alive for the first time in years. Everywhere Allyn touched him sparked with fire. He sizzled and his cock grew painfully harder with each nip of her teeth, each brush of her tongue. Sparks danced in front of his eyes and he couldn't get enough of her.

His palms glided over her silken skin from her arms to her hips and back up, delighting in the sweet, little purring noises Allyn made in the back of her throat. "Say it, Allyn."

She lifted her head and fixed him with a sultry look. "I want you inside me."

Every ounce of blood in Keane's body zinged from his head to his cock. He tried to lift her in his arms, but she resisted.

"Here," she instructed, pointing to the grass. "Right now." Lowering the zipper on her pants, she tugged her jeans over her hips while Keane held his breath. He waited, knowing what he was about to see would prove his undoing.

Allyn stood before wearing nothing save a scrappy piece of lace, more string than material. She'd put the thong back on! Through the wispy panel, he could see the dark outline of her pussy. His legs went weak as if all of his energy had been drained from his body and when Allyn hooked her fingers in the thin straps, lowering the thong, his breath left his lungs in a loud exhale.

She defied perfection. Pure honey and silk, she stood before like a goddess, carved with infinite care. Then, holding her hands away from her body, she whispered, "Is this what you wanted to see?"

"This is what I wanted to feel," he returned, yanking her back into his arms. His hands couldn't stay still. They stroked, tickled, caressed, before diving into the moistness between her legs. The calloused tips of his fingers massaged her clit and Allyn's head fell back while her hips pumped against his palm.

He couldn't stand any more so he carried them both to the bed of soft grass, covering her body with his. She smelled of honeysuckle and cinnamon, but it was the soft, musky scent of her pussy which called to him. And he answered the summons immediately, drifting down her body until he could hover over her there.

Allyn lifted her legs and placed them over his shoulders, granting permission much as a queen gives audience. Keane groaned low in his throat and accepted the invitation, lowering his head, his mouth until his tongue could make contact with her softness. Beneath him, she quivered and gasped, holding her breath with anticipation.

Then he stroked her. Just one light touch. Enough to taste. But it would never be enough. He sank into her. Feasting. Suckling. Tormenting. His tongue danced around her clit, lavishing the sensitive bud with seductive strokes. Her muscles grew taut as her legs clenched around his shoulders.

"Oh," she whispered, hands grasping fistfuls of earth.

Keane raised his head. "Look at me, Allyn. Look into my eyes. I want to see you come."

She opened her eyes and met his gaze. Keane kept his tongue on her while their eyes locked. He circled, swirled and Allyn exploded, unraveling with whimpers and cries.

Then the sun broke through the clouds over Newgrange and the Fates smiled their approval.

Also by Rachel Carrington

ೱ

About the Author

ೱ

Don't you hate having to find something clever to say about yourself? As a writer, you'd think words would come easy to me. Not when it comes to touting my own abilities. So a short and sweet bio would be, well, um, give me a minute. See, my problem is I never do anything short. And as for sweet, well, that'd be telling. But I'll give it a shot. I'm long-winded, aggressive, outgoing, charming as hell and have a BS degree. I like to take long walks down by the shore, listen to country music, drink wine—no, wait. That's the personal ad I'm writing. See? I told you I'm no good when it comes to talking about me. If you want to know more, what little there is to know, you can visit my website. Happy Reading!

Annie welcomes comments from readers. You can find her website and email address on her author bio page at www.ellorascave.com.

CHRISTMAS CASH

Maggie Casper

Chapter One

There was a definite nip in the air, enough to chill but not enough to freeze just yet. Standing on the street corner in a jacked-up costume on the day after Thanksgiving wasn't Noelle Jacobs' idea of fun, but it was necessary.

Since hunk extraordinaire, Cash McCain, refused to give her a job at Raising Cain, the McCain family bar, Noelle had no choice but to take the seasonal work.

It was bad enough she'd decided on the spur of the moment to move back home with no job lined up. The decision left her no choice but to accept the graciousness of her parents and the small apartment above their garage.

But as wonderful as her parents were, Noelle wasn't thrilled about moving back home at the age of twenty-six. Especially when her parents were sure something horrible had happened to bring her back home.

She tried to tell them there was no huge tragedy in her life. It was simple, really. Noelle was just tired of the hustle and bustle of city life. She yearned for home.

Poking her eyes out with fiery hot nails seemed preferable to asking her parents for money. Instead, she'd swallowed her pride and asked Cash, who also happened to be her best friend's brother, for a job.

She'd gone into Raising Cain before opening time, intent on leaving employed, but Cash had not so nicely shot that idea to hell with some lame excuse about her being too young to work in a bar. Their heated conversation and all that took place that day still made her ears ring and her core ache with need.

"How can you say that when Casey works here?" Noelle looked around the dimly lit interior of the bar, loving the rustic atmosphere. It had a definite traditional country feel to it. Everything about the place reminded her of Cash.

He'd shrugged his massive shoulders, pulling Noelle from her thoughts, then crossed his arms over the wide expanse of his chest. "She's a McCain."

He'd evidently thought that little fact to be explanation enough, but once started, Noelle was like a dog with a bone. She didn't easily give up.

"Oh give me a freakin' break. What in the hell does that have to do with working at a bar? We're the same damned age, Cash, and you know it."

Her words seemed to irritate him, causing a frown to crease his brow. His next words were spoken in a low, menacing voice.

"Everyone around here knows causing harm to Casey wouldn't be good for their health."

"You're nuts if you think her name is the only thing keeping her safe and the lack of it would make me a target. Think about how damned stupid that sounds, Cash!" Noelle was feeling a bit irate. Men could be such annoying bastards.

Noelle opened her mouth to continue her argument but was cut short when Cash pushed off the bar to stand directly in front of her. He grasped her upper arms, turned and lifted her until her ass landed firmly on the bar.

All thought of arguing fled when Cash wrapped his arms around her lower back, pulling her to the edge of the bar. When his head dipped toward the juncture of her thighs, Noelle thought she'd shatter into a million pieces.

He was so sinfully close Noelle could hardly catch her breath. His scent wafted around her, drawing her deeper under his spell. He nipped at her clothes, catching her thin pants and panties between his teeth in the process. Noelle couldn't help but gasp when Cash let them go with a snap. He seemed to enjoy teasing her.

The fingers of one hand kneaded her ass but it was his other hand that caught her attention and kept it. With sure, deft movements, Cash rubbed her through the thin barrier of her drawstring pants. He had to feel how hot and wet she was.

Noelle was so consumed with lust it never even dawned on her that she might want to say something, to insist he stop. When he used his thumb, adding pressure against the already sensitive bud of her clit, Noelle nearly shot off the bar her climax was so sudden.

She was a boneless heap when Cash pulled her from the bar. "Careful," he murmured against her ear as he turned her away from him.

The feel of his warm breath against her neck sent shivers of delight coursing through her body even though his mouth didn't actually touch her.

"This," Cash growled while pressing the thick length of his cock to her ass, "is why you can't work here. You're a distraction I don't need or want."

His words struck like lightning, cooling Noelle's ardor as if she'd been doused with a bucket of cold water.

"You…you…" Noelle hadn't been prepared for the impact of Cash's refusal or how he'd go about doing it. She was so angry forming a coherent sentence seemed impossible.

"This conversation…this *lesson* is over, Noelle. The answer is no. You should know me well enough to know I won't change my mind."

The damned man was built like a brick wall and had the mentality to match. There was just no swaying him once he made a decision, and he certainly wasn't known for his willingness to compromise, which was why Noelle found herself standing on the street corner dressed as Mrs. Claus and ringing a stupid bell.

The only joy she got out of the whole damned fiasco was the knowledge that she'd been stationed right across the street from Raising Cain. Knowing Cash was trying to sleep in his apartment above the bar made everything bearable.

The giggle that escaped her chilled lips was one of sheer wickedness. Cash McCain was going to have a miserably annoying Christmas season if she had anything to do with it.

Noelle rang her bell with enthusiastic cheer, smiling at every passerby as if they were her best friend. Even though she was always prompt, Noelle was going to be extra responsible in the days to come. Showing up early for work every morning might not get her a bonus, but it was sure going to make things much more fun.

When the front door of Raising Cain slammed open ten minutes later, Noelle was digging through her duffle bag for lip gloss. The errant thought running through her mind to bring a purse instead of her duffle bag was cut short by the vision of Cash standing there in nothing more than a pair of drawstring pants, which nearly knocked the breath out of her, but she was easily able to cover her near blunder with a wide smile.

It bit the big one that the arrogant ass knew just how much he turned her on. Now he'd probably take the information and use it against her, relentlessly teasing and torturing her with it.

The thought of Cash doing anything remotely close to teasing or torturing her made her nipples swell and ache. He was so big. Big hands, big feet, big all over. Noelle's feminine core couldn't help but wonder what the rest of him was like.

Would his cock be in proportion to the rest of his body? Noelle could almost picture it, thick and long with veins lying just below the surface. Her mouth watered just thinking about the utterly erotic possibilities.

She'd give just about anything to find out, but evidently Cash was hung up on age. At thirty-six Cash was ten years older than Noelle and therefore thought of her as off-limits. Of course, that didn't mean she was going to give up, it just meant she had to rethink her strategy.

Noelle loved a challenge. Hell, even her mama always said that if you didn't have to work for what you wanted, it probably wasn't worth having in the first place. The thought made her smile.

Knowing full well she had his attention, Noelle waggled her fingers in Cash's direction then loudly greeted those walking by.

Happy Holidays!

Cash wanted to murder someone. It was ten minutes after nine in the morning and cold enough outside to shrivel a man's balls. Undeterred by the cold, Noelle dressed in a tiny red dress with no more than a sweater on for warmth, stood on the corner ringing the bell from hell.

Her mile-long legs were covered in white stockings but they couldn't be enough to keep her warm in Cash's opinion. Hell, even the Santa hat perched on the top of her pretty little head sat at a jaunty angle. How was it possible for anyone to be awake so early in the morning, much less coherent and perky?

Cash wanted to march across the street and cover her in the bulk of one of his jackets. To haul her into the kitchen for a cup of hot chocolate with marshmallows on top just as he'd done when she and Casey were younger. It didn't seem possible that they were already grown women.

Especially Noelle. Hell, when she'd left town, she'd still been stuck between being a child and a woman, sort of gangly and awkward, a definite late bloomer. Cash closed his eyes briefly, trying to remember the last time he'd seen her up close and personal, and for the life of him, he couldn't remember.

Surely he'd seen her in the time between her leaving for school and her return home just a few weeks ago? Life had been grueling and busy back then, but that was no excuse. Cash felt a twinge of guilt at the knowledge.

The persistent ringing of the bell stopped, leaving nothing but the normal sounds of life. Cash opened his eyes to see Noelle squatting down in front of a child. A beautiful smile curved her lips, it looked nothing like the mischievous grin she'd bestowed upon him when young or the sneer she'd been aiming at him lately.

Realizing she was no longer the gangly teenager she once had been was like a blow to the solar plexus, stealing the breath from his lungs. Time had been more than nice to Noelle, filling her out in a way that made Cash's mouth water.

From her large, obviously real breasts to the nipped-in expanse of her waist, over gently curved hips and down the long, long expanse of leg she loved to show, Noelle Jacobs was all woman.

My woman!

The caveman in him growled. Cash would love nothing more than to drag her off to his lair to do with as he pleased. No matter how hard he fought it, Cash could no longer act like the responsible, big brotherly type toward Noelle.

She'd probably run as fast as her pink-tipped toes would take her when she found out the way he liked his sex. Being the impertinent minx she was, Noelle would probably plant her palm across his cheek, earning her an ass-burning spanking in the process.

"Dammit!" Cash muttered the curse as he backed into the bar. He didn't slam the door. To do so would only prove how much Noelle was getting to him. Something Cash wasn't quite ready to admit. Admitting he had feelings for Noelle, feelings that went deeper than he was willing to deal with, would open up Pandora's box and, sure as shit, all hell would break loose.

Cash made his way back through the bar and up the back stairs to his apartment. He enjoyed the dark wood and earth tones that seemed to engulf him every time he stepped through the door. No matter what was going on in his life, his apartment was always a place of retreat, his castle.

Cash showered and dressed even though he was nowhere near ready for the day. Coffee and food seemed to help but nothing could make the noise that blasted bell was making sound better.

At the end of his rope Cash stalked across the street. He didn't slow down to speak to those around him or acknowledge another soul. He didn't stop until he was face-to-face with Noelle, their chilled breaths mingling in the scant inches that separated them.

"What are you doing out here?"

She looked at him as if he'd grown horns. Then she began speaking slowly as if she were afraid he might not comprehend what she was saying. "I'm. Working." The damned imp even had the audacity to exaggeratedly move her lips. When she was finished mocking him on the street corner for all to see, she smiled.

She must be insane, Cash decided. Not many grown men were willing to go up against him, much less a woman who, when compared to his size, would be considered tiny.

Of course that didn't seem to stop her. Pulling herself up straight, Noelle glared at him before asking, "Why? What are you doing here?"

Cash wasn't certain how to answer the loaded question. If he admitted that her bell was driving him insane, she'd only ring it louder and even more obnoxiously. If he admitted that he didn't like the fact she was only partially dressed and standing out in the cold, she'd know he cared more than he should.

He knew she had a crush on him. She wasn't worldly enough to keep her emotions well hidden and even if she were, she'd never even so much as tried. Instead, she flirted shamelessly whenever the chance arose.

This one was going to be tricky. Cash was going to have to pull out the big guns and play the big overbearing brother, something he was very good at. If Noelle were anything like Casey, she'd be huffing mad in no time.

He was annoyed, just as Noelle had hoped. She had no problem with standing out on the sidewalk, freezing her ass off, if that's what it would take to make it impossible for Cash to ignore her. He never should have refused her the job, especially for some lame-ass excuse, because now she was on a mission, no matter the outcome. And to prove his point by using her sexuality was plain wrong. Noelle was going to make sure he knew it too.

It was bad enough that she had to stand on a street corner ringing a bell instead of working in the nice, warm interior of Raising Cain, but to have him waltz across the street all high and mighty as if he owned the whole damned block was too much.

She could be making a nice wage, but *nooo,* her sarcastic side chided, the almighty Cash McCain had to go and refuse her. The more irritated Noelle became, the more calm her outer appearance seemed. She was raging on the inside, but kept her smile sweet and charming. Deep down, she knew it was the only way to deal with the larger-than-life man, especially if she had any chance of opening his eyes to the truth.

I might be the same age as your baby sister, but there is nothing childish about me. Not the things I want to do to every inch of your muscular body, or the things I want you to do to mine.

If only she could say the words aloud. Noelle inwardly sighed, knowing it wasn't going to happen anytime soon. If there was one thing about her that would turn Cash off, it would be blatant forwardness.

So, she'd walk right on the edge, be just forward enough to irritate the hell out of him, flirting and sashaying about every time she was in his presence, not giving him any choice but to see her for the woman she was. And she'd do it all without crossing the line.

Who knows, Noelle thought to herself, maybe her actions would push him over the edge and he'd take her in a frenzy of angry sex.

The thought made her shiver.

"It's too cold out here to be dressed the way you are."

His words caught her off guard, surprising the smile right off her face. "So either you go home and change or—"

Noelle couldn't help but laugh. Not a giggle, an outright laugh. "Or what, you'll put me on restriction?" she taunted, not at all believing the man really thought she would just fall in line and do what he said, just because he said it. It was unreal.

Cash didn't seem at all amused by her outburst. Noelle wiped tears of mirth from her eyes, but the laughter just wouldn't stop. She wheezed and snorted and just about the time she thought she had herself under control, she would look up, see his face and it would start all over again.

Cash on the other hand, had evidently had enough. "Noelle." His tone was undeniably peeved and brooked no argument.

"Oh sorry," she muttered, straightening from her doubled-over position. Noelle wasn't at all sorry, but when it came to Cash, it was best to act a bit repentant.

A dark brown brow arched over green eyes flecked with gold. "Either you change or you come to Raising Cain for a thicker coat, one that actually fits." Cash gestured to her too thin sweater.

His look of exasperation quickly changed to one of lust. His hooded lids spoke of something dark and sensual. He seemed to be in a trance, as if he couldn't pull his eyes away from her chest, no matter the consequences.

Following his gaze, Noelle lowered her eyes only to find her nipples prominently displayed through the lace of her bra and the thin fabric of her dress. Instead of crossing her arms over her chest in an attempt at modesty, she slowly started buttoning her sweater, from the bottom up.

When her fingers reached the button at the rise of her breasts, Cash's gaze snapped up and locked with hers. His eyes were dark and his pupils dilated. Color rode high on his cheeks and Noelle would bet it had nothing at all to do with the cold.

It didn't matter how hard she tried, Noelle couldn't keep her eyes locked on his. Not when the possibility of glimpsing his straining erection made her mouth water. She lowered her eyes to his fly, not even trying to hide where she was looking.

Damn!

She'd always known he was going to be awe-inspiring, beautiful even, but the sight of the thick ridge straining against the zippered fly of his jeans was just too much.

"Goddammit, Noelle! Knock that shit off." Cash's voice thundered through the haze of lust clouding her thoughts. Never before had he been able to embarrass her, and yet, this time he'd accomplished it without even trying.

She cleared her throat, trying to hide her discomfort then looked around her, hoping no one had witnessed her blatantly gawking at Cash's crotch. "All right, already. I'll come to the bar and borrow a heavier coat."

Huffing a huge sigh of relief when Cash turned away from her, Noelle wondered for the first time since returning home if she was getting in way over her head.

Chapter Two

She was following him. Cash knew it even though he had yet to turn and see for himself. Her scent enveloped him like a gentle breeze, tickling his senses while making his cock throb to life. Knowing she had the ability to make him as stiff as a fence post without even trying irritated Cash to no end.

If Noelle ever really set her mind to seducing him, Cash knew he'd be screwed. Literally.

He opened the door to Raising Cain for Noelle. He had to hide his grin as she stomped through, making her anger known. She was a stubborn piece of baggage, that was for sure.

"Go on up and find something...warmer in my closet." Noticing once again the peaked tips of her beautiful breasts made Cash stumble over his words.

He didn't follow her up or offer to help. To do so would be asking for trouble Cash didn't need. Besides, it wasn't as if his place was so big she wouldn't be able to find the closet, he reminded himself as he set about making hot chocolate.

Noelle returned in moments. She looked utterly adorable and devastatingly sexy all but swallowed whole by his coat. She didn't look too happy, however.

"This is never going to work, Cash. Dammit! I can hardly move."

Noelle flapped her arms like a bird taking flight to make her point. The sleeves of his coat stopped several inches below her fingertips. The hem didn't stop until nearly her knees.

Perfect.

"Watch your mouth and come here so I can roll the sleeves, darlin'. Unless you want to pack up and head home?"

By the look on her face, Cash knew Noelle didn't much care for the choices he'd given her. "I'll be staying. Hurry up so I can get back to my post."

Noelle kept her eyes glued to the front window. Chaos was a small Texas town, with family-oriented folks but just like any other place on earth, there was occasional theft. She'd brought her little red money pot with her but her belongings sat on the sidewalk right where she'd left them.

"You brought a duffle," Cash commented, motioning across the street, "but not a coat?" He'd never understand women and the way their minds worked.

"It has my stuff in it and a change of clothes. I'm supposed to wear this getup while ringing the bell but I need something else for after and didn't want to have to drive all the way home."

Cash thought about her words for a minute. He wanted to know what she needed a change of clothes for but knew asking would raise her ire to an even higher level. She'd think he was being the bossy big brother again, when in reality, Cash was worried she might need the change of clothes for a hot date or something similarly wicked.

Jealousy won out. "What's the change of clothes for?" Cash winced at the gruffness of his voice.

Noelle raised a perfectly arched blonde brow at his tone. Could she tell he was getting jealous? Did she have any idea what the thought of her with another man did to him deep down inside?

"Jeez, lighten up already. I'll be job hunting after I finish my shift and I don't think this outfit is appropriate for the occasion."

Cash punched down the guilt threatening to choke him. He'd refused her a job because it was what was best for the both of them. He wasn't ready for anything permanent and even if he were, Noelle, as the best friend to his little sister, was off-limits.

"Come on over after you're done and use my apartment to change." He made the offer while mentally kicking himself.

Once finished rolling the sleeves of the coat Noelle was wearing, he took a few steps back.

Noelle opened her mouth. Cash was sure it was to argue and didn't give her the chance. Arms across his chest, stance wide, he narrowed his eyes. "It's warmer here than a public restroom and cleaner, so don't argue."

She just stood there staring at him for a minute before she gave a single sharp nod of her head. Then, instead of stomping her foot or pouting as he expected, Noelle moved impossibly close to him. Heat radiated off her voluptuous body in waves, nearly pulling him in. It was her finger poking his chest that brought him back.

Her closeness was overwhelming as was the feel of her finger touching him. Even if it was just to poke at him. Cash caught her wrist on its next pass toward his chest and used it as leverage to jerk her body against his.

She was warm and pliant in his arms, a sure sign she was more than willing for anything he cast her way. Damn, the woman was going to be the death of him. Cash wasn't sure it was possible to get close enough to ease the ache in his groin but he'd damn well try.

Without warning, Cash slanted his mouth over hers, licking and nibbling at her. "You taste so good," he growled against her lips. "Open up for me, darlin'."

Noelle parted her lips, taking everything he had to give as if they were made just for each other. When Cash finally broke the kiss to bury his face in the curve of her neck, Noelle was panting.

Erotic visions of Noelle and him together danced through his mind. Cash was sure some of the things he wanted to do to her delectable body were illegal.

When Noelle pushed closer, all but climbing his body, Cash lifted the hem of the jacket she still wore then pressed a knee between her thighs. She was hot against his leg. Her heat seeped into his body causing his balls to draw up close to the base of his shaft in anticipation.

Noelle whimpered low in her throat. The contact between their bodies wasn't enough to get her off and Cash wanted to see her fly apart. He needed to see the bliss on her face before he once again sent her off.

Just thinking about pissing her off again or even worse, making her cry, left him breathless and not in a good way. It was like a fist squeezing his insides, cruel and unusual, but there was no way around it because there was no future for the two of them together.

"Ride me, darlin'. Show me how pretty you look when you come."

Noelle's glazed eyes fixed on his face as he used her hips to pull her close, lifting until she was on the tips of her toes. When she gasped and rocked forward, increasing the pace Cash had set, he knew she was getting close.

"That's it, baby. Come on. Come for me, Noelle."

Cash dug his fingers into her hips, pulling her hard against him and she shattered. Her cry of completion as well as the scent of her arousal would haunt his nights for years to come.

Taking a deep breath, Cash tried to steel himself for what was to come. With a wealth of regret, he set Noelle away from him then, swallowing the bile that threatened to rise, he said, "Go finish your shift then go home, Noelle. This is no place for you."

"I'm not your little sister, Cash. Never was and never will be, so stop treating me like a goddamned child."

She was pissed and hurt, that much he was sure of. Her eyes shot green lasers at him. If looks could kill, he'd be six feet under in no time.

"Then stop acting like a goddamned child." Cash knew his words were harsh but she'd asked for it by throwing a fit. "I won't tell you again to watch your mouth either, darlin'."

Cash led Noelle to the door. Once outside, he turned her toward the street. She'd only taken one flouncing step away from him when Cash brought the palm of his hand down on her delectable ass.

Noelle yelped then looked around in abject horror as if being caught getting spanked was the worst possible thing in the world. Cash would have to keep that in mind.

"Watch your mouth, brat, and stop trying to push me. You won't like the outcome."

*****

It was hard to stalk across the street as if in a huff of anger when she was so wet her cream was surely coating her thighs. Her damp panties clung to the folds of her pussy like a drunken lover.

Cash had swatted her. Making her climax had been great, the kiss so passionate Noelle was sure she'd be dreaming about it for days, but he'd actually spanked her ass! Noelle's mind swirled with arousal even as the curve of her ass stung. Even through multiple layers of fabric, she could feel the burn. Imagining what he could do to her bare flesh made her shiver with delight.

Cash would probably head for the hills if he knew he'd just partially fulfilled one of her all-time favorite erotic fantasies, forget the fact that he'd just brought her to a raging orgasm without taking even a stitch of clothing off.

The original skirmish might have involved a job at Raising Cain but in Noelle's mind, the only way she could truly be the victor was by claiming Cash. A dreamy smile curved her lips. Noelle straightened for a minute. She had to remember that pacing herself was the important part. If she intended to win the war, she'd have to take things slow.

A thought so brilliant it nearly blinded her flashed through her mind. Noelle studied the street, allowing her gaze to drift up one side and down the other. There were several small shops sporting antiques and collectibles but the main attraction, besides Raising Cain, was the new sports bar Dooner's, which catered mostly to the college crowd.

It was rumored that the waitresses were all young ladies who wore low-riding jeans and tight sports-oriented T-shirts cropped at the bottom to show their midriffs.

Sounded like just the job Noelle needed to keep things interesting.

She hadn't applied there before out of loyalty to her friend Casey and the McCain family business but she'd been left with no choice in the matter since Cash refused to hire her.

She smiled again, a knowing smile the likes of which would make the devil himself tremble in fear. Happy once again, Noelle set out ringing her bell and spreading the holiday spirit with an extra boisterous flare.

Her voice was a bit hoarse by the end of her shift but Noelle felt light and springy. After loading her work-related supplies in the trunk of her car, she headed across the street to Raising Cain with nothing more than her duffle bag in hand.

"Hi, honey. I'm home," Noelle announced as she strode casually through the door.

Cash was behind the bar stocking bottles of beer in the cooler while talking to one lone customer. Red vinyl-covered stools stood beside the bar ready for the evening ahead, as did the chairs next to the tables. The floor had obviously been swept and mopped. On the floor, fresh sawdust had been scattered.

Noelle couldn't help herself. She was in such a good mood, knowing damned well she'd soon have the upper hand that she couldn't help but push her luck.

Cash had stopped working and was now just standing there staring at her, a confused look on his handsome face.

Noelle sidled up to him, happy to know she could shake him up just a bit. "Aren't you going to welcome me?" She laughed as she went up on tiptoe to kiss the side of his jaw.

She'd have preferred his lips or even his cheek but Cash was too tall.

His extremely large hands grabbed a hold of her arms. His touch was firm but gentle as he placed her away from him.

"Don't do that again." His voice was strangled, low and raspy in a way Noelle had never heard it before.

Knowing she had to take it slow didn't make it any easier. Deciding to lighten things up, Noelle smiled impishly. "Hey, you invited me to change my clothes, insisted really. Remember?" She batted her eyelashes for good measure.

Cash didn't laugh. Hell, he didn't even smile. He thrust a hand through his hair and sighed. "To change your clothes, Noelle. Nothing more."

Her fingers itched to feel his hair. Would it be silky soft or coarse? It didn't matter in the least. When she finally got the chance to clutch it between her fingers while Cash's face was buried between her thighs, she wasn't ever going to let go.

Noelle could feel her cheeks heat. Looking away from Cash's intense gaze damn near took an act of Congress, but finally she managed. Could he tell she was aroused? He'd probably bellow the roof down if he knew exactly what it was she'd been thinking.

"Just checking, big boy. Just checking." Noelle waggled her fingers just the way she knew would annoy him then fled to the stairs leading to Cash's apartment.

Once inside, she hurriedly changed her clothes. She wanted to get over to Dooner's before it got too busy. Maybe then she'd be able to talk the owner into taking on one more waitress.

If so, she'd be killing two birds with one stone. Not only would she have a decent paying job but, if she knew Cash half as well as she thought she did, it would piss him off to no end. What more could she ask for?

Noelle skipped down the steps light on her feet, her spirits soaring. With a smile on her face, she entered the cavernous room immediately searching out Cash. She finally found him in the storeroom with Connor and Carson, his younger twin brothers.

*****

"The truck ought to be here anytime. Why don't you two head out back and wait for it?"

Cash made the command sound like a request, but his brothers knew it for what it was worth.

"Sure," Connor started, his smile growing by the second.

"Whatever you say," Carson finished, his gaze bouncing first to Noelle then back to Cash.

Cash still found it funny the way they could finish each other's sentences. What he didn't find the least bit amusing was the way they were both staring at Noelle, looking her up and down as if she were a rich and creamy desert.

"Now would be good." This time, Cash left no doubt as to his feelings on the matter. After Carson and Connor left, Cash turned back to Noelle.

Her honey blonde hair was loose, swinging around her shoulder, framing her features in a way that made his cock throb to life. The pale green orbs of her eyes held a wealth of mirth. The vixen was playing him again.

Cash decided to continue with her lessons. He'd give her a taste of her own medicine. His mind screamed for him to retreat but his mouth insisted he move forward, just for a taste.

He'd just scare her a bit. Cash knew not all women craved their loving rough and messy the way he liked it, so he'd use that little bit to gain leverage. To make her forget she'd ever had a crush on him.

"Come here." Noelle's eyes widened and the smile slipped from her face. "Now, Noelle."

Her breath quickened at the sound of his voice, causing her breasts to bob enticingly beneath the confines of her too tight T-shirt.

She moved toward him slowly. Cash gave her no time to think or react before he gathered her close. Her hair swung around her shoulders as he jerked her against his chest, causing her unique scent to waft around them. Cash inhaled deeply, taking the scent of Noelle deep into his lungs.

For a second, her body stiffened against his tight hold. Cursing himself for a fool, Cash slanted his mouth across hers, plundering the moistness he found between her parted lips.

The urge to nip her lower lip was too enticing to fight. The feel of her warm flesh between his teeth was heavenly. Noelle's gasp at the sharp sting of pain was like music to his ears. Cash lapped at the hurt causing Noelle to all but melt into him. She was nearly purring in delight by the time he finished.

In mindless need, he clasped the finely rounded globes of her ass in his hands, pulling her close, grinding his hips against hers. Cash nearly came in his pants at the contact. The plan to run Noelle off had, in effect, backfired on him.

All thought of trying to salvage what was left of his sanity fled at the contact. Cash broke the kiss and stepped away from Noelle, but only for a moment, just long enough to lift her shirt above her breasts. The sight of her nearly naked chest made his mouth water.

Needing her nipples free for his mouth, Cash lowered the cups of her bra until her breasts spilled over the top, begging for his touch. Noelle shivered at the first touch of his tongue then groaned when he worried the erect nub between his teeth.

She seemed to enjoy the small bite of pain, a reaction that urged Cash on. He felt a bit of triumph at the dazed look on her face. Her normally clear eyes were glazed with lust and need.

Cash tried not to think of what it would be like to wake up every morning to the feel of her body snuggled against his, to take her every morning, in every way thinkable. Would she always look so luscious after he made love to her?

Cash's mind snapped back to the present. The need to be inside of her, to feel the fist-tight channel of her pussy throb around his cock made him mad with desire. Cash, knowing he was moving beyond the point of no return, wrenched her pants open. Then, dropping to his knees, he took them as well as her barely there panties with him.

As much as he wanted to taste her, to tease and torment her every fold, Cash just couldn't wait. He took only the time needed to unzip his fly and sheathe himself with a condom from his wallet before bending Noelle over the deep freezer sitting in the corner of the storeroom.

Within minutes Cash was balls deep inside her warm and willing body. He couldn't help but groan and shudder at the feel of her body gripping his so erotically tight.

"Fuck, baby, you feel good."

Cash pulled back then thrust home again. The slippery sounds of sex as well as their breath panting into the otherwise silent room urged him into a mind-blowing tempo guaranteed to have him seeing stars in minutes.

Noelle's white-knuckled hands grasped the edge of the freezer as if it were a lifeline. Her breathing was shallow and her body glowed with a fine sheen of perspiration. The sexy little sounds she was making grew louder as small spasms gripped and released Cash's cock.

Reaching forward, Cash braced a hand at the center of her back, holding her exactly where he wanted her.

"Hurry, Cash. Hurry!"

She didn't need to urge him on. Pistoning in and out of her body swiftly brought them both to completion. Light burst behind Cash tightly closed eyes, a growl of hunger tore from his throat as Noelle climaxed beneath him, taking Cash with her.

Cash didn't regain his bearings until Noelle squirmed beneath him in an attempt to dislodge his body. "Stay still."

Cash gathered her hands in his, placing them over her head, holding her in place. He wasn't quite ready to let her go yet and that knowledge made his knees weak with fear. He couldn't…wouldn't let himself think in long term.

"Let me up, Cash." Noelle didn't beg or whine. She seemed absolutely coherent, a thought that pissed Cash off to no end when he couldn't seem to string two thoughts together without feeling strangely panicked.

Reluctantly, Cash let her up. He removed and discarded the soiled protection into the nearest trash can then tucked his now flaccid cock back into the tight confines of his jeans before turning back to her.

Noelle seemed to be fine. Her jeans were back in place as was her shirt. Cash immediately missed the taste of her and wondered if he'd ever again have the chance to sink deep into her tight sheath.

"Wow!" Noelle breathed, looking at Cash from beneath her slightly lowered lids. She then ran her tongue across her swollen lower lip, all but inviting him to taste more.

Cash wanted to follow her tongue with his own. He'd made a huge tactical error. By tasting her and feeling her body against his, he hadn't put an end to what was between them, he'd merely upped the ante. For the first time, Cash realized there was no getting Noelle out of his system. He craved her like an adrenaline junkie needed a challenge.

Noelle stood before him, a woman who'd just been thoroughly fucked. There was a sparkle in her eyes that hadn't been there before and, for a moment, Cash was afraid she was going to jump him this time.

He'd just decided he wouldn't stop her when she said, "Well that was fun but I've got things to do and people to see. See ya later."

Cash stood there dumbfounded and irritated as hell as she walked out the door. His day, as well as the complicated mess of a fiasco only got worse when Connor and Carson both started snickering from the doorway behind him.

Chapter Three

Trembling legs were the least of Noelle's worries, but wonderful sex topped the list. She was pushing hard and although she knew her actions would end up biting her in the ass, she just couldn't seem to stop herself.

Cash was a commanding presence. Noelle had always known it, but the way he kissed her, nearly devouring her, took her breath away. Now that she was out in the chilled night air, catching her breath should be no problem.

Only that wasn't the case.

Remembering the way Cash had touched her, tormenting her with his hands, mouth, and the wicked length of his cock, left no denial as to how dominant he actually was.

Knowing she might very well be getting more than she'd bargained for sent shivers of anticipation up her spine. As soon as she finished speaking with the owner of Dooner's about a job, she'd go home and rest up for tomorrow.

If Cash thought he could touch her and kiss her the way he had, as a means of punishment or as a scare tactic, he was sadly mistaken. And Noelle planned to make sure he knew it.

It took a lot of concentration, but Noelle finally got her head on straight and her thoughts out of the gutter. By the time she reached Dooner's she was well prepared for what she hoped would be a lucrative waitressing job.

Forty minutes later, with a tray full of drinks in hand, Noelle began her training. She did well during the short, three-hour shift she pulled and planned to do even better tomorrow night when she came back for a full four hours.

Mona Sinclair, the owner of Dooner's, had hired her on the spot and within minutes, they'd come to an agreement. Noelle would work a four-hour shift, five days a week until the Christmas season was over and then move on to full-time. By then, she ought to have the lay of the land and know how to wield a tray with precision. At least that's what Mona had said.

Just knowing she was now gainfully employed took a bit of the pressure off. Now she'd be able to either find her own place closer to town or pay her parents rent for the small apartment above the garage she'd been occupying. Either way, she felt like life was finally taking a turn in the right direction.

"I'm off, Mona." Her new boss was a very stylish, forty-something-year-old woman with a wicked sense of humor. Noelle liked her right off the bat.

"Sure thing, missy. You take care."

Noelle headed out the front door and back up the street to where her car was parked. Although Chaos was a fairly small town without big-city crime, she still kept her eyes open for any danger, just as her daddy had taught her.

The drive out to her parent's small ranch took much longer than Noelle would have liked. She was so tired after her long day of working and flirting that it took everything in her to keep her eyes open.

She couldn't help but sigh tiredly when she finally reached the house. It was dark and quiet, perfect for thinking, but Noelle was too damned tired to think. Tonight she was going to sleep like the dead.

Tomorrow morning, however, would have her bright-eyed, bushy-tailed and hopefully as irritating to Cash as she had been today.

Unfortunately, things didn't quite work out the way Noelle had envisioned. She'd made her way up the rickety stairs to her apartment and into bed in a matter of minutes, but instead of sleeping, she'd tossed and turned. And dreamed.

* * * * *

The next morning Noelle stood post on her street corner and thought about the night before. Some of her dreams had been so erotic she couldn't help but blush just remembering them, even in the light of a brand-new day. Pushing naughty thoughts out of her sleep-deprived mind, Noelle fired up her boom box. Within seconds Christmas carols filled the crisp morning air.

She smoothed a hand down her shorter than usual skirt and unbuttoned another button on her white dress shirt then began setting up for the day. She had on a fuzzy, red button-down sweater over the top of her shirt. It wasn't thick by any stretch of the imagination but it was cover, and thus would keep her out of trouble while still showing off her assets.

Noelle smiled then checked her watch, curious to see how long it would take Cash to wake this morning. What type of a mood would he be in? So many different thoughts tumbled through her mind.

Her bell sounded merrily as did Noelle. She greeted those passing by as long-lost friends, even making a few new ones in the process. It was wonderful to see so many people giving to charity. Her little red pail seemed to be filling quite nicely. A surprise to Noelle since it wasn't quite ten o'clock yet.

Letting impatience get the best of her, Noelle rang the little bell in her hand as if her life depended on it. If Cash didn't show himself soon, she was going to have to resort to drastic measures.

Noelle wasn't quite sure exactly what those drastic measures were, but she'd sure the hell think of something if necessary.

* * * * *

Murder was too good for the bell ringer from hell. She deserved an ass whipping to outdo all ass whippings. He grumbled and complained as he climbed from the warmth of his bed. Two mornings in a row were too many as far as he was concerned.

Still pissed off from the night before, Cash yanked on a pair of faded jeans. He didn't bother fastening his pants much less putting on a shirt or shoes before making his way down to the bar where there would be a fresh pot of coffee.

Not for the first time in his life, Cash decided whoever had come up with the idea of putting a timer on a coffeepot deserved a medal of some sort.

He was enjoying a moment of bliss, eyes closed, warm coffee in hand when a burst of cold air came from the back of the building. Within seconds Cooper and Casey, the youngest two McCain siblings, made their way into the main area of the bar.

"Mornin'." Casey approached him for a brotherly hug. She always felt so tiny against him but not in the same way as Noelle. By height standards, Noelle was small but she was far from fragile with her overblown womanly curves.

Cash, disgusted with himself for comparing his little sister to her best friend—the same friend he'd all but devoured the evening before, stepped away from Casey so fast she stumbled forward.

"Oh hell," Cash cursed, placing a steadying hand out for Casey. "Sorry, Case."

She cocked her head to the side, her bouncy brown curls falling over her forehead in the process. "Everything okay?"

Cash thanked everything holy that she had no idea of what had been happening between Noelle and him. If Casey had even an idea, she'd be on him like white on rice.

"Yup. Everything's just fine."

"Good God, what is that awful racket?"

The disgruntled question came from Cooper, the youngest McCain brother, who also just happened to be the only staid one of the bunch. He liked numbers almost as much as he liked to be alone. Cash could only imagine how annoying Noelle's bell would be to his accountant brother. The thought made him smile.

"Ohhhh!" By the squeal of delight, and the way Casey was racing for the front door, Cash figured she'd just noticed Noelle across the street.

"It's Noelle. She's got a new job." Cash was actually enjoying Cooper's discomfort.

"You mean they actually *pay* her to make that noise?" The look on Cooper's face was just too much. Cash couldn't help but laugh.

"I don't think they pay her to make *that* much noise. I believe she gives it a bit extra for my benefit."

Cooper grumbled something about loud females on his way to the coffeepot to which Cash just shook his head. It was beyond comprehension the way Cooper acted toward women, as if he could take them or leave them and be perfectly happy either way. Nothing seemed to excite the man.

"Where's the pipsqueak?" Cash asked of his niece Autumn, Casey's five-year-old daughter.

"She's with Mike for the morning." Mike was Casey's ex-husband. It still made no sense to Cash how two people could divorce and remain good friends. To his dying day, he'd never understand it.

Cooper mumbled something else as he left the room making his way toward the storage room, which also doubled as an office, to do the bookwork. Without any further distractions, Cash was able to get back to work.

A couple of hours passed and before Cash knew it, it was time to open for the day. He went to the window to change the sign to "open" and couldn't help but notice that Noelle still stood across the street ringing her bell, although she no longer seemed in the high spirits she'd been in earlier that morning.

He was just beginning to wonder where Casey had run off to when she wandered her way up the sidewalk toward Noelle, a bag in hand. The transfer of the bag and goodbyes didn't take long at all. Within minutes, Casey was walking back across the street toward Raising Cain, a mischievous smile on her face.

Cash knew in that instant he was in trouble. Casey's first words as she strode through the door, proved it.

"Oohhh, you are so getting what you deserve for refusing Noelle a job." The smirk on his sister's face was over the top.

"You gonna tell me or make me guess, twerp?"

Casey wrinkled her nose at Cash's choice of endearment.

"Fine then, spoilsport. I'll tell you." Casey sucked in a huge breath warning Cash she was fixing to go into a long spiel on a subject that could probably be summed up in ten words or less.

"Well, you saw me across the street talking with Noelle, I'm sure."

Cash just nodded. There was no use in trying to talk, because once Casey got started, there was no getting a word in edgewise.

"Let me just say I'm not happy she's stuck on the corner ringing a bell. Then again, that doesn't really have anything to do with this, does it?" She didn't wait for an answer nor expected one, Cash was sure.

"I went to apologize *again*," she stressed, "for you not hiring her when she all but begged you for a job, and you know what she told me? She said it didn't matter because Mona over at Dooner's, the new place down the street, hired her like that."

The news was bad enough, but the way Casey snapped her fingers in front of his angry face made things even worse. Her next words sent him on a course that would surely change the relationship he had with Noelle for the rest of their lives.

"She even sent me to get her some more of those low-rise jeans and a few more T-shirts. Said her stuff wasn't sexy enough."

* * * * *

It was probably stupid to be so angry that Cash had ignored her all day long. How he'd managed to tune out *A Chipmunk Christmas,* blaring as loud as the tiny speakers on her boom box would allow was beyond Noelle.

As hour after hour passed, she'd gone from happily doing her job to barely managing a smile for those nice enough to stick money in her bucket. Damn if she wasn't peeved, with no real reason for being so.

Casey's visit almost made up for standing out in the cold without so much as a glimpse of Cash. Her friend was quirky and could talk an auctioneer under the table, but she was caring and had a heart of gold. Noelle made a mental promise to spend more time with Casey and her daughter Autumn as soon as the holidays were over and she was done ringing a blasted bell for a living.

The next few hours crawled by at a snail's pace. Checking her watch, Noelle was glad to see it was time to load up. Just as she had the day before, Noelle wrestled her belongings to her car where she stowed them into the trunk safe and sound.

Job completed, she grabbed the bag of new clothes Casey had picked up for her earlier in the day. She was debating whether to change at Raising Cain or Dooner's when she was startled by a sound behind her.

Cash stood there as still as stone, looking as angry as a thundercloud. "Uh, hi." Noelle licked her lips, nervous about the angry gleam in Cash's eyes.

"I was just fixing to—" Noelle's words were cut off, her breath sucked right from her lungs by a kiss so hot, so full of anger, she couldn't help but struggle against its intensity.

Cash's tongue vied for entrance and won. The heat between them grew until Noelle couldn't stand it. Rubbing her abdomen against the hard length of his erect shaft nearly buckled her knees.

Why was he so mad? Did it matter? Noelle was sure it did, but for the life of her, she couldn't fathom why. As abruptly as he started the kiss, Cash stopped it. He pulled his body away from hers, still holding her by the upper arms. "You are not going to work at Dooner's. Do you hear me?"

Noelle felt her eyes widen at his tone. "Let go of me, you jackass!" Noelle put action to her words. She pulled herself from his hold but refused to do the smart thing and take a step back.

With her one free hand planted firmly on her hip, she gave him her best no-nonsense look. "I don't answer to you. You didn't want me as an employee, so as far as I'm concerned, you've got no business butting into my affairs."

Something in Cash's stance changed. He went from boiling mad to calm in the blink of an eye. The way his eyes kept her rooted to the spot was extremely uncomfortable. He was quiet, too quiet. Noelle began to worry.

She thought of fleeing. Things had gotten quickly out of hand and she needed time to regroup and prepare for the next round. Cash must have caught the way her gaze skittered to her car because in the next second he had her by the hand, all but dragging her across the street to Raising Cain.

Casey stood on the sidewalk with several of the regulars. They were all watching intently, only Casey had a loony grin spread across her face. Noelle tried to stop Cash, to insist Casey tell her exactly what in the hell was going on, but the Neanderthal pulling her along, as if she weighed no more than a feather, was having none of it.

The only words he spoke as they made their way through the bar toward the stairs leading to the apartment were, "You'll answer to me all right, Noelle, and you'll never forget doing it."

His words alone, forget the deep, gravelly tone of his voice, were enough to make her panties damp with need. An aroused smile replaced the look of uncertainty she was sure had wreathed her face just minutes ago. Let the games begin, was her new motto.

Chapter Four

The feel of Noelle's fingers entwined with his made Cash's pulse skyrocket. He tugged her behind him up the stairs to his apartment. They'd no sooner crossed the threshold when he backed her against the wall, pinning her there with the full length of his body.

Instead of struggling against him or cursing a blue streak as he thought she'd do, Noelle dropped her bag of clothes then squirmed to get even closer. She snaked her free hand beneath the hem of his shirt, skating her fingers across his abdomen, causing the muscles there to bunch and ripple in anticipation. Her warm breath feathered across his neck, warning just how close she was getting to making him lose it.

"Put your hand by you side." If she didn't stop touching him, Cash was going to forget that he had plans involving the palm of his hand and the plump curves of her ass.

"Wh…what?"

"By your side, darlin'. Now."

With obvious reluctance, Noelle removed her hand from his stomach. Cash missed her heated touch instantly but wouldn't let it sway him. He was on a mission, a mission that could very well change his life, and he planned to get it right.

If the look on Noelle's face were any indication, she didn't like being told no, especially when it came to matters of sex. Her cheeks were flushed with arousal, her eyes heavy-lidded. She moved away from him, her arms crossed over her heaving chest.

Cash knew exactly how she felt, but he wouldn't let her huffy attitude deter him.

"Casey said you're working at Dooner's."

She gave a sharp nod of her head, causing the silky locks of her honey blonde hair to swing sensually around her face as if caressing her cheeks. "I don't see how where I work is any of your business though."

Cash rubbed a hand over the back of his neck as he made his way across the room. He wasn't sure whether to laugh or groan. Did she not see what she was doing to him? Or maybe she did, and being extra obnoxious toward him gave her great pleasure.

"It's my business because I chose to make it my business."

Damned if she didn't arch a brow then sneer, "Well, isn't that special."

Cash knew then and there that Noelle wouldn't be leaving without her tail end on fire. "Come here, Noelle." His tone brooked no argument and for the first time since stepping foot in his apartment she seemed unsure.

"Why?"

God, but she'd probably argue him into an early grave, he thought, as he moved closer to the only straight-backed chair in the place. "Now, Noelle. Make me ask you again and you'll have trouble sitting for more than just a few hours."

His words must not have sunk into her thick-as-hell skull because in the next instant, she was stomping across the room toward him.

"There. Happy now?"

This time, Cash couldn't help but chuckle. "No, but I will be real soon," he said as he sat and upended her over his lap all in one motion.

The palm of one large hand was all it took to hold her in place when she started flailing her arms and legs about.

"Let me up, goddammit!

Cash made a tsking sound. "Such language for a lady."

Noelle kicked and shrieked at his words. "This *lady's* going to kick your ass!"

Raising one hand high, Cash brought it down on her cloth-covered ass. It was enough to cause her to still, cutting off her foul tirade in the process. When Cash knew he had her attention, he continued.

First he lifted the hem her skirt until her ass was bared for his gaze. The sight of nothing more than a strip of red elastic that seemed to all but disappear between the fleshy globes of her ass was nearly his undoing.

"Holy hell."

"Cash? Don't."

Her voice quivered slightly as his fingers glided over her curves, dipping slightly into the well of warmth between her thighs.

"You want me to stop?" The guttural tone of his voice proved just how on edge he was.

When she made no move to answer, Cash delivered another stinging swat, this time to her bare ass. Noelle's yelp of surprise turned into moans of need as Cash slid a finger along the silk-covered folds of her pussy.

Her ass was already pink in stark contrast to the white of her thigh-high stockings. Cash brought his hand down again. *Whack!* Her smooth flesh heated beneath his palm, jiggling enticingly as he delivered yet another stinging swat. *Smack!*

Small swats landed repeatedly, peppering her ass. When Cash reached where the curve of her cheek met thigh, she gasped.

"You want me to stop, baby?"

She prayed he was kidding. *Please let him be kidding,* she pleaded silently. Noelle thought she might very well expire on the spot if he didn't finish her off.

"Answer me, darlin'. Do you want me to stop?"

"Nooo," Noelle wailed when Cash brought his hand down again, catching her off guard.

Nothing seemed to work, she'd tried it all. Rubbing herself on his leg only made things worse. With the way he was holding her, she couldn't open her legs wide enough to get her clit the attention it needed, and yet, every time she pushed her ass back, asking silently for more, he stopped.

Stopped spanking, stopped caressing, stopped touching. Noelle was sure she was going to die.

"Please."

"Please what, baby?" Was that smugness she heard in his voice? Probably, but at this point in time, it didn't matter. Later, she decided. She'd deal with everything later.

"Please fuck me. Make me come. Something!"

As the words tumbled from her mouth, Noelle felt a change in Cash. His touch became frenzied. The sheer force of the need she saw written clearly across his face as he lifted her from his lap, standing her before him, made her inner muscles clench and spasm with tiny pre-climactic tremors.

Cash's hands trembled as he pulled both her skirt and thong panties down her legs until they pooled around her feet. She quickly stepped out of them as well as her shoes, leaving her bare from the waist down except for her stockings.

"Leave them on." The huskiness of his command left Noelle no choice but to obey.

Cash reached into his back pocket for his wallet. He then quickly extracted a condom before discarding his wallet on the floor. When he held his hand out with the condom between his fingers, Noelle didn't hesitate to snatch it out of his grasp.

Kneeling between his parted thighs, she unzipped the fly of his jeans. She sucked in her breath when his erection sprang free, not a stitch of underwear in sight. The head of his shaft was large, welcoming and leaking copious amounts of pre-cum.

Noelle didn't even think before she leaned forward and licked him from base to head. She couldn't help herself. The sight of him, as well as the scent of his arousal, was overwhelming.

"Enough, darlin'. Put the condom on then come up here and ride me." His voice was a deep rumble, touching Noelle in places no body part could reach.

She did as Cash asked, eager to feel the thick length of his cock buried deep inside of her. When the condom was in place, she straddled his lap, staring into his eyes. They were so green—McCain green—a woman could lose her soul in them.

Cash's hand was beneath her thigh, guiding his length into her heat. The first nudge of his cock head against the sensitive folds of her pussy sent frissons of longing down her spine and, for a minute, Noelle thought she'd come before he buried himself completely.

"Hurry." The single word left her lips on a breathless whisper.

"Mmm," Cash growled into her mouth as his hands tightened on her hips. He plunged Noelle onto the full length of his shaft in one wicked thrust, wringing a gasp from the both of them.

In no time at all, Cash set a rhythm Noelle couldn't help but follow. Her body was hot with need and slick with perspiration. Her inner muscles spasmed around Cash's intruding length, urging him on.

His scent wafted around them, musk and man—unbelievably arousing. He was hot inside of her. Hot and hard, and so deep Noelle wasn't sure where he ended and she began. Her hips rocked back and forth, stimulating her clit just right. The feel of his large hands grasping her hips so tight Noelle felt the hold all the way to her core was the little bit extra she needed to send her right over the edge.

"Oh! Oh, God." Noelle was sure her scream of completion could be heard for miles but it didn't matter. Nothing mattered except for Cash and her and the mingling of their bodies.

Cash thrust home one last time, lifting the both of them off the seat, then collapsed beneath her, a huge masculine heap of a man.

Noelle ran her hands along his face, twining her fingers in the hair at his temples. The wavy brown locks were thick between her fingers. Noelle gave a little tug then basked in the deep growl that rumbled from his throat. She then proceeded to cover his face and neck in kisses. She'd have liked to taste his chest, to lick and nibble until he was hard inside of her once again, but that was impossible since he was still dressed.

The now uncomfortable feel of his zipper beneath her ass told the story of just how dressed he was. Noelle flushed at the reminder of just how hot they were for each other.

Memories assaulted her. She'd acted like a sex-crazed woman. One used to asking for exactly what she wanted, a woman used to being erotically spanked and giving sensual delight in return. How far from the truth that actually was made the whole thing funny.

She'd by no means been a virgin, but then again, she'd also never acted so…so… How had she acted? The only word that came to mind was wanton. For some reason the old-fashioned word made Noelle giggle, which caused Cash to stir beneath her.

His flaccid cock twitched inside her making Noelle's internal muscles quiver in response. She laid her head against Cash's chest but couldn't stop the moan of delight his involuntary actions caused.

"Something funny?" Cash was sated, loving the feel of Noelle's soft body molded intimately to his.

"Nope, nothing." Her words were mumbled against his chest.

Cash felt her hips flex before the rest of her body moved. He tightened his grip, not wanting her to separate their bodies just yet. "Where you going?"

The thought of her just leaving after all they'd shared was too much for Cash to take in. Had Noelle felt the same intense heat he'd experienced during their wild ride?

"Nowhere just yet, but I need to get up before I end up with permanent zipper marks on my ass."

Noelle wiggled to make her point then winced when the metal of his zipper bit into her tender flesh. Feeling like a cad, Cash helped her to her feet. Once she was steady, he strode to the bathroom where he discarded the soiled condom before moving back to her side.

She'd already dressed and was smoothing down her skirt, covering herself from his gaze. When she came close enough to touch, Noelle lifted herself to her toes, and this time, Cash took advantage of her eagerness by taking her mouth in a slow kiss.

He flicked the tip of his tongue over her lips then as slowly as he could possibly go, Cash traced the curve of her neck to the soft pink shell of her ear. When she shivered, he smiled.

She was so damned soft and so responsive that her moans alone would keep him hard for hours. Cash tore his mouth away from hers, intent on inviting her to stay for the night. So many things had changed in such a short time. There was so much they needed to talk about.

"Yummm." Noelle licked her kiss-swelled lips. Her gaze, when she looked up at him was searching, even hesitant.

"I need to change and then I've got to go."

Cash should have known angry sex wouldn't make her forget. Not his Noelle, she'd keep at it until one of them died of exhaustion. And he loved her for it.

My Noelle? Love?

The thought struck Cash funny. After all the time he'd spent trying to run her off, now he had her right where he wanted her, knew he'd love her until he took his dying breath and now she planned to leave. Although still uncomfortable with the fact that Noelle was the same age as his sister Casey as well as her best friend, Cash would no longer let that come between them. She was his now. Forever. That's just the type of man he was.

"No."

The minute he said it, he knew he'd chosen the wrong way to go about getting his way. He should be getting used to her narrowed eyes staring up at him, open and hostile.

"You're offering me a job, then?"

Cash shook his head. Trying to keep his patience tightly reined in, Cash paced across the room and back. "I told you I don't want you working here. It's no place for a young woman without protection."

He could have sworn her eyes swam with unshed tears before she snapped her spine board-straight, grabbed her bag and headed for the door.

Cash caught up to her just as she wrenched the door open. "I said you're not going back to work at Dooner's." He all but yelled the words at her.

Noelle gave an unladylike snort. "You said a lot of things, Cash. You said you didn't want me to work for you and you also pretty much said that I couldn't work here because none of you big, bad McCain men give a shit enough to protect li'l ole me. Now. Please move. I'm going to be late for work."

Her voice cracked, making Cash's chest ache with regret even as his anger boiled over. "That's not what I meant, dammit, and you know it."

"This conversation is over, Cash. You were right, you know. For whatever reasons, this never would have worked."

She turned from him then, intent on leaving his apartment, intent on leaving him—only Cash was having none of it. He'd bide his time, give her the space she thought she needed, but by no means were things over between them.

There was no way he'd let it be over. Hell, they'd just started.

Chapter Five

Leaving was the hardest thing Noelle had ever done. She never should have assumed that just because they were having sex all would be well and all of a sudden her life would come up looking rosy.

Instead, she felt like everything was going to shit. She was unequivocally in love with her best friend's brother, a man who obviously didn't feel the same way. Hell, from the looks of it, Cash didn't care about anything except the fact that her pussy was warm, tight and wet.

Noelle sniffed, trying to hold her tears at bay. She refused to cry over Cash. If he didn't have feelings for her, then she'd just have to deal with it. No more pushing, no more teasing, no more Cash.

The thought tore at her heart as she stalked her way up the street toward Dooner's. Once inside, Noelle made her way to the restroom where she quickly changed her clothes before clocking-in to begin her shift. It was hard to keep a smile plastered across her face but she managed it. At least she managed it until Cash strolled casually through the door.

Noelle stopped dead in her tracks then wildly searched the room for Mona. Her boss had yet to ask any questions but it was only obvious she knew something was wrong with Noelle.

"I've got him, missy. You go on about your business as if he ain't here."

It wasn't hard to like Mona. Noelle squeezed her hand in thanks as Mona walked by on her way to Cash's table. She served drinks, listened to the fun banter between the patrons, all while stealing quick glances toward where Cash and Mona sat speaking.

It wasn't long before Mona shook Cash's hand then left his table. And yet, Cash stayed put. Noelle couldn't help but wonder why he wasn't leaving. He was making her nervous the way he followed her with his eyes.

"Why isn't he leaving?" Noelle blurted the question as soon as she had Mona to herself.

"The boy's got it bad, missy. Best if you put him out of his misery right now."

Noelle couldn't believe what she was hearing. "The only thing that ass has bad is a temper. He's probably just pissed because I didn't follow his orders. Well, you know what? He can go to hell for all I care!"

Noelle knew she was being childish but it didn't stop her from stomping away like a teenager in the throes of a hissy fit. It took her several minutes of deep breathing before she felt in control enough to work again without growling at any of the customers.

Coming out from behind the bar, a tray in hand, Noelle noticed Cash still sitting at an out-of-the-way table in the corner. He had a smug look on his face. It was as if knowing he'd hurt her and continuing to do so while pissing her off for good measure, made him happy.

Noelle wasn't sure if she'd ever understand men, Cash in particular. He wanted to make her cry, scream in anger and throw herself at his feet begging for even a little bit of his love all at the same time.

Just knowing he could so easily turn her life upside down pissed Noelle off and everyone knew working with the public while mad was not a good idea. If Cash got her fired, there was going to be hell to pay. Knowing she'd never make it through her shift with him watching, Noelle decided to bite the bullet and see what he wanted.

* * * * *

The way she kept stomping around was sort of funny. It made Cash want to paddle her ass again. To feel her warm skin beneath his palm, hearing the sound of flesh upon flesh while she writhed against him, first at the stinging pain and then at the arousal coursing through her body.

What Cash didn't like was the hurt look in her green eyes. She was trying to hide the hurt behind a veil of anger, but it wasn't working. Cash could clearly see how deep his words had sliced. He regretted every one of them. When Noelle disappeared into the storeroom, Cash feared he might never get the chance to tell her how much.

He didn't realize how tense he was, waiting and watching for Noelle until she appeared back in the main room of the bar. Cash wanted nothing more than to gather her close and insist she listen.

When she turned to him—her eyes pinned on his—Cash knew trouble was brewing. Noelle was looking at him as if she wouldn't mind seeing him roast in hell. Cash knew in that instant life with Noelle would never be boring.

She must have gotten tired of being stared at because before Cash could think of something irritating to say, she was across the room and in his face.

"What do you want, Cash?"

Boy was that ever a loaded question. Cash, however, knew when to keep his mouth shut so decided not to answer. Besides, from the look of her face, all red with anger, he wasn't going to get a word in edgewise.

"I mean, you spend half your time pushing me away..." Noelle looked around then moved closer. Lowering her voice, she added, "Except for when you're fucking me, then it's okay."

Whoa, that was a bit too much. "Don't say another word."

"Why? What in the hell does it matter? I mean, you're here watching me like a hawk. You think these people don't already have a clue?"

Cash watched Noelle's shoulders sag, her anger knocked completely out of her and wanted to fix it. "It matters, Noelle. It matters to me."

Her blonde hair swayed around her face as Noelle shook her head. "I don't understand you, Cash." Her voice was a mere whisper as if she didn't want to open up for fear of letting her emotions loose.

"I know, baby. Took me a while to understand it all myself but now I do. It's crystal clear and I feel like a damned big idiot for not getting it sooner."

A puzzled look crossed her face. Cash stood then gritted his teeth in irritation when Noelle backed up a step.

"Getting what, Cash? You're not making any sense."

"I'm making perfect sense, darlin'. You just aren't listening." Cash stepped closer to Noelle then without touching her, he placed his lips against hers, keeping the kiss sweet and innocent.

"What I'm trying to say," he murmured against her lips, "is that I love you, Noelle. With every breath I take."

Her head snapped back on her shoulders as if she'd been slapped. "Don't do that. Don't mess with me like that, Cash."

Her eyes were awash with unshed tears, making their green depths appear even more luminescent. Cash's heart ached for her, with her, but there was little he could do if she wasn't ready to listen.

Noelle held her hands up as a single tear streaked down her face. "Just go. Please," she pleaded when he opened his mouth to speak.

Cash, knowing he would only make things worse by staying and pushing her, cupped Noelle's cheek then wiped the single tear away with the pad of his thumb. "I'll go, sweetheart, but I won't go far or stay gone for long."

He heard her breath hitch at his words and knew she was fighting for composure. With regret running through his veins, Cash turned from Noelle. He left the bar, but instead of heading straight back to Raising Cain, he wandered aimlessly until he realized the moon was high in the sky.

Cash was thankful for his family and the fact that Connor and Carson were at the bar and would close up when he didn't return. He just needed some time to think, time to get used to being in love with Noelle, but most of all, he needed time to plan exactly how he was going to win her over.

Even when his body was so tired he could hardly drag himself home, Cash's mind whirled. He couldn't get visions of Noelle out of his head. The sight of her head thrown back in passion as she slowly took every inch of his cock within the tight depths of her warm and willing body made all his blood travel straight to his groin.

Once in bed, Cash took the length of his rigid shaft in hand and, with thoughts of Noelle, stroked himself to a groaning completion.

* * * * *

Noelle woke the next morning after crying herself to sleep, feeling completely out of it. She was so afraid to believe Cash's words of love. But something inside of her not only remembered but also held dear his words. The way he caressed her cheek, wiping away the tear she'd let slip, touched a spot deep within Noelle's soul, a spot that yearned to be loved unconditionally by Cash.

Afraid she was making too much out of Cash's spur-of-the-moment admission of love, Noelle readied herself for work. By the time she left her apartment, she was running on nerves and giving real thought to moving away from Chaos once again.

Ringing her bell didn't bring the same wicked delight it had been. She didn't want Cash to notice her, much less come storming across the street to complain about how she was dressed. What she wanted was to forget what a fool she'd been.

Luck was having none of it, though. Noelle had only been at her post for an hour when the front door of Raising Cain opened. Her pulse skyrocketed at the sight of Cash dressed as usual in faded jeans and a button-down shirt.

It wasn't until Noelle noticed the rest of the McCain family all but tumbling from the door that Noelle began to panic. Leaving them all on the sidewalk in front of the bar, Cash made his way across the street to her. He was almost nose to nose with her before Noelle found her voice.

"What's going on?"

Without a word, Cash gathered her against his solid chest. He was warm and comforting and smelled sinful. His face was cleanly shaven and smooth against the side of her face as he nuzzled her, getting closer and closer while arousing her to no end.

"Cash?" Noelle could have kicked her own ass for allowing her voice to quiver in such a way.

"You know how I feel about my family, right?" Cash didn't let Noelle do more than nod her head against his chest. "I got to thinking last night, trying to come up with a way to prove to you how much I love you, and the only thing that came to mind was to do it in front of my brothers, sister and whoever else in the town just happened to be watching. I thought maybe then you'd believe me."

Noelle couldn't believe what she was hearing. The impact of his words nearly blew her away. Cash really did love her. When he tried to pull away, Noelle couldn't help but cling to him, afraid if she didn't, he might very well be lost to her forever.

"It's okay, baby. Just give me a minute."

Noelle struggled to loosen her hold as Cash backed away from her. When he lowered himself on bended knee before her, Noelle let the tears flow.

"I love you, Noelle Jacobs, with everything I am. Be my wife?" Cash's tone was hopeful. Only Noelle saw the tenseness he held in check. When he pulled a simple emerald ring from his pocket, Noelle held out her shaky left hand, allowing Cash to place it on her ring finger.

"Did she say yes?" The hollered question came from Casey who was still standing across the street.

Noelle laughed, she couldn't help herself. Then, gathering Cash's face in her hands, she kissed him full on the mouth, deep, slow and sensual. When she was done, she smiled. "I love you, cowboy, and, yes, I'll marry you."

His hoot of excitement could have raised the dead. Cash got to his feet then lifted and swung Noelle in a circle. "She said yes." His voice was loud enough that no one could have misunderstood. Cheers came from all around them, from both family and friends. Noelle was finally home.

Epilogue

Cash carried her across the street and into Raising Cain where the rest of the McCain clan had set up a table full of appetizers and drinks. Folks continued to mingle and talk long after Noelle and Cash snuck away to be alone.

They'd made him wait, putting him through the misery of holding Noelle by his side yet never being alone with her long enough for much touching. And if that wasn't bad enough, Noelle had spent most of the time torturing him with whispered words and provocative wiggles.

Cash had decided she'd pay for her part in keeping him with a hard and throbbing cock for hours on end.

Carrying Noelle over the threshold, even before the wedding, would forever be a high point in Cash's life. He made his way through the apartment without slowing his pace then unceremoniously dumped her on his bed.

"Shh." He had plans for Noelle. Down and dirty, sexy as hell plans that didn't include talking, unless the sound of her screaming his name as she climaxed over and over was considered talking.

"No talking, huh? Just fucking," Noelle said, pushing with words guaranteed to get his attention, her voice hopeful.

"There's going to be plenty of fucking, darlin'. Now lift up so I can strip the bed down."

Noelle did as asked, her movements eager. Cash wondered just how long it would take before she was cursing with her need for release.

"Now for your clothes, they've got to go too." Noelle hesitated. Cash could only assume it was from the tone of command clear in his voice. He was on edge and in need, a man barely hanging on to his control.

"Now, baby."

Cash wasn't worried he'd scare her. The way her breath fluttered out in excited little bursts, not to mention the way her nipples pressed against the fabric of her shirt, begging for his touch, proved just how unafraid she was.

By the time Noelle was completely nude, Cash was so damned hard, he though he might keel over. Her breath came in panting little bursts as she waited on her knees in the center of the bed for his next move.

Cash was unable to get past the need to taste her, to fuck his tongue so deep within her depths he'd never be free of her essence.

"Face the wall on your knees and hang on to the headboard, sweetheart." Her pupils dilated. Cash was lost.

He climbed onto the bed behind her until they were touching, Cash's shirt-covered chest to Noelle's nude back. Her bare ass was cradled in his lap. Cash thanked his lucky stars he hadn't yet undressed because if he had, it might have all been over before it ever got started.

With his hands, Cash brought her to the brink by touching and teasing her soaked center but never allowed her to fall completely over. When she was pleading for release, Cash pulled away then settled on his back behind her. With deft movements, born of an intense need to taste and savor, Cash pushed himself to the head of the bed and comfortably between Noelle's thighs.

At the first swipe of his tongue, Noelle whimpered, "I... Oh, God, Cash." She nearly screamed the place down when he circled her thighs with his arms and sucked the swollen bud of her clit between his lips.

"Mmm." Cash knew his mumbled response would only add to her pleasure.

"Please, please, please."

Cash gripped Noelle's thighs tighter then pulled them down the bed just a bit. Their new position left her leaning forward, perfect for what Cash had planned.

Moving his hands from her thighs to caress the full, round globes of her ass cheeks was only half the fun. Her gasp of pleasure as he collected her own cream before sinking knuckle-deep into the ultra-tight channel of her ass was like music to Cash's ears. Her climax nearly sent him over the edge.

Within minutes Noelle was bucking back against his finger. Cash, unable to wait, pulled himself from between her thighs. It took every ounce of his self-control to reach for a condom and lube and not just plunge balls deep into her body.

Once protected, Cash moved back to where Noelle now lay sprawled on her belly. "Noelle." It was as close to asking for permission as he was able to grit out.

When she looked over her shoulder, blonde hair in wild disarray and smiled, Cash's pulse leapt. The intensity of their position only grew as he spread the pale cheeks of her luscious ass. With lubed fingers, Cash carefully prepared Noelle's ass for the thick length of his shaft.

Inserting first one finger and then a second, Cash stretched Noelle's tight channel until she lay panting for breath, her skin covered in a light sheen of sweat. When he was sure she could handle his girth, Cash sank into her inch by inch until he could go no farther.

"Oh…oh! Please hurry! Hurry!" The last came out as a shrill scream. Cash couldn't hold back, powering into her body over and over, as she spasmed around his cock, he came with her.

After they were sated, lying with their bodies entwined, Noelle asked. "Why, Cash? Why would you want to marry me?"

It wasn't like Noelle to be so cautious, so unsure, but when it came to loving Cash, she had to know.

"Besides the fact that I love you more than words can say?" Cash asked, as he started beneath the sheets once again.

"Oh yes," Noelle gasped not at all sure if she was answering Cash's question or urging him on his wicked journey down her body.

"I figured it was the only way I could get you to stop ringing that damned bell."

Also by Maggie Casper

ℰ

Maverick's Black Cat – with Lena Austin
O'Malley Wild: Hayden's Hellion
O'Malley Wild: Honoring Sean
O'Malley Wild: Zane's Way
O'Malley Wild: Tying the Knot

About the Author

ℰ

Maggie Casper's life could be called many things but boring isn't one of them. If asked, Maggie would tell you that blessed would more aptly describe her everyday existence.

Marrying young and being loved by a great husband and four gorgeous daughters should be enough to make anybody feel blessed. Add to that a bit of challenge, a lot of fun and an undeniably close circle of friends and family and you'd be walking in her shoes.

Speaking of challenges and fun, when not writing, Maggie's alter ego spends her time fighting fires and treating patients as a Lieutenant and Advanced Emergency Medical Technician with the local fire department. These awesome people are like her second family, no picking and choosing, they're just stuck with her.

A love of reading was passed on by Maggie's mother at a very early age, and so began her addiction to romance novels. Maggie admits to writing some in high school but when life got in the way, she put her pen and paper up. Seems that things changed over the years because when she finally decided it was time to put her story ideas on paper, the pen was out and the computer was in. Took her a while to catch up but she finally made it.

When not writing, Maggie can usually be found reading, doing genealogy research or watching NASCAR.

Maggie welcomes comments from readers. You can find her website and email address on her author bio page at www.ellorascave.com.

WISH LIST

Sylvia Day

ജ

Dedication

ꟼ

To Raelene Gorlinsky, for giving me the opportunity to write a Christmas story. It was very high up on my list of story themes I wanted to write. And to fellow Brava author and lawyer, HelenKay Dimon, who very helpfully answered my questions about law firms. All factual errors are mine alone.

Trademarks Acknowledgement

ꟼ

The author acknowledges the trademarked status and trademark owners of the following wordmarks mentioned in this work of fiction:

BlackBerry: Research in Motion

Grand Cherokee: DaimlerChrysler Corporation

Chapter One

Nicholas James, the hottest man on the planet, was bare-assed naked with a bow covering his cock.

Steph gaped. And not just any kind of gape, but a "bug-eyed, mouth hanging open to catch flies" kind of gape. Before she could even think twice, she flipped up the red bow and then drooled at what was under it. *Oh. My. God.*

"Jesus, Steph," muttered her paralegal Elaine, bringing her sharply back to the festive conference room and the sounds of Frank Sinatra singing holiday songs. "Your Secret Santa gift can't be that bad. Let me see it." She held out her hand and beckoned with her fingers, showing off long acrylic nails with airbrushed snowmen.

Hugging the silver foil box to her chest, Steph thrust over the restaurant gift certificate that had concealed the photo beneath—the photo with the clever little bow strategically glued with just enough hinge to afford her an eyeful.

"Ooohhh, nice. I love Dominico's." Elaine's red painted mouth curved in a smile. "You should take me. All of my dates are too cheap to go there."

"Uh." Turning her head, Steph searched the crowded conference room for the naked man of her dreams. Of course, Nicholas wasn't naked right now. Not at the Mitchell, Jones, and Cline annual Christmas party. No, right now he was wearing beautifully tailored slacks in dark blue, a crisp white shirt with blue tie and white silk vest. She loved that he wore three-piece suits. Somehow, the urbanity of his clothing only served to accentuate the raw masculine power of his body. He was single and gorgeous, and like most single and gorgeous men, he led an active lifestyle which kept him in fine shape.

Just the sort of man most women were wildly attracted to. She, however, avoided him like the plague. She'd learned her lesson the first time.

Her breath caught.

There he was. By the door.

You could hardly miss him. Not when he was so tall and broad shouldered. His dark hair gleamed under the glow of blinking strings of Christmas lights as he leaned his lanky frame casually against the doorjamb. He was staring at her with a wicked half smile.

Then he winked.

Realization hit her hard and made her gasp.

Somehow, he'd found her wish list. The fantasy one. The silly stupid *naughty* wish list.

Oh. My. God!

* * * * *

Nick knew the exact moment Steph caught on. The flush spread up from the low V of her teal silk blouse and then colored her cheeks.

Finally! After almost a year of flirting that got him nothing more than the occasional inconvenient hard-on, he was getting what he really wanted for Christmas—the opportunity to prove he was the man for her. He wished he could say it was his charm that won Stephanie over, but that wasn't the case. No, he'd had to wait for fate to step in and slip her name into his hand for their law firm's annual Secret Santa draw. He'd opened up the folded slip of paper, saw *Stephanie Martin* and grinned like an idiot.

For about one second.

Then he'd realized he'd have to come up with not only a great gift, but a great gift she'd have to share with *him,* and not one of the other drooling Lotharios around their firm. He'd walked through endless crowded malls, surfed a hundred online shopping sites, grilled every one of his ex-girlfriends and female relatives—all to no avail. They couldn't understand why he didn't just ask Stephanie out, instead of trying to plan something elaborate to make his point.

The answer was really very simple. He had a reputation as a ladies' man. She'd heard about it and didn't want anything to do with him because of it. So straight up asking for a date wouldn't work. He had to show her he was serious first.

Steph's reticence wasn't a new experience for Nick. Most of the women who were strictly platonic friends were ones who'd made it clear they were looking for Mr. Right. Not Mr. Right Now. Starting in high school, Nick had learned how to give the "not going to settle down" vibe pretty well. Not that he didn't have committed relationships. He did. They just weren't the forever kind of commitment.

So he'd tried to respect Steph's obvious non-interest, but the gnawing craving in his gut wouldn't go away. He wanted her—wanted that long dark hair wrapped around his fist, wanted those dark brown eyes burning with lust, wanted that lushly curved body out of the business suits and arching naked beneath him. And even though he knew it was never going to happen, Nick couldn't stop dreaming about it.

Steph was gorgeous, beautifully built, confident and intelligent. She knew her assets and showed them off. She also knew her worth and wanted a man who did. What had she said to him once?

Any man who has one foot planted firmly outside the door never really comes in.

But he wasn't a fly-by-night kind of boyfriend. He took damn good care of the women he dated. He paid attention to what they liked and didn't like. It wasn't so hard. It just took a little effort, and Nick enjoyed making that effort. Enjoyed watching their surprise when he remembered their favorite author, favorite song, favorite places to be touched and caressed. Because of this, most of his exes were still his friends.

"You're staring," teased a soft voice beside him.

He tore his gaze away from Steph's wide eyes to look at the woman next to him.

"Looks like she liked your gift," Amanda said with a fond smile. "Why didn't I ever get naked pics of you when we were dating?"

"You never asked."

Stephanie hadn't either, at least not in the verbal sense. He'd been staying late one night working on his billable hours. The goal was twofold—to get a decent cushion for the holiday time off work and also to forget about how he couldn't find a damn thing to give Steph that would get his foot in her door. The ploy wasn't working, so he'd stood and began to pace the hall that formed a ring around the center receptionist's desk and elevators.

That was when it caught his eye. The small, crumpled ball of paper missed or dropped by the nighttime cleaning crew. It was wedged next to the polished wood leg of their waiting room sofa. He'd picked it up with the intention of tossing it when a bit of red and green caught his eye. Steph had been using a cute little stocking-shaped notepad ever since the first of the month. Christmas was obviously one of her favorite holidays, if the tiny decorated tree on her desk was any indication. He knew instantly the festive bit of trash had once belonged to her, and it took on new meaning just because of that.

So feeling a bit guilty but unable to help himself, Nick opened the bit of trash...

And he'd been thanking his lucky stars ever since.

At the top of the striped paper were the words *Wish List* printed in a font designed to resemble a child's scrawl. Below that were the beautifully formed letters he recognized as Steph's handwriting.

Mom – new bread maker

Dad – deep sea fishing

Sam – gift card

And then she'd run a slash through that list and begun a new one.

My Wish List – (naughty)

Nicholas James naked and wrapped in a bow.

Nick kissing me senseless.

Nick cooking me dinner naked. (so I can stare at his ass)

Going down on Nick. (yum)

Nick going down on me. (double yum)

Fucking Nick until he can't walk. (OMG!)

The shock of that list had hit him so hard he'd stumbled into the nearby couch. He'd understood then that Stephanie had been fooling him the whole time, just like she would a jury. Acting unaffected when she was really as hot for him as he was for her. No woman had such detailed sexual thoughts about a guy she wasn't totally into. She'd obviously been thinking about him for awhile.

Images inspired by her words filled his mind. His cock swelled and he wondered how he'd make it back to his office, let alone the parking garage eighteen floors below.

He needn't have worried. Her next shakily written line took all the heat out of him and left him cold.

My Wish List – (good)

Forget about Nicholas James or transfer.

In that moment he'd discovered two things. One—no matter how much she wanted his body, she still didn't want anything to do with *him*. To the point where she was considering transferring to their firm's other office across town.

Two—the thought of not seeing her nearly every day struck him like a physical blow. Too painful for his interest to be merely casual. He'd realized then what the tight knot in his gut was trying to tell him.

Somewhere along the way, the purely sexual desire he had for her had become something more. Maybe it'd happened when they'd worked that last case together and she kept blowing his mind with her brains. Or maybe it was when she'd cried over a verdict and hadn't tried to hide it from him. Whatever it was, he'd be damned if his past got in the way of what they both wanted.

This Christmas, not so saintly Nick was making sure all of Stephanie Martin's wishes came true.

Chapter Two

Steph left the conference room party the moment Nick's attention was drawn away. She had the next two weeks off. If she could just slip out of the office, she could get out of this mortifying situation.

She'd had a feeling when she threw out that stupid scrap of paper that she should rip it up first. Or burn it. But then she'd told herself she was just being paranoid. The damn thing was in the trash. Who was going to see it? Certainly not Nick. He didn't dig in trashcans. Or so she'd thought.

As her temper rose, her step quickened and she reached her office in record time. This was ridiculous. Those were private scribblings made during an especially boring meeting. She hadn't been able to concentrate with Nick sitting across from her and looking as impossibly gorgeous as ever. Instead, she'd been totally absorbed in staring at the small part of his wrist visible at the edge of his cuff—hair-dusted dark skin next to the gold of his watchband and the white of his shirt. That little flash of *nothing* had made her hot and damp between the thighs.

There was just something about Nicholas James. Maybe it was the dangerous beauty of his face. Or that tall, well-honed body. Perhaps it was his amazing intelligence and aggressive stance in the courtroom. Or maybe it was his pro bono work for the Abused Women's Program… Shit, she didn't know why. She just knew his track record with women was bad news and she'd already had enough bad news to last a lifetime.

She growled. That damn list had been a form of purging therapy. None of it was ever meant literally. Still, as she shoved documents into her briefcase, she grabbed the silver box with the X-rated photo of Nick and shoved it in too.

"Merry Christmas to me," she muttered.

"I'm just getting started," purred a deep voice in her ear. The delicious sound hit the top of her spine and then curled all the way down.

Mouth open to protest, she spun to face her tormentor.

And found herself hauled up against a rock-hard body and kissed senseless.

Taken completely off guard, by the time her addled brain figured out who was accosting her and what he was doing, she didn't want him to stop. As her senses filled with the scent of aroused male, the hands pushing against Nick's shoulders slipped around them instead.

God, he was good. Equal parts demanding and tender. His lips were warm, the inside of his mouth soft. His hands slipped between her jacket and blouse, splaying on either side of her spine and pulling her closer. When his touch slipped lower to cup her ass, heat flared outward and flushed her skin.

"Don't," she whispered against his mouth.

Groaning softly in answer, Nick tilted his head and deepened his already drowning kiss. He tugged, stealing her balance so that she tumbled into him. Taking the advantage, he lifted her and sat her on the desk, wedging his lean hips intimately between her thighs. Instantly the throbbing that had begun the minute he touched her turned into an all-consuming ache. "Nick…"

His damp forehead rested against hers, his panting breaths hot against her swollen lips. "Let me give you what you want for Christmas, Steph."

"I don't want you."

"Liar." His hand came up and cupped her breast. Expert fingertips found the hardened nipple that betrayed her. Kissing his way to her ear, he whispered, "I bet you're creamy for me."

"Jesus, Nick!" She shivered but couldn't deny it.

"I locked the door…"

"Are you crazy?" she shot back, pushing his wandering hand away.

Nick caught her hips, pulled her to the edge of the desk and fit the hard length of his cock directly against her pussy.

"Yes." He moved his hips, nudging her clit through the soft fabric of their dress pants. She whimpered.

"Don't you know how crazy I am about you?"

"You're crazy about all women."

"No," he argued, thrusting against her with greater urgency. "I *like* women. I'm crazy about you."

The sweet friction of his dry fucking made her cunt spasm with need. With her heart racing and her breathing labored, she pushed at him weakly. "Stop that… I can't think…"

"You think too much." He held her in place as he rubbed his cock against her. She hadn't bothered with the lights when she'd entered, since moonlight lit the room through the floor-to-ceiling window. But even in the semi-dark, his eyes burned with a hunger that made her throat tight. Holding her still, he stroked the impressive length of his cock up and down her slit. He was so gorgeous, so determined, just watching him pleasuring them both was nearly orgasmic by itself. "I want you, Steph. I've wanted you a long time. And you want me too."

On the verge of coming, Steph set her hands on the desk and swiveled her hips into that large straining bulge, stroking him with her pussy. Nick's raw, pained moan was the impetus that pushed her over. Crying out, she rode the waves of pleasure that spread through her veins and made her dizzy.

"That's it," he praised hoarsely, rocking into her, making it last. "Ah, sweetheart. You're so beautiful."

She sagged into his chest as the tension fled. With her hot face pressed against his throat, the scent of his skin was nearly overwhelming. "Oh my God," she groaned, wishing the earth would open up and swallow her whole. The last thing Nick's ego needed was her hair-trigger orgasm.

"It's been awhile for you, hasn't it?" His large hands stroked the length of her back, gentling her.

"You're not going to take credit for that?" She couldn't hide her surprise.

"Me?" He pulled back slightly. "I wish. That was all you. But the next one's on me."

A laugh escaped against her will and she buried her face in his shoulder to hide her smile. He was charming, she'd never denied that. "There's not going to be a next time."

His embrace was nearly crushing. "Whatever. You really had me fooled. Until I saw that wish list, I thought you didn't like me."

"It's not about whether I like you or not, Nick. In fact, I think you're a great guy, but—"

"You're looking for someone to get serious."

"Actually, I'm not looking for anyone."

"I could get serious." Cupping her face in his hands, he used his thumbs to stroke her cheeks. "There's no reason I can't. But we'll never know if you don't give me a chance."

"Why?" She pushed him away. "Because we have the hots for each other? Being horny isn't the basis for a relationship and I don't want to be your experiment in monogamy."

"There she is," he said softly, stepping back so she could slide off the desk. "The exterior woman who doesn't want me, while the real Steph inside does."

She winced. The real Steph had learned to give up some of the things she wanted. It was a sacrifice she'd accepted gladly when she made it. "Are we done here?"

"No way. Not nearly." He ran his hand through his thick, glossy hair.

She regretted that she hadn't touched it when she had the chance. "You didn't get off, but I don't feel too guilty about that. You can have any of the girls in the conference room."

"Fuck you, Steph," he said gruffly. "This isn't about getting laid and you know it."

She snorted. "This is all about getting laid."

Suddenly he straightened, his eyes lit with a dangerous glint. "Give me a couple days to go through your wish list. Then, once you've lived out your fantasies—all of which happen to be mine as well—we can get back to business as usual. Minus all this sexual tension."

"That's not going to work." But her stomach did a little flip at the thought.

"Then you switch offices anyway, like you planned. But at least we got to have wild, sweaty, dirty sex before you go. If this is all about getting laid, let's do it."

Oooh, he was good at arguing a case. He knew he'd had her from the word "wild" too. She could see it in his eyes. "A hotel?" she suggested, resigned. A girl had only so much willpower and faced with a watertight argument, what else could she do?

At least that's what her inner devil said.

"My place," he said smoothly, having the grace not to gloat. "I've got everything I need to cook dinner—" He flashed a dazzling grin. "Naked."

"Oh, Lord…" She was blushing, she could feel it. That he knew her secret longings was embarrassing in the extreme. And a major turn-on, which was dangerous. She had to keep the two separate—the lawyer she admired and the playboy she wanted to fuck. "Let's just keep this simple."

He reached into his pocket and pulled out a folded slip of paper. Tucking it in her hand, he brushed his lips across hers. "No. You've been a good girl, so you deserve to have your wishes come true." He kissed her again and it didn't escape her for a second that he was the star of her sex dreams. "Come on, Steph, play along. It'll be fun."

Fun. Guys like Nick were always having fun.

"That's directions to my condo. I'll be waiting."

* * * * *

By the time Steph got to Nick's place, she was balls to the wall committed to having a good time. If she was going to binge, she was gorging. Period. So when she rang the doorbell and Nick answered wearing nothing but a Santa hat and an apron that said "Kiss the Cook", she didn't hesitate. She dropped her mini-duffle at his feet and jumped him.

"Shit." He stumbled backward in surprise but managed to shove the door closed before spinning his way to the nearest couch. They fell into black leather in a puddle of semi-naked gorgeous male and determined female.

Straddling him, Steph leaned forward and kissed him hard and deep. His scent inundated her senses and her nipples hardened into aching points.

Nick groaned.

She sat up atop the hard ridge of his erection, an obvious sign that he was as ready as she. Digging into the pocket of her billowy gauze skirt, she pulled out a condom and tossed it on his chest. "Hurry up and put that on."

Blinking up at her, Nick sputtered, "Just like that? Wham, bam, let's fuck?"

"You complaining?"

"Hell, no." As she lifted to her knees to pull up her skirt, he fumbled for the foil package with comical haste. Then he glanced up and stilled, his gaze riveted between her legs. "Oh man. Steph… You're not wearing panties."

"Ooops. Must have forgotten those." She tucked the trailing hem into the elastic waistband.

Dropping the condom, he licked his lips. "Whose wish list are we working on here?"

The heat banked in his heavy-lidded eyes made her shiver. His Santa hat was askew, his dark hair pushed over his forehead. Adding in the apron, he should have looked silly. Instead, he looked edible. His arms were sexy as hell, the skin still bearing the remnants of a dark summer tan, the muscles beneath beautifully defined.

"Come here." The command was issued in a seductively husky voice that made goose bumps cover her skin despite the fire crackling in the fireplace.

"Come where?" she teased softly.

"Come in my mouth, sweetheart. I want to lap you up."

Oh. My. God!

Forcing herself to crawl over him slowly so she didn't look desperate, Steph kneeled astride his head. With one knee on the sofa armrest and the other on the very edge of the couch, she was spread wide, affording him an unhindered view. His warm hands slid up her thighs, his breath gusted over her sex. He squeezed her ass. She whimpered her excitement…

And then he licked her cunt in a long deliberate lap.

She clutched the back of the sofa like a lifeline and moaned.

Kneading the backs of her thighs, he settled in to feast, gliding his tongue through her slit. Dipping inside her. Finding all the places that made her cry out and concentrating there before drifting away to find somewhere else. And then returning to stroke back and forth across her clit.

"Don't come too soon," he murmured as her legs began to shake.

"Are you kidding?" she gasped, her hips rocking into his busy mouth. "Don't be so good at this."

His chuckle was filled with pure masculine satisfaction. "I want to be fucking you when you come."

She shuddered violently. "You better hurry up with that condom then."

"I'm ready whenever you are."

"Huh?"

Nick's grin was pure wickedness. "I guess you were a little distracted."

Glancing down the couch, her eyes widened. He'd flipped up the apron and sheathed the object of her day and night dreams. Long, thick and arching up to his stomach, his cock made her mouth water. No wonder the man had that air about him that screamed *I know how to fuck your brains out.* The picture hadn't done him justice.

She swallowed hard and moved to straddle his hips. He angled his cock upward solicitously. Her chest tight and heart racing, Steph paused just above him. It was the point of no return. Nothing would ever be the same between them once they had sex. Could she handle that? Could she keep the distance she needed?

"Steph."

Her gaze shot up to meet his.

"Remember your list?" Nick's handsome face was flushed and his lips were slick with her cream, but despite the blatantly sexual look about him, his blue eyes shimmered with just as much compassion as lust. "It's okay to take what you want," he said softly. "Especially when it's given to you."

She took a deep breath. Suddenly, she registered the holiday music playing softly and the smell of pine from the small, undecorated tree in the corner. If she went home, she'd be alone right now. Or she could spend the night with Nicholas James.

She'd wanted this, wanted him. It was Christmas, damn it!

Slick with desire, she sank onto him slowly, taking the only thing she'd asked for this year. The only thing she'd asked for in many years. To be touched and held. To be wanted.

"Oh yeah," he groaned, his hands stroking along her thighs, his back arching. "God, you feel good."

Steph bit her lower lip as the languorous glide continued. His cock filled her too full. The heat and hardness of it stole her breath. The wonderful length and width… As her buttocks hit his muscular thighs and the head of his cock struck deep, the sound that was torn from her was raw and needy.

"I've got you," he soothed gruffly as she leaned over him, shaking. He stroked the length of her spine, murmuring, "Lift up a little… Shush, I'll give it to you… Right there. Now don't move."

His hips lifted, stroking her cunt with a breathless thrust.

"Nick. Oh my God!" She buried her face in his neck, her pussy spasming around him.

He lowered and lifted again, fucking upward into her greedy depths. "How's that feel?" he panted.

"Like I'm losing my mind." She lifted her head and looked at him. His chest rose and fell harshly against her breasts, making her wish she'd taken the time to get naked so she could feel him skin to skin.

"Good. I'd hate to be the only one." Holding her hips steady, he quickened his pace, surging upward in a relentless rhythm, withdrawing until only the thick head breeched her and then plunging balls deep with primal grunts.

Keening softly, she clutched his shoulders and braced herself for the slap of his hips against hers. He felt so good… He smelled delicious…

Nick spoke through gritted teeth, "Don't wait for me." He punctuated his order with a brutally hard thrust that caught her clit in just the right spot.

Her orgasm was stunning. She was paralyzed, unable to move, every cell in her body focused on the rippling of her cunt along his endless length of hard cock. He jerked beneath her then crushed her to his chest, growling in her ear as he came.

Holding him, she listened to the violent beating of his heart and the soft sounds of music, and she felt cared for.

For the first time in a long time it felt like Christmas.

Chapter Three

Nick held Stephanie close and tried to focus his eyesight on the cobweb that hung in the corner. It was almost impossible. His brain and body felt like mush, which was really saying something considering how energized he'd been while waiting for her to arrive. He'd been worried she might not show and if that happened, there would be no way he could track her down until the office was open again. He had no idea how to reach her outside of work.

Then she'd rang the bell and he'd run to the door, feeling like a kid on his first date. And when she'd tackled him, he felt like a king.

He'd always known she would be like that, warm and open and sexy as hell. No shyness about her when it came to getting down and dirty. Just like when she argued a case, she gave one hundred percent to everything she did. Lucky for him, he got to be on the receiving end of that attention to detail.

And he wanted it to stay that way.

Steph wiggled just a tiny bit and it was enough to remind them both that his cock was still buried inside her. His balls gave a last weary twitch and his eyes slid closed in contentment. It'd been a long time since he'd come that hard and even longer since he'd cared this deeply about the woman he did it with.

"Nick?"

"Hmm?" He nuzzled against her neck.

"You didn't have anything on the stove, did you?"

Groaning, he said, "Nah, but the oven's on for the breadsticks."

She sighed. "We should probably go check on that."

It was the "*we*" that got to him. He'd wanted to be a "*we*" with Stephanie Martin for the last several months. Looking back now, he thought he knew when it'd hit him. She'd been standing in the break room talking to Charles from Entertainment and while laughing at something said to her, she'd met Nick's gaze and winked.

In that little blink of an eye, he'd fallen hard.

That tiny wink had said so much. It was playful and affectionate, and it had warmed him on the inside enough to know that out of all the women in his world, she was the one he wanted to spend his down time with.

Sliding off him carefully, Steph rose to her feet and wobbled a bit. When he stood, the same thing happened. His legs felt like jelly.

"Jeez, Steph," he said, laughing and clutching her close. "You wrung me out."

Her blush was lovely and he hated to let her go, but he had dinner to cook. He needed to charm her with more than his bedroom skills. So after a quick kiss on the nose, he moved toward the kitchen. Catching up her duffle on the way, he set it on a dining chair and took note of the luggage tag.

"Stephanie Donovan?" he asked as he pulled off the condom and tossed it.

She was righting her skirt and didn't look up. "My maiden name."

"I didn't know you were divorced." He turned on the faucet and studied her as he washed his hands.

"It's not something that comes up and I don't like to talk about it."

"That bad, huh?"

Nick dried his hands then turned to light the burner beneath the waiting pot of water. "Want some wine? A beer?"

"A beer would be nice, thanks." Steph took a seat on a barstool at the breakfast bar. "It wasn't bad. It just wasn't good."

He grabbed a couple longnecks out of the fridge, twisted off the tops and set one in front of her. "How long ago did you break up?"

"A couple years. Should have been sooner, but we were both too stubborn to admit it wasn't working."

Catching up her hand, he gave it a squeeze. "You hate to give up. It's what makes you such a damn good lawyer."

"Thanks." Her dark eyes sparkled with warmth at his compliment. "Tom and I never should have gotten married. We were friends in law school, nothing more. He was such a player, I never took him seriously. Then somehow we ended up together and I still can't figure out how or why."

"Love?"

"I thought so, but really I think we did it just because it was 'time', you know? Tom felt like he was at the age where he should get married. All of his colleagues were married and I think he started to feel a little out of place."

"I can see that," he admitted, resting his elbows on the granite countertop.

She wrinkled her nose and it hit him suddenly that he'd just been inside her, holding her, touching her however he wanted. It was the first time he could remember where he didn't forget the sex as soon as it was done. Fucking Steph was an addition to an already established relationship and not the entire reason for it.

Now if he could only change their professional relationship into a personal one. He had to admit, he was usually actively working to do just the opposite so he was out of his depth.

"Do guys have a marriage clock?"

He laughed. "Like a biological clock?"

"Yes."

"I guess there is some peer pressure after awhile. If you're thirty-something and single, even women start to think there must be something wrong with you or else some chick would've snapped you up." Turning away, he opened the fridge and pulled out the produce he'd chosen to make a salad with. He was a simple guy. Spaghetti, salad and breadsticks were about as much as he could do with confidence in a tasty outcome. "I personally don't care what people think."

"I would say that's pretty obvious."

The humor in her tone had him looking over his shoulder at her.

Steph was grinning. "This whole wish list thing is really a bad idea, but I have to admit, it's worth it to see you dressed like that."

"You're not laughing at me, are you?" He'd been a little nervous. Like anyone, he didn't want to look stupid in front of someone he wanted to sleep with. Bent over like he was, he knew she was getting an eyeful of every damn thing he had to offer.

"No." Her gaze was mischievous and warm. "I'm actually really impressed with you. You have enough confidence to wear that. I know I wouldn't be able to do it."

"Personally..." He turned with an armful of vegetables, which he dumped on the counter. "I'd like you in just the hat. That's my Christmas wish."

"You know—" Her fingers toyed with her beer.

"I know what?"

She sighed. "I really thought getting the sex out of the way would make me more comfortable."

"The sex isn't '*out of the way*'," he retorted, pulling a knife out of the wooden block next to him. "Just say what you're thinking. I'm the one wearing nothing but a Santa hat, apron and a smile, so you've got no business being shy about anything."

"Thank you," she blurted, her gaze focused on the beer label she was removing from the bottle. "I don't care why you did it. I don't care if you just want to get laid. I'm flattered you went to all this trouble."

Nick paused with his knife halfway through a cucumber and stared at her. "It wasn't any trouble, Steph. I like giving you what you want, I like seeing you smile."

She blew out her breath and fiddled with her collar. "Do you need my help with anything?"

It wasn't like her to be so nervous or to switch subjects because she was uncomfortable, which told him she wasn't dealing too well with tonight's events. He knew it was a lot to throw at her—the photo, the wish list, the sex. Before the Secret Santa exchange they'd been nothing but distant co-workers. Now they were lovers. He'd had a couple months to adapt to his changing feelings for her. She's had a couple hours. She was asking for a little space and he had no problem giving it to her.

"No, I've got it covered. Go watch TV or something. It won't be too much longer."

"Okay. I'm going to wash up then."

He gestured toward the hallway with a toss of his chin. "First door on the right."

Steph locked gazes with Nick for a long moment and knew she was in trouble. He didn't have that air about him that said, *Thanks for the fuck, you can go now*. No, his vibe was very homey and relaxed. And she was falling for it like a ton of bricks.

Somehow she made it down the short hallway to the bathroom, where she leaned against the vanity and stared in the mirror. The glazed look in her eyes and the flush on her cheeks made her wince.

Damn it, she didn't need this right now! A relationship was completely out of the question on a good day, but to fall for a guy who had "temporary" written all over him was just plain stupid. Hadn't she learned anything at all from her years with Tom?

Apparently not.

When dinner was done, she was going home. They'd both gotten what they wanted.

It was time to minimize the damage.

* * * * *

"That was wonderful."

Steph smiled at Nick as she set her fork down, not the least bit concerned that she'd cleaned her plate. They'd eaten together many times over the last year and after the first time he'd praised her hearty appetite, she'd ceased being concerned about appearances.

"You're either too generous or you were really hungry." He stood and picked up her plate from the small oak dining table. Featuring a pine centerpiece lit by three red tapers, it was both inviting and unexpected. There was so much about him she didn't know. But she wanted to learn. Nick wasn't good relationship material, but he was a fascinating guy, a great lawyer and a good friend from what she'd heard.

She watched him walk into the kitchen, his fine ass flexing as he took each step. Occasional glimpses of his cock and balls kept her hot, and she grabbed her napkin to dab at the fine sheen of sweat that misted her forehead. He was also a fantastic and generous lover, but then she'd always suspected that and heard innuendo to the same.

The urge to bolt she'd felt in the bathroom earlier was now suddenly overwhelming.

It was time to go.

Standing, she reached for her duffle. It was rude to leave without offering to clean, but maybe a little animosity between them would be a good thing.

"What are you doing?" he asked behind her, the volume of his voice telling her that he was still some distance away.

"I'm going to head out," she said with forced casualness, even as her heart raced. "Thanks for a great evening."

Suddenly, she was crowded into the table from behind by a very hard body. "Talk to me, Steph." His palms flattened on the surface, caging her in place.

"We've been talking all through dinner."

"About everything except us."

"There is no '*us*'."

One of his hands reached into the pocket of her skirt.

"How many condoms did you bring? Feels like you've got half a dozen in here." He tossed one onto the tabletop. "You were planning for a busy night. Now, all of a sudden, you're done?"

"Yeah, well." She took a deep breath. "I didn't expect you to be so good. You took care of things the first go-round."

"Bullshit. You're as hot for it now as you were when you jumped me." Wrapping a hand around her throat, he tilted her head back. He nipped her ear with his teeth and she shivered. "What's got you running scared?"

She stiffened. "I'm not scared. I just think we both got what we wanted and it's best to end the night before it gets complicated."

"Guess what?" Nick bent his knees and rubbed the hard length of his cock between the cheeks of her ass. Somewhere between the kitchen and the dining room he'd lost the apron. With only the thin layer of her gauze skirt between them, she felt every millimeter of his arousal. "I'm not finished getting what I wanted and it's already complicated."

"Nick…" Her eyes closed on a whimper as he cupped the weight of one breast. Heat flared across her skin. She was suddenly more than hot, she was burning up, melting. He smelled like heaven and felt even better. She'd had a ton of daydreams about him, but they'd always been raw. Carnal. Fucking on her desk or his. Buttons flying everywhere. Rough hands and bruising lips. Never had there been this gentleness, this concern for her feelings and pleasure.

"You had a wish list, Steph. Fantasies about me. Tell me why you don't want to live them out anymore." The pads of his fingers brushed across her nipple and it peaked into a hard, aching tip.

"Fantasies aren't meant to come true."

"Mine did. Yours too."

"That's the problem," she muttered.

His hand left her breast and lifted her skirt, bunching it in his fists. She should stop him, wiggle away. He wouldn't keep her against her will, despite the forearm that crossed between her breasts and the grip that held her neck. But the energy she needed to escape just wasn't there. It had been so long since she'd been held with such tender lust, she didn't have the heart to reject it.

"Did I become too real?" he breathed in her ear. "Do you like me, Steph? Just a little?"

A little too much.

Cool air hit her buttocks the moment before he stepped closer. His cock was so hard, so hot against her skin.

His open mouth nuzzled against her throat. "Stay with me." Reaching beneath her skirt, he parted her and stroked her clit. A soft fluttering touch, circling then pressing. Rubbing. "Be with me."

"Nick." Her eyes drifted closed on a soft moan. She was wet, nearly soaked, and she ached for him. She was starving for the affection he gave so freely. It scared her how needy she was. Until tonight, she hadn't realized how lonely her life had become.

"Open the packet," he urged, his voice like rough silk.

She reached blindly for the condom, steeling the reserve she'd had when she arrived. *Enjoy him,* her heart said, and she would. One last time.

"We're so good together, Steph." Nudging her legs apart, he slipped two fingers inside her, moving in and out in a deep glide. "In every way that matters." The hand at her throat lowered to cup her breast again. It was heavier, full with desire for him. Expert fingers stroked over her nipple, pinched it, fondled it through her thin shirt and satin bra. That teasing touch radiated outward and left her gasping.

"Here." She thrust her arm back with the open packet in her hand.

Nick reached for the condom with shaking fingers. Steph had been ready to leave. More than ready. She'd been nearly out the door. And he knew in his gut if he couldn't get through to her before she left, he never would.

"Bend over," he said gruffly.

When his fingers left her soaked pussy, she made a soft sound of protest. "Hush," he soothed, pushing gently until she bent across the table. "Let me give you my cock instead."

He stared at the erotic view as he sheathed himself in latex. All the times he'd watched her at work and thought lewdly, he'd never quite pictured the view correctly. Her lips were flushed, swollen, glistening. He wanted to lick her again and did, a quick swipe of his tongue that had her writhing. Taking himself in hand, he used the tip of his cock to tease her clit, to make her cream, to see her squirm for him.

And then he caught her hips and slid deep into her.

"Oh my God!" she breathed, her fingers scratching at his table.

Her cunt was burning hot and tight as a fist. "Fuck, yeah," he groaned, his balls drawn up tight and aching. He withdrew and watched his thick shaft slide out of her, slick with her arousal, and then groaned as he pressed back in. Holding her hips, he stared at the place where they joined, arrested by the sight of him fucking her as he'd wanted to for so long.

"Nick."

The sound of his name spoken so morosely tugged at his heart. Hunching forward, he laced his fingers with hers and began thrusting in short shallow digs, his stomach rippling against her lower back. Her pleading gasps goaded him, incited him to bend his knees so he could stroke her pussy high and hard with the broad head of his cock.

With his cheek at her shoulder, he asked, "How can you give this up, Steph?"

She answered with a whimper and then hitched her hips up higher so he could pump deeper. Widening his legs, he gave her the long deep plunges that made her moan helplessly and drove him crazy. He released her hands, moving one of his to cup her breast and the other to pin her hips in place so he could swivel his pelvis and screw his cock through her grasping ripples.

"Give me a chance," he gasped, shuddering with the need to come, with the need to keep her close until he could change her mind.

"You don't…know…"

Reaching beneath her, he pinched her clit and thrust balls deep. With a cry she came, clutching his cock in her depths, milking him in a sensual massage. "Give me a chance, damn you."

Her "*yes*" was a whisper, but he heard it. His release was silent, his teeth gritted, his cock jerking as it pumped his cum into her.

He should have felt relief. He should have felt some sense of security.

But he didn't.

Chapter Four

It was the sounds of shuffling paper that woke her. Stretching on the black leather sofa, Steph opened her eyes and turned her head to find Nick wrapping gifts. Or trying to.

"You're mangling that wrap job," she murmured, vaguely remembering being lifted in the dining room and carried to the couch. The fire still crackled merrily, music still played softly. Despite the fact she was in a strange place, it felt like home.

Dressed in worn gray sweatpants, Nick sat within touching distance. He twisted at the waist and tossed his arm over her legs. "I'm trying not to, but the more effort I put into it, the worse I seem to do."

"Need some help?"

He nodded and gave her a boyish smile. With evening stubble along his jaw and finger-mussed hair, he was almost too gorgeous. Angled toward her like he was, the beautifully defined muscles of his chest and arms stood out in stark relief. She hesitated and then gave in to the urge to touch his hair. It was thick and silky, making her shiver with renewed desire. Then he turned his head to kiss her wrist and her stomach did a little flip.

It was going to take her a long time to get over him.

Blowing out a resigned breath, she sat up and maneuvered herself into position straddling his back. He leaned into her and yawned. Shooting a glance at the clock on the mantle, she saw it was two in the morning.

"Being tired might be the reason you're not wrapping well," she said dryly. "Why don't you go to sleep and we'll go over how to wrap in the morning?"

He linked his arms around her calves and looked at her upside down. "If I go to sleep, will you still be here in the morning?"

"Oh, Nick." Steph leaned her cheek against the top of his head. "Don't be silly."

"You're talking to a guy who cooked dinner naked."

Nuzzling her mouth into his hair, she changed the subject. "Do you have double-sided tape?"

"Huh? That sounds kinky."

She laughed and fell a little in love. "For your presents."

"Oh… Bummer. No. Just the regular clear stuff."

"Okay, sex maniac." She looked over his shoulder. "Let's see what you've got."

He turned his head and kissed her cheek.

Her heart clenched, and she had to clear her throat before she spoke. "You have too much paper on the ends. That's why it's hard for you to fold them without bunching it up."

Nick took up the scissors and cut. "Like that? Is that enough?"

"Yeah." She slipped her arms beneath his and demonstrated how to tuck the corners. "Now put some tape right there."

"Here?" His voice had deepened. With her breasts pressed to his back and her nose by his throat, their position was unbearably intimate.

"That's perfect," she breathed, releasing the gift and drawing back. He caught her hands before they left his lap.

Cupping her hands over his pecs, Nick whispered, "Touch me."

She swallowed hard as his skin heated under her hands. The tips of her fingers found the flat points of his nipples and rubbed gently. Groaning, his arms fell to his sides.

He leaned his head back into her lap and the sight of his face lost in pleasure was too much for her. Steph looked away, taking in the glass-topped coffee table, the flat-screen TV and the bare Christmas tree by the sliding glass door.

"Don't you have any ornaments?" she asked.

"No." His voice was a low whisper of sound. "I bought the tree for you and forgot the damn ornaments."

Her hands stilled. "For me?" *Oh my God, I'm going to cry.*

"Yeah, I knew from that notepad of yours and the little tree on your desk that you must really like Christmas. I do too, but since I'm going to my sister's for holiday dinner, I hadn't bought one for myself. For you, though, I figured it wouldn't be much of a Christmas wish if it didn't feel like Christmas around here."

Wiggling around, she switched from straddling his back to straddling his hips. Face to face, they stared at each other.

"I'm sorry I forgot the ornaments," he said.

And then he cupped the back of her neck and kissed her.

Unlike the deep possessive kiss he'd given her in her office, this kiss was coaxing, his lips brushing, his tongue flicking softly. Steph wrapped her arms around him and kissed him back with everything she had. In gratitude. In lust. In love.

She pulled away and gasped, "What do *you* want for Christmas?"

"This. You. Making love with you." He rocked his hips and she felt how aroused he was.

A gift that required no wrapping. No words. She lifted her skirt, he tugged down his sweats. She sheathed him. First in latex, then with her body. He groaned, she cried out. They moved together, without the haste that had marked their previous encounters. Her hands on his bare shoulders, she took him deep, rising and falling in tempo with the sounds he made. Clenching her muscles to stroke his thick length. Pulling off her shirt and bra to press her bare skin to his.

"I've wanted you," he said hoarsely, guiding her hips with shaking hands. "So badly… God, you feel amazing."

Steph made it last, in no hurry for their time together to end. But it did, of course.

Dawn came too swiftly. As the pink light of the early rising sun came into the room through the sliding glass door, she tucked a blanket around Nick and picked up her duffle.

"Merry Christmas," she whispered, pausing on the threshold a moment before shutting out the view of Nick asleep on the couch.

The clicking of the latch said the goodbye she couldn't.

* * * * *

"Well, this is a surprise," Amanda said as she pulled the door wide. "It's been over a year since you last darkened my doorstep, Nicholas James. And you looked a hell of a lot better then than you do now."

He gave a curt nod before dropping a kiss on her forehead. "I need a favor, Mandy, and I hope to God it doesn't make me an asshole for asking. Do you know where Stephanie lives?"

The petite blonde blinked up at him. "Wow. Okay, hang on a sec. That hurt a little." She blew out her breath and stepped out of the way. "Come in."

Nick stepped inside but hovered by the doorway. Three damn days had passed since he last touched Steph and if he didn't get to her soon, he was pretty sure he'd go insane.

Mandy stared at him a moment and then walked to the kitchen counter where her purse waited. "I'm over you, I swear I am." She pulled out her BlackBerry and a pen. While writing she said, "I still have to ask why Steph's the one that got to you."

"Hell. What kind of question is that?" He ran his hand through his hair.

"I don't know. I guess I'm just wondering if what they say about *The Rules* is true. Is playing hard-to-get the way to land the great guys?" She came toward him and held out a business card with an address on the back.

Relief flooded him. He tucked the precious card in his pocket. "Maybe in the beginning the chase is fun. Now it just sucks. Thanks for this, Mandy. Really."

"Hey, Nick."

He paused on the threshold, his impatience nearly overwhelming. "What?"

"You're not heading over there now, are you? Steph and Kevin were—"

"Who the fuck is Kevin?" Every muscle tensed at the sound of Stephanie's name linked with another guy's.

Amanda's eyes widened. "Oh shit… You don't know."

"Obviously not." He strode back into the living room. "But you're going to tell me."

She sighed. "You better take a seat."

* * * * *

Nick watched out the window of his car as Stephanie exited her Grand Cherokee and started up the icy walkway from her driveway toward her front door. The house where she lived was quaint and cozy, with soft touches that were clearly Steph's that made the residence a home. She looked sad and he knew why. He'd watched her leave with Kevin Martin just an hour ago. Now she was alone.

Steph had a family.

He was the outsider.

Steeling himself inwardly, he stepped out into the chilly afternoon air and shut his door with enough force to catch her attention. She looked over her shoulder and came to an abrupt halt. He walked toward her with a purposeful stride, part angry and part really fucking hurt.

"What are you doing here?" she asked, her voice low and slightly panicked.

He didn't answer. Instead, he pulled his hands out his coat pockets and pulled her close, his mouth finding hers. The moment her lips met his, he groaned. When her momentary hesitation melted into desperate ardor, he knew he had a chance.

She still wanted him.

Lifting her feet from the ground, he carried her to the door. "Open it."

"Nick—"

"I suggest you hurry up if you don't want to shock your neighbors."

Fumbling nervously, Steph shoved the key in the lock and when the knob turned, he crowded in behind her, kicking the door shut with his booted foot. She turned and he pushed her against the foyer wall.

"I've missed you," he said hoarsely, his hands wandering restlessly in an attempt to feel her through the bulky jacket she wore. "Every goddamned minute since you left me, I've missed you."

"Don't do this, Nick." She leaned her head back and then gasped when his teeth scraped her neck. "We had a deal. The wish list and then we'd be done."

"But we're not done," he argued. "We're nowhere near done. And if I have anything to say about it, we'll never be done."

"What?"

Stephanie stared up into Nick's gorgeous but pissed-off features and felt like she was going to pass out. His jaw was shadowed with stubble, his blue eyes rimmed with red. His hair was spiked from agitated fingers and his beautiful mouth was harshly drawn. He simply looked like hell, but her heart swelled with happiness at the sight of him.

"I love you, Steph." He caught her hand and pressed it over his heart. "Feel that? That's panic. I'm terrified you're going to say that's not enough, when that's all I've got to give you."

Tears welled and dripped from her lashes. "Kevin..."

"You should have told me about your son, Steph. I've been going nuts trying to figure out why I can't have you." Catching her zipper, Nick tugged it down and shoved her jacket to the floor.

"Now you know why this isn't going to work," she said, her voice shaky.

"I don't know shit, Steph. Because you didn't tell me." Shoving his hands beneath her top, he squeezed her breasts and she melted in his hands. "Think quick. The bed or right here on the floor."

"Oh my God."

She stumbled away, backing down the hallway as he stalked her. With wide eyes and a racing heart, she watched as he shed his jacket and then his shirt. When he reached for the button fly of his jeans, she swallowed hard. The tender lover she'd known three nights ago was gone and the thrill that coursed through her made her dizzy.

"Nick..."

"I'd lose the sweater if I were you. You'll be sweaty enough without it." He shoved his waistband just low enough to free his fully engorged cock and heavy balls. Then he reached into his back pocket for a condom and sheathed himself even as he stalked her.

Yanking her sweater over her head, she faced forward and nearly ran the remaining distance to her room. Nick was right on her heels. She was barely to the foot of her bed before she got her bra loose and then he was on top of her, his long lanky body sinking into hers. The crisp curls of his chest scraped her nipples and she gasped, opening her mouth to his questing tongue. A low groan rumbled deep in his chest and he tugged at her jogging pants.

"Off."

She squirmed desperately, kicking. "I'm trying."

"Try harder."

Laughing, she wiggled free and then his hand was between her legs, stroking her pussy and rubbing her clit. She wasn't laughing anymore—she was whimpering and arching up into his hard body.

"Did you miss me?" he growled, biting her earlobe.

"Yes… Ummm… too much."

Two fingers slipped inside her and stroked, making her cream.

"Spread your legs."

Nick came over her, nudging her thighs wider with his lean hips before he took her in a deep, breathtaking thrust. Then he wrapped his fist in her dark hair and began to fuck her within an inch of her life.

"Nick!" Steph writhed beneath him, trying to move but held still by the prison of her bound hair and his pumping cock.

He leaned his weight on one elbow and used his free hand to pull her leg over his hip so he could plunge to the hilt. She watched him, every nerve ending in her body hot and tingling, her breath panting. The waistband of his jeans rubbed against her inner thighs, a constant reminder that he couldn't bear another moment without being inside her.

"This isn't about getting laid," he insisted hoarsely.

"I know." Her hands clung to his straining, sweating back.

"This isn't temporary."

"I-I…" Her cunt fluttered along his cock. "I know."

Burying his face in her neck, he said, "I love you" against her ear and she melted. Into the bed, into him, into an orgasm that made her cry out his name. And he filled her with love.

With hope.

* * * * *

Nick tucked her cheek against his damp shoulder and said, "Talk to me, Steph. Tell me what you're thinking so we both get on the same page."

She gave a lame shrug. "I don't know where to begin."

"Start with the ex," he suggested. "Tell me about him."

"Tom's a great guy. He's handsome and charming, a caring dad. But he couldn't commit to me. I think he really wanted to, but he couldn't."

"Sweetheart, I'm not like Tom. Just because I waited for you to come along doesn't mean I've got commitment issues."

"He's got a new girlfriend every month," she rushed on. "Kevin has a little notepad he takes to his dad's to write down their names so he doesn't mess up and use the wrong one. He did that once and it was a mess." She reached down and stroked his bare hip. "I can't do that to him, Nick."

He nuzzled against her. "I'm not asking you to do that. I'm asking you to let me in. Make room for me in your life, someplace permanent. Let me love you, be with you. You won't regret it."

As his blue eyes began to glisten, something inside her softened. "I'm scared. For my son. For me."

"I know. I'm scared too." He pressed his lips to hers. "I'm scared you're going to send me away because you can't trust me."

The last three nights without him had been hell. She'd missed the feel of him holding her, making love to her, making her feel special and cared for. She missed the way he made her laugh and how good she felt when she was with him. "I want to trust you," she whispered.

"Then do it! Listen to me, Steph." He rose up on his elbow to look down at her. "Being a single mom doesn't mean your life is over."

"It means my needs come second. I can't—" She closed her eyes. "You don't understand. It was hard for Kev. I was a wreck when Tom and I broke up. And I didn't even love him anymore."

"But you love me." Nick cupped her face in his hands. "A little. Enough to be scary. And I'm glad you love me because I'm head over heels for you."

The look in his eyes told her he was laying it all out there, making himself vulnerable.

"I-I don't know what to say."

"Say you'll give us a chance. You're used to running the show, and you can keep on running it. I just want to be the guy you lean on when you need to recharge. I want to be the guy who holds you when you're tired and makes love to you when you're not. I want to be the guy you come home to every day."

"There won't be any sleepovers for awhile," she warned, needing him to cast aside any romantic illusions.

"We'll take long lunches."

"A lot of nights you won't see me. I can't do the dinner and date thing often. Kevin only goes to his dad's every other weekend and part of every holiday."

"I know I'll take the backseat to your son. I'm okay with that. In fact, I love you for that."

The tears wouldn't quit and the knot in her throat made it hard to speak. "Kevin might not warm up to you right away."

Nick pulled her closer. "I know that too."

Steph frowned. "Have you dated a single mom before?"

"No. But my friend Chris just married into a similar situation. We met for lunch today and talked about it. I talked to his wife, Denise, too so I could try to see things the way you do."

"You did?" The image in her mind of Nick approaching his friends to discuss his feelings and fears made her cry harder. She hugged him tight, silently conveying her endless gratitude.

"I wanted to know what to expect. I wouldn't have come here like this without doing my homework. That wouldn't be fair to any of us."

"So you know it won't be easy."

"I'm not asking for easy, sweetheart. I'm asking for a chance to make you happy."

She didn't know whether to laugh or keep crying. So she did both. "You're *The One*." Kissing his face, she pressed him back and climbed over him. "This whole year you've been right here and I couldn't see it."

"I love you, Steph." His lopsided smile made her heart race. With a lock of dark hair falling over his brow, he looked younger and vulnerable. Lying on her Christmas quilt, he was the most perfect present she could ever imagine.

She pressed her lips to his. "You made all my wishes come true."

"Actually…" He grinned. "We missed one."

"Did we?" Thinking back, her eyes widened as her mouth curved. "Yes, we did."

Licking her lips, Stephanie slid down his body.

Nick closed his eyes with a contented sigh. "Merry Christmas to me."

Also by Sylvia Day

ℬ

Kiss of the Night

Misled

About the Author

ℬ

Sylvia Day is the multi-published author of highly sensual romantic fiction set in historical and futuristic settings. A former Russian linguist with the US Army Military Intelligence, she now writes full-time. When she's not working on her next erotic romance, you can find her chatting with visitors on her weblog, message board and chat loop http://groups.yahoo.com/group/SylviaDayBookCafe.

Stop by http://www.sylviaday.com to say hi and meet all her bad boy heroes.

Sylvia welcomes comments from readers. You can find her website and email address on her author bio page at www.ellorascave.com.

SPECIAL AGENT SANTA

Denise A. Agnew

ॐ

Chapter One

Special Investigations Agency
Christmas Eve
Top-Secret Facility
Somewhere in Colorado

Tinkling, disgustingly cheerful Christmas music echoed throughout Finance Services.

Kat Langdon returned to the spreadsheet on her computer that she'd tried to finish for the last hour. Instead, all she could think about was one maddening SIA agent extraordinaire.

Boone Granger. Or, as many women in SIA referred to him, the long, tall Texan. She often wondered if the women of SIA meant his cock or his considerable height. Her face heated at the conjecture.

Boone. His name sounded like a country and western singer or an old-west gunfighter. He'd invaded her thoughts for too many days lately, and too many nights. What made her think of him today?

Maybe because she didn't have anywhere to go on Christmas Eve. She imagined him visiting family around a twinkling Christmas tree, his wide smile gleaming as he laughed. Her body heated ruminating about the gorgeous agent. At the same time, deep sadness threatened. She wished Boone happiness, but she longed for a similar joy for herself.

Oh, yes. It would be bliss to touch him. Kiss him.

Face it, Kat. It would be flaming fantastic to fuck him.

Thinking about the crack special agent sent her heart into a chaotic pounding and her stomach dancing with manic butterflies. The flush migrated like a solar flare from her face down her neck, to chest, to her belly with maddening attention. Nevertheless, she refused to buckle under to the treacherous desires that slammed her at the mere thought of him.

If Boone decided to visit today—God, not right this minute, please—she'd be a goner. Okay, goner didn't exactly describe what would happen. *Nothing* would happen, as usual. Boone would walk into the room, smile and nod civilly or make some jokes—horrible jokes—and she'd lose her ability to form a coherent sentence as she always did when he appeared. Top that off with her wildly out of control hair, dark circles under her eyes, and the fact she'd worn sweats, and her sex appeal fell to a one on a scale of one to ten.

She remembered a weird saying one of her friend's teenage daughters said one day, "I'd like to break me off a piece of that."

Oh Lord. Yeah, she could imagine getting a piece of him. Her mouth wrapped around his cock, sucking him until he spewed down her throat. She tried to envisage the vital, sexy, strong man ever depleted of his high-test sex appeal. Nope, just couldn't happen.

She heaved a deep breath. Damn, she needed to get back to work. Kat returned to her spreadsheet. She felt the pressure behind her eyes. Tiredness flirted with her body, warning that she'd gone too hard, too fast, for too many days. She'd worked overtime during the holidays for several years now and avoided holiday parties like the plague.

One person she could count on for the holidays was her friend Christabel. But she'd taken off over a week ago for a bus tour through the Central American country of Puerto Azul. Kat had resigned herself to a quiet holiday season, and when Christabel came back before New Year's Eve, they planned to get together.

Worry made her pause with her fingers above the keys. Christabel had promised to call her yesterday but hadn't. When she'd expressed her concern to her boss, Lanny, he'd told her not to worry. No doubt Christabel was having so much fun she forgot to call. She'd probably phone later tonight to say Merry Christmas.

Brushing aside worry about Christabel, her mind popped back to the delectable Boone. Why did she have such an obsession with the man? It couldn't be because the man was too damned sexy for words. No, he had other qualities that she liked. Integrity. Intelligence. A sense of humor even if he couldn't tell a good joke. Kat sighed and saved the half-finished work. She'd never complete this project if she didn't stop thinking about Boone.

A huge yawn cracked her jaw.

Numbers ran through her head in a scramble as she entered more data into the spreadsheet. Another yawn caused an annoying squeak to leave her throat. Tears caused by the yawn blurred her vision. She leaned back against the executive-style chair, appreciative of the high back. After one more jaw-stretching yawn, she closed her eyes.

A second later, a fantasy passed through her mind. A very vivid, descriptive, inappropriate for the workplace, delight. The world started to fade. Even sounds muted. Keystrokes on computers, phones ringing, footsteps in the hall, the scent of freshly brewed coffee, the heater spewing warm air from the vent above her desk. All faded away in the face of her daydream.

Boone sauntered into her office in slow motion, his handsome mouth tilted in sardonic appreciation. His dark blond hair fell straight around his face to about chin level and reminded her of a disreputable pirate. His blue eyes twinkled with a secret, his day-old growth of beard providing a thoroughly roguish appearance. He wore a black leather jacket, blue denim long-sleeved shirt and black jeans that curved over his narrow waist, hips and muscular legs. His hiking boots gave him that "I'm a country boy" fashion statement that cemented the fantasy. Why, oh why, did she find him so gorgeous? Her heart tripped as he planted his big hands on her desk and leaned forward.

"Wake up, Sleeping Beauty."

She jolted awake.

Standing right in front of her, hands planted on the desk, *was* Boone.

He'd stripped off his navy blue winter coat and tossed it on the chair in the corner, rolled the sleeves up on his red flannel shirt to reveal bronzed, strong forearms. Heat filled her face and spread straight down her chest into her stomach in a wild whirlwind of arousal. Her gaze pinpointed to his shirt collar, where dark blond chest hair peeked out. She could almost smell a hint of earthy man. Nothing intrusive, but she couldn't ignore the delicious scent either. God, he was so maddeningly distracting with that teasing grin and sparkling, ocean water eyes.

"Boone," she finally managed to say with a scratchy voice.

He straightened and tucked his thumbs in his belt loops. He winked. "Hey, darlin'."

His drawl held enough hint of the South to make a woman wonder. He rarely laid it on thick unless he wanted to tease her.

His brow creased, and a second later he cruised around her desk and squatted down. He planted one hand over hers as it rested on the chair arm. Renewed heat shot up her arm and tingled.

"Everything all right?" he asked, eyes worried.

She smiled, gratified not only by his concern but the tenderness in his usually gruff voice. "Of course."

His brows drew together, doubt planted in his gaze. "I've never come in here and seen you fast asleep."

"I didn't have my eyes closed more than a few minutes." She shifted in the chair, and he released her hand and stood. "Thanks for your concern, though. It was sweet of you."

He snorted. "Nothin' sweet about me. Nothin' at all."

She almost spouted a "yeehaw", then thought better of it.

"Lanny called me on my I-Doc and wanted to see me," he said. "I was off until later tonight, but he said to get my butt in here. It's about my latest assignment."

"You missed him. Lanny ran out of here an hour ago and said he had some errands to do before the snow got too bad. Last-minute Christmas stuff. Why would he want to see you about your assignment?"

He grinned. "I think I spent too much on my costume."

Her eyebrows went up. "Costume?"

"There's this Christmas Eve party I need to infiltrate, and I needed a costume for it." His gaze twinkled, wicked and spiced with amusement. "Last month I was a homeless man, this month a Santa."

He headed to the one chair opposite her desk. Boone eased six foot four inches of brawny male into the dainty chair.

"One of these days that chair is going to protest your treatment, Boone."

His cockeyed grin and sparkling eyes declared he didn't care. "I've sat in this chair dozens of times. It can hold me." In a flash, his amused glance changed. He tilted his head as if he had a brand-new idea. "Now, you and I both sitting in this chair…that might break it down."

Despite the nonchalant tone in his voice, she knew exactly what he meant. Fire burned her cheeks as she visualized his naked body in the chair, cock pointing straight up and waiting impatiently for her to straddle his lap and impale herself on several thick male inches. Searing heat rushed through her body at the thought. *Oh God. Yes.*

For six long months since he'd started work at the SIA, he'd waltzed into this office and made statements this side of suggestive. No matter what he said, she could never think of anything equally clever to say. Today a yearning built within her that made her want to connect with him on a deeper level, a respite against one more Christmas Eve spent alone.

Before she could respond to his flirtatious statement, he winked. His gaze, a disturbing cloudless sky she could fall into easily, turned warm and appreciative. "You look pretty in that sweat suit. What is it? Velvet?"

Bemused by the fact he cared, she shook her head and looked down at the plush emerald green material. "Velour."

"Looks soft." His voice lowered, husky and sensual, his gaze holding hers. His eyes took in her sweat suit again, fixating on her bust area. "But those goin'-to-Sunday-meetin' pearls don't do you justice."

She flushed and tugged self-consciously at the pearl necklace. "These are my mother's pearls."

"Mmm. Well, they're pretty, but you need something less conservative."

Damn, would she ever get used to his outrageous comments? She clasped her hands in her lap. "Boone, it's none of your business what I choose to wear."

"True. Don't tell anyone I said that about the pearls, though. If you do, the guys will all think I'm gay as hell."

"I thought you didn't care what other people thought."

"I don't." He shrugged those big shoulders again. "Except maybe for you. I care what you think." He stood and with one eyebrow cocked in question, he touched the doorknob. "Mind if we talk in private?"

"No, I don't mind."

He clicked the door shut then locked it. Warmth stole into her belly and she inhaled deeply to calm her racing heart.

"Why did you lock it?" she asked, a weird sense of apprehension mixed with excitement.

"Because I want privacy for what I'm about to ask."

"Okay." This sounded serious, and the teasing light that shimmered in his eyes disappeared.

He returned to the chair. "I need your help."

He sat in typical male abandon with his legs spread out. He crossed his arms. Even under a long-sleeved shirt, she could see his muscles bunching and rippling. An over-the-top reaction to Boone drove her nuts because she couldn't stop it now she was alone with him. His flattery and knee-buckling, I-want-to-eat-you look made strident arousal tug low in her stomach. Moisture trickled between her legs and she clenched her muscles in reaction. *Oh God.* She needed to stop this reaction before she did something or said something incriminating.

"What were you saying?" she asked.

"The costume I bought for this next assignment is a pain in the ass. Requires wrestling to get the damn thing buckled, strapped, you name it. Anyway, I was hoping you could help me put it on."

"Oh…uh, well." *Come on, get with the program. Of course you want to help him. Say it. For once say what you really want to say to him and stop dancing around it.* "I don't know. Why me?"

He leaned forward. His salacious grin and the hot attention in his eyes almost sucked the breath from her. "There's something else I need, Kat."

"Oh?"

"A date for the party. It's undercover, but only for a few hours. And there's no danger, I promise."

Surprise almost choked off her breath. "What?"

His eyebrows knitted together. "I realize it's last minute, but there aren't any other agents available to help me."

She narrowed her eyes, picked up a pencil and started to twirl it nervously in her fingers. "That's hard to believe."

Jumpy, she stood and walked to the window, watching the snow blanket the pine forest around them.

He rose from his chair and ambled toward her until he stood a foot away. She inhaled his tangy, musky scent again and her stomach did that funny swirling dance.

He leaned close to her. "There isn't anyone else. But even if there was, I'd still ask you."

A tiny thrill tickled her lower belly. "Why?"

He edged nearer, and she took a step back and found herself up against a wall. He towered over her five-foot-six frame, and a subtle shudder rippled over her skin. Boone always made her feel delicate and feminine. She could be outraged by her response to him, but she didn't feel helpless…just womanly.

He leaned one palm on the wall near her head. Oh, he was way, way too near for comfort. Excessively close for office etiquette. Thrilled and scared, she didn't move.

His voice dropped even lower, a whiskey and velvet sound so husky and sexy she considered melting on the spot. "I just can't take it anymore. Tonight I need you. Only you."

"Me?" She almost choked on the word. Her hand went to her throat.

He touched the side of her neck, his fingers sending pure arousal into her belly and even lower in her pussy.

"Your pulse is racing. You feel the same way I do." His voice held a husky plea that heightened the growing fervor inside her.

She did feel the same way, but enjoyed the desperation in his voice for a few more minutes. Moist warmth pooled between her legs as the excitement of having him so close quickened her breath. She dared look deep into his eyes. Rampant desire sparked in those baby blues. Whoever said blue eyes couldn't look hot and intense hadn't seen Boone's eyes. Oh, yeah. He wanted her all right. Several emotions ran through her at once. Amazement. Happiness. Toe-curling craving. All inhibitions started to crack and fall away one by one under the knowledge he cared for her and wanted her.

"You should leave work early." Boone's voice held the soft, encouraging nuance of a man in charge.

But she didn't want him in charge—not of her, anyway.

"Boone, I have work to do. We both need to get back to our business."

His gaze dropped to the pearls around her neck, then lower. She wondered if he could see down the zip front of her sweat suit top. Her heart continued that ridiculous pitter-patter.

"It's my day off, darlin'. But tonight I'm back to wheelin', dealin' and playin' games under the covers."

She about swallowed her tongue. Under covers. Not undercover. Playing games, eh? What if he played a game with her right now? Let's fluster the sexually frustrated single woman. God, she hoped not.

His hand came up to cup the side of her face in one big, warm palm, then let his fingers trace her jaw. A strong quiver racked her frame.

"Cold?" he asked.

"Definitely not," she said, her voice a breath of sound.

He frowned, a purely worried look on his face now. Gone was the mild-mannered charmer. "You're not afraid of me, I hope?"

She should be. His body radiated power and assurance. "Of course not. I just don't think you need help getting into your costume."

He winked again, the roguish tilt to his grin charming enough to sideswipe the most reluctant virgin. Not that she was a virgin, but she came as close to reconstituted as a woman could get. Working long hours at the office the last few years in Finance Division put a dent in her dating life.

"My costume is damned hazardous," he said.

She stifled a laugh. "You're irrepressible. A rogue."

His voice softened to a husky purr that made her insides heat. "You mean the idea of me in a Santa costume doesn't turn you on? All that padding, and the big boots and the damned beard. Hell, it's a nuisance, but with your hands touching me, I think I can take it. Darlin', don't you see, I'm dying to have you touch me."

Molten desire slid through her body, curling in her belly.

The more she heard from this rogue, the more she liked what he said, and in one way that scared the bejeebers out of her.

"Now did you say something about me bein' indispensable—"

"Irrepressible. There's a big difference."

"Damn. Irrepressible. I think I like the sound of that."

"Don't get a swelled head."

His eyes twinkled with humor. "Too late."

"Uh-huh." She plunged all her doubt into that word, unwilling to allow his charm to derail her before she was ready.

Amusement left his eyes and his mouth. Worry replaced it. "Please leave the office early with me. This storm is turning into a blizzard. I'll worry like hell if you're out there without me."

Pleasure danced through her system at the low, husky concern in his liquid voice. She felt naked and without defense or pretense in that moment. His gaze danced over her, searching for answers she didn't know if she wanted to provide. On the other hand, part of her rejoiced at the attention, the overwhelming knowledge a man desired her with such force and conviction.

Damn it, Kat. You're thirty, not thirteen. Chin up.

"Kat?"

She tilted her small chin and stared him down. "I'm not helpless, Boone." She poked his chest with her index finger. "I'm perfectly capable of driving through snow. I've been doing it for years and so far so good." She poked his chest again, and raised her voice to stern and determined. "And second, no one orders me around."

She took a deep breath to steady her pulse—the man's scent and his nearness continued to unravel her one thread at a time.

A warm connection flowed between them, an intimacy she never expected and liked very much. She breathed deeply. He smelled so tempting and if she inhaled one more dram of his masculine aroma, she figured she'd pass out on the spot from intoxication.

He said, "Honey, I don't want to boss you around. I want to spend time with you. Lots of it. We've got chemistry, Kat. For six months I've been wondering what it would be like to get to know you better. I've had one assignment after another keeping me away from you. You know what I thought about late at night when I turned out the light? It would make you blush."

She inhaled deeply, becoming braver and more willing to jump off the edge. "Are you sure? Tell me what you thought about late at night."

Without remorse, his voice thick with passion, he said, "I imagined kissing you here in the office. Pushing you up against this wall."

Her heart slammed in her chest. "Oh, my."

"I'd rip your shirt off." His heavy-lidded gaze drew her in until she couldn't look anywhere else but into his mesmerizing eyes. "I'd free your beautiful breasts and play with your nipples. Suck and lick them until you beg me for more." His gaze dropped to her breasts and the heat in his eyes blazed higher. "I'd make sure you were naked, then I'd cup your ass, lift you up and slide you down onto my cock."

She almost came unglued then. Almost grabbed him and demanded he do everything in the fantasy he'd created. Tension rippled and stretched between them. It wouldn't take much to send them both to the point of no return.

"What would happen then?" she managed to ask.

His heavy-lidded gaze traveled over her face to her lips. "Then we'd have a wallbanger so fucking loud people might hear us."

She not only blushed, she felt the heat radiate from her pussy all the way up her belly, over her chest, across her aching nipples, and straight into her face.

"Oh my God, Boone."

His hands planted on either side of the wall next to her head. What would it be like to explore his power? To caress it? To taste him?

Her heart pounded. She licked her dry lips. "So loud people could hear?"

"Oh, yeah."

Boone watched her with a hunger he could no longer deny. She didn't know it, but he could read every tiny nervous twitch she made. Did she think she could hide anything from him with wide eyes a sparkling green-blue, clear and beautiful as Caribbean waters?

Mischief twinkled in her eyes. "But maybe I'm not as attracted to you as you think I am."

"I didn't fall off the turnip truck yesterday, darlin'. You feel something for me and won't admit it."

Damn, he'd said it. Shit. His physical need for her went off the chart. Feelings? Well, those grew every time he saw her until he would do anything to make the fantasy he'd described come true.

Her small chin quivered, and he caressed her perfectly oval face with admiring eyes. Did she understand how much he wanted her? Had wanted her for six, agonizing, long months? He'd been a damned fool not to approach her sooner.

He allowed his gaze to wander over her delicate features. Her small nose, her long lashes. Only a little eye shadow, maybe mascara. She always looked natural. Her sweat suit fit her just right—not too tight across her full breasts or nicely rounded hips. Once, he'd like to see her in something slinky, sexy. Something he could slip off her shoulders and watch it pool around her naked feet.

A tiny panic welled up in her eyes. "How do I know you aren't trying to take me for a ride?"

He grinned slowly. "Oh, I am. A very long, hard ride."

Because he couldn't wait any longer, he dove in and took the kiss he'd wanted for what seemed eternity. His hands speared into her hair, and he cupped her head at the same time his mouth covered hers. Heat roared through his veins as he devoured her hungrily. As her lips parted and clung to his in response, a low growl of satisfaction rumbled in his throat.

Yes.

His tongue stabbed deep into her mouth. She moaned softly as he explored, thrusting his tongue against hers, pumping into her with an inflaming sexual cadence. When Kat met his dance with her own and tangled her tongue with his—well, his cock went rock-hard in seconds. She tasted as hot and delicious as he'd imagined.

He'd wanted to kiss her, fuck her for six agonizing months. Now he had Kat in his arms, he didn't plan on letting her go. His breath hitched as her body arched, her breasts full and soft against his chest. He wanted to cup the round globes, pinch and tug her nipples, lick them until her eyes closed in ecstasy. Tenderness sideswiped him at the same time as physical yearning. His hands slid down to her neck, where he allowed his thumbs to caress her collarbone. She trembled under his fingers. No matter what, he'd make sure she reached sexual peak over and over again.

The phone rang.

Chapter Two

Kat almost came out of her skin.

Boone released her with a gasp and backed away.

She snatched up the receiver before it could ring a third time. "Kat Langdon."

Kat frowned deeply, hating the fact they'd been interrupted. She took care of the call, reassuring the person on the other end of the line she'd have the spreadsheet ready for a meeting on Monday. When she hung up, she turned to him. His gaze held a slumberous, sensual quality that stirred her the way no man had before. He glanced out at the snow outside.

"Conditions are getting rough out there. We need to leave soon. Besides, if I don't get you out of here, I'm about to do something unprofessional as hell," he said.

Heaven help her, but she liked the fire in his eyes, the on-the-edge cut to his jaw and mouth. She stood her ground. "Oh? Something more than what we've already done?"

His gaze blazed with a new fire. He heaved a deep breath and his broad chest and shoulders moved. He walked up to her and stopped with almost no space left between them.

"Kat." His voice, so husky and almost aching, drifted over her lips. "You're driving me nuts. I have dreams about you at night. Hot, wet, sexy dreams. I can't take it anymore."

He leaned in and kissed her again. His mouth molded, shaped, teased. She burned everywhere, her body going up in flames as he pressed his tall length to hers. His hands gripped her shoulders then swept upward to cup her face. Every inch of his fantastic body rippled, moved, seduced with power and confidence. As she parted her lips and joined in the kiss, he took full advantage. He dipped into her mouth, caressing her tongue with a masculine assurance. His hands trailed down her neck, over her shoulders and arms and finally cupped her ribs. He explored with unabashed male interest. As his kiss deepened, his tongue thrust and retreated in a timeless tempo, testing her depths until she felt each stroke like a fine brush in her belly. If his first kiss ignited passions she didn't know she had, this one fanned flames so powerful she reeled with the intensity.

She ached, her core clenching and releasing with a desire to have him there, for the thick erection pressing against her belly to fill the void. Again and again he stroked, his tongue dancing against hers. His thumbs caressed her cheeks. She slipped her arms around his narrow waist and moaned against his lips.

He walked her backwards until they bumped into the wall again. Pure heat and happiness washed through Kat as she enjoyed the strength of Boone's body. Sensations encompassed her from every side like a blanket both comforting and riotously unpredictable. Potent male animal, he tantalized her with his rugged appearance, touch and raw possession. His hard, sculpted muscles embraced and protected with a spine-melting heaven.

Twisting his mouth across hers, he tasted with a hunger full of lust, staggering in passion. Her folds moistened, heated with slick, hot evidence of desire while her nipples tingled. Tracing his broad back, she smoothed over the taut muscle that bunched and rippled beneath her fingers. She flushed from head to toe, burning up with a brazen craving that stirred in her belly and demanded fulfillment. Their breaths came hard. His cock was a demanding blade of masculine need that prodded at her stomach, and she wanted it with a driving craving that broke over her like a wave.

As she leaned against the wall behind her, Boone broke the kiss. He unzipped her sweat suit top and peeled it back to reveal her plain white bra. He flicked open the front clasp. As he revealed her breasts, his eyes flamed with a ravenous urgency. When he cupped her breast, his fingers tenderly brushed her nipple. Wildfire pleasure made her gasp and shiver.

He leaned in and captured one tight, aroused nipple in his mouth. She gasped again, startled by the intense desire darting low and deep in her stomach. His tongue flicked, his lips nibbled. When his hand came up to capture her other nipple between his fingers, she writhed in double enjoyment. She couldn't bear it, yet she couldn't stand for it to stop. Continually he tweaked, pulled, rubbed one nipple while sucking deep, hard and long on the other.

"Mmm," he moaned against her nipple, licking and laving with tormenting rhythm.

Kat buried her fingers in his hair and closed her eyes, breathless with swiftly rising exhilaration.

He slipped his fingers down her belly, and she held her breath in anticipation. He wedged his fingers under her stretchy waistband and skimmed his way downward, his fingers exquisitely gentle as he discovered her folds plump and wet.

Delicate shivers coursed through her frame as he feathered his fingertip with the lightest touch over her clit. He kept up his maddening torment on one nipple, suckling and tonguing.

She gasped and her eyes closed. "Oh."

He released her nipple. "You gotta be quiet, darlin'. There are people outside who might hear. You want them to know what's happening?"

Excitement burst over her, illicit and heady. *Oh, yes. Yes.* People might hear. She smiled and opened her eyes.

His answering smile looked cocky and pleased. "I think you kinda like that idea, don't you? Do you like the idea people might know what we're doing?"

"That would be..."

"Wild?"

"Yes."

"Fucking exciting?"

"Yes." She closed her eyes again and sighed. "Yes. It's so...forbidden."

He chuckled, the throaty sound sexy. His fingers found her clit and caressed.

Her hips twitched and jerked as bliss cascaded through her. Aching, throbbing, her flesh demanded completion. She fell into an untamed paradise as his lips touched her throat, teasing her flesh in a torment she couldn't stand and yet didn't want to escape. His fingers probed, stroked, thrust. He slid one finger deep inside. At the hot caress, Kat moaned, squirmed. With slow, undemanding movements, he found a spot deep inside her and rubbed.

"Oh my God," she said with a cry of surprise.

She'd imagined feelings this astonishing before, but nothing she'd experienced in her sexual life so far compared to these invigorating, out of control demands her body made. When he took her nipple in his mouth and sucked, she cried out again.

Closing her eyes, she fell into the sensation, aware of nothing but his heat, his strength, and the heady delight. Without remorse, he fucked her with his finger, nudging that spot, caressing. She panted, crazy with a need so strong she almost didn't recognize it. He withdrew his touch and she groaned with disappointment. She opened her eyes to find him looking down on her with a mixture of lust and enjoyment so profound it stunned her.

He plied her clit, teasing over the sensitive bud with circling motions. She groaned, caught in a mind-splitting glory that surged then broke over her body in a dizzying wave. Her fingers clutched at his shoulder in desperation. Her head falling back as ecstasy grew with every gentle sweep of his finger over her clit. Arousal spilled from her in a slick hot juice.

"I've got to have you, Kat." His voice, low and thick, made her tremble.

As much as his fingers tormented her, she ached so much she must have him thrusting inside her or lose her mind. "Please. I'm on the patch. And I know we've tested safe."

His nostrils flared a little, his lips parted. "Jesus, sweetheart. That's music to my ears. God, you are so beautiful and I want you so much."

Impatient, she said, "Tell me later. Take me now."

Within seconds, he'd removed her boots then stripped her sweatpants and panties from her ass. Rapidly, in jerky movements that showed his impatience, he unbuttoned and unzipped his jeans. He shoved his jeans and briefs down to his thighs. His cock sprang free. Thick, long, and spike-hard, he lived up to the "long, tall Texan" adage without a doubt. Her mouth watered.

"Put your arms around my neck, Kat. When I lift you, wrap your legs around my waist."

She was going to do it. They were going to play out his fantasy.

When she put her arms around his neck, she closed her eyes and waited. His fingers dug into her ass as he lifted her off her feet. As he propped her against the wall, her legs came around his waist. The fabric of his shirt brushed against her nipples and teased them unmercifully. The thought that he was mostly dressed and she was mostly naked sent her arousal into the stratosphere. When his cock probed between her pussy folds, the broad tip pushed just inside her. She gasped as the thick invader pressed relentlessly forward. *Oh, that felt fantastic.*

"So fucking wet and hot," he said huskily.

Without hesitation, he shoved hard. She cried out as his broad cock spread her wet core wide and deep. He kissed her to muffle the sound.

"Ah, Jesus, God." He panted against her neck. "All right, darlin'?"

"It feels so good." Her voice sounded rusty, and she licked her lips. "So good."

She opened her eyes and looked into his smoldering gaze. Nothing would stop them now. People outside could break down the door and they wouldn't stop. The thought of her coworkers just on the other side of that door maybe hearing them fuck made her pussy clench and release over his length buried inside her.

He hissed in a breath. "Hang on."

He pulled back, sliding out until the tip barely rested inside her pussy lips. She squirmed, her hips twitching. "Boone, I can't stand this."

With one powerful stroke, he slammed forward. Again, she stifled a cry. Once more he pulled back with excruciating slowness, then thrust hard and fast. Her head fell back against the wall. Without mercy, he jackhammered inside her, his cock pounding out a rhythm between her thighs. Each thrust rubbed high inside her, the friction fast, relentless, out of control. Her body screamed with need for release. Sex had never been this good before.

Oh God, yes. It doesn't get any better than this. She moaned again and again as thick, amazingly hard cock drilled her thrust after thrust. Tingling, rapidly growing heat surged into her pussy along her vaginal walls, and the dam was ready to break loose. Her pleas came in whispers so no one but him could hear. As he fucked her with steady, unrelenting power, her mind and body reached for the goal hanging just out of reach.

"Boone." She sobbed out the word, her hips writhing as he increased the pace of his thrusts.

Finally, she could take no more. Orgasm burst inside her pussy, rolling in waves as she quivered and shook with breath-stealing rapture. Boone kissed her hard, and she screamed into his mouth. He thrust hard and stayed deep inside her, pressing his hips against hers.

His tongue plunged deep as he absorbed her ascent to the top. When he let her up for air, she continued to quake with small pulsations deep in her pussy. Kat knew she wasn't finished coming. Not by a long stretch.

"Sweetheart, that was beautiful," he said.

He eased his cock from her as her legs slid from around his waist. She moaned. "Why did you stop?"

He grinned. "There's much more where that came from."

He reached between her legs and felt the swollen folds. She hissed in a breath as he tested oversensitive flesh. Then his fingers left her pussy, creamy wet with the arousal that had inched from her steadily.

Sex scented the air, and a wave of heated embarrassment and elation combined inside her. Then he did something so carnal it shook her down to the secret, most primal sanctum of her being.

Boone licked her essence off his fingers. She tasted musky and clean. His cock twitched, hardened even more. Suddenly he couldn't get enough. "I want more of you. We're not done yet."

Fuck, she looks like a goddess. A well-pleasured, hedonistic woman who took her enjoyment in full stride. Yet he saw an uncertainty in her eyes that showed she didn't do things like this every day. Certain knowledge made him want her with a strength so profound he ached.

Boone liked the way she flushed. Hell, he more than liked it. He'd never seen anything sexier than Kat Langdon. Her hair fell in mussed chestnut waves around her shoulders, not exceptionally long and not short. Her slim, oval face looked delicate, china porcelain he was almost afraid to touch. Lips reddened, her sweatshirt unzipped, bra hanging loose, and those beautiful, tight brown nipples. Shit. His cock was still so hard he figured he could use it to hammer nails. Urgent, pounding desire drove him. He tugged her into his arms again and kissed her hard. With each deep plunge of his tongue, he tasted her, and she tasted him. She didn't hesitate, and something inside him broke free and rejoiced. *She's mine. Mine.* He lifted her into his arms.

He found a clear spot on her desk and sat her down. "What are you doing?" she asked, her eyes a little wide.

"I'm going to taste you."

Oh my God. She couldn't believe they were doing this. But she wanted it, ached for it. Frightened as hell and yet exhilarated beyond her wildest dreams, she gave into the swirling desire that swept her into this crazy fantasy come true.

"Lean back," he said.

She leaned back on her elbows. Breathless with anticipation, she closed her eyes. For a moment, all she could hear in the room was their heavy breathing. He got down on his knees, parted her thighs, and dove in to devour her.

The first hot lash of his tongue over her folds sent her heart into a staccato beat, her whimpers of enjoyment stifled as she remembered someone might hear. She centered her feelings inside her pussy, condensed to a pleasured woman needing him more than she needed anything in life. As his tongue swirled and flicked over her folds, she clenched the muscles in her pussy, then released. Each contraction created more heat along her pussy walls, more wonderful satisfaction. Kat kept her eyes closed to concentrate on his tongue swirling, darting along her folds, then over her clit with steady, massaging movements.

"Please." She didn't care if she begged.

Nothing mattered but coming and coming hard. Not today. Not tomorrow. Only pleasure.

With hungry attention, he feasted upon her. She shuddered and moaned. The moist heat of his tongue circled her clit then he lapped at her with undeniable enjoyment. He ate her like a dessert, like a succulent sugar, delicious and addicting. When he pushed two fingers slowly and deeply all the way into her sex, she put her hand over her mouth and moaned.

After what seemed endless seconds, his tongue strummed her clit repetitively while his fingers massaged her slippery channel. Her body shook in a fever-like delirium, the sensation so mind-blowing she couldn't suppress a strident whimper. When he enveloped her clit in his mouth and sucked strongly, her hips arched. She lay back on her desk and several items fell off onto the floor. The wet heat against her aching clit burst over her in a relentless wave. Panting and on the verge of coming, she gasped for air.

"God, you're delicious, darlin'." His voice became hoarse. "Do you want my cock?"

Any more waiting, and she'd lose her mind. "Please, Boone."

A cocky grin touched his mouth. "Please what?"

"Take me," she almost gritted between her teeth.

"Climb off the desk. We're doing this doggie-style."

She scrambled to leave the desk. She tossed her velour top and bra onto the chair. Stark naked, she leaned down, put her forearms on the desk and presented him with her ass. Boone caressed her ass cheeks, and she shivered with exhilaration.

"Shit, you have a pretty ass."

"Boone," she practically sobbed in frustration.

"Easy." His husky rasp, full of assurance, only served to drive her crazier. He urged her thighs wider.

Before she could take a breath, he eased his cock between her folds and pushed. She groaned softly as his cock tunneled to her depths. But if she thought this time would be slow, she was dead wrong. He drew back and rammed forward. His hips started a forceful fucking, his cock massaging her inner walls with every heavy, pistoning movement inside her. Jolted by his unmerciful thrusts, she shook under the impact. She reared back, wanting him harder, deeper, faster. Every thrust asked more from her already fiery arousal. Their rhythm turned frantic and Boone's hips gyrated as he pumped, strained, plowed her. He reached under her and cupped her breasts, his fingers dancing over her nipples.

Seconds later she ignited.

She gasped, thrashed, surrendered to the climax raging inside her. With a snarl he shuddered, thrust hard. He moaned low in his throat, and she felt hot streams of cum spurting inside her pussy. He lay over her back, kissing her shoulders, tugging her nipples.

"That was incredible," she said, panting and dazed. For a minute she was dizzy.

"Mmm. More than incredible. Fucking fantastic." His voice sounded gravelly and thick.

He slowly removed his cock from her, and she turned around. Desire blazed down at her from the soul-deep questions in his eyes. Her breath sluiced from her throat, her lips plumped from his kisses, her heart pounding.

Boone's mouth curved in one of those self-assured and companionable grins she associated with him and loved. He helped her climb into her garments again. When he said nothing more and propped his forehead against hers, his fingers caressed her shoulders and then he kissed her forehead. She needed wiggle room to figure the baffling sensations and feelings crashing around inside her. She pulled back from his embrace and glanced at the snowstorm growing into a blizzard.

"I can't believe we just did that," she said, half alarmed and half thrilled.

His eyes narrowed. "Do you trust me?"

His question took her off guard. "Why is it so important to you?"

He hesitated, and she detected a new emotion in his eyes. Fear. Genuine uncertainty. "Because it hurts to think that you don't trust me. That you'd believe I'd hurt you. Is it because of what we just did?"

A blush heated her cheeks. "Maybe."

"We didn't do anything wrong."

"No? We…"

"Kissed."

She smiled. "That's an understatement."

He returned her look with a nonplussed face. "Do you regret it?"

She swallowed hard. "No."

His lazy grin made her heart speed up. "Do you know how excited it made me, how much it turned me on to see you come?"

More heat flooded her face. "It was so…"

"Raw."

"Yes."

"Real."

"Yes."

He nodded. "You could hurt me, Kat. Hurt me so damned deeply I don't know if I could get back up again."

Startled by his confession, one part of her pretended she didn't hear it and didn't believe it.

She tried to imagine anything she did hurting him, and shook her head. "I've never met a man I could damage."

He cupped her face with one big palm, and the heat turned molten in her stomach. "I think you could put a hole through me ten feet wide."

Speechless, she waded into the deep end and dared to sink into his eyes. It scared the hell out of her to allow him to see this much. "Now that sounds like a Texas-sized exaggeration, Boone."

Before he could retort, the public address system came on and a pleasant female voice informed them all but essential personnel could leave for the day to celebrate the holiday and avoid the worsening weather.

He grabbed her hand. "Come on. Let's get out of here."

Chapter Three

Boone drove his SUV up the long driveway leading to his log cabin home.

They crested a rise in the road and the two-story cabin came into view. Surrounded on three sides by tall pine trees and nestled along the crest of a huge mountain, his home was beautiful.

Large and comfortable-looking, the cabin wasn't near any other homes in the area. From without it screamed masculinity and fit Boone's personality. Would she find awkward male touches inside that passed for decorating, or had someone decorated it for him? Another woman, perhaps?

As they walked into the wide hallway off the kitchen from the two car garage, he said, "Make yourself at home."

He pulled off his coat and put it away with her down coat in the hall closet.

Instead of speaking right away, he locked the door and set the security system. She observed the living room as he turned on the lights. Emerald greens mixed with eggplant and burgundy, dark wood and rustic southwest designs that looked authentic rather than designer-instigated. Large portraits of mountain scenes dominated the living area. Despite his carefree attitude, his cabin showed attention to detail and a sense of home that wrapped around her in exquisite comfort.

He glanced at his wristwatch. "We've got three hours to get to the party, so I guess we have time."

"To do what? Get naked and sweaty?" she asked, teasing him.

He smiled. "You don't believe in beating around the bush, do you?"

"Not when it comes to serious matters."

"Hmm." He cleared his throat, and his masculine drawl lured her with its liquid sound. "Very serious."

"I think we're alike that way." She tilted her head to the side and appraised him, taking in his strong body that had given her staggering pleasure.

He reached up and cupped her face in his big hands. "Let's find out what else we have in common."

Boone kissed her aggressively, his mouth smothering hers and his tongue plunging deep. A flash fire of sensations assaulted Kat. Under Boone's kiss, she came alive. He lay back on the couch and drew her down until she lay on top of him. His big hands pressed her hips into his, and as her thighs fell open, his jeans-clad hips pressed upward. She moaned into his mouth as his hard cock pushed between her legs and pressed against her clit. Clamping her in place, he slid his hands past the waistband of the stretchy sweat suit material and under her plain cotton panties to contact naked flesh. As he cupped her ass cheeks and smoothed his palms over her bareness, she sighed in pure delight. She broke their kiss to look into his eyes.

Uncertainty flickered in his eyes for an instant. "Please tell me this isn't one-sided. I know you care for me but—"

"Shhh. I'm falling for you, too. I think I've been half in love with you for months."

Potent desire boiled in his gaze. "What do you want to do first? Talk, or just get down to business?"

"I think we can save talking for later. Besides, we've been talking for six months."

He winked. "You probably thought I was all talk and no action?"

"I was beginning to wonder."

She smiled at him then looked around as an idea came to mind. She spied a big recliner next to the couch. "I think you need to sit in that chair for me."

A huge grin broke over his face. "You want to see whether it can take the weight of two people?"

"I do."

"I don't think we're going to get to that party tonight."

"Do you care?"

"Shit, no."

"What about the Santa suit?"

"Honey, if you want to fuck me while I wear the suit, that's fine with me."

She laughed. "Sounds intriguing."

He grinned widely. "Now?"

"I'd love that."

"Darlin', if that isn't the kinkiest suggestion I've heard in a long time." He left the couch and headed for the stairs.

Feeling breathless and excited, she said, "Hurry."

"Roger that."

"You didn't need help with the suit either, did you?" she asked.

"Hell no."

She chuckled then sat on the couch to take off her boots. Kat had never wanted to make love to a man with such fierce and overriding passion. Unbridled lust and complete trust flowed between them. While she enjoyed his flesh, she wanted to give him more than a spine-melting orgasm, she wanted his heart, his affection. She'd heard and seen the need in his voice as he'd taken her earlier, and she knew it wasn't only a physical connection between them.

By the time he returned a few minutes later, she was naked and sitting in his chenille recliner with her legs primly crossed. She frowned as he walked toward her. Along with wearing a shit-eating grin, he sported the Santa hat, and the red pants held up by suspenders. Absolutely nothing else. *Oh, yes, yes, yes.* She took in his broad, tanned shoulders, impressively sculpted arms, a wide, muscled chest, and the delineation of a muscled stomach and slim waist. Her gaze coasted over his chest, with its peppering of dark blond hair fanning over his pectorals and down over his stomach.

"I should have said this earlier. You're gorgeous," she whispered. "Even with that ridiculous hat."

He smiled. "Thank you. Come here."

She stood and went into his arms. His broad chest brushed Kat's breasts with exquisite movements designed to tease. His cock, trapped in the Santa pants, prodded her stomach like a hot brand. His fingers brushed through her hair.

"What next?" he asked.

Excitement winged through her. "Undo your pants and sit in the recliner."

When he unzipped the pants, his cock stood out proud and ready. This man was incredible on many levels, but his sex drive was obviously through the roof.

She'd planned to sit on him, impale herself on his gorgeous masculinity. Instead, she urged him to sit down. Then she parted his legs, knelt between them, and grasped his cock in her left hand.

"Holy shit," he said with a moan and a gasp. "I won't last if you do that."

She winked, wanting to torture him with her mouth the way he'd tortured her. "Who said I wanted you to last? Besides, you're a very bad boy, Boone, and deserve punishment."

She stroked his cock, moving up and down with firm pressure. He groaned, his hips twitching. "Yeah? How bad?"

"You didn't wear your Santa beard or the top."

"What's that going to cost me?"

"A severe fucking, at least."

He closed his eyes. "God, I hope so."

Kat leaned in and licked a drop of pre-cum off the reddened, broad end of his cock. She'd never seen a man so erect, so hard. Boone's cock was symmetrical perfection, thrusting out of a bush of dark blond hair. His silk over steel length pulsed under her touch. In response, her pussy wept moisture, her body aching to jump him and sink his thickness far inside her empty pussy. Instead, she encircled the base of his cock in her hand and covered as much of his hot flesh as she could with her mouth.

"Ah!" His hips jerked upward.

She worked his cock with steady pumping, her fingers slick as she combined the wetness of her mouth with the pre-cum leaking from his tip. Reaching below, she massaged his balls. When she removed her mouth from his cock and licked his balls, he sucked in a harsh breath.

She was going to kill him, the little wench. Emotions slammed him at the same time his mind reeled from screaming pleasure. His breath wheezed from his throat and his thigh muscles quivered. His hands clutched at the chair. She grinned and picked up the pace. He wouldn't last long under her assault. As Kat lapped at his length like a cat licking a delicious meal, he plunged his fingers into her hair. His hips started to move, fucking the hot, slick, wet depths in her mouth. Whether he wanted to or not, he was going to spew like a boy during a wet dream, out of control. He writhed, tortured by the unwavering cadence of her lips, tongue and hands. When her fingers caressed his balls with featherlight pressure, he thought the top of his head would come off. He couldn't get his breath. He opened his eyes and saw her gazing at him with slumberous eyes. Normally he hated losing control, but with her testing his restraint, he knew all bets were off. His darlin' liked meting out punishment, by God. On the receiving end of her unrelenting strokes and hot sucking, he fell into a heaven he never wanted to leave.

Yeah, he was a fucking dead man.

When her pace turned fast, her hand and mouth working in tandem, he lost it completely. "Damn it, Kat. Oh, shit, yes. I'm going to—"

He growled low in his throat as his hips thrust upward, further into her mouth. Boone writhed as pleasure rocked him, ripping through his body. Again and again his hot cum filled her mouth. She swallowed and lapped and the wet heat of her lips and tongue soothed as much as they drew blasts of cum from deep inside him. She released him and sat back on her heels, looking totally pleased with herself.

"Enjoy that?" she asked innocently.

Boone managed to pant a few words. "You are…beautiful…fantastic…incredible." His heart banged furiously in his chest. "But now it's your turn to get punished."

Her eyes widened. "I don't think so."

"Yes."

She giggled, and he liked the silly sound as it came from her lips. He reached for her, but she darted to her feet and backed away. He slipped the suspenders off his shoulders, yanked the stupid red felt pants off his legs, and stood.

Kat's coy smile said whatever retribution he gave out, she wouldn't make it easy for him to apply it. "Come here, sweetheart. We have some talking to do."

Cautiously, she stepped forward until his arms came around her, and he kissed her.

Every kiss Kat had experienced over the years paled in comparison to his drugging, incredible taste that sent waves of arousal straight to her womb. Her breasts tingled, aching for him to touch them. Watching Boone lose total control as she gave him fellatio had excited her more than she thought it would.

He stopped kissing her and with slow, slow motion, he cupped both breasts. Her breasts weren't too big or too small, and yet the nipples were a large and dusky brown. Tight and aroused, they poked out, ready to be licked, stroked, tasted.

Her whole body throbbed with needs. Her clit throbbed, the very walls of her pussy clenched, released and ached. His fingers drew together and pinched lightly. She gasped. Oh, yes. She threw back her head and enjoyed as he massaged her nipples with tender, delicate strokes and sweet plucks that sent her breath into overdrive and her heart pounding out of her chest.

As he looked into her eyes, she saw the building affection, the growing love. "You're the most gorgeous woman I've ever seen." He kissed her eyelids. "Your eyes are so dark and mysterious it makes a man wonder." He brushed his lips over her nose and then her chin. "And your face…your skin is so smooth."

Kat trembled, brought to the edge by the care he took with her. Before she understood his intent, he swept her into his arms.

"Boone!"

"Easy, darlin'. Don't you like to be carried?" He headed toward the stairs. "Just enjoy it."

And she did. She looped her arms around his neck and savored the power under her fingertips. His arms felt so warm, so strong, so protective that primeval female instincts took over. Once upstairs he headed for the end of the hallway. Her heart pounded as he reached a bedroom now barely illuminated with late afternoon winter light. A large, dark cherry wood four-poster bed dominated the big bedroom. At the bed, he released Kat so that she slid down his body. He kissed her lightly then looked deep into her eyes. Fascinated by the masculine planes of his face, she brushed her fingers over his unshaven jaw. His nostrils flared, his eyes blazing with a building desire. His mint-scented breath touched her cheek. She wanted the hot and fluid pressure of his body to encompass and soothe the crazy desire overruling every thought within.

"Give me your heart," he said softly, his lips near hers.

As they locked eyes, her eyes filled with happy tears. "You have it."

"And you have mine."

She reached up and cupped his face, bringing him down for a consuming kiss. Boone's tongue dipped inside as he groaned a harshly erotic sound. He edged them back toward the bed until her knees bumped into it and they tumbled in a tangle of arms and legs. Rubbing, smoothing, flowing against each other, Kat gloried in the sensation of his hair-rough thigh pressing her pussy. Hot and fluid, slickness flowed from her core. Sensations melted together as his hands traveled over her body in a restless search.

He left the bed, went to the highboy and fumbled around in one drawer. He came away with four lengths of what looked like silk. The hell-bent-for-leather grin on his mouth made her heart skip a beat. *He didn't mean to – oh, shit. He probably did.*

"What are you doing?" she asked, even though she thought she knew.

Would he spank her? Tickle her? God, she didn't think she could stand not knowing.

She'd never seen any man more gorgeous, his chest heaving, a taut hunger over his almost brutish expression. His gaze raked over her with brazen intensity. She wanted him so much she ached deep in the pit of her stomach and between her legs.

"Turn over and get ready to take your punishment."

Wildly stimulated and yet uncertain, she turned over onto her stomach.

"Spread your arms and legs out wide," he said.

Before she knew it, he'd tied her arms and legs to the four posts on the bed. The soft coverlet felt warm and comfortable against her face, her breasts, her stomach, but her mind wondered what dangerous things he had in mind. "Oh, Boone, this is…what are you going to do?"

"Wait and see."

He touched the slick bud in her folds, then grasped it gently with his fingers and began to stroke and pull. Dark sounds left her throat. A few seconds later, the friction became unbearable.

"Oh, my. Oh, oh, God." Her body tightened, her eyes closing, her lips parting. Another orgasm threatened. "Please, please."

Kat panted, her heart pounding frantically.

"Mmm." His voice went husky and deep. "You're so pretty down here. So wet and soft."

Mindless with need, she pleaded. "Do something. I'm about ready to scream."

"Go ahead and scream. I'm not done with you yet." When he left the bed, she almost cried out for him not to go. He went into the bathroom and returned a few moments later with condoms and lube. *Condoms? Lube? Hmmm…* What did this wicked man have in mind?

She turned her head to watch him as he ripped a condom package open, rolled it down over his erect cock, and smeared a generous supply of lube over his length. Then he added lube to the fingers of his left hand.

"I think you're going to like this," he said, a self-satisfied sound in his voice.

A few seconds later he slipped his fingers between her ass cheeks and caressed. Her hips twitched as the illicit touch sent curls of bliss straight to her pussy.

"Boone, oh, Boone." He kissed her ass cheeks then slowly but surely wedged one finger into her tight hole. "Oh!"

"All right, darlin'? I'm not hurting you, am I?" he asked huskily.

"No. God, no."

As he thrust his finger back and forth, he created an exquisite friction. "Anyone ever touch you like this before, Kat?"

Her breathing quickened as the pleasure heightened. "No."

"Tell me if you don't want this, honey. You know I wouldn't do anything to hurt you."

"I've always wanted it, but the men I've...slept with didn't want it."

He snorted a laugh. "Shit. You're kidding me?"

"No."

With a gentle insistence, he pressed another finger into her ass, and she gasped at the pinching sensation that soon turned to satisfaction.

"They must have been insane not to want inside this pretty ass. It's tight and so hot."

His flattery—no—his compliments emboldened her. "Are you going to..."

She couldn't say it, suddenly finding herself a tad embarrassed by the concept at the same time she wanted the experience.

His soft laugh rumbled low in his chest, a sound promising sensual delight yet undiscovered. "Fuck your ass?"

"Yes."

"Only if you want it. If it excites you. Makes you come for me."

"Yes," she said without hesitation.

For several long moments, he treated her tender flesh with sweet care and ensured when the time came she'd find only pleasure in his possession. His attentions drove her wild, the silky restraints around her wrists and ankles heating her blood. His other palm smoothed over her ass cheeks, the sensation almost a tickling.

He slipped his fingers from her well-lubed ass. "I'll go slow. Tell me if it hurts."

The blunt tip of his cock touched her ultrasensitive tight hole. Kat's breath rasped in her throat as he pressed forward and penetrated the smallest increment. She gasped softly, almost surprised when his broad length slipped in with ease. He withdrew then pressed forward again, his cock finding entrance a bit at a time. With each small movement, the thick head of his cock made headway. She felt her flesh stretching to accommodate him. Boone's arms held his weight up as he worked the tip of his cock in and out.

"Good?" he asked, his voice hoarse with pleasure.

Panting, she managed to say, "Great."

She grabbed the restraints and clutched for dear life as the maddening sensation of his cock inching back and forth inside her sent throbs of pleasure to both pussy and ass.

"I've imagined this," he said, "From the first day I met you."

Heat flashed through her as her breath rasped in her throat. "The first day?"

"And every day since, darlin'."

With a last thrust, his entire length filled her ass with a smooth slide. Filled by his cock, she let out a soft exclamation of enjoyment. Bracing himself over her, he thrust with deliberate yet tender strokes. He took his time, moving languidly to a beat known only to them. He never pushed too hard and his care for her comfort heightened her already aroused state. They moved to a silent dance that built inside them thrust after thrust. She gasped, she moaned, she begged for release. The restraints stimulated, the vulnerability, the implied dominance in their mating a catalyst designed to blow her mind. Seconds blended until she felt nothing but his cock plundering her most forbidden place.

As her moans increased, he rasped out, "No one else can hear us. Take what you want."

Bliss surged into her on a tidal wave so strong, she shrieked. As his cock caressed her tight channel, she fell into the climax, her pussy throbbing, her ass clenching. Breath tore from her throat as she convulsed, whimpered and sank into the most beautiful orgasm she'd ever known.

She expected him to take his pleasure, but he pulled away from her and disposed of the condom. When he returned, he undid her restraints and turned her over on her back. Without delay he climbed onto the bed with her, lay between her thighs, and thrust hard and deep.

She arched, her hips bucking upwards as she aided penetration. Her breath hissed inward as she clenched him within her depths.

With tender attention, he peppered her face with kisses. Her forehead, her cheeks, her chin, her nose. "Ah, God. Tight. You're fuckin' tight." A tiny frown wrinkled his brow as he captured her within his blue gaze. "All right?"

A sweet, sensual laugh slipped from her throat. "Better than all right."

His gaze flared, passion bringing him into tempo as his hips started to move. Each steady, push and pull within her cleft started a trembling within her pussy. Arousal immediately quickened inside her in a mindless, hot rush. He kissed her, his tongue exploring. She writhed, her moan into his mouth a pleading sound. He felt so excruciatingly good she couldn't stand it.

"I can't wait." His guttural statement fired her libido. "I want you so badly. I want you."

She lost control, so excited by the thick, smooth hardness that thrust deep into the fist of her womb. Without hesitation, he deepened his strokes, his sex heavy and hot moving into her in a hard dance that caressed her sheath. She looked up at his face and saw the surrender, the tumbling, building, taut hunger suffusing his handsome face. And it freed her in a way she'd never experienced, never knew.

Boone thought he'd lose his mind as he fucked her. He closed his eyes as he moved inside her tight, soaked heat.

She whimpered, throwing her head back, clutching at the firm globes of his ass. Their movements increased, the primal, hot rush, swelling in raw glory inside him. He grunted, he groaned against her mouth, his animal need evident. He rocked hard, his fucking feverish. She titled her hips, planting her feet to push up and join the ride. She bucked, and fierce desire crashed through him in sharp waves. Kat thrashed in mindless fever as Boone fucked her. His sex seated fully, ramming to the hilt with each flex of his hips. He wedged his hands under her ass and made last, powerful thrusts.

He flushed hot, his heart thundering as his deep, urgent strokes sent a hot rush of building, glorious pleasure spreading through his body. As her pussy clenched and released around him, he heard her cry out—the piercing delight so shattering she sobbed and her entire body shook.

With a feral growl, he made one last hammering thrust, shouted in harsh pleasure. Hot spurts of semen jetted from his cock as he exploded deep inside her.

Chapter Four

Boone woke with Kat nestled against his chest, and he couldn't remember feeling anything as good as holding her in his arms. When her hot, wet pussy had swallowed his cock, he'd almost lost it. Plowed into her with every hot, slamming thrust he could manage. Her plump breasts, curvy hips and long legs had cushioned him, wrapped him in an embrace more exiting than any he'd experienced. Now that he had Kat in his arms, his feelings intensified.

He glanced down at her head resting on his shoulder, her slim, beautiful hand lying between his pecs, and one slim leg thrown over his thigh.

Kat's fingers threaded through his chest hair, and he tilted his head down to smell her intoxicating scent. "Kat?"

"Mmmm?" Her fingers stroked lower, down to his stomach.

He trembled under her touch. "What are you doing to me?"

"Enjoying your body. You have the most gorgeous body I've ever seen, Boone Granger. You're not plump Santa material."

His chest puffed up. Literally. "Thank you. Believe me, I work hard at it."

Her touch drifted lower to his cock and he sighed in pleasure as she encompassed his flesh at the root. "God. I've created a monster."

She laughed, the sound sweet and mischievous. "You didn't create anything, Granger. I've always been a sexual person. But I don't throw around my sexual favors."

"That's good to know." He caressed the back of her head with reverent brushes. Then he frowned. "How sexual?"

Another low, gentle laugh escaped her. "I've had two serious relationships."

"How serious?"

"One engagement while I was twenty-one and in college, and a fairly complicated relationship that lasted six months. That one was about three years ago."

He couldn't stem the rising tide of jealousy, and said, "Damn it. I can't believe this."

"What?" She propped up on one elbow and released his cock. A frown pinched her lips.

"I'm fucking jealous."

She smiled. "And you're admitting it? I think I like that."

"That I'm jealous or that I admitted it?"

"Both."

Satisfaction filled her. "I've never had a man jealous over me before. And thank you for being honest with me."

"I'll always be honest with you, Kat."

"Can I be honest with you, then?"

"Of course."

"Well, your Santa costume needs some improvement. Like a big fat stomach, facial hair, that sort of thing."

"Hmm." He cleared his throat. "So how would you like to hang around for a while and help me with my other disguises?"

She kissed his chin, then her lips wandered over his chest to land on one nipple. He moaned at the cock-pleasing sensation of her mouth tugging on his flesh. "What kind of costumes?"

"Executive. Freeloader. Nerd. You name it, I've played it."

When she stopped manipulating his chest and glanced up at him, seriousness played over her features. "Which one are you now?"

"Boone Granger. Nothing more, nothing less. In the flesh, baby."

"I think I was worried about that."

He frowned. "Wait a minute. You mean we danced around each other for six months because you didn't know who I really was?"

She nodded. "It wasn't just me dancing around you. You kept your distance from me, too."

He caressed her face. Her features held a youth far smoother than thirty years, and yet her eyes held wisdom far beyond. His heart flipped over and squeezed. "I'm sorry, Kat. I was an ass."

She grinned. "No, you were cautious. You didn't want to get hurt."

Did he want to admit that? Yes. "Yeah, I think I was."

"I'd never hurt you, Boone." A sheen of tears welled in her eyes. "I'd never hurt the man I love."

His heart thumped, his breath coming shorter. He knew the words he wanted to say and that he felt deep in his soul. "I love you."

The glow on her face told him what he needed to know. He'd made her happy beyond words. Kissing her with a deep, satisfying intensity, he tightened his arms around her. Now was the time to confess. All he could do was hope she didn't kick his ass out to the doghouse once he finished explaining himself.

"There's something I've needed to tell you," Boone said.

She propped up on one elbow and looked down on him, apprehension building inside her. "What is it?"

A no-nonsense expression clouded his normally clear eyes. "Lanny told me about your friend going on the tour to Puerto Azul."

Puzzled, she sat up. "And?"

"He also told me that she didn't call you yesterday. I thought I'd do some checking through my contacts down there."

Her heart started a slow, almost painful thumping as dread spiraled through her body. "Why did you do that?" Boone's expression altered in a way that was just discernable. If she wasn't good at reading faces she would have missed the tiny change. "Boone? What are you leaving out?"

"Christabel's tour bus was taken hostage by insurgents a few days ago. Then, for some reason we don't understand, she was separated from the others and taken in a different direction."

Her hand flew to her mouth as she stifled a gasp. Gut-wrenching fear rose inside her. "Oh my God. When did—how did—"

"We're not sure. I came into your office today to tell you about Christabel and to tell you how I feel about you."

Unease mixed with anger and fear. "I've got to help her."

He caressed her shoulder. "That's why I didn't say anything to you while we were still at the office. Because I knew if I did, you'd run off to Puerto Azul."

Tears prickled her eyes. "Damn right."

"Honey, a SIA black ops military team is already in country to rescue the hostages."

His calm tone threatened to irritate her. Maybe because she could feel a tiny panic welling within her for her friend.

Tears filled in her eyes, and she gulped down a deep breath. "Damn you, Boone Granger."

His soft laugh caressed her ears. "Why am I damned?"

"Because I'm going to Puerto Azul to help her."

A hard as ice look came into his eyes. "You don't know the first thing about the area, Central America, or fighting insurgents. You'll get hurt or killed, and that's not going to happen as long as I have a breath left in me."

While her emotions in the last few minutes meandered from pulverizing him to walking out the door, another emotion arose that was certain, primal, and true.

"Come with me, Boone. Help me find her."

His expression didn't alter. He brought her hand to his mouth and kissed the palm with the sweetest, most delicate taste. He sighed. "Fuck it. I knew you were going to say that."

With a watery smile, she said, "Then you know that you have to go with me. Because I'm going whether anyone else wants me to or not."

He closed his eyes. "Shit." When he opened his eyes again, he said, "I knew you were trouble from the first moment I saw you at the water cooler."

"Humph." Braver now, she continued. "Are you trying to pour on that sticky Texas charm and lather it on thick?"

His eyebrows arched. "I'm not from Texas. Where did you get that idea?"

She sputtered. "Well, the ladies in the office call you the long, tall Texan."

His head fell back as he burst out laughing. "Long, tall Texan? That's a compliment, I hope."

"Where are you from, then?" she asked.

"Georgia. Down near Savannah. But I haven't lived there in...let's see...about twenty years. My family left there years ago." He shrugged. "When I wanted to know more about you, I got Hetty over at Personnel to let me see your file."

She gasped. "That's unethical."

He winked. "I never said I was a saint."

"How did you bribe her? She's an ancient curmudgeon with a steel bra."

"I smiled at her."

She sighed, and a laugh slipped from her despite everything. "Georgia charm. You charmed her into it, didn't you?"

"Nah. She's from Georgia, too. I think that might have something to do with it."

"God, you are—"

"I know. Irrepressible."

"Exactly."

"Your file told me some things that made me care about you even more. I read about your family life. How you were tossed from one member of your family to another. How your daddy ended up in prison for extortion and your momma wasn't much good for anything but abusing you. That's why you stay so controlled, isn't it? You think you're like the rest of your family."

He'd hit the proverbial nail on the head so accurately, new tears filled her eyes and rolled down her cheeks. She couldn't control them.

"Ah, darlin'. No, don't cry. Damn it." He drew her into his arms and held her.

She nestled into his strong shoulder and his powerful embrace cradled her as if she was the most precious thing in the world to him. She'd never felt as cherished and protected as she did in this man's arms. He massaged the back of her neck, caressed her hair, gave her comfort she'd never experienced before with a man.

She lifted her head and looked into the softest, warmest eyes she'd ever seen. She saw more than lust, more than desire. It thrilled her to recognize the genuine compassion deep in his expression. That this big, tough man cared for her so deeply sent waves of delight growing inside her.

Courage to speak her truth welled up. "Then you won't be angry when I tell you that I bribed Hetty about a month ago with a box of chocolates to let me see your file."

His glower surprised her. "You what? Then you already know I'm from Georgia."

She nodded. "Yes. It made it easier for me to understand why you've got this incredible intensity. You've had a tough life, too."

His glower didn't disappear. "Not so bad. So my parents were dirt-poor. So I had to scrape and save to make it through college."

She shook her head and reached up to touch his bristly cheek and jaw. "There's more than that. What about the accident?"

He sighed. "My parents were in the wrong place at the wrong time. Bad shit sometimes happens."

Her heat swelled with sadness. "You had loving parents. I can't imagine watching their car pushed off the side of a cliff by a semi. It's bad enough it happened, but the fact you and some of your brothers were in the car behind and saw it all." She kissed his jaw. "It's horrible."

Another sigh shuddered through him, and this time when she looked into his eyes, she saw matching tears. He gave her a wobbly grin. "Maybe that's why my brothers and I are so damned close. Maybe it's why you and I mesh."

Her eyebrows twitched. "Mesh. Mmmm. I like the sound of that. Now, how many brothers do you have?"

"I'm the youngest of six children. I have five older brothers. We're all damned nuisances in one way or the other. Especially my oldest brother. He's the biggest clown there is. And you thought the youngest was supposed to be the wackiest, right?"

"That's what they say."

"Well whoever *they* are, they're wrong. Don't you agree?" he asked.

"About what?"

"That *they* are wrong sometimes."

"Oh, oh yes. Definitely. Absolutely wrong sometimes."

His arms, which had never left her, drew her nearer once more. His mouth was a hairsbreadth from hers. "I ought to punish you for looking in my file."

She gasped in mock indignation. "Punish me? Like you did earlier? You like to use double standards?"

"Damn right."

"Brat!" She took the plunge and fluttered her fingers over his ribs and hoped he was ticklish.

He started violently and laughed. "Oh, no you don't."

Her protest was muffled under his lips as he kissed her aggressively, his mouth smothering hers and his tongue plunging deep. She smiled against his lips, but humor disappeared under the sensual onslaught.

A flash-fire of sensations assaulted her. Under his kiss, she came alive. Inhibitions broke loose and refused to pen up. The steady arousal that burned inside Kat demanded a finish.

They loved deep into the night, and Kat came so many times she lost count. Boone couldn't seem to get enough of her. She expected soreness after their continual loving, but her body craved him after months of desiring him. Insatiable, he thrust into her and stayed there, his cock tunneling with slow, tender movements for what seemed a lifetime until neither of them could stand it any longer. He'd plowed her, fucking with inexorable hammering strokes until she'd screamed herself hoarse with the pleasure.

She hesitated to leave his arms right away, even though she had plans to make. She glanced out the huge skylight above the bed. Low sunlight filtered through the snow flurries blowing across the window. Before she could slip from his arms, Boone stirred and rolled her over on her back.

"You're not thinking of sneaking out and stealing my car to get home, are you?" he asked.

She laughed softly. "It's snowing like hell out there. And I think I like being right where I am."

"Good." He kissed her, and moments later, he lowered his hips between her thighs and with a sharp thrust, he took her.

"Oh my God," she gasped out. "Boone."

"I can't get enough of you." His voice sounded raspy. "I want to fuck you for days."

"Mmm. Please do."

With passion-glazed eyes, he looked down on her and said, "You aren't going anywhere without me, darlin'."

She closed her eyes and savored the slow back and forth motion of cock through creamy wet folds. She barely managed, "Then let me go with you to Puerto Azul to find Christabel. You know I'll find a way on my own."

When she opened her eyes again, he gave her a lopsided grin. "Damn it, I know you will. Okay, you've convinced me." He pushed deeper, hitching higher and spreading her thighs wider. He rocked his hips, building up speed.

"I didn't think it would be that easy," she said between panting breaths.

"It won't be. If you go with me, it'll be dangerous. A hard road."

She looped her arms around his neck. "I never expect anything else. As long as you're with me, I can handle it."

His hips picked up speed, powering with fierce, rutting thrusts until orgasm took hold of her senses. Seconds later, her pussy shivered, contracted, burst through with exquisite, shattering pleasure.

His hips jerked, his body quaking as he roared out a guttural completion.

* * * * *

The phone rang, and Kat startled out of her sleep. Boone fumbled for the bedside light and snapped it on. Mind fogged by sleep, she listened in a half daze as he reached for the phone and mumbled into the receiver.

"Hey T.J. Where the hell are you?" Boone asked. "What? That's fuckin' fantastic! Is she okay? Kat's going to be happier then hell. She's right here with me. Hold on a minute."

Kat opened her eyes and blinked at Boone. "Who is it?"

He smiled as he handed her the phone. "Someone special."

As she frowned in confusion, he scooted off the bed and headed for the bedroom door. She watched his broad shoulders, back and tight ass parade through the door.

She heard a female voice on the phone, sounding tinny and far away. "Hello? Kat?"

At first Kat couldn't believe what she'd heard. "Christabel? Is that you?"

Christabel's clear laugh came over the phone. "Yes."

Joy spilled through Kat's heart. "Oh God! Are you all right? How did you escape the terrorists? What—?"

"One question at a time." Christabel laughed again. "It's a really long story. Sounds like you have some explaining to do yourself. What are you doing hanging with an SIA agent on Christmas Eve?"

Kat sank down into her fluffy pillows. Her face heated. "That's classified."

Christabel sounded doubtful and amused. "Right."

"Where are you?"

"Still in Puerto Azul. After the insurgents took my tour bus hostage, they decided it would be fun to take me off by myself. I spent some time in a rat-infested hut until T.J. Calhoun came to my rescue."

"Your old friend from way back? That T.J?"

"The very one. He's a soldier in the black ops unit of SIA. We fought our way through the jungle, Kat. It was the most terrifying and amazing thing I've ever experienced."

"Wait a minute. Why are you still in Puerto Azul?"

Christabel cleared her throat. "Well…um…T.J. is debriefing me."

It took Kat a moment to comprehend then she chuckled. "Is that what they're calling it these days?"

They talked a few minutes more, with Christabel admitting that she'd fallen in love with T.J. and he with her. As long it was confession time, Kat decided to admit to Christabel that she'd gotten more than cozy with Boone. By the time she hung up the phone, Kat was grinning broadly.

Boone strode into the room and slid back under the covers with her. He gathered her close in his arms and pressed a kiss to her forehead. "Everything okay now?"

"More than okay. It sounds like she's not only been rescued from the bad guys, but she's in love."

One of his eyebrows twitched upward. "Just like you are?"

"Oh, yes."

He kissed her thoroughly then let her up for air. "I'm damned glad we aren't going to Puerto Azul."

She sighed. "Me, too."

As they rested in each other's arms, he said, "I want you with me forever, Kat."

Her heart sang with new excitement.

"Together always."

And he kissed her again.

The End

Also by Denise A. Agnew

ഩ

By Honor Bound *(anthology)*
The Dare
Deep is the Night: Dark Fire
Deep is the Night: Haunted Souls
Deep is the Night: Night Watch
Ellora's Cavemen: Tales From the Temple IV *(anthology)*
Men to Die For *(anthology)*
Special Investigations Agency: Impetuous
Special Investigations Agency: Over the Line
Special Investigations Agency: Primordial
Special Investigations Agency: Sins and Secrets
Winter Warriors *(anthology)*

About the Author

ഩ

Suspenseful, erotic, edgy, thrilling, romantic, adventurous. All these words are used to describe award-winning, best-selling novelist Denise A. Agnew's novels. Romantic Times Magazine called her romantic suspense novels *Dangerous Intentions* and *Treacherous Wishes* "top-notch romantic suspense." With paranormal, time travel, romantic comedy, contemporary, historical, erotica, and romantic suspense novels under her belt, she proves her gift for writing about a diverse range of subjects. (Writing tales that scare the reader is her ultimate thrill.)

Denise's inspiration for her novels comes from innumerable sources, but the fact she has lived in Colorado, Hawaii, and the United Kingdom has given her a lifetime of ideas. Her experiences with archaeology have crept into her work, as well as numerous travels throughout England, Ireland, Scotland, and Wales. Denise currently lives in Arizona with her real life hero, her husband.

Denise welcomes comments from readers. You can find her website and email address on her author bio page at www.ellorascave.com.

FIRST AND LAST

Suz deMello

ജ

Glossary

Bet Din: group of community elders charged with judging issues

Chanukah: Jewish holiday, eight days long, commemorating an historical event when Jews (again) narrowly escaped destruction; celebrated by a combination of prayer and partying

cheder: school

chuppah: traditional Jewish marriage locale, a decorated canopy under which the ceremony takes place. Symbolizes the overarching presence of God.

dreidel: a four-sided spinning top used at Chanukah

ema: mother

goy: non-Jewish person

kinder: children

Kosher: food that is Kosher complies with strict Jewish ritual and law as to its content and preparation.

latkes: potato pancakes, traditional Chanukah food

maydel: Shayna maydel, a pretty girl

menorah: nine-branched candelabrum used at Chanukah

meshugah: crazy

mishegass: craziness, insanity

moil: person who performs ritual circumcisions on male Jewish babies at the age of eight days. These days, usually a pediatric urologist

shaygetz: non-Jewish man

shidduch: arranged marriage

shiva: part of the Jewish ritual of mourning, during which mourners gather in the home of the bereaved and remember the departed.

shtup: to shag

yenta: busybody

yeshiva: secondary school

zaftig: pleasingly plump, voluptuous

Trademarks Acknowledgement

The author acknowledges the trademarked status and trademark owners of the following wordmarks mentioned in this work of fiction:

Clue: Hasbro, Inc.

Chapter One

New Brooklyn, Luna
Chanukah, 2114

Thank God it was the end of the evening. Turning her back on her date, Shayna wiped her mouth on her sleeve and closed the sli-door to seal the pod with a disgusted flick of her finger, then stomped into the kitchen, where the mild aroma of hydroponically grown coffee lingered.

"So what was wrong with this one?" Shayna's mother asked, cradling a mug.

Shayna bent to kiss her mother's cheek, hiding her blush. She wasn't going to discuss her date's make-out style with her *ema*. "He, umm, he hovers."

"He *vacuums*? Shayna, what are you talking about?"

"Not Hoovers, *ema*, he hovers. He practically breathed down my neck when I ate my *latkes*." Shayna carried her mother's empty mug to the sonic cleaning unit. Hoovering didn't begin to describe what her date did with his mouth. Shayna had considered herself lucky to escape him with her tongue, teeth and tonsils still in their proper places. She liked deep kissing, but spraining her tongue at the root was a no-no.

"Such a nice boy, and a doctor to boot."

"He'd make me *meshugah*."

"You'll have to go to the matchmaker for a *shidduch*."

Shayna's jaw tightened as she put the mug inside the unit, then tapped a button. The soni-cleaner hummed. "Please, no. I'm capable of finding a husband for myself."

"You've been dating since you were sixteen. You've gone out with every single man in New Brooklyn, most more than once," her mother said. "I don't know what you're looking for."

Shayna's mind flashed on the image of a tall dark man with smiling gray eyes and a demanding kiss.

Her mother continued, "This one hoovers, that one's too short…there's no alternative. If you don't marry soon, you'll have to go live on Earth. You know the rules."

Shayna cast a fearful look upward. She'd never been to her home planet, and didn't want to go. Earth consisted of armed enclaves surrounded by post-Apocalyptic *mishegass*. On Earth, a Jew was safe only in Beverly Hills, Miami, and Israel.

Those who'd created New Brooklyn had dreamed of completely safe, wholly Jewish outposts on a pristine worldlet. In exchange for their security, stringent rules governed conduct. Skilled personnel were at a premium, forcing the able-bodied to work and produce young to continue this, their great experiment. At twenty-four, Shayna was pushing the age limit.

"All right." She sighed. "I'll try a *shidduch*."

* * * * *

Trained as a cultural anthropologist, Dr. Rivka Markowitz was a valued member of New Brooklyn, not merely because she kept the peace and the laws as a member of the *Bet Din* ruling council, but she played matchmaker. In a small, tight community, the strength of family bonds was crucial. The young men and women who had to marry and bear children while young had to be assured of appropriate mates. Thus, the value of a skilled matchmaker who could create a successful *shidduch*, an arranged marriage that would flourish.

The next morning, Shayna tapped at the sli-door of Rivka's tiny office. The door opened, revealing Rivka's podlet, cluttered with bones, skulls and other unnerving detritus of the anthropologist's calling. She sneezed, the dust from the artifacts tickling her nose.

Rivka, a diminutive brunette dressed in the same silvery Slicksuit everyone wore, looked up. "Ah, Shayna Goldstein. I've been expecting you."

Grumpy, Shayna moved a stack of infodiscs and sat in the armchair Rivka indicated. "And which of the gossipy *yentas* infecting this town tattled?"

"Your *ema* phoned ahead. She thought it would be polite." Rivka smiled. "But I'd expected you long before this day. Couldn't handle the way Harold Mechlin smells, or how Jim Abrams kisses?"

Shayna burst out laughing. She bet that Rivka was good at her job. She'd put Shayna at ease in the wink of an eye. "I needed a towel, the way he slobbers. And the sucking! I had to check to make sure my teeth were still in place."

"So I've heard. I'll get him married somehow," Rivka said. "All of the *emas* think that their sons are such princes that they won't come to me. But everyone ends up here eventually."

"Everyone?"

"Just about. Very few on Luna entrust their futures to a random selection process based on hormones." Opening her drawer, Rivka withdrew a carved wooden box. "Sometimes they merely want their choice confirmed. Others, like you, can't quite make up their minds." She passed the box to Shayna.

Shayna lifted the lid, then raised her brows. "Tarot cards?"

Rivka winked. "Most people don't know the tarot is based on the Zohar, ancient Jewish mysticism. These cards have been modified to receive the emotional and mental vibrations of the user, and have been previously programmed with the identities of all the single folk on Luna. Go on, take them out."

The tarots felt peculiarly heavy and greasy in Shayna's hands. If they were programmable, that accounted for their weight since each card would contain chips or computers of some sort. Dubious, she flipped them through her fingers. They vibrated gently, perhaps responding to her thought waves, or whatever. Sounded kinda hocus-pocus to feet-on-the-ground Shayna.

"Divide the deck into three on the desk, here."

Shayna followed Rivka's direction.

"Turn over the top card on each stack."

Shayna obeyed. "Colonel Mustard, in the library, with the candlestick?"

Rivka frowned as Shayna mocked the old and honored game of *Clue*. She tapped a finger on the first card, which depicted a dark moon beneath a sky full of stars. The Earth, normally a constant companion in the heavens, was absent.

"You are to go to Farside," Rivka said.

"Farside!" A chill zipped up Shayna's back despite her Slicksuit, designed to keep body temperature stable.

Rivka tossed the second card at Shayna. It showed a circle of dancers surrounding a *menorah.* "The Chanukah party at Farside. You will see your intended there."

"How will I know him?"

Rivka held up a third, last card, which depicted a dark man. A head taller than his companions, he regarded them with an air of authority. Another shiver chased the first up Shayna's spine. This was her mate, her one true love?

A dark man. Could it be…?

"Michael Jordan?" Shayna hid her nerves with a quip about the first African-American president of the now-defunct U.S. republic.

Rivka glared.

"Sorry." Shayna shrank back into her seat. "But there are many dark males here. I'm sure Farside is no exception."

"Your intended will know you. Few moon children are redheaded, remember?"

"But who is he?"

Rivka smiled. "The only possible mate for you." She shuffled the tarots together before putting them away.

"But I don't want to live on Farside!"

Rivka's smile disappeared. "Why not?"

"I want to stay in New Brooklyn. I was born here. This is my home." Shayna rose to pace, as best she could, Rivka's tiny podlet office.

"Apparently it's time you left the cocoon." Rivka tapped the top of the carved box. "The programming in these tarots has a reliability factor of over ninety-nine and forty-four one-hundredths percent. I assure you, your mate is correctly selected."

"But why do I have to go?" Shayna wailed.

"'Whither thou goest, I shall go.'"

Shayna's shoulders slumped as she recognized the ancient words from the book of Ruth.

"It is time for you to commit to something beyond yourself, *Shayna maydel*."

Chapter Two

Shayna boarded the ziptrain to Farside with both dread and excitement warring in her soul. A quasi-military outpost, the Farside colony, new and primitive, was populated by many peoples, not only Jews. Shayna, born a moon child in New Brooklyn, had never met a *goy*. She couldn't be fated to marry a *shaygetz*, but what Jew would separate himself from his people? More than a religious enclave, their community held life, culture, laughter and, most of all, freedom. Shayna had seen ancient flix of Old Earth, where her people had nearly been persecuted out of existence by the prejudiced. Why would one wish to live among the hateful?

The ziptrain passed the remains of a burned-out shell of a hut, which Shayna could see clearly through the thick Plexiplus windows. She winced as she remembered what that hut had been—a storage structure, kept separate from the rest of New Brooklyn by their strict rules. A single spark struck from two banging metal canisters had sent the entire hut, which had contained gas cylinders, up to space in a massive explosion. Four people had been lost, blown to bits, including one of Shayna's *cheder* friends. The entire community had sat *shiva* for days, mourning the deceased, yet comforted by the presence of others.

What Jew would want to separate himself from his people?

The desolate moonscape outside the train reflected the chill fear in Shayna's heart. She loathed uncertainty, and until she met her mate, her future was clouded. But she wanted to marry, and not only because she desired to stay on the moon. The truth was, she was just plain horny. Though she was technically a virgin, she knew married couples, had dated plenty, and fooled around enough to realize she wanted to make love. She needed it. She dreamed of it every night, but wouldn't give herself to just anyone. She was picky.

Lulled by the train's smooth movements, her mind wandered to the first time she'd been kissed—really kissed—by a male.

When she'd turned thirteen and started at *yeshiva*, the secondary school she attended after graduating from *cheder*, she hadn't a clue about what was going on between the boys and girls. The air was constantly charged with a tension she now understood was born of sexual repression. Flirting and gossip about boys had dominated conversation.

And the prime topic had been Gideon Landers, even though *boy* had been the wrong word for him.

Gideon. Tall and dark, broad-shouldered and handsome, with a deep voice at age eighteen, he'd already matured. A Terran, Gideon and his parents had moved to New Brooklyn when the pogroms had wiped out the Jewish community on most of the Atlantic rim. Who knew what he'd seen and done? The girls whispered about the bulge in his Slicksuit, his burgeoning beard…he already shaved, and everyone wondered if he was still a virgin.

Shayna had tried to ignore the gossip. She'd claimed that he was arrogant, although her day didn't seem complete without seeing Gideon's smile, bright against his tanned skin, at least once. So she'd bantered with him, telling him jokes and anecdotes, just so she could see his smile. Years later she'd realized that she'd had a schoolgirl crush on him.

He'd graduated and joined the Officers Corps, but had returned to *yeshiva* to talk with students about joining the Corps. She'd been sixteen, and for the first time she'd seen him as a man, and a very sexy one at that.

He'd asked her out to coffee. They'd stayed late, closing the place down. When it was deserted, he'd pinned her in a chair with his much larger body and kissed her.

She remembered the strange sensation of someone else's tongue caressing her lips. Her mouth had opened in surprise, and he'd pushed his insistent tongue all the way in. Because he'd been straddling her and holding her close, she'd felt his heart pound through their Slicksuits. As his pulse speeded up, it seemed to echo her racing heart.

Everything in her body, every cell, every vein, seemed to ignite with a fire she'd never before experienced. Electricity zipped along her nerve endings. She'd become hot, her armpits had dampened, and sweat had slid along her skin. Though she knew her Slicksuit would convert the perspiration to usable water, she was still embarrassed. Was she supposed to react this way? She'd kissed boys before and this had never happened. Would he see how she was sweating and be repulsed?

He stroked her neck and the gentleness of his touch disarmed her completely. She'd grabbed onto his shoulders with shaking hands to anchor herself in the tumult of emotion and pushed her tongue back against his.

He'd taken that as some sort of signal and begun to move his tongue inside her mouth in a mesmerizing dance. She didn't know the tune, but improvisation seemed to be okay with Gideon. Their tongues played together endlessly, it seemed, and she could have kissed him forever. She reveled in his flavor, his unique scent…was it sandalwood? She didn't know, but she liked it.

Desire flamed through Shayna's body, bringing her back to the present. She tugged at her Slicksuit's collar, opening it. The ziptrain's recirculated air, a little stale, cooled her but still she squirmed in the seat, driving her wet pussy against the cushions. She was glad that the train's car was empty except for her, she could have an orgasm right here and now, and no one would know. And it would be easy. Just the memory of Gideon Landers' kiss turned her on.

He'd wanted more, had wanted to go further, and had. He clasped her breast, and she thought she'd go right out of her mind when one of his fingers flicked back and forth across her nipple. Even through her Slicksuit, it was the best thing she'd ever felt.

He'd eased his mouth away from hers to flutter kisses down her neck…oh heavens, was he going to kiss her breast? That would be too much for her. Would the Slicksuit dry out before she went home? How could she explain a big wet spot to her *ema*?

She'd pulled away, and he'd bitten her neck. With a yelp, she'd convulsed, driving a knee up and into him.

"Shit, Shayna!" Gideon howled.

"You bit my neck!" She'd been outraged.

"It's called a hickey, little girl." He massaged his crotch.

Stung, she snapped, "Don't call me a little girl, and don't do that in front of me."

He shot her a resentful look from beneath dark brows. "I'd like to do a lot more."

"You'll never get the chance."

After that awkward interlude, he'd left to continue his career in the Officers Corps. She assumed he'd be stationed very far away.

But now, looking back, she realized that she'd compared every subsequent kiss to that one. No man had come close to lighting her up the way Gideon had, damn him.

Leaning back her head and allowing it to be cradled by the seat's back, she let the memories of Gideon's touch envelop her. She ground her pussy into the cushion as she recalled his cool gray eyes, eyes that crinkled at the corners when he smiled or laughed.

Now, facing an arranged marriage, she wished she'd let Gideon go as far as he'd wanted. What could have happened?

He reached for the zipper at her neck, and slowly slid it down, revealing her breasts to his intent gaze. Cool air washed over her naked flesh, and her pink nipples tightened. He covered them with his big, sinewy hands. "Oh, God, Shayna..." he breathed. "You're so beautiful." He squeezed the globes, pinching the tips.

A moan escaped her lips as she palmed her breasts and imitated her fantasy lover. Her hard nipples peaked against the thin film of her Slicksuit. Desire raced to her core and her clit twitched with need. It rubbed against the Slicksuit, heightening her pleasure.

He lowered his head and took one nipple into his mouth, tonguing it harder, then gently closing his teeth over the aching nub. He pressed her breasts together and kissed each nipple... When his kiss intensified into a strong sucking, a fiery bliss shot from her breasts to her core.

She gasped, feeling the heat increase and her clit throb.

He sucked on her while his free hand insinuated itself between her legs, caressing her pussy. Even over the Slicksuit, his touch was knowing and experienced. He brought her to her first orgasm with sure strokes, holding her in a close and loving embrace.

Tension gripped every muscle, and Shayna looked around to make sure her car was still empty before opening the slit in her Slicksuit's crotch. She sought her pussy with needy fingers, first dipping a finger into her slit, delving for cream, then spreading it on her clit. Wanton need whipped through her body and her heartbeat sped as she imagined Gideon making love to her.

He unzipped her Slicksuit with steady hands. It fell away, revealing her naked to a man for the first time. But she didn't feel scared or shy. She wanted to please him, and knew she could. She reached for his zipper and drew it down, down...

She squeezed her clit between two fingers, wondering what Gideon's body looked like. As a teenager, he was lean but fit; all Luna's residents were. There wasn't enough food for anyone to be fat, and stringent requirements existed regarding work and exercise.

No doubt Gideon had grown into a perfect specimen. He always had been handsome, and maturity would have improved his looks. He'd have broad shoulders, narrow hips, muscular legs. Did he have a big cock? Thick or narrow, straight or curved?

Though still a virgin, Shayna and her friends sneaked around the rules by frequently indulging in oral sex. She knew the kind of cock she liked in her mouth—not too big, and if her date was thoughtful enough to shave his privates, so much the better.

Gideon's open Slicksuit revealed a perfect body. He'd retained his Terran tan, and a masculine mat of chest hair furred his developed pecs. She stroked his chest, marveling in the satiny softness of his skin overlaying muscle, solid as metal plates.

She slid her fingers down his hips and tore off the Slicksuit. His cock sprang out like a live thing, with a drop of pre-come glistening on its tip. She leaned forward and took him into her mouth all the way to the root.

With just a few strokes of her talented tongue, Gideon came, throwing back his head and crying out her name...

Shayna thrust a finger into her pussy and moaned. Fire scorched her nerve endings as she fantasized about making Gideon come. She curved her finger, seeking her G-spot, and rubbed it while caressing her clit with her thumb.

She was close, oh, so deliciously close, when a hiss told her that the ziptrain's door had opened. Sharp and hot, her orgasm whipped through her. Quivering, she slouched in her seat, hoping that whoever had entered hadn't seen what she was doing. Turning her head, she saw in the window's reflection that a young couple had entered the car. The man was holding the woman around the waist and was gripping her breast with his other hand. Giggling, they collapsed into seats to continue their love play, apparently without seeing Shayna, who hastily closed her Slicksuit.

She rested in her seat, letting her orgasm reverberate around her body, but her bliss was short-lived. Nothing could relax her busy brain. As wonderful as her memories of Gideon made her feel, she resented the hold that one kiss had on her imagination. She couldn't help dreaming of Gideon Landers, fantasizing about him, and that wasn't good.

Now she had a *shidduch*. But what if she didn't like the way this one kissed? What if he slobbered, or sucked too hard, or drew blood? How could she give herself to someone who couldn't even *kiss*? What if he couldn't match the brief moment she'd shared with Gideon? Away from New Brooklyn, her friends and family, she'd be alone with only a loveless marriage and old memories to sustain her.

What if her only satisfaction would come from a fantasy lover?

She dropped her face into her hands and sucked in deep breaths. You're a moon child, she told herself. A pioneer, committed to a greater goal than your stupid happiness. If it's to be, it's to be. So stop whining!

The efficient ziptrain stopped at Shayna's destination all too soon. She'd wanted more time to contemplate her future. That she'd soon meet her husband, she had no doubt. Rivka Markowitz's matchmaking skills were legendary.

A map in the ziptrain showed that Farside consisted of several globular, metal domes connected by sealed Plexiplus tubes, with the ziptrain station at the hub. At least, Shayna hoped that everything was properly sealed. She adjusted the cuffs of her Slicksuit, pulling out the retractable gloves to cover her hands. Shoving her braid down her back, she lifted her transparent cowl to encase her face and head before stepping out of the ziptrain onto the platform. The suit would recycle all her bodily wastes and convert them into usable gases and liquids; the wearer could survive in the chill vacuum of the moon for several days, if necessary.

Then she noticed she was the only person on the platform suited from head to toes. Feeling like a fool, she pushed the gloves back as a dark man standing on the platform laughed in her face.

Shayna stiffened as she met a pair of amused gray eyes belonging to Gideon Landers.

* * * * *

Gideon had recognized her the moment she'd stepped off the train, though he hadn't seen her for years. Redheads were rare but, more significantly, Shayna had made an impression on him. He often remembered when he'd pinned her down in a chair and kissed her silly. She'd seemed to enjoy it before he lost control and bit her neck. Then she'd kneed him where it counted, hard. Much later he'd realized that his eagerness had frightened Shayna, a young sixteen.

The moon children often said Terran girls were easy, and after moving to New Brooklyn, he'd realized they were right, at least by lunar standards. Even as a teenager he'd gotten a lot more action on Earth than he ever saw on the moon, with its rigid religious culture.

Hopefully Shayna had gotten over that incident.

She'd grown into a knockout, a bit *zaftig*, maybe, but he didn't like scrawny women. Her Slicksuit defined an hourglass body with breasts that deserved the adjective "glorious". The air filtration system bore her scent toward him. She wore a subtle flowery fragrance that didn't disguise the aroma of a very sexy woman.

Her hazel eyes met his and shock blanked her face. He grinned, enjoying her discomfiture when she recognized him.

Shayna tugged down her cowl before shooting him a long, cool look. Then a flush spread beneath the freckles dotting her creamy skin. "You're not—you're not—"

"I'm afraid so. Rivka Markowitz strikes again." He offered her his arm.

Horror suffused her features. She apparently hadn't forgotten that one little nibble.

"But—but he's dark." She pointed at a rasta-haired maintenance worker. "Rivka said a dark man!"

"Shame on you. You'd marry a *shaygetz*? Marlon's a Rastafarian."

She blinked. He'd bet a lunar c-note she'd never heard of a rasta.

He continued, "Besides, you're the only carrot-top in this place, and my tarots were very clear. It's you and me, kid." He hauled her toward a trans-tube.

She followed. "Why aren't you married yet? You must be twenty-nine, at least."

"Thirty, and I'm flattered you remember. Officers get a special dispensation to delay marriage."

"Where are we going?"

He was pleased to see how easily she fell into step with him. "To the old folks' common room. I want you to meet my mother."

Shayna stopped short. "I'm not going to marry you to take care of your *ema*."

Heedless of anyone who could be watching, he spun her against the Plexiplus wall of the tube, trapping her with his body, molding her soft, warm curves against him. Twisting her braid around his hand, he eased her head back and kissed her indignant, pouting mouth until it opened and she returned the kiss. He forced one knee between her legs so she sat on his upper thigh.

Lifting his head, he made sure the tube was empty. "I'm not marrying you for my mother's sake," he ground out. He'd been unbearably excited when he received Rivka's email. Shayna Goldstein! Marrying Shayna could make his favorite erotic scenarios come to vivid life.

Because of the lack of action on the moon, Mary Palm and her Five Fingers often had to suffice, and as he pumped his cock, his favorite fantasy was of Shayna. In his dreams she'd been a little older, more experienced, and very willing to let him have his way with her.

And he did, often. In his imagination, he'd done Shayna every possible way in every possible position. He wondered how she'd react if she discovered she'd been his fantasy lover for years.

"Why do you want to marry me, then?" she asked.

"For this." He kissed her, cupping one of her wonderful globes. Sweet heavens, she was a dream come true. He longed to feast on her breasts, push them together into a tunnel for his questing cock, and when he was done, pillow himself on them and rest…then wake up and make love to her again and again.

Her female scent intensified, arousing him all the more. He gripped her breast with a desperate palm, then slid his other hand down her body to her hip, where he pressed her crotch against his erection, hot and hard beneath his Slicksuit. He moved, searching for the sweetest spot. When she jerked against him, he knew he'd found her clit. "Bless Rivka and her magic cards," he murmured.

Shayna gasped. Gideon's strength, his male potency, overwhelmed her. Though he was her favorite fantasy, she'd forgotten his intensity, and hers, when they were together. And he was even more handsome than she remembered. He'd lost his Terran suntan, but maturity had given his face a hard angularity that was both commanding and sexy. She liked his pleasant sandalwood fragrance. Yes, it was sandalwood she remembered, and the scent brought back all her memories of how wonderful Gideon could be.

He ground his pelvis against hers, hitting her clit on just the right spot. He rubbed his hard-on back and forth, massaging her already happy pussy toward another orgasm while he explored her mouth with his tongue, demanding and tender at the same time. She thought she'd faint, but at the same time she'd never felt so alive.

Gideon knew he'd been the first man to kiss her and, by God, he'd be the last, her one and only lover. He didn't stop caressing her until her body wrenched against his as she came in his arms. A delicate moisture beaded her brow.

He kissed the sexy sweat of her release, delighted by her response. "Yes, baby, like that. Every day and every night. You and me." When could he get her into bed? She'd come, but he was tense with need.

She continued shaking in his arms, then sagged against the wall. "Like that? Every day?"

"Like that, and you know, there's a lot more." Smiling into her beautiful hazel eyes, he hugged her close, letting her feel his arousal.

Shayna recovered herself with a deep breath. "I know that. I'm not a little girl anymore. I'm not completely inexperienced." She shoved her hips against his, a blatant signal.

Yes! "Really? Show me."

"A challenge? Interesting." She narrowed her eyes, then pushed him against the wall before kneeling at his feet. She reached for his Slicksuit's crotch and opened the slit with nimble fingers.

"Ohhh, Shayna…" Gideon let his head sag against the clear Plexiplus wall, glad that no one inhabited Farside's eternal night. Clearly Shayna was no stranger to blowjobs. Maybe New Brooklyn girls had learned a thing or two since he'd left to pursue his career.

She started slow, teasing his cock's tip with tiny flicks of her tongue. He throbbed, wanting to bury himself deep inside her mouth, ram all the way back to her throat. But at the same time, he wanted to experience what Shayna had to offer. What kind of a lover would she be?

Evidently not a shy or tentative one, since she knew her way around a man's cock. Her pink, sensuous lips wrapped around his cock head and she sucked, her cheeks hollowing. His rod got harder…he was damn close. Normally he could last a long time, but this was Shayna, his fantasy woman, and damn, she was good.

No, she was great. She took him in all the way, then opened her mouth, allowing his cock to rest on her warm tongue while she breathed, washing the top with a blast of cooler air. The effect was electric, galvanizing, and he lost control. He grabbed her head and pushed into her throat, forcing her to take him deep. He rocked from side to side to heighten his sensations. Hot and sweating, he scrabbled at his zipper, pulling it down to cool his chest.

About to come, he swelled in her mouth. She grabbed the base of his cock and gave him a firm pinch.

"Whoooaaa..." It felt good, but stopped his orgasm. Gideon swore. "Where the hell did you learn how to do that?"

Laughing, she pulled out to lick the underside of his glans. That was his most sensitive spot, and he again dug his hands into her hair, desperate to drive deep for his release.

Damn her, she eased away again to rub her face on his balls. The soft skin of her cheeks against his tender scrotum was unbearably stimulating, and he groaned, "Please, Shayna, please..."

She looked up at him and winked. "Okay," she said.

But she wasn't going to bring him off quickly, Shayna decided. Now that she had Gideon begging, she was going to make him wait. Maybe it was unfair, but he was going to pay for that "little girl" remark he'd made years ago.

She licked the base of his balls, than ran her tongue up his rod to the round head and rimmed it. Gideon had a gorgeous cock, not too long or too stubby, and just the right thickness for her. Dark, like him, it was straight and sexy. She imagined his cock entering her, and heat arced to her pussy as she sucked him again. Gideon's groans increased in pitch, and he thrust his hips forward, seeking the back of her throat. *Not so fast, officer,* she thought. *You're mine and I'm gonna keep you right where I want you.*

She did it again, then licked his sweet cock as though he was a lollipop before taking it in. Instead of sucking, she rotated her head so that it knocked around the inside of her mouth, hitting teeth, tongue, lips and the insides of her cheeks randomly while she clenched her fist around its base.

His cock head swelled, and she tasted the unmistakable flavor of pre-come, felt its sticky texture on her tongue.

"Yessss..." Gideon began to come in her mouth, and she let go of him to deep throat him, bury her face in his pubic hair, smelling his good male scent, a scent she'd never entirely forgotten. She gulped, swallowed, licked her lips, pleased she'd taken all of him, everything he had to give.

She stood and stretched, regarding Gideon with satisfaction. He was slumped against the Plexiplus wall, eyes closed, looking as though someone had whacked him over the head. His limp cock lay against his Slicksuit, and she bent to give it a tender little kiss before tucking it back inside and sealing the slit.

He opened one eye and looked at her, still visibly stunned.

She winked at him. "So let's think about getting married. Perhaps Rivka's right."

"I, uh, yeah." He roused himself and hauled away from the wall, zipping up his Slicksuit. "Of course she's right. When has she been wrong?"

"Never, as far as I know."

He reached for her and slid an arm around her waist. "Thank you."

She raised a brow. "For what?"

"That was the most fantastic b.j. ever." Reclaiming his self-control and his manners, Gideon took his hip flask and offered her a sip of water.

"Thank you." She sipped daintily. "So you'll never again call me a little girl?"

"Hell, no. Hey, let's set a date."

"Maybe we'll marry, but with one condition." She handed back the flask.

His smile slipped. "What's that?"

"I want to live in New Brooklyn." Shayna's mouth had taken on a mulish twist.

He sucked in a breath. "I can't promise that, love. I'm an officer. I have to go where I'm sent. Besides, what's wrong with Farside?"

"What's right with Farside?" Pulling away, she put her hands on her hips.

He tried not to be insulted, but he felt he and his companions had done a good job at the colony. "Farside is fascinating. It's full of new people and new things."

"I want to live in New Brooklyn with my people."

"There are plenty of Jews on Farside," he said with exasperation. Had she given him that blowjob with the hope of softening him up for this demand? And what the hell was wrong with her? For the first time, he doubted Rivka's selection. As the commander's wife, Shayna would have to mix with all kinds of people and get along with everyone. "How can you be so narrow? Can't you give us a chance?"

She stopped short, a pensive look stealing over her face. "I—I suppose you're right."

He took her arm again. "I promise you, you'll find New Brooklyn dull after you've experienced Farside. Come with me."

Chapter Three

Holding her hand in a firm grasp, he led her back to the ziptrain station, then took a different Plexiplus tube to another area of Farside. As they headed toward the dome, Shayna could smell a variety of aromas—*latkes* frying, a woman's perfume, disinfectant. She guessed they were heading toward Farside's residences.

"How many people live here?" she asked.

"About twenty families per dome. We learned from the errors of New Brooklyn, and instead of large domes with hundreds of families, we constructed Farside as a series of hives surrounding a central core, the transportation center."

"Why do you consider New Brooklyn to be poorly constructed?" She couldn't help sounding huffy, but her father had been one of New Brooklyn's original engineers.

He sighed. "Shayna, if you're going to take offense at every remark I make, this is going to be a difficult relationship."

"I'm not offended, just curious." She squeezed his hand, just to show him she really wasn't upset.

"It's easier to build slowly, provide services to people a few at a time. Granted, there's some replication of machinery, but it seems to work out. There are fewer breakdowns because the equipment isn't as stressed." He gave her a slight smile and squeezed back. "Your father would have approved. He designed Farside, you know."

"I know. Farside's schematics were his last project."

He led her up an escalator to the dome's top. Pressing a pad at a sli-door, Gideon opened it and led her inside…inside what?

The interior was dim. Above, the transparent dome exposed Farside's dark sky, rippling with stars. The Milky Way spread across the black heavens like a diamond bracelet, furnishing the only light in the room.

She tipped her head back. "Where are we? The observation dome?"

"A good guess, but no." Releasing her hand, Gideon flicked a switch. A soft glow illuminated a comfortable sitting room. "This is my—our—home."

Overwhelmed, she put both hands to her face. "Oh, my goodness." She walked around slowly, looking at objects, occasionally touching one or another. Again, he let her explore. Wonderful how he seemed to instinctively sense that she needed to accustom herself in her own time.

After she'd looked her fill, he went to her and took her in his arms. More commanding than ever, Gideon's embrace demanded her response. Enveloped in his heat, Shayna reached for his head, framing his beautiful face between her palms. "I can't believe you're not married. Farside girls must be stupid."

He chuckled. "I was waiting for you, Shayna."

She knew when she was being mocked. "No." She turned away.

He pulled her back. "Yes. Believe it. Don't you remember when we kissed?"

Telltale warmth suffused her cheeks. "Um, well, yeah."

"You weren't the only one who found it memorable."

She reached between his legs, touched him, found him hard and ready. "Memorable for the right reasons, I hope."

He groaned and pushed himself against her, filling her hand. His length, his heat, his thickness turned her on to an unbearable pitch. She wanted him, and she could tell from the expression on his face that he knew it.

"You didn't hurt me, if that's what you mean." His voice sounded odd, a little raspy.

"Good. I could tell earlier that you're in, uh, good working order." She bit her lip and squeezed his hard, heavy rod.

"Shayna, unless you want me to put this inside you, please stop."

"I want you to."

Shocked but delighted—heck, this was Shayna Goldstein hitting on him *again*—Gideon gripped her shoulders. "I thought you weren't sure about us, about marriage, and living in Farside or wherever the Officers Corps sends me."

"I'm not sure." Her voice was low and tense. "I'm not sure about the future at all. But I'm sure about wanting you. I always have been."

"Oh, baby." He reached for the zipper of her Slicksuit and tugged down the tab, eager to see the luscious breasts he'd so often imagined in his dreams. With shaking hands, he opened the silvery suit encasing her and released them.

Big white globes popped out, tipped with pale pink nipples. Dizzy with delight, he passed one hand over them and sighed with pleasure when her nipples stiffened, growing hard and hot at his slightest touch. He bent his head and sucked the nearest one into his mouth.

Shayna moaned, arching her back so more of her tit thrust into his mouth. "Gideon, please, please make love to me."

Yes. This was how he'd win her, by making their first encounter perfect. A sensuous woman like Shayna wouldn't be able to resist the lure of great sex. She was experienced, but she obviously hadn't found the right lover...otherwise, why would she still be single?

Gideon was sure he was the man for her, and vice versa.

He lifted her in his arms and carried her to his bedroom. Again, the room was lit only by the heavens in their glory. He laid her on his bed, then knelt between her spread legs to look at her. The half-open Slicksuit framed glorious breasts, with one nipple wet and hard, the other pink and soft, waiting for his eager mouth.

But he didn't want to rush. He reached for her long red braid and brushed the end over her breasts until both nipples stood at attention.

The subtle caress ignited Shayna's sensitive skin, and she wanted more. She rocked her torso back and forth. "Oh God, Gideon."

He wanted to use the braid to bind her breasts, make them peak high and pointed, but couldn't, it wasn't long enough. So he eased off her Slicksuit down to the waist and wrapped the suit's arms around one globe and then the other, tightening the stretchy fabric until her breasts stood like sexy little mountains on her torso. He pinched her nipples, watching the blood flow into them until they elongated. Then he sucked, hard, first on one and then the other. The engorged flesh hardened and he rubbed his stubbly cheeks over her nipples to heighten her pleasure. A moan told him that her breasts were as sensitive as they were beautiful. He was delighted that Shayna's breasts loved to be touched as much as he loved to touch them.

He clenched his hands around her incredible tits and lowered his head between them, then pushed them together, creating a fragrant nest he never wanted to leave. Untwisting her Slicksuit from around her breasts, he watched them soften and release. He couldn't resist those yielding, pillowy mounds, and he again rubbed his face against them, sighing with pleasure.

Shayna ran her fingers through his hair, then pushed his shoulders, creating some space between them. Sitting up, she reached for him with frantic hands. She tore his Slicksuit's zip down, then ran her fingers over his chest, visibly delighting in the rough texture of his curls adorning it and the solid muscles beneath.

While she explored him, he continued to caress her, cupping and fondling her breasts, pinching the nipples until fire shot through her from her tits to her clit. She gasped with pleasure. "Please, please kiss them some more."

He pushed her back onto the pillows and pressed her breasts together, taking both nipples into his mouth, rubbing his face in her cleavage. The rasp of his beard lit her on fire, and she writhed beneath his weight. Running her hands down his sides, she grabbed his Slicksuit and started to wrestle the tight fabric off his body. She was desperate to see him naked, desperate to have him, to feel him inside her.

He pulled away and stood. Bereft, she stared at him, wondering what was going on. He put his hands on his hips, slid his thumbs under the Slicksuit and slowly eased it off, shimmying his hips, giving her a show she'd always remember. Though lit only by starlight, his body was amazing, the most perfect of God's creations, lean but sculpted. He wiggled the Slicksuit down, and it caught on his erection. She couldn't take her eyes off the fascinating sight.

He chuckled. "Interested, huh?"

She was already hot, and embarrassment heated her even more. "Um, yeah, so?"

He shoved the Slicksuit down to his ankles and off. Freed, his cock gleamed, long and hard in the starlight.

"Oh, my." Now the reality of what they were doing hit her, and she scrambled back against the headboard, both scared and thrilled.

"Shayna, after everything else you've done…are you still a virgin?"

"Uh, yeah."

He shot her a mock frown. "When were you gonna tell me?"

"Whenever it came up." She eyed his cock.

"Oh, it's up, all right." He laughed. "Don't worry, baby. I'll make it good. It'll be great, I promise."

Gideon used his weight to pin her against the pillows and kissed her until the tension in her body eased. Then he laid her flat on the bed and again attacked those bounteous breasts, kissing, nibbling and loving… He'd never tire of the flavor and feel of her nipples in his mouth, but when she moaned and bucked beneath him, he sensed she was ready for more.

He licked down the midline of her body until he came to her Slicksuit bunched around her waist. As he kissed her belly, he tugged it down and off, with Shayna cooperating by lifting her pelvis.

Now she was naked, and although he longed to feast on her juicy, red-furred pussy, he took a moment to appreciate Shayna nude—her hourglass body, perfect white skin, and shapely hips crowned by that enticing red muff.

"Turn over, love, I want to see your, umm…" *Ass* might be too vulgar a word for Shayna. "Backside," he said.

Chuckling, she obeyed, then turned her head to fling him a come-hither look and a wink. "So, do you like your Kosher piece of ass?"

Startled, he laughed. "Shame on you, Shayna Goldstein. Using a crude term like that in a holy moment like this one."

"This is a holy moment?"

"For me it is. You're my dream come true." He sat beside her and ran reverent fingers over the curves of her ass and up her spine, admiring the delicate skin. He dropped a light kiss on each butt cheek before rolling her over.

He scooted to the end of the bed near her feet and spread her legs. A flaming beacon, her muff beckoned him. He slid forward and kissed her pussy, then pushed his tongue between her labia. "Mmm, good, but not enough." He opened her thighs, opened *her*, to his gaze.

She was gorgeous. Her engorged clit reddened as he watched, changing from a delicate pink pearl to a hard red ruby, almost as though it sought to reach his mouth.

"Oh my God." She pressed her palms to her face.

"Enjoy, baby. This is just for you." He licked her clit.

Groaning, she spread her legs wider and bent her knees, shoving her pussy harder against his mouth.

He thrust his tongue inside her, then raised his head to say, "God, you're tasty."

She laughed a little breathlessly. "I am?"

"Oh, yeah, baby. You're delicious. Try it."

"What?"

Gideon crawled up her body and kissed her on the mouth.

"Hmm. Salty. Yeasty, and maybe a little sweet. Interesting."

"Delicious is more like it." He dived back down for another bout, determined to get her off before he took her. He licked her sweet little clit, took it between his lips and sucked while thrusting a finger into her.

Hot, wet, tight. He closed his eyes, dreaming of the moment—very soon—when he'd sink his cock into her sweet virgin flesh. He eased his finger in and out of her while continuing to suck her off. Shayna's hips banged up and down in time with his finger's rhythmic movements. Her cream flowed, drenching his hand. Though her channel flexed around him, she'd loosened…was she starting to come?

Her moans and sighs increased to panting gasps. He pulled out his finger, and her eyes popped open. "Oh, don't stop!"

"Trust me, baby." Kneeling between her legs, he lifted her hips and shoved a pillow under her so he could put his cock head to her slit. Her moan increased in pitch as he penetrated her, feeling her tissues part for his rod. She squealed and squirmed.

He stopped. "Too much?"

"No—yes. I don't know! It hurts, but oh God, it's so good…" Her voice trailed off into a groan.

Better a fast tear than a slow, agonizing pain, he decided, and thrust all the way inside her to the balls. The pleasure blasted him into outer space, but she shrieked, grabbing his shoulders and digging in her nails. He groaned and slid one hand between them, fumbling for her clit. He found the swollen nubbin and rubbed it between his fingers until her sobbing breaths evened, then rose into pleasured whimpers and sweet little cries of completion.

Though he'd come, he decided to stay inside her until she had another orgasm.

Shayna felt him swell again inside her tender sheath and she wondered, *how can he do it? He's come twice in the last hour or so and somehow, he's hard again…can I keep up?*

"This is just for you, baby," he murmured into her ear.

He nipped the lobe and ground his pubic bone against her clit. She raised her legs and spread them wide, giving him greater access. He thrust fully into her and she moaned, tightening herself around his burgeoning cock. It hurt, because she was sore from being taken so hard, but she was wet with her cream and his come, so it was good. She could tell that the longer she had sex, the better it was going to become.

"This is incredible… Why did I wait?"

"You were waiting for me," he growled into her ear. "Admit it. You're mine, and we'll marry."

She didn't say anything, wanting to keep him on the edge. And how could she be so sure so soon? The sex was overwhelming, threatening to swamp her good sense. She couldn't make a decision with Gideon inside her.

With an impatient grunt, he swiveled his hips against her, and she moaned, the pressure on her clit turning her on yet again.

"Tell me." He rammed his cock in and out.

She moaned, incoherent, as lightning blasted through her, shooting her up to the stars, toward another orgasm.

He pulled out of her and turned her over. "Get on your hands and knees."

His voice was impatient, rough, and she was afraid, but only a little. But another part of her wanted whatever Gideon had in store.

He kneed her legs apart and reached for her pussy, fingering her, opening her...she felt the swollen tissues part for his hand. Then he entered her again, and this way was different, a sharper pleasure than with him on top of her. It should have been demeaning, animalian, but oh, it was so sexy that she came fast and hard, banging her hips back against his. He reached around her and gripped her clit, rubbing their combined sex juices into it, fueling her orgasm so it went on and on. Grabbing her hips, he came in her. "Ahh, Shayna..."

She collapsed beneath him. He rolled to her side and pulled her in close. A minute or two later, she could tell by his breathing that he'd gone to sleep.

Overwhelmed by what they'd done, Shayna couldn't rest. The choices she faced still oppressed her. Yes, lovemaking was extraordinary, and there was no doubt in her mind that Gideon was the perfect lover and husband for her. But how could she leave her mother and her New Brooklyn friends? Could she adapt to life on Farside?

Chapter Four

A squawking voice from an intercom summoned Gideon back to consciousness and to awareness of his obligations. He groped for Shayna, who should have been by his side. Blinking, he saw her step out of his bathroom, hair neat and Slicksuit encasing her lush body, the body that now belonged to him.

"What's up?" she asked.

"We gotta go, babe." He cleaned up and dressed. He hated letting her out of his bedroom, but duty called, so he led her to the Community Dome for the Farside Chanukah party. The room was decorated with silver and blue streamers, six-pointed stars and cutout paper *dreidels*. A long table, laden with goodies, extended along one wall, while a circular platform with a large *menorah* dominated the center of the space. The room was filling with Slicksuited Farsiders.

"I thought we were going to visit your mother," Shayna said.

Gideon smiled. "We spent more time fooling around than I thought we would. We had to be on time for the party. Excuse me a moment." He didn't normally concern himself with the details of community events but wanted to ensure all would be flawless today. Shayna's introduction to Farside society had to be perfect.

Shayna, left on her own, adjusted. "Hi, I'm Shayna Goldstein," she said to the nearest person, a small man with surprising golden skin. She knew Asians, or Orientals, existed, but they never came to New Brooklyn. She tried not to stare at the fellow's honey-colored flesh and dark, almond-shaped eyes, but he looked so much like Mr. Sulu, in her favorite old vidflix, that she didn't want to tear her gaze away.

"Tadeo Kiramoto." He extended a hand covered with small scars and healed burns. "I think I remember your name. Are you related to the late Sam Goldstein?"

The condition of his hands told Shayna that Mr. Kiramoto was probably an applied engineer; they experienced myriad small mishaps in the course of their careers. "Sam was my father. You're an engineer?"

"Yes, I am. Your dad taught me everything I ever knew." His smile dimmed.

Shayna didn't need psychic cards to divine the golden man's thoughts. "It's okay. It's been a long time since my father passed on." She guessed that Mr. Kiramoto had been one of Sam's many protégés. Her father's apprentices had been devastated when he died back in 2109.

Kiramoto shook his head. "I'm sorry, but I'll never forget what happened…or your father. Long life to you, Shayna Goldstein."

Shayna, again surprised by the golden man, stammered, "And—and to you." That the Asian knew the proper ritual phrase was a real eye-opener. That her own father had known and worked with such an unusual person amazed her. Why had they never met?

"Welcome to Farside." Mr. Kiramoto's mood seemed to lift as he gestured to the food table. "Shall we? The candle-lighting ceremony will take place in a few minutes after the kids arrive."

Shayna edged closer to the goodies, moving carefully due to the soreness between her legs. It was a good soreness, though. She liked being reminded of Gideon's lovemaking with every move she made. But the ache in her pussy didn't mask her hunger. She hadn't eaten since before she'd boarded the ziptrain to Farside. Everything on the table looked familiar, except some slabs of what appeared to be raw fish. But that couldn't be. No Jewish dish consisted of raw fish. Smoked, definitely, but not raw. And this seemed to be slabs of raw fish placed upon chunks of sticky rice, bound together with—what? She sniffed. Seaweed?

"Try my sushi." Taking a plate from a stack at the end of the table, Kiramoto loaded it with gefilte fish, *latkes*...and also some of the odd food he called sushi.

She didn't want to upset him, because he seemed so nice. And, she thought, why not? She took a bite, then another, chewing the sweet, tender fish slowly and thoughtfully.

"It's good." Suddenly, something hotter than horseradish hit her tongue. She swallowed fast and hard. About to cough, she didn't want to spew half-eaten raw fish around the room. Eyes tearing, she turned an accusing gaze on Kiramoto.

Laughing so hard she thought he'd split his Slicksuit, Gideon appeared, a glass of water in hand. "A new experience for sheltered Shayna?" Handing the water to her, he winked at Kiramoto. "Didn't tell her about wasabi, did you, Tad?"

Kiramoto grinned at her, apparently unrepentant. "Commander." He nodded at Gideon, then tactfully slipped away.

Commander? She drank, then set down the glass on the nearest table. "People aren't telling me about a lot of things, are they?" she murmured to Gideon. "No wonder your quarters are so deluxe, Commander."

He gave her a cocky grin. "That would have been boasting. I am what I am, Shayna, and I won't apologize for my career." He took a piece of sushi from her plate. Lifting the fish off the rice, he showed her a greenish paste. "Wasabi mustard. Like horseradish, only more so."

"Made from a hydroponically grown vegetable?" Discovery of water deposits beneath the lunar poles had made civilization independent of Earth feasible, as had the gases found in pockets under lunar seas. Life here was precarious, but possible.

"Of course, just like the fish and the rice. Better, it's Kosher. What do you think?" He held the sushi to her lips.

"I like it." She took a bite, chewed and swallowed.

He ate the other half of the sushi. She raised her brows at the intimacy. But why not? Rivka's recommendation, along with Shayna's advancing age, made marriage a foregone conclusion. Then there was that scene in his quarters. She'd had no idea she'd succumb to Gideon so quickly, but she'd dreamed of him for so long that lovemaking seemed so natural, so right. She wouldn't have done that with any man unless she intended to wed…but she wasn't sure she wanted to marry him, was she?

She retained her concerns about Gideon's work. She liked Farside, found it interesting. But did she want to live here, away from her own people? And what of the future? The Lunar Officers Corps, charged with the protection of the moon's colonies, didn't have any retirees. Everyone seemed to die in action or, worse, be lost.

Shayna sighed. Her father had been killed, as had many on Luna. No assurance of a long future existed for any moon child.

Her thoughts scattered as Gideon kissed her, in full view of everyone in the crowded room. As much a declaration of intention as his proposal, or their lovemaking.

She kissed back. "You're the commander of Farside, so everyone's probably watching us." Gideon a commander, the commander of Farside. If she cared about social status, she'd be proud. Instead, she worried.

"Yes, I am, and yes, they are." That cocky grin again. "Get used to it."

Their conversation was interrupted when a gaggle of kids poured into the room. "*Cheder's* out," Gideon murmured into her ear, wanting to lick the delicate whorls. He tried to control his burgeoning arousal. Fantastic that she turned him on so much…he'd just had her, and now he wanted her again.

She nodded, a maternal smile covering her face. "They're only a little older than my kids."

"You teach school?"

"Yes, and sometimes work in the nursery. Wherever I'm needed."

"You like children, then. Good." Gideon imagined a baby, his son, suckling one of her magnificent breasts. His Slicksuit drew so tight at his crotch that if Shayna had cared to look, she could probably guess the angle the *moil* had held the blade at his ritual circumcision. He slipped behind her, hoping no one would notice.

She turned, her maternal smile replaced by a scowl. "Don't push me, Gideon."

His Slicksuit loosened. Damn. Shayna had grown into a tough cookie, feminine instincts notwithstanding. It would take more than great sex to manipulate Shayna. Good. He didn't like weak women. He needed a strong wife.

"Now, *kinder*!" One of the teachers accompanying the children tapped a spoon on a glass, drawing everyone's attention away from *dreidel* games, *latkes* and flirtation. "Before we light the candles, who wants to tell the story of Chanukah?"

Screeches arose. "I do! I do!" A field of waving hands sprang from the group of kids.

Gideon smiled. This was why his family had moved to Luna, so they could worship and learn in peace.

One boy, no more than eight, said breathlessly, "The bad Greeks and Syrians didn't want us to pray to God anymore an' they made us eat pig an' everything!"

"And they killed bunches of us!" Another kid chimed in.

Gideon saw Tad Kiramoto grin at the children's antics. This was why Gideon had joined the Officers Corps. He enjoyed working with people who were different, watching cultures collide, merge, then create something new and greater. He'd never live any place as boring and stultified as New Brooklyn. How could someone as intelligent as Shayna Goldstein stand it?

The teacher said, "That's very good, Nelson. Who can tell us about the miracle of Chanukah?"

"I can!" a little girl screamed. "The oil lamp in the temple lasted eight days instead of only two."

"Thank you, Dvora. Next time, please raise your hand. Rachelle, what's the true message of Chanukah?" The teacher pointed at a shy redhead with hazel eyes, much like Shayna at age thirteen.

The girl hesitated, tugging at a fat curl. "The message is tolerance." She had an unusual, deep voice.

"Tolerance?" Shayna asked, sounding surprised. "I always thought the message of Chanukah was God's ability to perform miracles."

"Not to me," Rachelle said. "The Greeks weren't wrong because they worshipped Zeus, but because they didn't allow us to pray to the Almighty, blessed be He."

Shayna blinked, her face taking on a thoughtful expression. Gideon wanted to drive the point home, but lost his chance when candles were lit by the children, prayers intoned and hymns sung. When the hubbub had calmed, he caught her sneaking toward the door.

He grabbed her arm. "Where are you going?"

"Home."

"Not yet. We're not done."

She blinked again. "We aren't? Haven't we done enough?" She shot him a flirtatious grin.

He tugged her out of the party room into a deserted corridor. "We'll never do that enough, but more importantly, you haven't given me an answer."

She kissed him, using a lot of tongue and rubbed her mound against his burgeoning erection. "Haven't I?"

"You had that condition. Don't you understand? I like it here."

She drew in a deep breath. "I like it too. I think. It's different and scary, but it's exciting and fun, isn't it?"

"Exactly! Oh, Shayna, I'll make you so happy!" He threw his arms around her and started to dance with her up and down the tube.

"Rivka told me I had to leave my cocoon and commit to something beyond myself. This is what she meant, wasn't it?"

"You're a smart girl, Shayna Goldstein."

She grinned, sliding her arms around his neck. "And there's this, too, isn't there? Every day and every night."

"Every day and every night." He bent his head to kiss her.

About the Author

ஐ

An award-winning, best-selling traditional romance novelist, Suz deMello uses a pseudonym to protect her privacy. But if you're a romance fan, you've probably read her books or have heard of her. She's known for layered, compelling novels charged with humor as well as emotion.

Of her journey to the steamier side of writing, Suz says, "I love writing traditional romances, but after several years in the same mode, I felt that I really needed to cut loose as a creative artist and write hot, sexy books that reflect the wilder side of being human."

Suz's books are fast-paced with seductive situations, complicated characters and a whole lot of kink!

Suz welcomes comments from readers. You can find her website and email address on her author bio page at www.ellorascave.com.

ONE NIGHT OF PLEASURE

Lynn LaFleur

Chapter One

He saw her standing with a group of three other women. Lust hit him like the force of a size thirteen combat boot rammed into his stomach.

That lust quickly dropped several inches, making his cock swell.

Jason Devereux tipped up his bottle of beer and took a healthy pull of the cold, foamy brew. He'd refused at first when his friend Austin had invited him to this party. Being alone on New Year's Eve wasn't exactly his idea of fun, but an evening of trying to be polite with people he didn't know held no appeal either.

Seeing her made him glad he'd changed his mind.

Long, light brown hair with a hint of wave. Ivory skin. Full lips made for kissing, and for sliding down his hard cock. Slightly above average height, probably about five-foot-six. She'd fit nicely against his six-foot frame.

He couldn't see the color of her eyes at this distance, but he'd bet they were green.

Jason's gaze slowly moved down her body. She wore a short-sleeved, vee-necked purple dress made of some slinky material. It clung to her curves, emphasizing her wide hips and generous breasts. Those breasts were large enough to fill his hands, and his hands weren't small.

He wondered if she had a round ass to match those luscious tits.

She laughed and turned toward one of her companions. Jason groaned to himself when he got a glimpse of her ass. Definitely round and as full as her breasts…perfect to hold while he pounded into her sweet pussy.

His cock swelled more at that mental image.

Austin had told him there would be plenty of women here who would spread their legs as soon as they were tapped on the shoulder. That sounded crude, but it was exactly what Jason wanted tonight.

One night of pleasure.

His love life lately had been nonexistent. Long hours at work left little time for play, plus he'd only been in North Texas for a month. A night of hot fucking with a warm, willing woman sounded perfect.

He wanted *her* to be that warm, willing woman.

It'd be rude of him to interrupt her while she talked with her friends. No matter. He could be very patient if he had to be.

Jason had no doubt she'd be worth the wait.

* * * * *

"He's still staring at you," Wanda said into her ear.

Gail Baxter looked over her shoulder. The tall, dark-haired man stood ten feet away, leaning against the end of one of the three bars set up in the large living room. Their gazes collided. With a crooked grin on his gorgeous mouth, he gestured at her with his beer bottle.

Gail sighed. What an incredible looking man. Thick, dark brown hair that almost touched his shoulders. Dark eyes. At least six feet tall. Broad shoulders. Wide chest. Flat stomach. Strong thighs. A healthy bulge between those thighs.

She'd bet her next paycheck that he knew exactly what to do with that bulge.

Wanda nudged her side. "You should go talk to him."

Returning her attention to her friend, Gail pushed her hair behind her ears. "I can't be so forward."

Diane snorted with laughter. "Since when?"

Eyes narrowed, Gail glared at her friend. "Are you insinuating I'm pushy?"

"Yeah, when you have to be. That's why you're such a successful doctor."

"Besides," Wanda said, "you came to this party to get laid."

Even though that was true, Gail didn't want it broadcast to everyone in the room. "Shh. Must you be so loud?"

"Who can hear me over The Rolling Stones?"

The fourth woman of the group, Lily, touched Gail's arm. "That man is hot and obviously wants to get in your panties. Go for it."

Lily was right and Gail knew it. She'd never had any trouble going after what she wanted in her professional life. She'd known from the time she was six years old that she wanted to be a doctor. She'd realized that dream. Now, at thirty, she was on staff at North Texas Highland Hospital in Fort Worth and very well respected in her field of cardiology, despite her young age.

Unfortunately, her personal life wasn't as successful. Her last relationship ended almost four months ago. The breakup was one of the reasons she'd moved to Fort Worth.

She drained her glass of Chardonnay. "I want a refill. Anyone else?"

Diane grinned wickedly. "You just want to get closer to that hunk."

Gail returned her grin. "Maybe."

Lily shrugged. "Like I said, go for it. You've been working twenty-six hours a day ever since you came on staff two months ago. You deserve a break with a hunky man."

No one knew better than Lily how many hours Gail worked. Lily was a surgical nurse at NTHH with Gail. Diane worked in Human Resources, Wanda in the lab.

Her friends were right. She *did* deserve a break with a hunky man…a break that included an entire night in his arms.

* * * * *

Jason straightened from his casual position and watched her walk right toward him. Her gaze connected with his a moment before she looked away. He continued to watch her as she walked past him and up to the bar.

The bartender smiled at her. "What can I get for you?"

"Chardonnay, please," she said, setting her empty glass on the bar.

Her soft voice wrapped around Jason, making him think of cool sheets and sweaty bodies. Oh, yes. This was definitely the woman he wanted to be with tonight. He took a step closer to her. "Hello."

She turned her head toward him and smiled. "Hello."

"I'm Jason."

"Gail."

"Here you go, ma'am," the bartender said as he set her glass of wine on the bar. He turned toward Jason. "Another beer, sir?"

"Sure. It's a party, right?"

"It's a *loud* party," Gail said.

"Music too much for you?"

"A little. I'm used to something…softer."

"How about if we go outside where it's quieter? I don't think the cold front has hit yet. It's still warm enough to stand on the patio."

She smiled again. "I'd like that."

After picking up his fresh bottle of beer, Jason took Gail's elbow and steered her toward the French doors that opened to the patio. He rubbed his thumb lightly over the inside of her elbow. Her skin felt as soft as velvet.

He longed to find out if her skin was as soft on other parts of her body.

Several people stood on the patio, laughing and talking. Jason led Gail to a corner so they'd have privacy to talk. He didn't realize a couple stood next to the house, sheltered by a large potted plant. They'd apparently slipped behind the plant to engage in some heavy necking.

It wasn't the first couple Jason had stumbled across tonight in the throes of passion.

Her blouse was unbuttoned, her bra strap pulled down her arm. The man cradled her bare breast in his hand, his thumb rubbing over her hard nipple. They kissed passionately while he caressed her. She didn't appear to mind the fondling one bit.

Gail cleared her throat. "Maybe we should go somewhere else."

"Yeah," Jason said, his voice raspy. He watched the couple another moment, his gaze focused on the man touching the woman's bare breast, before looking back at Gail. "Would you like to take a walk? I've never been here, but my friend told me the grounds are huge and well lighted."

"A walk sounds good."

Taking her elbow again, Jason guided her through the people on the patio and down the steps leading to the backyard. He used the crowd as an excuse to keep her close to his side.

"Does your friend own this place?" Gail asked.

"No. Austin works for Verilar Enterprises. This is the CEO's house."

"I think 'mansion' is a better description."

"True."

He led her through the maze of small tables that had been set up across the lawn to the last one. Pulling out a chair, he waited until Gail sat before taking the chair across from her. "It's a beautiful place, but I can't imagine living in something so big. I'd probably get lost on my way to the bathroom. That could be embarrassing."

She giggled. "I know what you mean."

Jason leaned forward, holding his beer bottle between both hands. "So, tell me all about you."

"I thought that was *my* line. Don't men love to talk about themselves?"

Her eyes twinkled with laughter. The lighting was too dim for him to make out their exact color, but they weren't dark enough to be brown, like his. He was still betting on green. "I'll admit I've been known to bore a person from time to time with my life story."

"I find that hard to believe."

"Ah, got you fooled already."

She sipped her wine. Jason almost groaned when she licked the wine from her top lip.

Damn, he wanted to fuck her.

"Do you live here in Dallas?" he asked.

Gail shook her head. "Technically, in White Settlement. I work in Fort Worth."

"Where?"

"North Texas Highland Hospital."

"So you're a…lab tech? Nurse? Doctor?"

"Doctor. Cardiologist, to be exact."

The lady was intelligent and successful as well as lovely. "I'm impressed."

"Don't be. It's a job, just like any other."

"I imagine your job is a lot more exciting than mine."

"Which is?"

"I own a plumbing company."

She swirled the wine in her glass. A hint of a teasing smile touched her lips. "That could be exciting when a sewer backs up."

He chuckled. "I've definitely worked on my share of those."

Leaning forward, she rested her elbows on the small table. "But you said you own the company. Don't your workers do the actual jobs?"

Her position caused her dress to gape, exposing a generous amount of her cleavage. Jason had to concentrate to keep his gaze on her face. "I work with my guys. I won't ask them to do something I'm not willing to do."

"Now *I'm* impressed."

Her praise only made him want her more. He reached out and touched the back of her hand with one forefinger. "Thanks."

A loud giggle made Jason look over his shoulder. The couple he and Gail had caught on the patio were walking toward them. Or rather, waddling toward them. They'd obviously overindulged on the free booze. She stopped waddling ten feet away from the table and jerked the guy to a stop. Wrapping one arm around his neck, she openly fondled his penis through his pants while kissing him deeply.

Jason glanced back at Gail. She watched the couple's display while biting her lower lip. He couldn't tell if the scene bothered her, or excited her.

The couple stopped kissing and staggered by the table, heading toward the back of the property.

Jason ran his finger over her hand. "I guess there's no doubt what they're going to do."

"No," Gail said softly, "I guess not."

"Did watching her touch him bother you?"

"Bother me how?"

"Disgust you."

She shook her head.

Taking her hand, he turned it over so he could caress her palm with his thumb. He took a chance and asked the question he wanted to ask her. "Did it excite you?"

She bit her bottom lip again. "Maybe a little."

Honesty. He liked that. He wanted to be just as honest with her. "Every time you bite your lip like that, I want to kiss you."

Her eyes widened a moment, then turned sultry. That teasing smile touched her lips again. "Really?"

"Yeah, really."

"Then why don't you?"

Loud laughing and inventive cursing from a nearby table of young men made Jason frown. He couldn't seduce Gail the way he wanted to with an audience nearby. "Let's walk some more."

"Okay."

Leaving his beer on the table, Jason stood and pulled out Gail's chair so she could stand also. He intertwined his fingers with hers and steered her toward the lighted path that wound through the property.

It'd been a long time since he'd felt so at ease with a woman. His last relationship had left his heart and ego bruised. He'd been reluctant to try again, reluctant to take a chance on having his heart trampled once more. Being with Gail, holding her hand, felt right.

Maybe taking another chance wouldn't be a bad idea.

They remained silent as they strolled among the many flowers, bushes, and trees. Instead of searching for something to say, Jason was content to simply walk with Gail without talking. Several moments passed before he spoke again.

"I imagine your work schedule is pretty hectic, being a doctor."

"Yes, it is."

"Doesn't leave a lot of time for dating, huh?"

"No, not really. Relationships have been…strained."

"Are you involved with someone?"

"I was. My schedule got in the way. I worked a lot of hours since I'm the new kid on the block. I still do."

"I can tell by your speech that you aren't a native Texan. Did you recently move here?"

"Two months ago. I used to live in northern California, near San Jose."

They came to a fork in the path. Jason elected to turn left. "What brought you to Fort Worth? Aren't there great hospitals in California?"

"Yes, there are, but NTHH is the leader in the country in cardiology. I wanted to be where I could do the most good for people."

"The guy you were involved with. He lived in California?"

She nodded.

"Did you love him?"

She looked Jason straight in the eyes. "Yes. Very much."

"If he knew that, then he should've been more supportive of your career."

Gail sighed. "It isn't always that simple. I neglected him. I know that. Yes, my schedule has been crazy since I started my internship, but I should've made more time for him."

"Is he part of the reason you moved to Texas?"

"I thought a fresh start would be good for me, and I wanted to work at NTHH. When the opportunity to be on staff there was offered to me, I accepted it."

"So you made a fresh start in a new state. Are you ready for a new relationship, too?"

Gail stopped walking and faced him. "I don't like being alone."

Jason cradled her cheek with his free hand. "I don't like being alone either."

Slowly, he lowered his head until his lips touched hers. He kept the kiss soft, gentle, unsure if she'd pull away from him.

She didn't.

A soft moan from deep in her throat traveled straight to Jason's cock. It lengthened, thickened, as if in anticipation of slipping into her sweet pussy.

The thing had always had a mind of its own.

He slipped his hand around her neck and tilted her head. His tongue touched her lips, silently asking for entrance into her warm mouth. She parted her lips an inch, answering the intimate caress with the tip of her tongue.

She tasted of the wine she'd drunk, and of desire.

Growing bolder, he slid his tongue along her bottom lip, then the top one. Gail parted her lips a bit wider. Jason took advantage of her softening and darted his tongue into her mouth.

She moaned again.

Tightening his hold on her neck, he deepened the kiss, thrusting his tongue past her lips over and over in a simulation of lovemaking. She gripped his waist as she returned his passionate kisses. Each stroke of her tongue against his, each panting breath she took, sent his desire soaring up another degree.

His cock felt as hard as a pipe wrench.

Gail stopped the kiss with a final swipe of her tongue across his lips. She buried her face against his neck. He could feel her hot breath on his skin. Sliding his hand down her back, he gripped one round buttock and squeezed it.

"You're quite a kisser, lady," he rasped.

"So are you." She kissed her way up his neck to his jaw, then back to his lips. This time, she clasped his neck while devouring his mouth.

He had no problem with her taking the lead.

Jason wrapped his arms tightly around her, pulling her body flush against his. She had to feel his erection pressed to her pelvis, evidence of how much he wanted her. How easy it would be to push her up against the large oak tree three feet away, peel off her panties, and thrust inside her. Her intense kisses were proof she was as hot for him as he was for her.

He took a step forward, intent on directing her to that tree, when she stopped their kiss. She stared into his eyes. Here, so far down the path, the lights were spaced farther apart, but he could still see her face. Her eyes clearly showed her desire.

"Maybe we should walk a bit more," she whispered.

It took Jason a moment to clear his brain of lust before he realized what she said. "Walk?"

She nodded. "Please?"

No matter how sharply desire clawed at him, he would never expect a woman to have sex with him if she wasn't ready. He cleared his throat. "Sure."

Taking her hand, he once more led her down the path. He wasn't sure what to say after the kisses they'd shared. Resuming the conversation about their jobs after experiencing her passion seemed...backward.

Gail suddenly stopped walking. "What's that?"

"What's what?"

"That noise."

Jason's eyebrows drew together. "Noise?"

"Listen."

He stood still and strained to hear whatever Gail had heard. A moment passed before he heard the sounds. A moan. A grunt. The unmistakable rhythm of flesh slapping against flesh.

Someone nearby was fucking.

Jason's hand tightened on Gail's as he looked into her eyes again. "You know what's happening, don't you?" he asked.

She nodded.

"Do you want to watch?"

Biting her lower lip, she nodded again.

He dropped a quick kiss on her mouth. "C'mon."

Following the sounds, Jason soon discovered the groping couple from the patio occupying one of the lounge chairs by the tennis court. He pulled Gail into the shadows of the trees and brush so they wouldn't be seen. Their position, less than five feet from the couple, gave them a clear view of the action.

She was on her elbows and knees, her dress up around her waist. The man's pants and underwear lay in a pool on the cement. He straddled the lounge, his hands gripping the woman's waist, as he pounded into her pussy.

Gail gasped softly. Jason quickly placed his hand over her mouth to quiet her. "Shhh," he whispered directly into her ear. "Just watch."

Chapter Two

Gail stared, entranced by the sight before her. She'd seen pictures in magazines and on the Internet of people in sexual positions, and adult movies that included every type of sex imaginable, but never two live people having sex.

The sight made her clit throb and her pussy moisten.

She shouldn't be looking at them. They were sharing a very private moment…or as private as they could be completely out in the open.

Jason still had his hand over her mouth. She could smell him…that wonderful scent of man. Parting her lips, she touched his palm with the tip of her tongue.

He slid his hand to her jaw, his thumb caressing her chin. His other arm encircled her waist, his hand flattening over her stomach. "Looks good, doesn't it?" he whispered.

His warm breath in her ear sent goose bumps scattering across her skin. She'd never felt quite so…wicked. "Yes, it does."

"Have you ever watched two people having sex?"

She shook her head.

"Neither have I." He nuzzled the sensitive area by her ear. "It's exciting, isn't it?"

"Yes."

He brushed his hard shaft against her buttocks. Gail's eyes crossed. Between the feel of his erection in her cleft and watching the couple fucking, she felt bombarded with sensation. Her body grew warm, her skin damp with perspiration. Her nipples pressed against the lace of her bra.

She'd never been so turned on in her life.

"Oh, yeah," the woman said. "Harder. Give me that big cock."

"You got it, baby."

The man gripped her hips and pounded even harder into her pussy. Gail could hear the slap of his flesh against the woman's. Opening her mouth wider, she pulled Jason's thumb inside and sucked on it.

He drew in a sharp breath. "I'd like to feel your tongue on my cock instead of my finger."

In answer to his request, Gail sucked harder on his thumb. She closed her eyes as she imagined dropping to her knees before him, licking the head of his penis, sliding it between her lips. She wanted that. It'd been four long months since she'd been with a man.

She'd missed sex a lot.

Jason's hand traveled up her stomach to her breast. Eyes still closed, Gail continued running her tongue over his thumb while he caressed first one breast, then the other. He squeezed one full globe.

"Damn, your breasts are big."

She let her head fall back to his shoulder when he slipped his hand inside the vee of her dress. "Don't you like big breasts?"

"I *love* big breasts." Sliding his hand inside her bra, he cupped her firm flesh. A soft moan escaped from Gail's throat. "And your nipples are hard. Very nice."

She swallowed. Her breasts had always been sensitive to touch. She'd never come from having her nipples sucked, but she'd been close many times.

"Look, Gail. Watch what he's doing."

She had to struggle to open her eyes again. The woman lay on the lounge, her legs spread wide. She held onto the man's head while he lapped at the folds between her thighs. Gail could see the man's hard cock, wet with the woman's juices, jutting upward toward his stomach.

"Look at that. He's really into it." Jason continued to fondle her breast while his other hand journeyed down her stomach. "Do you like having your pussy licked, Gail?"

"Oh, yes."

He kissed her ear, her neck, her shoulder. "I'd love to do that to you. I'll bet you taste delicious."

Gail whimpered. The mental image his words created made her legs weak. She had to lock her knees to remain standing.

Gail threatened to collapse when Jason's hand cradled her mound.

"I can feel how wet you are right through your dress and panties. Watching them is really turning you on, isn't it?"

"Your touch is turning me on."

"Mmm, I like the sound of that."

"Right there, baby," the woman moaned. "Oh yeah, right there."

"Jesus, that's hot," Jason growled as he squeezed Gail's breast. Watching the couple having sex, along with Gail's passionate response, pushed him past his limit where he no longer thought. Now it was time to *act*. He burrowed his hand beneath her dress. "I've got to touch you."

He slid his hand inside her panties. Warm, thick cream coated her swollen feminine lips. Jason buried his face in her hair, trying to rein in his desire. Ignoring his body's needs wasn't easy, but he had to. He wanted to give Gail pleasure first.

Running his fingers up and down her slit, he covered the tips with her juice and transferred it to her clit. He rubbed the hard button lightly, until she clutched his wrist and pressed his fingers closer to her.

"Harder?"

"Please."

"Like this?" he asked.

"Mmm, yes."

"Back and forth or in a circle?"

"Back and…oh!…for-forth."

"Slow or fast?"

"Fast."

"Slip off your panties so I have more room to touch you."

Jason kept his hand on Gail's pussy while she pushed her panties past her hips and down her legs. She stood upright again, clutching the small scrap of nylon in her hand.

"I'll take those." Plucking the panties from her hand, Jason stuffed them in his pants pocket. "Now hold up your dress for me and spread your legs."

He smiled to himself when she instantly obeyed him. He continued to caress her clit as he lowered the zipper on the back of her dress. A flick of his fingers loosened the snaps of her bra. Tugging the silky dress to her waist, he tunneled his hand inside her bra, pushing it up, and once more cradled her bare breast.

"Much better." He rolled her nipple between his thumb and forefinger. "Now I can touch you the way I want to."

Gail leaned back against Jason, unable to stand on her own any longer. She watched the display before her while her body heated from Jason's caresses. The man had stopped licking the woman's pussy and returned to fucking her. The sounds from their activity increased along with Gail's temperature. The woman's back arched and she released a keening moan.

"Yes, yes, *yes*!"

The man threw back his head and slammed his hips down hard against the woman's. "Yeah, baby. Oh, *yeah*!"

"Sounds like they're coming," Jason whispered in her ear. He rubbed her clit harder. "Come with them, Gail."

The orgasm slithered down her spine and exploded in her womb. Gail bit her bottom lip to keep from crying out. She closed her eyes and shuddered as the climax washed over her entire body.

When she opened her eyes again, she saw the couple straightening their clothes. They shared a passionate kiss, then turned and walked toward the house on a different path.

"My God, you are *hot*." Jason nipped the side of her neck. "You okay?"

No, she wasn't okay. She was incredible. It'd been a long time since she'd had such a powerful orgasm.

The slow descent from the heavens made her able to think again. The first thing she realized was that Jason's erection still pressed between her buttocks. She'd been satisfied, but he obviously hadn't.

She turned in his arms. His gaze fell to her bare breasts, exposed by her unfastened bra. He inhaled sharply.

"Beautiful." He cradled both globes in his hands, his thumbs coasting over the stiff nipples. "Absolutely beautiful."

Gail laid her hands over his. "Thank you. I needed that."

He smiled. "My pleasure."

"I want it to be your pleasure." She slid one hand over his muscular chest and down his flat stomach. Looking into his eyes, she traced his erection with her fingertips. "I want you inside me."

Jason tunneled his hands into her hair and kissed her, long and deep. A gentle nibble on her bottom lip. A swipe of his tongue along the seam. A quick dart inside her mouth to play with her tongue. Gail's knees weakened all over again. He certainly knew how to kiss to make a woman's head swim.

"Where?" he asked.

Instead of answering him with words, Gail took his hand. She led him past the lounge chair where the couple had made love and into a small building she assumed was a changing room for anyone who used the tennis court. Inside the room, she spotted an overstuffed sofa near a window. The room would give them privacy, yet the window would let in the moonlight.

Perfect.

"Sit down."

Once he was seated, Gail slipped off her bra and let it drop to the floor. She watched Jason's gaze snap to her chest.

"Are you a breast man?" she asked as she pushed her dress past her hips.

"Breast, ass, legs. I love everything about a woman's body. There isn't an inch of you that isn't beautiful."

His words warmed her ego and her body. Despite experiencing a powerful orgasm mere minutes ago, she longed to feel his hard cock inside her.

The silky dress fell to the floor. Naked, she dropped to her knees between his spread legs. His chest rose and fell rapidly as she unbuttoned his shirt. Spreading the cloth wide, she ran her hands over his chest. A light dusting of dark hair tickled her palms.

She'd always loved hair on a man's chest.

She followed the trail down his stomach with one fingertip. When she reached his belt, she raised her gaze back to his face. Staring into his eyes, she unhooked his belt and unfastened his pants.

Jason's breathing deepened. Slowly, Gail pulled down the waistband of his briefs. His shaft popped free, long and thick and very hard. Her eyes widened.

"Oh, my," she whispered.

He chuckled. "Does that mean you approve?"

"Definitely."

She tugged his briefs farther down until his tight balls were free of the cloth also. She licked her lips. Grasping his cock at the base, Gail parted her lips over the head. Jason released a deep moan. He lifted his hips, pushing his penis into her mouth.

"Yeah," he rasped. "Damn, that feels good."

It certainly did. The intimacy, the closeness, the trust. Gail enjoyed everything about oral sex. She inhaled deeply, savoring the musky scent of desire and man. Her eyes drifted closed. How she loved that scent.

She slid her lips halfway down his shaft before making the return journey to the head. On her next pass, she slipped farther down his penis. Inch by inch, she took more of his cock until she had all of him in her mouth.

"Damn, babe," Jason hissed.

Gail massaged the sensitive area between his cock and anus while she sucked him. She looked up from her pleasant task to see Jason resting his head on the back of the sofa, his eyes closed. His clenched fists lay on the cushions next to his hips. His chest rose and fell rapidly, proof that he was enjoying this as much as she.

She wanted to take him beyond enjoyment. She wanted to make him crazy.

Cradling his balls in one palm, she caressed his shaft with her other hand while running her tongue all around the crown. Jason raised his head and opened his eyes as he began to pump his hips. The tip of her tongue darted into the slit. Her teeth lightly scraped the crown. She squeezed his balls and ran her tongue up and down the thick veins.

"*God*, Gail."

She circled the head once again with her tongue. "Do you like this?"

"Yeah." He cradled her jaws, his fingertips caressing the skin behind her ears. "I'm close to coming. You'd better stop."

"Uh-uh. I don't want to."

"I'm not kidding."

Instead of doing what he said, Gail took his cock in her mouth again, all the way to the base.

Jason's breath hitched. His hands tightened on her jaws as his thrusts picked up speed. Using both hands, Gail caressed him while he pumped into her mouth. She slid her lips to his balls and back to the head once, twice. The third time, he released a heavy moan.

"Shit!"

His seed filled her mouth. Gail greedily swallowed every drop. Jason's thrusts slowed, then stopped. He sat sprawled on the sofa, his legs spread wide, his chest and stomach shiny with perspiration.

He was the most handsome man she'd ever seen.

Chapter Three

Jason sat still, trying to get his heart to stop pounding while the blood slowly returned to his brain. Every drop had fled south, making concentration impossible.

Being able to think was highly overrated anyway.

The soft licking on his cock made him open his eyes. Gail remained on her knees on the floor, slowly running her tongue over his softening flesh. He watched her for several moments, enjoying the intimacy of her touch, before he touched her cheek. "Hey."

She smiled. "Hey back."

"That was very nice."

"I'm glad you approved."

"Oh, yeah. I *definitely* approved." He caressed her lower lip with his thumb. "You said you wanted me inside you."

"You *were* inside me."

"You know what I mean."

She grinned before swiping her tongue across the head of his shaft. "Well, I was hoping you might be able to…go another round."

Jason chuckled. "Trust me. Going another round won't be a problem at all." He leaned forward and took her hand. "Come here."

She climbed up and straddled his lap. Her wet pussy cushioned his cock. Jason hissed as his shaft responded to the warmth surrounding it.

No, another round wouldn't be a problem at all.

The moonlight shining in the window behind him illuminated her face. Jason swallowed. When he'd decided to find a woman at the party for one night of pleasure, he'd never expected to find one so lovely. Or sexy. Or one who made his heart pound with a simple kiss.

Cradling her jaws in his hands, he drew her face closer to his. He traced the outline of her lips with the tip of his tongue. "Kiss me," he whispered.

She did…lightly, sweetly. Jason slowly caressed her spine as she made love to his mouth. She nipped at his lips. A soft lick soothed the tiny bites. Gentle pecks turned into full, open-mouthed kisses. Gail clutched his hair while she devoured his mouth.

He loved every second of it.

"I need to get inside you," he rasped when she stopped kissing him for a moment to breathe.

Gail lifted her hips a few inches. Looking into his eyes, she grasped his cock and impaled herself on it.

"Oh, *fuck*!" Jason hissed.

"Exactly." She shifted her pelvis, driving him deeper inside her body. "Mmm, that feels good."

It certainly did. Her pussy was hot, tight, and very wet. Jason held Gail by her waist as she began to ride him. He tried to stay still so she could take her pleasure however she needed to. The intense sensations flooding his system made remaining still impossible. Tightening his hold on her waist, he lifted his hips while she lowered hers. He established a rhythm with her, one that drove up his blood pressure with every thrust.

"You fill me so completely." Clutching his shoulders, she threw back her head and rode him faster. "Harder. Fuck me harder."

Jason dug his fingers into her ass. He rammed his cock upward into her pussy while she slammed her pelvis down on his.

"Oh, *yes*! Like that. Right there. Jason! *Yes*!"

He felt the walls of her pussy contract around his cock. Her orgasm triggered his own. Tightening the hold on her buttocks, he groaned out his release.

Moments passed while Jason tried once more to remember how to think. He held Gail close to him, caressing her back and hips. Her skin felt so smooth, so soft. It'd been much too long since he'd held a woman in his arms.

He wanted to change that by holding Gail all night long.

She raised her head from his shoulder. "Wow."

Jason chuckled. "Liked that second round, huh?"

"Very much."

He ran his hands up and down her arms. Her skin felt pebbled with goose bumps. "Are you getting cold?"

"A little."

"I think that cold front has finally hit. Maybe you should get dressed."

"No, not yet. Can't you just...hold me for awhile?"

He smiled. "I'd like that."

Gail rose from Jason's lap. Muscles shifted beneath his skin as he shrugged out of his shirt. She sighed softly. He was so gorgeous.

He lay back on the sofa, holding up one hand to her. Gail took it and stretched out beside him. He covered her with his shirt before wrapping his arms around her.

"How's that?" he asked before dropping a kiss on her temple.

The warmth from his shirt seeped into her chilled body. "Perfect."

She lay in his arms, content to be quiet and still after making love. She had no idea of the time, but she didn't care. All that mattered was lying here beside Jason.

He kissed her temple again. "Tell me more about this guy you left in California."

Gail shifted her head on his shoulder. Talking was easier when she wasn't looking at Jason. "We were together two years. We had some…problems that we couldn't work out."

"Like your job?"

"That was the biggest one, yes." She drew circles on his chest with one fingertip. "I put everything into my job. I had to. Medical school isn't easy. Neither is internship or residency. I had to work a lot of long hours."

"Meaning you didn't have time for him."

"Meaning I didn't *make* the time for him. That was wrong. So very wrong."

Jason's arms tightened around her. "What other problems did you have?"

"Kids. He was ready to start a family. I wasn't. I want to be able to spend a lot of time with my baby when I have one. I couldn't do that as an intern."

"Surely he understood that."

"He was hurt because I wouldn't get pregnant. He never said so, but I believe he took my refusal to have his baby as a sign that I didn't really love him. That wasn't true. I loved him so very much."

He rubbed his cheek against the top of her head. "What else?"

"He was trying to build his own business, so he worked a lot of long hours, too. When I managed to get a day off, he'd be busy."

"And you resented that."

Gail hated to admit it aloud, but it was true. She'd been wrapped up in her career, but hadn't wanted her guy to be too busy for her. "Yes, I did."

"Did you tell him that?"

"No."

"Why not?"

She shrugged one shoulder. "We didn't talk much. We made love even less. Not at first. When we first got together, we couldn't keep our hands off each other."

"Not unusual for a couple in a new relationship. New couples usually fuck like rabbits."

Gail giggled.

He laid his hand over hers on top of his stomach. "Was the sex good?"

"Incredible. He was an amazing lover." She entwined her fingers with his. "I should've told him that."

"Maybe he knew how you felt."

"I still should've *told* him. Words are important. There were so many things I should've said to him that I didn't, so many things I should've done. But hindsight is always twenty-twenty, right?"

"Sounds like you're beating yourself up over it. It takes two to make a relationship." He kissed the top of her head. "I had similar problems in my last relationship. It's easy to get into a rut, take someone for granted. That happens a lot. It's probably the main reason why so many couples get divorced. Life gets in the way and people forget to do the little things to show their love."

Gail tilted her head on his shoulder so she could see his face. "Like?"

"Like…flowers. A man should give flowers to the woman he loves just because he loves her. He shouldn't wait until her birthday or anniversary. Silly cards. A note left next to her car keys. A phone call in the middle of the day to tell her he loves her. Stuff like that."

"You're a romantic."

"I am now. Losing the woman I loved made me learn my lesson." Lifting their hands to his mouth, Jason kissed her palm. "I made mistakes, too, just like you. I lost the woman I loved because… Well, because of a lot of reasons. I swore I'd never make those mistakes again."

"Easier said than done."

"But worth it. Loving someone and having them love you in return makes life worth living."

"Yes, it does."

"And losing someone you love hurts like hell."

"Yes, it does," she whispered.

He kissed her palm again, then her lips. "If he wanted another chance with you, would you take it?"

"In a heartbeat."

"Yeah, me, too." He touched her hair, running his fingers through the strands. "If I could get another chance with the woman I loved, I'd take it."

Jason kissed her lips again. One kiss led to two, then three. Gail slid her hand down his stomach and clasped his cock, still exposed by his open pants. He moaned as it began to harden.

"Again?" she asked against his lips.

"Definitely again," he said, his voice husky.

Jason shifted on the sofa, tugging Gail beneath him. He hadn't yet paid the attention to her beautiful breasts that they deserved. Very large, round, ivory in color with dark pink nipples. Cradling them in his palms, he pushed them together and upward to create a deep cleavage.

"These are incredible." He scooted down on the sofa so his mouth was even with her breasts. He watched her face as he kneaded her firm flesh. Her lips parted, her eyes drifted closed. A soft gasp came from deep in her throat when he whisked his thumbs across her nipples.

"You like this?" he asked as he thumbed her nipples again.

"Yes. Mmm, yes." She opened her eyes and lifted her head from the sofa. "Suck them."

"With pleasure."

Jason drew her left nipple into his mouth while he continued to caress the right one with his thumb. Gail moaned softly, then gasped when he clamped his teeth on her nipple and tugged.

"Oh!"

He soothed the bite with his tongue. "Did I hurt you?"

"No. You just…surprised me."

"I like to bite." He nipped her again, a bit harder. "You okay with that?"

She arched her back, pushing her breast closer to his mouth. "Bite me. Suck me. Hard."

Alternating between biting her nipples and sucking them, Jason moved back and forth between her breasts. Each swipe of his tongue made her breathing quicken. She grabbed fistfuls of his hair, as if to hold him in place.

He had absolutely no intention of moving from his very pleasant task.

She spread her legs a bit wider, making more room for him between her thighs. Her womanly scent drifted up to his nostrils. Jason inhaled deeply. He loved the aroma of an aroused woman. Smelling her desire changed his mind about moving. He gave each nipple one last hard suck, then started dropping kisses down her stomach. His tongue flashed by her navel, tickled her abdomen, ruffled through her pubic hair. He touched her clit with the tip of his tongue.

Gail lifted her hips, pushing his tongue farther into the folds of her pussy. Pulling her lips apart with his thumbs, he drove his tongue deep inside her.

She was wet with both her juices and his. Jason lapped at her labia and clit, loving the taste of her. Tangy. Sweet. Salty.

Delicious.

He lapped her pussy for several moments, then slowly made the journey to her anus. He pressed his tongue flat against the sensitive hole.

"Oh, *yes*. Lick my ass."

"You like this, baby?"

"Mmm-hmm. More."

Only too happy to comply, he licked her from anus to clit and back again, over and over. When he thrust his tongue inside her ass, Gail bucked and grabbed his head.

"Like that. Oh, Jason, just like that."

"My God, you're hot," he said before laving her slit again. "Spread your legs wider."

Hooking her hands behind her knees, she pulled her legs toward her chest and far apart. Jason slipped his hands beneath her buttocks to lift her even closer to his mouth. He speared her ass with his tongue.

Gail's moan urged him to continue. He began tongue-fucking her ass while he caressed her clit with one thumb. Her moans turned to pants, her pants to gasps. She had to be close to coming again.

Not without him.

Quickly crawling up her body, Jason thrust into her heat. "I want to be inside you when you come."

No sooner had he said the words than he felt her walls clamp around his cock.

"Jason!"

She threw back her head and arched her back. The tempting sight of her neck was too much to resist. He sucked on her silky skin, lightly bit the pounding pulse. Gail shuddered beneath him. Her walls convulsed around his shaft again.

Jason remained still, enjoying the sensation of her pussy contracting on his cock. When the last contraction died, he began to move, lazily pumping into her channel.

Gail's hands slid down his back to his buttocks. Taking that as a sign that she wanted more, he increased the speed of his thrusts.

"You feel so good, Gail." He kissed her ear, her jaw, the point of her chin.

"So do you." Her breath hitched. "I can't… I can't get enough."

"Then I'll give you more."

Slow was no longer enough for Jason either. Digging his fingers into her ass, he pounded into her pussy. He pushed her hair away from her neck and darted his tongue into her ear.

"Come again, Gail," he whispered. "Come while I'm fucking you."

She wrapped her arms around his neck and met him thrust for thrust. He felt her fingernails dig into his shoulders. The sharp bite of pain made him hotter, took him closer to the edge. Cradling one breast in his hand, he squeezed Gail's hard nipple between his thumb and forefinger.

"Ahhhh!" she cried out. Her pussy clamped on his cock again. It was enough to send Jason over the edge into bliss. Burying his face in her neck, he groaned out his release.

He struggled to catch his breath. His heart pounded in his temple. His sweaty skin stuck to Gail's. It must be uncomfortable for her, but Jason didn't think he could move. Every bit of his strength disappeared with his orgasm.

The sound of firecrackers and whistles penetrated his muzzy brain. Propping himself up on shaky arms, he looked into Gail's face.

"Sounds like it's midnight."

"Mmm-hmm."

"Happy New Year."

She smiled. "Happy New Year."

Jason kissed her softly. "Did you get enough?"

Laughing, she ran her fingers up and down his spine. "Definitely."

"Good, 'cause I'm wiped."

"So am I. It was amazing."

"Yeah, it was. How many times did you come?"

"About three hundred."

Jason whistled. "Damn, I'm good."

Gail laughed. "Yes, you are."

Turning serious, he caressed her cheek with his thumb. "Come home with me. I want to wake up in the morning with you in my arms."

She smiled tenderly. "I'd like that."

Chapter Four

Jason propped up one elbow and watched Gail sleeping. She lay on her stomach, her face turned toward him. Muted sunlight filtered through the mini-blinds and touched her hair, giving it a reddish look. The tousled curls begged for his touch, but he didn't want to wake her. It was still early, and they hadn't gone to bed until after two.

Even after going to bed, they hadn't fallen asleep until making love again. He'd needed to feel her wet pussy surround his cock one more time. Gail hadn't complained at all when he'd said he wanted her again. She'd been in control, pushing him to his back and straddling his hips the way she had in the changing room at the mansion. She'd teased him with slow thrusts and pecking kisses. She'd touched her own breasts, plucking at her hard nipples.

He'd always loved watching a woman pleasure herself.

Jason had endured her teasing for several minutes before the need to be the one in control had erupted inside him. Grasping her upper arms, he'd practically thrown her to her back and fucked her furiously until they'd both exploded in orgasm.

He'd never had a better, sexier lover.

Jason shifted to a more comfortable position. The covers slipped from his shoulder. He shivered. With the unseasonably warm temperatures North Texas had experienced the last few days, he'd had no reason to turn on the heat in his apartment. The cold front had blown in from the north shortly before midnight. The biting wind had made Gail and him run from the tennis court's changing room back to the mansion. Today held much cooler temperatures and cloudy skies. There was a good chance of sleet or snow before noon.

He didn't care what the weather did. It could snow three feet and it wouldn't matter to him. Despite not turning on the heat last night, he was warm and cozy with Gail next to him.

Wanting to kiss her awake but not wishing to bother her, he decided to start coffee instead. He cursed softly when he climbed out from under the covers and the cold air hit his nude body. Heat first, then coffee.

The short amount of time it'd taken for him to start the coffee hadn't given the heat the chance to warm the apartment. By the time Jason climbed back into bed after starting the coffee, he felt like he'd played outside with the north wind barreling straight at him. He cuddled up as close to Gail as he dared without waking her.

She stirred and turned her face away from him. A moment passed, then he heard her inhale and exhale deeply. She turned her face back his direction, a frown turning down her lips and wrinkling her eyebrows. Jason chuckled to himself. It obviously wasn't easy for her to wake up.

Her eyelids fluttered. Her frown deepened a moment before she opened her eyes. She blinked twice, as if to bring him into focus. A slow, sleepy smile touched her lips.

"Good morning," she said, her voice rusty.

"Good morning." Jason dropped a soft kiss on her lips. "How did you sleep?"

"Like a rock."

"Oh, yeah? Pardon me while I pound on my chest."

Gail giggled and rolled to her back. Her shifting blessed him with a glimpse of one creamy breast and pink nipple.

He planned to give that nipple a lot of sucking today.

"Do I smell coffee?" Gail asked.

"You do. It should be ready in a minute."

"That gives me enough time to borrow your little girls' room."

"Help yourself."

Jason sat up and watched Gail rise from the bed and cross the room, thoroughly enjoying the view of her naked body. He'd always preferred a woman to be more voluptuous than slender. With Gail's large breasts, wide hips, and rounded tummy, she definitely leaned toward the voluptuous side.

He had no complaints.

At the door, she smiled at him over her shoulder and wiggled her butt. He laughed and rubbed his hands together. "Hurry back so I can paddle that luscious ass."

"Ooh, baby!" She wiggled her butt again before disappearing through the doorway.

Smiling, Jason fell back on the bed. He liked her sense of humor. He liked the way she bit her bottom lip when she was unsure about something. He liked how free she was with him sexually.

He wanted a lot more from her than one night of pleasure.

The sound of a door opening drew his attention. He looked at the doorway to see Gail run into the room. She jumped up on the bed, scampered over him, and landed on her butt on her side of the bed. Quickly, she burrowed back under the covers.

"Damn, it's cold! Didn't you pay your electric bill?"

"I just turned on the heat a few minutes ago."

"I can tell. It'll take me an hour to get warm again."

"No way. Turn over. I'll help you get warmed up."

She turned her back to him and pressed her cool buttocks against his groin. Jason wrapped one arm over her breasts, one low over her stomach. She sighed when his thumb brushed her nipple.

"That's nice."

"It certainly is." He pressed his hardening cock against her buttocks. Nudging aside her hair with his nose, he nibbled on her earlobe. "You feel good."

So did he. Gail loved the feel of Jason pressed up against her back. She'd missed this closeness with a man the last four months.

"What are you thinking?" he asked after nipping her earlobe again.

"About how I've missed this closeness. Waking up in your bed is really nice."

"I've missed it, too." He kissed her jaw, her neck, her shoulder. "Waking up alone isn't any fun."

"That's for sure."

He tightened his arms around her. "So what now?"

"You mean other than getting warm?"

His chuckle so close to her ear sent shivers down her spine. Gail hunched her shoulder. "Don't blow in my ear. It tickles."

"You didn't mind me blowing in your ear last night."

"I was horny last night."

"You aren't horny now?"

"Right now I'm...content."

"Content. So getting some early morning nookie is out?"

"It isn't out. It's just...postponed for a while." She looked at him over her shoulder. "So tell your cock to calm down."

"I can't tell it anything. It never minds me. Just ignore it."

"I can't ignore something poking into my back."

"Would you rather it poke somewhere else?"

Gail rolled over to face him. She laughed at the hopeful expression on his face. "You're insatiable, do you know that?"

"Guilty as charged." He slowly caressed her breasts and stomach. One finger dipped between her thighs and brushed her clit. "Can I help it if this body turns me on?"

They'd been teasing with each other, but his words sobered her. "Does it?"

"You know it does. It always has."

His sweet declaration brought tears to her eyes. Jason cradled her jaw in his hand. "Why tears, Gail?"

"I was afraid you'd…never want me again."

"I never stopped wanting you. I never stopped loving you."

"Even after I was so horrible to you?"

"We both made mistakes. We were both wrong about a lot of things. What happened between us wasn't your fault, nor mine." He caressed her cheek with his thumb. "Your eyes look like emeralds when you cry."

"They can't look like emeralds. My eyes aren't green."

"They are, too."

"Jason, they're hazel. I can't believe we've been married for two years and you still don't know the color of my eyes."

"Whatever color you want to call them, they're beautiful. *You're* beautiful, both inside and out." He kissed her tenderly.

"So my idea worked?"

He nodded. "It did for me. We agreed to start fresh, to pretend we didn't know each other at that party. It was like we met for the first time."

"One look at you made my heart melt, just like it did the first time I saw you."

"One look at you gave me a hard-on."

Gail burst out laughing. "Will you be serious?"

He grinned, but his grin quickly faded. "Okay, I'll be serious. We let life and our jobs and petty disagreements interfere with our love for each other."

"Some of those petty disagreements were pretty intense."

"All right, I'll admit some of them were fights. The main thing is we took each other for granted." He cradled her cheek, his thumb brushing over her lips. "I promise you I'll never do that again."

"Does that mean I can expect flowers and love notes now?"

"You can expect a *lot* of things."

"I don't need 'things', Jason. I only need you."

"You got me, for as long as you want me."

"Forever works for me."

"Then forever it is."

Jason kissed her slowly and thoroughly before he sat up and opened the drawer of the nightstand. Gail propped up on her elbows so she could see what he was doing. He removed something from the drawer and closed his fingers around it. Turning back to her, he opened his fist.

Two gold wedding bands lay on his palm.

"I think," he said, picking up the smaller band, "it's time we put these back on."

Tears filled her eyes and flowed down her cheeks. Nodding, she held out her left hand to him. He slipped the ring on her finger, then kissed it. Gail took his band from his palm and placed it on his finger. She, too, kissed it once it was back where it belonged before kissing her husband's lips.

How she loved him.

Once their lips parted, Jason pulled her into his arms, her back to his chest. "I rented this apartment on a very temporary basis. We'll have to start house hunting. I'll ask around, try to find a real estate agent we'll like."

"I rented my apartment hoping it would be temporary, too. House hunting with you sounds wonderful." She ran her fingertips lightly up and down his arm. "Are you sure, Jason? You gave up a very successful plumbing business in California to move here."

"I sold that business and made a nice profit. I've already started another business here and have three guys working for me. NTHH is tops in cardiology in the States. This is where you need to be. If you wanted to move to Greenland, I'd go. I don't care where we live, as long as we're together."

"Greenland is definitely out. I get cold too easily."

Jason chuckled. "That's true."

"It'll be different here, Jason, I swear. I won't ever neglect you again."

"I know that," he said softly. "We started fresh last night, Gail. No more regrets, no more rehashing of the past. Our marriage officially begins now."

She drew tiny circles on his arm with one fingertip. "Maybe…maybe we could talk about starting a family."

He'd been tweaking her nipples while they spoke. Her words must have shocked him for his fingers stilled. "What?"

"I wasn't ready two years ago, or even a year ago. I'm ready now. I'm established in my job. My hours are still long, but I have more say-so about my schedule now. I doubt there would be a problem with me taking off some time after the baby is born."

"Gail, are you sure? I want us to have a baby. I want that more than anything. But I'd never push you. I did that once and drove you away from me. I won't do it again."

"You don't have to push me. I want to have your baby." She reached her hand back and squeezed his hip. "So let's talk about it."

His hand slid down her stomach to between her thighs. "Talking isn't how it's done, sweetheart."

Gail giggled. "Well, I thought we could talk first, then do the other stuff."

Jason pushed two fingers inside her pussy. "You can talk while I feel around."

She swatted his hip. "Behave! I'm being serious here."

"So am I." He pushed his fingers farther inside her. "Believe me, I'm *very* serious about fucking you."

"Jason… Oh!" She gasped when he pressed her G-spot. "You aren't playing fair."

"I know."

His smug tone made her laugh, despite the intense sensations his caressing was causing in her body.

She knew exactly what to say to make that smug tone disappear.

"I'm not on the Pill anymore."

He stopped rubbing his cock against her buttocks. "What did you say?"

Gail grinned to herself. She knew that would get him. "I stopped taking it when I moved here."

He cleared his throat. "Where are you in your cycle?"

"I started my period two weeks ago."

"Two weeks…" Jason jerked Gail to her back and loomed over her. "You could be pregnant right now."

She nodded. "As regular as I am, that's very possible."

Jason remained silent. Gail bit her bottom lip, worried that he'd think she tricked him. "Are you angry I didn't tell you before we made love?"

"No. *God*, no, I'm not angry. I'm…" He chuckled. "Hell, I'm speechless."

"Well, *that* doesn't happen very often."

"True." He rubbed his hand over her flat stomach. "But you know, we should be sure. I mean, just because your cycle is regular doesn't mean you'll get pregnant the first time. We should do everything we can to make sure you *do* get pregnant."

He settled between her legs. His erection pressed against her pussy. "You think we should make love again?"

"Oh, yeah. Probably all day. The apartment will be warm soon. I have plenty of food. It's gonna snow soon, so we have no reason to go outside."

"You have it all figured out, huh?"

"Absolutely. In fact..." He slipped his hands beneath her buttocks and lifted her hips. His cock slid inside her. "We should probably make love as often as we can for at least a couple of weeks. Just to be sure."

"Only a couple of weeks."

He grinned. "To start."

Gail arched her back as he began a gentle thrusting. Spreading her legs wider, she wrapped her arms around his neck. "You always have such good ideas."

The End

Also by Lynn Lafleur

ꕥ

Enchanted Rogues (*anthology)*

Happy Birthday, Baby

Holiday Heat (*anthology)*

Rent-A-Stud

Two Men and a Lady (*anthology)*

About the Author

ꕥ

Lynn LaFleur's writing career has included winning several writing contests. She was a semi-finalist twice in the prestigious Golden Heart Contest of Romance Writers of America. She served on the board of the RWA Chapter in Sacramento, California, for four years, as secretary and activities director.

Lynn can't imagine ever writing anything except romances. "I love writing about a man and a woman falling in love. If you enjoy the story I tell enough to smile in places, shed a tear at times, or get a warm and fuzzy feeling, that is my greatest reward."

After living on the West Coast for twenty-one years, Lynn is back in Texas. She works for her small-town newspaper during the day and writes books of romance at night.

Lynn welcomes comments from readers. You can find her website and email address on her author bio page at www.ellorascave.com.

Why an electronic book?

We live in the Information Age—an exciting time in the history of human civilization, in which technology rules supreme and continues to progress in leaps and bounds every minute of every day. For a multitude of reasons, more and more avid literary fans are opting to purchase e-books instead of paper books. The question from those not yet initiated into the world of electronic reading is simply: *Why?*

1. ***Price.*** An electronic title at Ellora's Cave Publishing and Cerridwen Press runs anywhere from 40% to 75% less than the cover price of the exact same title in paperback format. Why? Basic mathematics and cost. It is less expensive to publish an e-book (no paper and printing, no warehousing and shipping) than it is to publish a paperback, so the savings are passed along to the consumer.
2. ***Space.*** Running out of room in your house for your books? That is one worry you will never have with electronic books. For a low one-time cost, you can purchase a handheld device specifically designed for e-reading. Many e-readers have large, convenient screens for viewing. Better yet, hundreds of titles can be stored within your new library—on a single microchip. There are a variety of e-readers from different manufacturers. You can also read e-books on your PC or laptop computer. (Please note that Ellora's

Cave does not endorse any specific brands. You can check our websites at www.ellorascave.com or www.cerridwenpress.com for information we make available to new consumers.)

3. ***Mobility***. Because your new e-library consists of only a microchip within a small, easily transportable e-reader, your entire cache of books can be taken with you wherever you go.
4. ***Personal Viewing Preferences.*** Are the words you are currently reading too small? Too large? Too... ANNOYING? Paperback books cannot be modified according to personal preferences, but e-books can.
5. ***Instant Gratification.*** Is it the middle of the night and all the bookstores near you are closed? Are you tired of waiting days, sometimes weeks, for bookstores to ship the novels you bought? Ellora's Cave Publishing sells instantaneous downloads twenty-four hours a day, seven days a week, every day of the year. Our webstore is never closed. Our e-book delivery system is 100% automated, meaning your order is filled as soon as you pay for it.

Those are a few of the top reasons why electronic books are replacing paperbacks for many avid readers.

As always, Ellora's Cave and Cerridwen Press welcome your questions and comments. We invite you to email us at Comments@ellorascave.com or write to us directly at Ellora's Cave Publishing Inc., 1056 Home Avenue, Akron, OH 44310-3502.

Cerridwen, the Celtic Goddess of wisdom, was the muse who brought inspiration to storytellers and those in the creative arts. Cerridwen Press encompasses the best and most innovative stories in all genres of today's fiction. Visit our site and discover the newest titles by talented authors who still get inspired - much like the ancient storytellers did, once upon a time.

ELLORA'S CAVE
ROMANTICA PUBLISHING